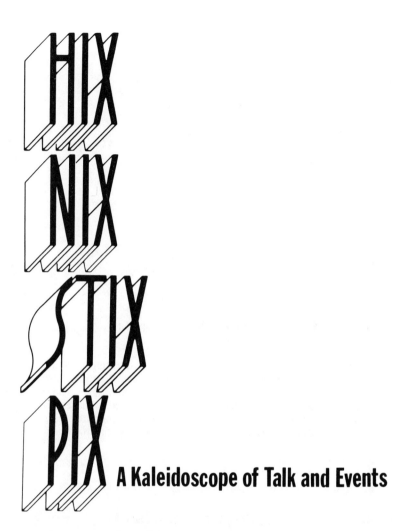

HIX NIX STIX PIX

A Kaleidoscope of Talk and Events

DAVID LLEWELLYN BURDETT

E. P. DUTTON, INC./ SEYMOUR LAWRENCE
New York

Published in the United States by E. P. Dutton, Inc.,
2 Park Avenue, New York, N.Y. 10016
Published in Canada by Deneau Publishers, Ottawa and Toronto

Library of Congress Cataloging in Publication Data

Burdett, David Llewellyn
Hix Nix Stix Pix

I. Title.
PR9199.3.B784H5 1984 813'.54 83–8920

ISBN: 0–525–24202–3
OBE

10 9 8 7 6 5 4 3 2 1

First Edition

To Mr. James Porter

AUTHOR'S NOTE

THIS LOVE STORY embraces a very wide area, with momentous events happening almost simultaneously in places far apart. Hollywood is its center, the place which is at the heart of so much modern romance.

With regard to the historical persons depicted, care has been taken to adhere as closely as possible to the facts. If readers should wish to know more about the people of whom they get a glimpse, they will find a store of good things in *Inside Europe* by John Gunther (Hamish Hamilton, 1936).

The history of the Federal Theatre as depicted in Hallie Flanagan's *A Theatre is Born* (Federal Theatre, 1944) will never lose its fascination.

Those wishing to know more about the trials and tribulations of the acting profession should consult the theater and fun pages of the *Quiver*, the *Penny Magazine*, the *Union Jack*, *Jones's Theatre* and the *Musical Home Journal*. Much of the source material is obscure. Many anonymous newspaper cuttings and pamphlets (especially pertaining to EPIC) are contained in the large collection of scrapbooks at the British Museum.

Lines quoted on p. 323 from the song 'Papa's Got a Job' (Ned Lehac, Robert Sour and Hector Troy), © copyright 1939 Edward B. Marks Music Corporation, copyright renewed, are used by permission. All rights are reserved. The quotation on p. 315 from David S. Hull, *Film in the Third Reich*, published by the University of California Press in 1970, is also used by permission.

It is hoped that finally Clarence Williams will be instated in the annals of great American oratory.

All the costumes in the story were designed by File.

PREFACE

SOMETIME AT THE END OF THE 1890s J. M. Barrie, author of *Peter Pan*, the boy who wouldn't grow up, first saw the beautiful Llewellyn Davies boys. He was out strolling in Kensington Gardens, and discovered them standing by the round pond with their nurse. He stopped to look and admire. A vast cloud picture reflected itself in the water. Plants growing under the surface, eating into the skin of the living picture, the boys smiling down at themselves, their reflections swaying like slow flags. Barrie was inspired by the sight and struck up a conversation; soon they were all taking regular walks together. Sitting on a bench one day, he started to weave the story of Peter Pan for them. As he talked the boys listened, their lips parted in amazement, eyes shining. They looked like children fresh into a dream, and the ecstasy of that dream would never quite dry from their faces.

On November 6, 1905, after its London run, *Peter Pan* opened in New York under the supervision of the impresario Charles Frohman. Maude Adams played in the title role. Mark Twain wrote to her, "It is my belief that *Peter Pan* is a great and refined and uplifting benefaction to this sordid and money mad age." For many years *Peter Pan* toured Canada and America, and the boy became a national hero to millions. The North Americans transformed him from an English stage creation into the best loved of all children. To the audiences, the never-never land in the story came to symbolize the New World, while Peter Pan was seen to represent the spirit of youth and freedom calling the children of the Old World to leave their antiquated nurseries and fly away to the never-never land of liberty. Once asked what he would like to be remembered for, Frohman said, "Bringing *Peter Pan* to the world, it is enough for any man."

The horror of J. M. Barrie's adolescence had been the realization that he would finally have to grow older, become an adult, and live in a world where he would no longer be protected from pain and death. If only he could discover loopholes in time where part of him might secretly escape. If clocks couldn't be made to go backward, could they be brought to a standstill? That terrible clock, the instrument that severs the neck of the passing hours. Clocks gloat and tell us time has gone, time to get up, time to go to bed, coffin time; no wonder we scowl. Most men who build castles in the air do so merely to astonish their friends. Barrie built his architectural extravagance of *Peter Pan* to live in, and he built it to last for centuries. While the decades march past, his castle was to be forever anchored in a still and invisible place somewhere out of time. Its inhabitants, permanently young, come from the unknown air, occasionally straying into our torrents of life and consciousness. Moving from mist to mist across the song of night and moon they roam astray. No ominous hour knocks at their door with bad news, for they are far away in another dimension where desire, fear, and time have no meaning.

A new Barrie play opened in London in the early part of 1915 and flopped. The author asked Frohman, due in London later in the year, to come over early and try to salvage the production. The impresario agreed and sailed out of New York on the *Lusitania*, saying as he boarded ship, "I don't fear U boats, only IOU boats." The actress Rita Jolivet, who was on board and survived the torpedoing, said that Frohman's last words were Peter Pan's. "To die will be an awfully big adventure."

PART ONE

'Twas grace that taught my heart to fear
And grace my fears relieved.

"Amazing Grace"

A WEEK AFTER AMERICA entered the First World War, a conference was in progress on the small, newly founded lot of Drewstone Films in Hollywood. A group of executives was looking through some western stories with the company founder, trying to find one suitable for a film. Each man was loudly advocating his particular preference. They had to find something quickly, as the star of the production, Phillip Inshroin, and some of the film crew were leaving for France in fifteen days. The star was present at the meeting, and he sat silently at the back of the room as everybody around him argued and bickered over the potential of each story. Above his head was a large framed print of the company motto. IF YOU HAVE A GOOD STORY ABOUT A BAD GIRL, TURN IT INTO A BAD STORY ABOUT A GOOD GIRL, AND KEEP HER IN FRONT OF THE CAMERA ALL THE TIME. Finally when an uneasy silence fell after all the choices had been rejected by Drewstone, the actor said: "I've got something, Chief, that I think is interesting."

John Drewstone looked up from the pile of stories in front of him on his desk, and stared at the speaker. The actor's face was expressionless, but it seemed to hide no weakness. Under the skin lay broad bones—and the eyes: miles on miles of blue. His look didn't associate itself with the placid Christian name Phillip, and most people at the studio took Drewstone's cue and addressed him by his surname. "Have you? I don't usually like my performers to suggest a story for a film, Inshroin. Most of them don't know what the public wants, or understand the technical problems involved." He put his hand up behind his head. "But as nobody has come up with any-

3

thing, and you say it's interesting, I'll make an exception. Let's hear some of it." He took his hand from behind his head, and shifted his pants so they didn't bite so hard into his crotch—the dark heavy grape of his prostate was giving him painful trouble.

"You'll all enjoy this," said Inshroin. "I'm pretty good when I get going. The last time I did a public reading was on stage in London. On that occasion a man in the audience was especially delighted with my performance. He was so delighted he wanted to give me an egg, but the hall was packed and he couldn't get down to give it to me, so he had to throw it."

The actor ordered a beer from a drinks waiter who hovered in the background. There was the sound of paper rustling as he began to read.

"The place is a—"

"What's it called, first?" asked Drewstone.

"*The Outlaw in the Reign of Gun.*"

"That'll have to be changed. What's it about?"

"It's about two men who rob a small town bank, and what happens to an innocent girl when they get away with the cash." Someone tittered, but Inshroin didn't look up. He waited until the room was silent.

Orchestra full into title theme. Then a series of swift ascending questioning chords. Shimmer under for . . .

The place is a station at a Midwest town in America, a setting completely in harmony with an outlaw romance a year after Billy the Kid was killed.

At ten o'clock on a midweek evening, a young man stepped down from the train, and stood flagellating circulation into his body. His hair was blond and thick. At the front a huge cowlick curled down between his eyes, and whenever there was a slight breeze, the rest stood up on top of his head like a Sioux war bonnet.

The stationmaster watched him carefully, as he was the most expensively dressed passenger among the people who had got off.

The two men approached each other and came face to face in the middle of the platform.

"Are there any good lodgings in town?"

"Plenty, just walk up Main Street and take your pick."

The stationmaster came closer. "Haven't I seen you here before?"

"I passed through a month ago, and I've come back for a longer look around."

Then the young man spat, jerking forward stiffly from the neck to shoot clear of the shirt ruffs. After that he joined the crowd moving out of the station.

"Lot of temperament there," said the stationmaster to himself, "in fact he looks all mane and temperament with a pair of legs dangling underneath. If the hair gets much longer, he'll need someone walking behind to hold it off the ground . . ."

Inshroin continued reading. At the same time, over on another lot, the more established D. W. Griffith was shooting the battle scene for one of his films. Five hundred men were fighting and struggling, and so inspired were they by Griffith's voice through the megaphone, most of them were actually fighting almost to the death. The battle was to climax in and around three burning towers. Several men were sent to the lot gates to prevent curious or unwelcome intruders getting in, and the order was given to start the fires. Clouds of black smoke billowed up into the sky. As the battle swayed backward and forward up the burning stairs of the towers, some of the actors became trapped in the highest turrets by the flames. Through the megaphone Griffith called them down, saying dummies would be substituted and thrown over in their places. But the actors, completely immersed in their performance, wild and reckless with excitement, refused, jumping down themselves to add realism. Several broke arms and legs as they landed, and were carried to one side by quickly organized stretcher parties. After a quarter of an hour of filming, the flames were so high, the fire brigade saw the blaze and sent over engines to put it out. The guards at the gate stopped them getting in until the last frame was shot, and the towers reduced to smoldering ashes. After that the gates were opened and the brigade poured in. Fights broke out between actors and firemen who were furious because they hadn't been allowed in on the production. Finally they had to console themselves with spurting water on the heaps of smoldering ashes before they left.

Inshroin was concluding his reading of *The Outlaw in the Reign of Gun:* "The young woman was taken around to the

5

stable where Garrett had brought his horse. A noosed rope was thrown over a beam. Her eyes flashed around on the crowd as she declared in broken English that she would do the same again to any man who treated her in such a fashion. Taking long blond hair in her hands, she held it out at arm's length while the rope was placed around her neck. She then allowed it to flow its whole length down to her knees, and so died without a sound." Inshroin stopped reading and looked up.

"How much longer is it?" asked the Chief.

"That's it, the story finishes on that scene. I think it's very dramatic."

"Do you?"

Inshroin called the drinks waiter over.

"Do you enjoy your job with Mr. Drewstone?" he asked.

"Yes sir, very much."

"Earning enough to feed the family?"

"Yes sir."

"How long have you been working here?"

"Six months sir."

"I see," said Inshroin, "then you are not the man who took my order. Do you think I could have that beer now? I'm very thirsty."

Drewstone got up from his desk, went to the window and lifted the blind. The California sun lunged in and bent a long shadow of him up the wall behind. The room remained silent as he stared out onto his lot—a collection of wooden barnlike structures and huts. At the rear of the property the ground ascended steeply and disappeared into a fringe of rocks and scrub that covered the area as far as Van Nuys.

Trails of foam trickled down the sides of beer glasses and soaked into the coasters underneath. As was his habit in these situations, the Chief maintained the air of a man about to let a guillotine blade fall. Finally he turned back to the room, and said, "Well, what do you others think about it as a story?" The room still remained silent, and everybody sat with their mouths open. They looked like Punch and Judy puppets after the operator has taken his hand out.

"Such a to-do, then no to-do. Must be a deaf and dumb institute near here, and this is founders' day. Rolf, you've been looking at scripts for a year now, what do you think?"

"Think? Think?" replied Rolf. "I've got a few talents useful to the industry, but I'd never go as far as to call myself a thinker."

"I see," said Drewstone. "As far as I'm concerned it's completely unsuitable for an outlaw photoplay. Where did you get it from?"

"My old theater agent in New York sent it to me."

"Yes, I imagine he would, it's very typical of the theater, much too wordy. You're not on the stage anymore Inshroin, you're in films now, and that's a different thing altogether. If that's the kind of stuff the theater likes, no wonder it's dying. The people in the story are unreal, not true to life. Also it's too complicated, too intellectual. Our art has no sound, there's no place for a lot of words, so a story should be simple and direct."

Drewstone shook his head, the executives took the cue, came alive, poked each other in the ribs, and laughed.

"It's a ridiculous story, Mr. Drewstone."

"A real gaffe."

"Never take off, Chief."

Everybody was enjoying the opportunity to sneer openly at Inshroin. Although the actor was becoming popular with the filmgoing public, he was not liked in the company. He had a capacity to laugh at himself. It made him racy, and took away from the serious work of concentrating on the drive to success.

In the 1930s when things will get difficult for the actor, he will turn to liquor for support. There will be no slow and steady decline, just a sudden physical collapse. He will come apart, full of self-criticism and self-parody.

Inshroin stood up, "I think it's a good story, and I noticed that I managed to get through it before you said anything."

"It wasn't the story," said the Chief. "I was enjoying the sound of your voice. I was thinking what I could make of it if we had sound in pictures."

Inshroin smiled. "A lot of people tell me I love the sound of my own voice, but it's not true, basically I revel in a childlike delight at being a voice-owning personality. Anyway, whatever you say about the story, the author has created an atmosphere that is real and true to the times and daily lives of people living in small-town Victorian America. We always looked to Europe for our styles and tastes, and he's tried to show that. If you remember, Lincoln was watching *Our American Cousin* when he was killed. It was the hit of the season."

" 'Europe,' you say," said the Chief. "I was in Europe once, did the whole trip. After three weeks of museums and art, I couldn't move for cultural constipation. I had to get back to the States to have a good crap."

He gazed intently into the distance. His own brand of inspiration was sinking in and mixing at a great depth.

"I'll spell it out for you, Inshroin. Basically what you've read to me is a story about a successful bank robbery, and a girl who doesn't end up happy ever after. It breaks all of my rules. A girl always ends up well clothed and happy ever after in my photoplays, and nobody steals money without getting caught. The women in an audience want to see a lot of cash spread on a girl's back and imagine it's happening to them. The men want to see that too, but in addition they want to think they're the ones doing the spreading. Nobody can do either without money in the bank."

He raised his eyebrows. "So how could I allow two robbers to steal a town's entire savings and get away with it? No, I'm afraid your story doesn't fit the bill either."

"Seems to me you've got a lot of faith in happy-ever-after," said Inshroin.

The Chief's facial contortion resolved itself into a strained smile.

"It's my ultimate faith for the country," he said. "The secret of my success is that I know the American public like I know my own fly buttons. People flocked to this country because they believed happiness was easily obtainable here. In the Old World, millions are not certain of happiness because they've struggled so long against the oppressor. My job is to offer them something they can see and understand, which will help them fulfill the raw desire for a better life. In doing so I, we all, make money."

"From the way you're talking," said Inshroin, "I'm convinced you've got a mandate from Christ."

The Chief ignored the remark as he was fumbling in the side drawer of his desk. He took out a script and stuck it toward Inshroin. The actor took it and flicked through the pages.

"I'd like you to read some of that to me. It's a story by an American at the war front in France. I know it's not a western, but it's an example of what I consider direct and exciting material. I'd use it myself, but the author has already sold it to Biographic."

Inshroin glanced down the first page, as the Chief sat watching him, tapping a pencil on the desk. "Out loud and from the beginning," he said.

As Inshroin started to read, the Chief got up and stood behind his chair. The words were having a liquorlike effect on him. He clasped his hands behind his back, convexed his chest, and stared down his columnlike legs. After a few minutes of recitation he said, "Read that bit once more."

" 'Here come the Huns again!' exclaimed Frank Sheldon, as from the American front line, his keen gray eyes searched the land ahead. 'Bad habit they have, we'll have to try and cure them of it. It's a pity they've come back for more. What we did to them last time was a shame.' "

"That's powerful stuff," said the Chief. "With that story we all know where we are. The author has laid down a barrage while throwing himself into his dramatic task in an intense way. Nothing of lasting human interest has escaped him. He works like a fire department and military attaché combined. He remains tireless and sleepless, moves forward, misses nothing, mops up, and brings home the final victory!"

The Chief's eyes seemed to revolve in their sockets, then righted themselves.

"When big events like these are happening, this company must march with them."

He sat down in his chair, as the executives watched him, sipping their beers.

"Now Inshroin," he went on. "I know you're interested in the production and writing side of things, but I see your principal function as our photogenic figurehead. It's the main reason I'm sending you with the film crew to France. Your job will be to keep out of danger, follow them everywhere as an observer, absorb everything you can, and get your picture in as many papers as possible. You'll have a lot of competition. Walter Long from *Birth of a Nation* is already in Europe, and his company will make as much out of it as they can."

The Chief looked up at the ceiling. "I'm convinced that *Over There* can be turned into a fine pic, if we get the right background material, to show how our American principles compare with what the Hun is doing in France. And you're the star who will roll up his sleeves and show the world this country's biceps. My God, what a chance it is for you! I'd go to France myself, but firstly I'm a little too old, and secondly, somebody has to stay here at the helm. Anyway it's a good thing our young men are doing the fighting. They have no fear, are stronger, and better able to stand up to things with fierceness. Older men like me calm down quickly, and are liable to forgive suddenly. Our army needs a raw anger that burns furiously; otherwise they won't have the heart to kill."

"Hear, hear," said one of two voices.

"Good," said the Chief. "I'm glad that's understood. But it still doesn't solve the problem of the western. Luckily, while we've been talking I've come up with a plot that's a mixture of three of the stories we've been looking at, and it's a good one."

The executives looked relieved, finished their beers, and allowed a butler to refill the glasses.

The plot Drewstone thought up at the meeting materialized into a story called *Heart of a Gambler*.

Still sneering, Luke the gambler called Jake a vile name. Jake's trigger finger itched, but he said, "Get up and we'll shoot square."

Suddenly, like the treacherous snake he was, the gambler made a false move toward his hip. Jake fired twice and the gambler pitched forward. He was as dead as a stone. Jake had shot him through the lungs.

With Inshroin playing Jake, the film was shot in two days and in the theaters in four.

On the day it opened all across the country, Inshroin went into a Hollywood drugstore.

"Do you have a copy of Pater's *History of France*?" he asked the clerk. "I'm off to the war, and need to know something about Europe."

"We don't sell books, sir, this is a drugstore."

"I'm not particular whether it's leather- or clothbound."

"We don't sell books, sir, this is a drugstore."

"Actually I told a small fib, it's a present for one of my relatives, so wrap it beautifully."

"We do *not* sell books, sir."

"Gift wrap it as you would for your own brother. When I get home I'll write something endearing on the flyleaf."

"We don't sell books, sir," screamed the clerk.

"I see. I quite understand, a history of Germany will do just as well."

The shop clerk went over to the manager, who was by now peering anxiously out from a small office at the back of the store. There was an anguished and tense conversation in which Inshroin heard the word "insane" used several times.

The manager left the clerk standing by the office door and came over.

"Can I help you, sir?"

"You're the manager?"

"I am."

"Good, I'm going to France on a visit and need some sea sickness pills. Do you have any in stock, your assistant didn't seem to know."

"Certainly, sir," said the manager, handing over a box of pills.

As he took Inshroin's money he looked over his shoulder, and gave the clerk a series of withering looks.

Hollywood will expand quickly as a film center. The theater seems to be in a state of decline. The spotlights of Broadway (that some people had known individually by name) are becoming just a flashlight flicker aimed at the movie capital. From there a more powerful beam is starting to reach out and throw an image of a performer around the world.

Real estate is cheap in California, and the long, sun-filled days are necessary to a revolution that hasn't yet reached the point where it can use artificial illumination. Light is as important as a painter's palette. In Hollywood, actors no longer walk in front of backdrops with light and shade painted on them, they stand in front of a camera, ensnared in shadows naturally created for their bodies by the sun.

There was the matter of talk about mothers, for example, I can't imagine this being the case in a volunteer army of American boys, but not once during fifteen months of British army life did I hear a discussion of mothers.

J. N. Hall
Kitchener's Mob

TWO WEEKS LATER Inshroin and a camera crew were in London en route to France. By the time they got there in the fall of 1917, the Canadians had just consolidated the first great victory of the war at Vimy Ridge, and their commanding officer had been knighted in the field by George V.

Men were marching away to new and bigger assaults, and the women left at home were making the loveliest ammunition in existence. The bullets were so precise and beautiful they could have graced a modern art gallery, while the heavy shells lived and breathed, each one looking chaste, chic, and nunlike.

For the first three years before America became involved on a national scale in the war, US volunteers had come across as Canadians. A sheriff had arrived at a depot in England with men, gun, and a badge. His corps was called the posse, and he informed the press he had come to arrest the Kaiser in the name of the State of Illinois.

Inshroin and the crew left for France from a central London station crowded with troops and women. A mute people—a stammer, a stutter, and a fight against the tears. Most people looking at each other silently, hearts full, mouths empty. A soldier standing with his parents patted his mother on the shoulder. Inshroin saw that she trembled but made an effort to hide it. "You didn't have a proper shave this morning," she said. All three started to talk about a play they had seen together the previous evening. The parents made such an effort it actually sounded as if they were really interested in the theater. They talked against time, pressing out the words. Then silence fell. When the guard blew his whistle, the young man said, "Well, I think I'd better be going." He kissed his mother, who embraced him. Then he turned and brushed his lips gently on his father's cheek. The man raised a hand quickly to the spot as if he had been burned.

Inshroin stood aside to let a middle-aged officer and a nursing sister get on the train first.

"Mind you don't let my lads get free and easy with your nurses," he said.

"I don't think you need to worry," replied the sister, tapping her forehead confidently. "My girls have it up here."

"I don't care where they have it; my lads will find it."

The battle Inshroin and the Drewstone film crew were to observe would last a week. Preliminary attacks to probe the German defenses had started on Monday and would go on till Friday, when the bulk of the army would attack.

As the Hollywood men arrived, half a million soldiers were strewn across the French countryside. Young officers strolled around acting the part of Victorian governesses, and sergeants barked like sheepdogs at their flocks.

From the first day a padre started burials in a running funeral that never stopped. The lines of dead crept from the hospital tents to the cemetery like a tide. Deserters were being shot; the order was passed down to put gas masks on backward, so the firing squad didn't see the faces moving of those found guilty, nor hear them calling to their friends.

Two privates were in the process of being court-martialed.

"Why did you kick the general?"

"I have quick reflexes in my foot, and the man behind stepped on my heel causing the foot to shoot out."

"I see. And you, why did you kick the general?"

"I didn't know about the problem with this man's reflexes. When I saw him kicking the officer, I thought the war was over, so I kicked the general too."

After the crew had stacked their equipment in a hut office, Inshroin walked past the animal hospital, and went to one of the many tent bars for a drink.★

★The Royal Army Veterinary Corps and the RSPCA (Royal Society for the Prevention of Cruelty to Animals) successfully treated, through four years of war, 725,216 horses and dogs wounded in action. At the height of the war, one hospital was equipped with stalls for 2,500 patients, a motor ambulance to bring in the wounded, an operating room, and messes for officers and men.

The officers' mess was very luxurious, with tables and chairs set up in front of the main tent. Inshroin sat down at one of the outside tables, ordered a Scotch with water.

Without warning he had his first experience of light German shelling, when two missiles wobbled through space in his direction. The first sounded like a steam whistle. The noise of its approach started on a low note, which rose quickly to piercing intensity and finished in a crash behind him. The other shell was heavier and rolled across the sky making a noise like an approaching express train. Suddenly he swore it was coming directly for him. He felt a strong inward urge that compelled him to put his hands over his genitals and whistle a tune. Don't hurry—get it finished before the explosion and he would be safe.

The tune was finished in time, but he felt a rush of panic. There would be more of them coming over. He glanced around to see if anybody had noticed his fear. Officers continued drinking and talking. When the Scotch arrived, he took a gulp as if he were trying to throw the contents of the glass straight into his stomach.

Outside the mess tent, in full view of everybody, a private was going through strange contortions. To Inshroin he appeared to be holding an imaginary bucket of water out at arm's length, one hand at the top, one at the bottom. He took it down to his side, then threw the contents up over his shoulder. He completed the sweep with a golfing mannerism, bending one leg at the knee and going up on his toe. This went on for about five minutes—languidly. The imaginary bucket down to his side, up over his shoulder, knee bent, up on his toes.

A sergeant approached the man. He asked him who he was, and what he was doing.

"Brian," said the private, "and I'm undertaking bayonet practice—stabbing people."

The officers' club fell silent, and a conversation ensued between the two men in which the sergeant seemed to be doing most of the talking.

Inshroin heard everything clearly, because those were the days when sergeants spoke to privates as if they were trying to pick a quarrel with them. When one opened his mouth, a raw recruit was supposed to feel as if he had been raked by gunfire. The private was asked if he expected to sleep with the Germans, and whether he would like some eau de cologne for his bayonet. He learned that the implement was to be driven deep into a man's balls or stomach so he would dig his own grave as he squirmed around dying. Under instruction he put his imaginary rifle out from the waist: "At the bollocks—*point*! At the bollocks—*point*!"

Inshroin heard a British accent behind him.

"This war has gone on for so long because the dregs of the socialist working classes are flabby with comfort, uppish, and pert with sheer safety. This life-and-death job in the field will do them no end of good."

Another British voice joined in. "I was stuck in a trench with a miner from Scotland last week. Funny person, his cock was as long as a cannon barrel."

"Not as long as that, I should hope!"

"Well as long as a rifle with a bayonet attached."

"Impossible."

"Then it was as long as your pistol—and dammit, I won't make it an inch shorter for anybody!"

"What the hell does he do with it?"

"Puts it where he damn well likes, I should think."

Inshroin got up from his table and walked across to the rear trench, the one farthest from the Germans.

He went down some steps and walked along a zigzag path twelve feet below ground level. Occasionally he glanced up as soldiers scissored across, silhouetted black against the sky. The trench was one vast suburban street full of watching neighbors, each man staying as close to the next as male pride would permit. They were a family, separated only in the job of each man keeping alive.

In one section Inshroin passed, men were lounging in armchairs, shelves had been put up, and flowers in pots swayed in the breeze. A coffin cut in half was full of foxgloves, and someone was turning over the soil with a little trowel. Inshroin turned a corner—two signs were nailed up: One pointed to a sandbagged hole and said LIBRARY; the other, LATRINES HERE PURELY ORNAMENTAL.

He lifted the flap of the library. It was a cave cut in the side of the trench lit by candles. There were four tables, chairs, and a shelf of books. A major was explaining a new process of war, and a group of young officers unversed in carnage stood around their superior listening religiously. Inshroin sat down by the entrance.

"You are professional misleaders now," the major was saying, "a privileged group, soon to be specialists in the art of deception. To you war must become a game of poker in which subtle bluff can win the jackpot. Our newly formed propaganda department will alter the course of this and all future wars.

"Propaganda can help make men hate and despise the enemy if the right subjects are used. The basic ideas are quite simple and are based on the old science of lying. There are three ways of lying. The first is unskilled lying, which is just using simple statements that are not true. The second is semiskilled lying, which is using statements part of which are true and part of which are false. The third method, the one we're going to use, is highly skilled lying. This consists of using statements that are absolutely true but are used to convey the wrong information." He smiled to himself. "In a nutshell it's a sophisticated interpretation of the old description of three classes of liars. Simple liars, damned liars, and expert witnesses."

The flap of the library was opened, and a young woman in the uniform of an ambulance driver stepped in.

"At it again, are you Bob," she said, "you and your new department. What you all want is to go through a battle that isn't really dangerous and come out from it with a wound that doesn't really hurt, I know."

The major smiled; they all smiled. The library was suddenly full of teeth.

"I've just come to tell you that we got the Charlie Chaplin film, and it's on tonight at eight."

"Nothing like a good comedy before a big push," said the major. "We'll be there."

As the woman turned to leave she glanced at Inshroin, put her mouth into an O and blew him a quick kiss. He nodded back as he toyed with a skull he had picked up from the shelf. It still had a little hair on the crown, and he ran his finger around a coin embedded just below the left eye socket.

That evening the tin hut used as a cinema was crowded with shouting and cheering men all through the Chaplin performance. As reels were being changed, a corporal entered and said a German plane was coming down, and everybody went out to look. The aircraft was on fire, and Inshroin got to the door just in time to see it hit the wire five hundred yards ahead. It bounced twice along the ground, then settled into a dozen pieces. Three men were sent out to look for survivors.

After the movie the audience filed out, and officers, medals covering their chests like shrubbery, shook hands with each soldier. It was a victory-just-around-the-corner grip, and was longer than usual.

The reels of film were wrapped carefully in oil paper and put in the back of the ambulance by the woman who had visited the library. As she got into the vehicle and started the engine, soldiers patted the sides. Moving off, she leaned out and blew kisses.

"Remember, boys, when you go into battle tomorrow, take no prisoners! Steal Fritz's helmet or any other souvenir you want, then let him go."

Sir Arthur Conan Doyle was visiting the front, and he was standing to one side with a major, watching the proceedings. A group of young privates passed the two men, and Conan Doyle, glancing at their shoulder tabs, noted they were from a public school battalion.

"I thought you fellows would be officers by now," he said.

"No sir, we like it better this way."

"Well, it'll be a great memory for you."

They all saluted and passed on.

"This war is looking up," said Conan Doyle to the major. "Even the mad cranks whose consciences prevent them from barring the way to the devil seem to be turning into men. I saw a batch of them working with a will by the road yesterday; they'll volunteer for the front soon."

A French general recognized Conan Doyle. "Is Sherlock Holmes a soldier in the English army?" he asked.

"He'd like to be general, but I'm afraid he's a little too old."

As Conan Doyle walked to his car, a battery of guns beside the road opened fire. One of the gunners was singing, but he couldn't be heard above the noise. His mouth opened and shut silently as he placed shells in the breach. Beside him four men were kneeling in a circle around a wounded messenger pigeon. It was being tenderly fed milk from an eyedropper. The bird lay on its back, claws folded and limp, wings spread, eyes flickering. Blood trickled from a small hole in its chest.

There is a tale of the trenches
Told when the shadows creep
Over the bags and traverses
And poppies fall asleep.

Shadow races with shadow
Steel comes quick on steel
Swords that are deadly silent
And shadows that do not feel.

And shadows recoil and recover
And fade away as they fall
In the space between the trenches
And the watchers see it all.

P. McGill

THE NEXT MORNING troops began to move into their forward positions. The brigade that Inshroin and his camera crew were with was integrated, and consisted of New Zealand, West Indian, and Canadian soldiers, with a young Canadian colonel in command. They marched through an empty landscape—in country with the topsoil shot away, the seasons had disappeared. A few dead trees, known as Kaiser Bill's flowers, stood up here and there looking like stripped umbrella frames. There was no sound, either; the birds had nothing to land on. Inshroin looked back. The line of men stretched away until it dwindled into a blur of abstract soldier.

Up in the sky, a balloon hung suspended from a single white cloud. The German observer watched the advancing column, then passed the information to a battery on the ground. A white cloud was created instantly above Inshroin's head. Without a sound it puffed into a perfect smoke ring. After that, there was a rushing sound that grew louder, then, one hundred yards ahead, a shell fell and built itself magnificently into body and skirts. The ground shook like a bowl of jelly.

Inshroin pulled the camera tripod he was carrying closer to his shoulder and trudged on. His part of the line soon came across a heap of bodies lying over the road, thrown around a

18

large hole. All were half-naked and the majority disemboweled. One man lay on his back holding his stomach region, making a noise like a slide trombone. The fresh troops going past gasped.

"Don't slouch," shouted a sergeant. "Hold those rifles up properly. If you don't like it, look the other way. We have to pay a price for the kind of hike we're on."

Most of the younger ones could only hold their tongues, and either looked away as they passed or stared speechless. Inshroin felt ill. The only blood he had known was a harmless substance the wardrobe department said could be washed off—or in a pinch swallowed.

They settled into their forward trenches late in the afternoon, and Inshroin and the crew decided to stay with the group they had come forward with. He walked over to the Canadian officer who was questioning the German lines with a pair of binoculars. Every now and again he would lower the glasses and report something to a sergeant standing at his side, who took it down in a notebook.

"Is this trench private?" asked Inshroin. "Or can anyone shoot from it?"

"Are you from Ireland?"

"Staten Island."

The officer grinned and waved his arm in a go-where-you-want gesture.

They set up their equipment, and started filming. Farther along the line, Lieutenant Garth (The Kid) Windslow, DSO, produced a pocket manicure set, leaned against the trench wall, and started polishing his nails. The officer who Inshroin had spoken to watched him.

"He's as mischievous as a puppy and as soft-hearted as a woman, but he knows his job."

"Yes sir," replied the sergeant.

"Last week he caused a hysterical exchange of official memoranda when he tried to send a machine gun corps he'd captured home as a souvenir. There they stood in the field post office, six big Germans, each with a label addressed to Garth's parents stuck in the middle of their foreheads."

The officer put his eyes back to the round OO of the binoculars.

"Yes sir," said the sergeant.

The filming proceeded. Sixteen frames a second, lots of

foreground, and because they had no telescopic lenses, they held their shots longer than modern filmmakers. Soldiers piled into one another as they stood in watch-the-birdie groups, a habit the world got into with the invention of photography.

A soldier who was positioning himself for a picture tripped and fell face down at the bottom of the trench. He quickly got to his feet and put a hand over his mouth.

"Jesus Christ! Wot 'ave I done! I flopped on a stinkin' corpse. 'E was 'uggin' an' kissin' me, the stiff cunt! Talk about rotten eggs bustin' in yer mouth!"

The Canadian officer came over. "If there's someone there, you'd better dig him up; we don't want to spread any diseases."

Taking a fold-up shovel out of his pack, the man who had fallen knelt down and dug into the ground. He unearthed a particle of clothing. A boot came into view, then a second. Finally an evil-smelling bundle of clothes and some decaying flesh were revealed.

The head was well preserved; the man might have fallen the night before. The nose was pinched and thin, turned up at the end, while the lips were drawn back tight around the gums. The teeth showed doglike.

"I suppose 'e copped a packet, dropped into the muck, then got trampled on."

"What does his cold-meat ticket* say?" asked the officer.

"Can't find one."

"Anything in the clothes?"

One pocket remained on the tunic, and inside was a letter. Soldiers closed in to listen as the officer read out:

Dear Major Wilson:

What about my son's blood money? I'm certain our Tony did a few Germans in, and he said we should get blood money for each one if our dear boy was killed. I'm sorry to write this, but I am a poor man unlike yourself, and have eight children to support. What about them trousers he had when he went away? Was he shot in them as I would like them back, they would come in handy for one of my younger lads.

Yours truly
Terrance Smith

* Identification disk.

20

Everybody looked back down, and as if animated by their gaze the remains moved. The belly heaved, and a rat scurried out of the carcass.

> Five yards left extend!
> It passed from rank to rank,
> And line after line with never a bend
> And a touch of the London swank.
> Doing their Hyde Park stunt
> Swinging along at an easy pace
> Arms at the trail, eyes to the front
> With the shrapnel right in their face.
>
> Sir Arthur Conan Doyle

EVENING CAME ON, and in the darkness Inshroin could see the shapes only of men standing close by, though hundreds of glowing cigarettes in every direction.

Plop went a light. Everybody flattened behind the slightest convexity. *Plop, plop, plop,* went other lights. The surrounding area was illuminated for a while, then the flares burned out, throwing off a shower of insulting sparks into the soldiers' faces. Once again everything was black.

"Fritzy keeping an eye on us," somebody said.

Somewhere in the distance a mouth organ played "Hello, Hello, It's a Different Girl Again" . . .

Out in no-man's-land a night patrol was probing an advance section of the German line. As they crawled forward, it suddenly started to rain. Without warning a German searchlight was turned on and swung a beam of light straight into the upturned faces. For a second of silence it held everybody frozen as pulses rose quickly to the elevation of risk, then the officer screamed, "Go for the light!" He started to run forward as machine guns opened up ahead. "Move! move! I want soldiers, not mice! Come on, you bullet eaters, get right into the teeth of the thresher, you whore-puss!"

The officer was hit in the neck, and he fell to his knees groaning. The rest of the men rushed past him.

Once into the enemy trench the patrol quickly and skillfully butchered the outnumbered Germans. A sergeant held the searchlight operator by the throat, and was pressing his head against a wall of sandbags. The German's eyes were strained open, while on his lips was a chalky line of dried spit.

"Who ain't stuck an 'un yet? Rowntree come 'ere!"

A child stepped forward as the other men stopped to watch.

"Ram that knife 'ome boy, come on ram it 'ome!"

The soldier spoken to made a halfhearted thrust at the German's chest. A *pop* of air escaped from a pierced lung.

"Harder, you cunt, harder!"

The German began to imitate the scream of shells with a treble shriek of his own.

"Wot a din," said the sergeant, "'ee's 'avin' a lovely time bein' at the center of so much attention."

The soldier with the bayonet looked around, and an uncertain grin wobbled toward his ears. Then he turned back and began to stab and stab . . . The rain came down harder, and mud from the top of the trench washed down the face of the victim and filled his mouth. The screams turned to a gurgle, the gurgle to a gasp, which finally stopped altogether.

The patrol's officer lay on his back under the night sky, a flesh canoe floating in a sea of pain and mud. His eyes were fishlike and glazed. Blood pumped out of his mouth as if it were being forced out by the strokes of an internal piston. The back was arched while the hands dug into the mud. There was a lightning flash, and a gray form darted over his face and disappeared. Another one jumped onto his chest, stopped and licked some blood. Within seconds there were a dozen of the gray forms moving round his head, sniffing and squeaking . . .

At midnight the rain stopped, and the British bombardment began from a mile in the rear. The sound was as startling as the cry of a newborn baby, and would go on for seven hours. The horizon came alive with thousands of tiny flashes of light, each one looking like a white fan being flicked open, then instantly closed. Occasionally, a searchlight swept the sky in a great arc; if it stopped in its swing and held steady, a warm spotlit pool was formed in the sky.

The armies tried to doze, and the rest of Inshroin's night was filled with men calling in their sleep, the sound of crying, urinations close to his head, and the din of the bomardment. Hungry rats smelled his body, biting him as he attempted to beat them off. Now and then one managed to push under his clothing, and he felt a tiny sawlike tongue licking the sweat that covered him.

At six the artillery barrage increased in intensity. The sound was an ear-bursting roar that seemed to be a condition of the atmosphere.

By ten to seven, the Canadian officer was glancing continually at his watch, and the sergeant was kicking the troops into activity. Some had managed to sleep, and when they awoke and remembered where they were, fear started to bubble through their clothing, while cold clung to the body like scales. After that, standing up was an act of pure faith.

A mobile canteen unit arrived, and as the men ate breakfast, a Scots piper began to warm up. He walked to and fro completely absorbed, with skirts flying and head swaying. Commanders in the rear imagined the Germans would be cowering back now, frightened by the strange sound of Allied troops grinding bayonets on their teeth.

It was the Canadian officer's first big push in control of a section of the line, and he wanted to do it well. (On leave in London he had taken to saying to female admirers, "Nightingales make a hell of a noise, while the sound of guns is music of a kind.")

"Two minutes to go." He was in an inward frenzy but kept his voice steady.

A shell fell on the parapet above his head.

"Jesus Christ!" He lost control of his features, ducked quickly, and looked straight into the face of a soldier, who was smiling.

"I should be careful, sir, you'll be pumping brown in a minute."

"I've never had diarrhea in my life, and I don't intend to start now," said the officer.

"One minute thirty seconds."

His voice was squeaky. He pretended to cough as the line looked in his direction. A sergeant came to the rescue and drew the attention away. "Holy Jesus, I'll kill any fucker who lets me down."

"One minute twenty seconds to go."

The officer went on counting but raised his foot and punched a hole two feet from the bottom of the trench; others followed his example.

German machine guns opened up deep in the mist ahead; the bullets almost level with their heads hissed across the top of the trench. The officer undid the flap of his revolver case, eased the gun out of the holster, then leaned forward and took hold of the edge of the trench.

"One minute to go."

To the left he suddenly heard laughter, and looking along the line, he saw a little man walking toward him down the trench. A funny little soldier with a moustache, and a white cane instead of a rifle crooked over his arm. He walked jerkily at sixteen frames a second, and as he passed along, each man tried to reach out and touch him.

The First World War was one in which men were weighed for a uniform, not measured for it, and this little man had a hard time disposing of extra cloth. The waist of the jacket came down to his knees, and twelve inches of sleeve had been rolled back up his arms. The boots were huge, and stuck out six inches in front and six inches behind. He looked as if he were standing on a pair of rockers after the chair had been removed. He stopped by the officer and climbed onto the parapet. Turning sideways like a duelist, he covered his lungs with an arm, thus presenting the narrowest possible target to an opponent's sword. Next he stuck a heroic pose, put one foot in advance of the other and, with the forefingers of the right hand rigidly extended, made violent stabs in the direction of the German trench. When he'd done this a few times, he moved forward at a jerky run, twirling the white cane stick as he disappeared into the mist.

The corps clergyman, who had followed the little man down the trench, started his battle prayer. "Fear not for I am with thee, I will uphold thee with the right hand of my righteousness."

Other machine guns joined in, shuttling more and more bullets back and forth across the Allied position. They poured along the ground making a noise like timber snapping crisply.

"Behold, all that were incensed against thee shall be confounded. Thou shalt seek them out, and they that war against thee shall be as nothing and a thing of nought."

"A-five, a-four, a-three . . ."

"Surely something's gone wrong?" Inshroin said. "You can't be going over the top in this?"

There was no reply. The officer was concentrating on his watch while his mind crumpled into disbelief. Eyelids hung fat and heavy over hollow cheeks. The skin had turned gray, and the perspiration trickling down his face gave the impression his head was melting. Precisely at 7 A.M. the British barrage stopped.

"*Birdlime!*"*

For miles in either direction, lines of soldiers rose up out of slits in the earth and moved forward at a steady funeral pace. It was all very orderly, very calm, very middle class.

In Inshroin's section, the men heaved themselves up into the full glare of bullets and shrapnel. The Scot went first, his pipes keening that elemental voice of crying for those who cannot be shielded. The officer turned and glanced back for a second, looking immense between the trench top and the sky. Last to go was the sergeant, who had started shouting again: "I'll kill any fucker who lets me down! Sorry about the language, vicar."

Then they were gone, and the whole trench was empty. Inshroin looked over the top. A ragged line of men was disappearing into thick banks of smoke, some fell and picked themselves up, some disappeared into holes and got out again. A few lay still.

The signalman had his backpack hit, and red and green flares were going off in all directions. He looked as if he were at the center of a huge Catherine wheel.

One boy had only managed to advance ten feet before he was badly wiped and took a red lesson. He lay on his side with his hands up around his head, then rolled slowly over onto his back, and banged the ground with his knuckles. The face was absolutely concentrated as if he had discovered something real. The machine guns were now sounding frenzied as the operators began to get masses of advancing flesh in their sights.

Inshroin reached out and took into his hand a butterfly that had landed on the trench wall. It was content to lie there, beautiful and motionless in the alien landscape of his palm.

*Rhyming slang for *time*.

25

He's so straight and slim and fair
More sweet than I can say
I sometimes think the guns who loved him
Have kissed his flesh away.

Hades Herald

INSHROIN AND THE FILM CREW waited for twenty minutes, and then, picking up equipment, started to move toward the German position.

Over a fifteen-mile front, the wounded lay in their tens of thousands, the majority machine gunned. All had fallen violently and suddenly—none had been eased down. Most tried to mark places so they could be picked up by stretcher bearers, and bayonets were stuck in the ground leaving rifles upright, with the butts pointing to the sky. There was a forest of them, along with jettisoned packs, until they were uprooted by shell bursts or knocked down like skittles by machine gun spraying.

The first line of German trenches had been taken—they only needed to overrun another three, and they would be in the enemy's rear. Surprisingly there were few dead, most of the opposition forces having fallen back before the Allied troops arrived.

Lieutenant Garth (The Kid) Windslow, DSO, nailed a piece of cardboard to the captured trench wall. It was in the shape of a label, with string attached, and read:

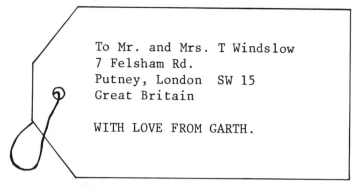

```
To Mr. and Mrs. T Windslow
7 Felsham Rd.
Putney, London   SW 15
Great Britain

WITH LOVE FROM GARTH.
```

Some prisoners huddled in a corner, and the German in command stepped forward and saluted. The Canadian made a polite attempt at conversation, asking him when he thought the war would finish. The officer replied that he didn't know, but when it did he could guarantee that it would be a few feet in any direction from where they were standing. After that he was taken into his own concrete bunker for questioning.

The sergeant went over to the group of prisoners who were laughing and winking with some of the New Zealanders. They were all looking at a photograph. The picture was of a woman lying back on a couch, she had one arm up behind her head, the other down at her side. She was naked except for a pair of stockings and tight steel garters that bit into the top of her thighs. Between her legs was a little Punch and Judy dog, wearing a thick ruff collar and a tiny hat with a bell on it. One paw rested on the woman's crotch as he rolled his eyes and tongue heavenward.

"Put that away," said the sergeant. "Give the prisoners shovels, and start them clearing mud from the bottom of the trench."

A cannon was brought up from the Allied lines and set up facing deeper into the enemy position. A German gun started to the right and fired once only. The piece of artillery that had just arrived answered back—the shell was a dud. It bowled fifty feet along the ground, then stuck on its nose in the earth.*

Inside the bunker, the cross-examining went on, while the pigeoneer sat with his basket of birds waiting to fly information back. As one of them was having a message attached to its claw, without warning there was a shattering explosion. The pigeoneer, his hands fluttering, leaped toward the ceiling; the candle flame flared and died. Complete silence followed. The camera crew, standing about thirty feet from the bunker, froze . . . The pigeons began to coo and flutter their wings gently, then the human noises started. Groans lapped up the side of the trench, and there was one continuous scream.

Fifty or so men jumped down into the trench and asked for the officer; some saluted the sergeant.

"Last of the Fifth, sir."

Candles were lit and held into the bunker. The doorway was blocked by a heap of soldiers, while the young Canadian officer sat in the middle of the floor, bolt upright, his legs scythed off

---

*Before the USA entered the war, duds were described as "American shells, too proud to fight."

below the knees. The hair, powdered with concrete, stood on end. Face muscles jumped up and down as he screamed and waved his arms in the air. The stumps were bound, and he was moved to one side. Another group of men rolled down into the trench.

"Last of the Fifth, sir."

A stretcher party appeared and stopped to pick up the Canadian. He was laid out carefully, and had MORPHIA penciled across his forehead. To get him over the edge of the trench, the medics upended the officer with the skill of furniture removers, climbed into the open, and disappeared towards the Allied lines.

"Garth's 'ead's been blown orf!"

There sat the kid supporting his head in his hands, blood streaming through his fingers. He had been hit by shell slivers. One piece had taken off the front of his skull, exposing the brain, while another had driven completely through his cheek, smashing the teeth of both upper and lower jaws. The entrance hole on the left side of his face gaped where the flesh was missing. On the right side, in the smaller exit hole, were embedded fragments of broken teeth. Another ragged puncture just below the jawbone had narrowly missed the jugular vein. His face looked like a sausage when it has burst in the heat of the frying pan.

"The top of my head's been blown away," said Garth. He got up and started to walk back to his own lines.

After he had gone, prisoners (elaborately instructed by pantomime) were ordered to remove the bodies to give some much needed space for a fresh start. Within twenty minutes there was no sign that the position had been filled with dead and dying soldiers.

A British tank crept slowly toward them from the direction of their own lines. For a second it seemed to swerve away, then it hitched itself around again and jerked forward. The animal kept coming . . . it rose over the top of the trench like a huge praying mantis, dropped its nose into the gap and stopped. Across the front, painted in white, were the words: TODAY I WANT TO WORK TOWARD A SWEET IF IMPOSSIBLE SMILE. Along the side was written: ONE OF HIS MAJESTY'S LAND SHIPS. A door opened in the middle of the word LAND and an officer stepped out.

"Good morning," he said. "Anything interesting happening up ahead?"

The sergeant saluted. "Thank Christ you stopped, sir, I thought the damn thing was coming down to look for food."

Some men led by a corporal appeared around the side of the tank. Two of them were carrying a wounded dog on a stretcher. When they saw the tank officer they stopped and the corporal saluted.

"Last of the Fifth, sir."

A messenger arrived and explained there was a massive buildup ahead, and a counterattack might succeed. When this news got around, shovels were taken away from the prisoners, and they were given cigarettes and drinks from hip flasks.

The Hollywood men had a quick discussion, and it was decided that as he wasn't of immediate technical use, Inshroin should go back with the cans of film they had already taken. He shook hands with the sergeant as he left.

"I 'ope you get some good pictures. We'll all be dead in an hour, but the country's proud of us. Best of luck."

Inshroin started to walk toward the Allied position, every now and then ducking into a crater when a shell dropped close by. Feeling like an elephant hiding behind a peanut, he lay beside a corpse in one mudfilled hole. The man was naked from the waist up, and his chest was covered with a huge tattoo—he looked as if he had been thrown down by its weight. Heat had blistered the face until it resembled gnarled bark. There was a glassy gleam deep in the eye sockets, and Inshroin leaned forward thinking he might be alive. The eyes had gone, however; ants had eaten through the back of his head: the gleam of light coming in from behind.

A helmet lay in the mud under the man's elbow. Across the front was painted the words: WELL HERE WE ARE. Inshroin picked himself up and, holding the cans of film tightly, started walking again. After another quarter of a mile, he came to a road where a line of carts and ambulances was pulled up. He noticed that the girl he had last seen at the film show was one of the drivers.

The first-assault dead were decaying as rapidly as horses' hooves, and a strange smell hung in the air. Some full carts were being drawn away, and Inshroin, watching, was surprised at the way bodies wobble when they are heaped one on top of the other. One corpse was being dragged toward the ambulance; the remains bumped along, with the arms out in the quarter-to-three position.

A doctor was kneeling beside the body of a soldier, going through his pockets. He pulled out a postcard and, holding it face down, could see the back was packed with words—a tiny neat hand that went all around the edges. At the bottom was a long row of Xs. He turned it over, and the face of a young woman stared up at him. It was a nicely taken picture and the doctor looked at it approvingly—he had wanted to be a photographer once, but he was a medical man in the big push now—and quickly put the card back in the pocket. He glanced at the man's face to see if he had finished dying and noticed the identification disk he had forgotten to remove. It was taken from around the corpse's neck. One side was blank, while on the other was stamped NO FLOWERS BY REQUEST.

The girl was the first to drive away, and Inshroin got a lift. She waved to a young doctor as they turned and pulled back toward the camp. "He's been good to me, that Englishman," she said. "When I first started this job and had to go out picking tags off the dead men, he'd find me ones wearing gas masks, so I didn't have to look at their faces . . . Quiet today. Sometimes casualties stick out the back like celery from an overloaded serving dish. Still, anything's better than the desert. I've got a friend driving with the British in Palestine; she tells me sand gets in everything, even into the most intimate parts of the anatomy. It's hardest on the girls," she winked at her passenger, "unless of course the man isn't circumcised."

Inshroin looked at her. Blonde hair tucked under her hat, a thin handsome face that just escaped being austere. He glanced at the uniform. She looked very soldierly, very solid, very concrete. He wondered if she had a lullaby bosom under the jacket.

"All that khaki camouflages you," he said.

"I don't understand what you're talking about. Do you mean that from the air I look like fields and trees?" She turned toward the actor and smiled. "My name's Lucy Armitage, by the way."

"And mine's Phillip Inshroin."

"I know, I recognized you that day I came into the library. I didn't say anything at the time because we don't talk about our civilian jobs out here. I really thought you'd made a mistake when I read you'd left the stage for films; I don't think they'll last. I can't see any future in a technique that shows moving pictures of a performer without being able to hear the voice. Actors will end up distorting emotions because they have to express everything with their faces and bodies."

"You seem to know a lot about it?"

"I want to go on the stage."

"Then why are you driving an ambulance in France?"

"I didn't find any work for a year after I left drama school, so when the war started, I thought I'd try something completely different for the experience. Somewhere in my deep and misty past I remember someone telling me war was man's ultimate theater."

"And what do you think of the war now?"

"It's not important what a woman thinks of war; how men fight is the important thing. Men belong to all this, and women belong to the peace afterward." She adjusted her rear-view mirror. "You'd be surprised how many actors like yourself there are dotted over the front. Walter Long is here somewhere. Know him?"

"Not personally," said Inshroin, "but I saw him in *The Birth of a Nation*. How's he getting on?"

"Pretty well from what I've heard. He's either a corporal or a general. There's an *a-l* in the title somewhere."

Out of the corner of his eye, Inshroin noticed a black curtain behind his head, separating the cab from the rest of the vehicle. It moved slightly, and the actor quickly fixed his eyes on the road ahead.

"Isn't this kind of work depressing?" he asked.

Lucy shrugged. "You can't say one kind of war job is any less depressing than another. I was depressed for the first three months I was here, but that was because I came to realize how shockable I was. I thought all men had minds like sewer rats. I was really upset when I first heard a man say, 'The second thing I'll do when I get home is take off my equipment.'

"I discovered later there are gentlemen, nature's gentlemen, drawn from all classes and all walks of life. I began to take an interest in things, watch the other girl drivers. Do you know some wouldn't even let a man squeeze their hands, were intentionally rude, and tried to ape the manners of rude male officers." She glanced at Inshroin and smiled. "And let me tell you, there are some rude male officers.

"I began to wonder if those women were any happier for being so prudish and cautious. The other kind, the sexual women, I started to find more human and companionable. Now I'm settled in, and as long as I can see my young men when I want to, I'm happy."

Lucy was now driving fast, or as fast as a vehicle of that kind would allow: like riding on wooden rims over railway ties. Inshroin sat back absorbing the bounces through his feet, knees, stomach, and elbows.

"This'll shake up the passengers," he said.

"They're all SAIK."

"SAIK?"

"Shot and Instantly Killed."

They started going uphill, and after ten minutes of slower driving, the road leveled off. Lucy stopped the engine and looked back.

"There's no loneliness so depressing yet so stimulating as a road deserted because of shelling," she said.

Out of a cloud of dust way back down the road a long procession had emerged. It looked like an endless snake, a gray reptile with red crosses on its back—crosses that dwindled as the snake diminished into the distance. At frequent intervals the line stopped squirming, and stretchers were lifted from its head. They were laid in rows on the earth, nurses fluttered about them, and the gray snake would crawl forward again. Two lines of troops crossed—one was reinforcements, the other wounded; to Inshroin they both looked like casualties.

"I was engaged once to a Canadian-born six-footer," said Lucy. "He loved fighting Germans, and the Germans shot him. He didn't ever think he'd be killed. I allowed my teeth to decay worrying about him. He was the first man ever to tell me I wasn't very feminine."

"How feminine are you with the men you've gone out with trying to forget him?"

Lucy smiled, and said quietly, "I've discovered I'm not too feminine."

She sat silently for a few seconds with her thoughts belonging to the dead soldier, then said, "Excuse me for a sec." She climbed out of the cab, pulled up her skirt, and squatted down. "Don't look!" she called.

Lucy got back into the driver's seat, restarted the engine, and they moved off. As the camp came into view over a ridge, the road dipped steeply, and she braked. The sudden movement of her foot caused Inshroin to glance down at her leg.

"You've got a huge hole in your stocking," he said.

"You would notice that."

"I could mend it for you."

"Get away with you."

"Everybody mends their socks in the trenches."

"Are you married?" she asked.

"Do I look married?"

"I haven't looked yet."

"Well, don't look now, or we'll end up in the ditch."

The ambulance passed through a fringe of trees and entered the camp, moving slowly down a plank road laid between rows of white and gray tents.

Lucy drove Inshroin to the Drewstone hut, and as the actor got out, he said, "We should see each other again. We can talk about working when the war's over."

"Shall we have a drink in the canteen mess tonight?" she asked.

"I'd rather not, the ones in this section are British, and they stink of charity."

"Come to my house then," replied Lucy. "I'm in the nursing section, hut twelve. Around eight."

She was about to put the engine in gear, when a French officer appeared on the driver's side of the cab.

"Oh hello," said Lucy. "Phillip, this is the chief of the French Medical Corps. We call him Old Bum Face; he doesn't speak any English."

The two men nodded at each other.

"Funny lingo," said Lucy, "but he means well with his *parlez-vous*. We ambulance girls like him because he's the only doctor who clicks his balls when he comes to attention."

The officer climbed onto the running board, and he, Lucy, and the dead soldiers bumped off toward the mortuary tent together.

That evening Inshroin arrived at Lucy's hut exactly at eight.

When he knocked, the door was opened by a young officer.

"Having a dinner party, is she?" asked Inshroin. "Are we both invited?"

The man shrugged. "There's no dinner party. I'm about to leave."

"Come in and sit down," called Lucy from somewhere in the interior. "I won't be a minute, Phillip. Meet young Colonel Bains. He's from Australia."

The two men shook hands and then they sat down, one at each end of a large sofa.

Lucy's "house" seemed to consist of two rooms. The one they were in was empty except for the large sofa and a mirror behind it on the wall; the other was obviously a bedroom.

Colonel Bains leaned across and started talking in whispers as if he were in a shrine or church.

"Did you know she's been awarded the Croix de Guerre with palms? It's the highest award the French army can give."

"No, I didn't know. How did she get it?"

"She was driving wounded into camp in a convoy of three ambulances, when they came under heavy fire. The other two drivers, both men, left their cabs and hid in a ditch; Lucy stayed. She drove her own vehicle to safety, then walked back and drove the other two out. Saved the lives of twenty men."

When Lucy appeared, she had changed her uniform for a long silk dressing gown; hair fell over her shoulders. She stepped into the room, languidly, like a giraffe, then stopped and stood behind the two men.

"I'm so pleased you could come, Phillip; I hope my complexion doesn't look too bad. When I'm driving my ambulance, I rub grease into my face, otherwise the skin would crack, but it takes hours to get out."

"I've just been telling him about your Croix de Guerre," said Bains, "and how you saved those soldiers when the two male drivers ran away."

Lucy patted him on the head. "I don't want to hear about the war tonight, in fact we all want a break from it." She came around and sat between them. "Get us some Scotch will you, Colonel? It's by the bed."

When he had gone, the two of them sat in silence for a few seconds. The sound of a bottle being opened came from the back room. She stretched out her hand and laid it on Inshroin's knee; he did the same to her. They stayed in that position for a while looking into each other's eyes . . . Lucy's face flushed, and leaning sideways she kissed him on the mouth. Inshroin pulled her across and began to kiss her neck.

They were only aware of Bains's return when he coughed politely. He came across the room carrying a little tin tray with a bottle and three glasses on it. Setting the tray on the floor, he fell on his knees beside Lucy, put his head on her lap, and rubbed his cheek on her dressing gown. As he had his face turned in the actor's direction, Inshroin could see tears welling up in his eyes.

Lucy continued looking at the actor while patting the other man's cheek. She puckered her lips, leaned sideways, and said, "Kissakissa," while mechanically rubbing off her tear-stained hand against the sofa.

Inshroin kissed her again.

From her lap Bains started talking. He said that Lucy should have wild apple blossoms in armfuls, and she would never have to worry about being a star after the war, because a whole nation would be anxious to see movies of her exploits. He said all the men he knew loved to dig her latrines and to share their rations with a woman driver who was doing such patriotic services. Lucy said nothing at first, continued patting his head, but raised her eyes toward Inshroin and mouthed "Help" toward him.

"That's not really true," she said. "When men are exhausted by a battle they hate women being near because they can't wash naked. We women close at hand mean an order to wear drawers." She shifted her legs. "Will you move a little? My word, you're heavy. You look like a tiny chicken; you must have big bones. Silly boy, you can always come and see me, that's part of my job, always to find time for officers like you."

Then she pushed him away, and he got off the floor blowing his nose. Bains sniffed, flicked the ends of his nostrils with a big handkerchief, and thrust it deep into his pocket.

"I'll have to go now," he said. "I'm back at headquarters in ten minutes."

"How's it going?" asked Inshroin. "Are we getting beaten?"

"No, just roughly handled. I've made a survey in a number of areas, and both the German dead and the Allied dead are facing in the same direction. The Germans in retreat, us in pursuit. There are a lot more dead Germans, so we've got the initiative. All we have to do now is keep at them and they'll go."

Inshroin got up and walked Bains to the door. Neither looked at the other as the first man left.

"I didn't do much for the Croix de Guerre," Lucy said. "Those other two drivers were only boys, and they shouldn't be criticized for running away. If I could have talked to them I'm sure they would have stuck it out. The kids just made a mistake in judgment."

"How are our American boys comparing with the other soldiers?"

"I don't know much about the French and Empire soldiers," said Lucy. "I've only been with the limeys and the septics. The big diff—"

"What's a septic?"

"It's British rhyming slang—septic tank, Yank. The big difference I notice is that British troops don't talk about their mothers; American troops don't talk about much else . . . except sex."

"That's because mothers dominate America," said Inshroin. "An old Australian professor once told me that; I hadn't realized until he pointed it out. His theory was that the patriarch had disappeared in America, and been replaced by the matriarch. Our country isn't a democracy or a meritocracy, it's a gynocracy."

"Your professor doesn't know what he's talking about," said Lucy. "American women don't have that kind of control."

"He didn't say women, he said mothers."

Lucy smiled, stood up, undid her dressing gown, and let it slip to the floor. She stood naked in the middle of the room, arms crossed over her breasts. "If you're one of those men who like big bosoms, you won't get much pleasure with me," she said.

Inshroin smiled. "You never know. Pleasure is a very mysterious thing. If you find it in one place today, you won't find it there tomorrow. You can't lay a trap for it, because pleasure has no logic, and it never treads in its own footsteps." He leaned forward as Lucy put an arm around his shoulders. "Pleasure comes unexpectedly and surprisingly, like a white swan onto a small village pond, then for no reason we can discover, it lifts itself away and is gone. All we are left with is its memory."

"That's very wise."

"Yes, it's J. M. Barrie, the man who wrote *Peter Pan*. I used to read him a lot."

Inshroin saw no more action. The following day he received a telegram from the Chief ordering him to Palestine, where he was photographed with T. E. Lawrence as the victorious British army entered Jerusalem. Then back to France, a week after Germany's surrender, the front once again, filmed wining, dining, playing soccer with the enemy.

On an evening toward the end of 1918, Inshroin strolled out onto what had been no-man's-land, where he stood smoking and taking a last look around. A clear sky, a cluster of clouds, the kind on which winged cherubs rest chubby elbows. The landscape flayed and raw. France was a giant petrified stew of machinery and barbed wire where once wheat had grown from horizon to horizon. A billion shell holes lay like giant soup plates scummed with motionless bubbles. Smashed signposts everywhere, headstones over the graves of towns dead and buried. Slowly, the citizens blinking and coughing emerged from their cellars and began digging up the bombs sown into their fields. There would be no more plowing until they had been removed, or a farmer might never reach the end of a furrow alive.

An English corporal going by on a bike pulled up and asked the actor for a light. He drew hard on the cigarette.

"Now the war's over, nuthin' will be done to the Kaiser, nuthin'."

"We didn't let Napoleon off scot-free."

"No, but 'e wasn't related to our royal family."

France softened and dissolved into the twilight. The last things to remain distinct were dead trees—their skeletons stuck out of the dimness, crooked fingers clawing at the rising moon. As the train pulled out of Paris on the way to the coast, Inshroin leaned out of the window of his compartment. He had a golf club in his hand, and with it he knocked off every officer's hat as he passed along the platform . . .

There are thousands of men in Europe today suffering from the effects of war, who can never hope to get better, and whose suffering is not known.

"You mean," she said, "they belong to the legion who dazzled us with their valour, and staggered us with their daring deeds?"

"Yes," I reply.

"Well," she says, "all is not gold that glitters. There must never be another grand parade. It isn't worth it."

Reader, it is simply a question of S.O.S. The Great War was the S.O.S. danger signal to civilization. If we ignore that S.O.S. and the lesson of war, civilization is doomed.

F. P. Crozier
A Brass Hat in No Man's Land

Wars are over, wrongs are righted
God is forgotten, soldiers slighted.

Hades Herald

A S SOON AS THE ARMISTICE WAS SIGNED, the medal distribution started, and dates were set for glorious anniversaries. In the streets of the winning nations, people were going wild with jubilation. There was a general desire to go back to a way of life that had existed before 1914.

The RSPCA was busier than ever. Nearly three thousand dogs had been used as messengers, and their owners began smuggling them back to the main Allied bases in Britain, trying to bypass the quarantine fees they couldn't afford. The RSPCA was inundated with letters regarding demobilized dogs. From a private in the Royal Engineers:

Dear Sir:
My dog is of no known breed yet his intelligence exceeds many human beings I have known, especially the officer class at headquarters. He has been my companion through many terrible times, and I cannot discard him on the day of peace. He has been a

faithful animal to me both in holding the line, and in attacking the German positions. He was wounded twice in going over the top. Kindly do your best for me, as I think he deserves to come back home to my family, because he has stuck to me through thick and thin. When I was wounded and lay out in no-man's-land, he stayed with me under a heavy barrage for nearly six hours. The little fellow also killed hundreds of rats. Many nights would have been a living hell for our section of the line if he hadn't been on guard twenty four hours a day. He was a boon to us all.

A council of the RSPCA met and concluded that if the soldiers who owned dogs had been paid at the same rate as munitions workers, they would have been able to pay the quarantine fees, and that it was unfair that they should have to do so. The organization therefore decided to accept responsibility for the cost of the dogs' upkeep and built five hundred quarantine kennels in Britain to house them.

All around the world, commanders of the armies were starting to write their memoirs of the conflict. Sitting in armchairs they stared intently into the distance, as if their eyes had grown binoculars, and they were back in the trenches gazing deep into enemy territory. The great task was to explain, without personal responsibility, a faith that had wanted to move mountains but had ended scarcely able to shift an anthill.

American and Canadian troops started to come home at the end of 1918. The first of the casualty ships arrived at Halifax in December, and townspeople and reporters turned out to watch. The liner was invisible for a long time, though her progress was followed by the sound of sirens. When she first appeared the crowd was silent, they could only make out the shape of her camouflaged bulk in the fog. Then people began to see the hundreds of soldiers swarming over the deck. Soon came the muffled sounds of cheering, which became louder as the ship got closer. Another few minutes and the sound filled the whole harbor, and from the shore came an answering roar.

The press ignored the first man off. He kept looking around repeating, "If I'd known what it was going to be like, I would have stayed at home and tried to sell something to the government."

Reporters wanted to see the ambulance girls. A group of YWCA women and an army major went down to the vehicle bay. Lucy was at the head of the line of ambulances, sitting on her radiator smoking a cigarette. The party stopped and stared.

"You're still in uniform," said the major. "Do you usually sit with your thighs crossed and smoke cigarettes while on duty?"

"My radiator's bitched," said Lucy.

The leader of the YWCA delegation looked surprised. The woman colonel in charge got out of a cab and came over. "Front-line woman, sir. We've got used to hearing coarse language; some of it is bound to have rubbed off. We've all gone through a period of disillusionment."

"If she was ever illusioned," said the major, "and after what I've seen of these girls, that's doubtful. I used to control cowboys in Mexico, that was a stiff proposition, but in comparison with these damn girls . . . I'd like to flog the lot of them. Are you coming down to meet the press, madam?"

As they went down the gangplank, a wharf hand came over and leaned against the hood of Lucy's ambulance.

"I'm sorry the war's over," he said.

"And what did you do in the war?" she asked.

He looked her up and down, then stuck out his chin. "What did I do? More than you, my pet. I made shells—dangerous work. I got ten dollars a week for more than two years; that's why I'm sorry the war's over. Same as you would if you were me, see?"

He tweaked her shirt collar.

"Were you afraid?" Lucy asked.

"'Course I was, who wouldn't be?"

"I was afraid, too."

"No need to be afraid now, the war's over. Life'll be safe and quiet after this."

On the dock, Lucy's commanding officer answered a few questions, then went to the town hall to speak to a group of clubwomen. She read a short prepared speech composed on the ship coming back to North America.

"When the war broke out, my three brothers had careers they could immediately transfer to the armed forces: My one career was to marry. As yet none of our women had enlisted in the ambulance corps because it had not yet become fashionable. At first it was difficult because men thought we could be spoken to as though we were chorus girls. Sometimes I wished I had been born with the face of a gargoyle. When the wounded are very ill, they don't care what nurses or ambulance drivers look like, but when they begin to recover, they stare, and occasionally make odious propositions: So many young men wanted to be kissed. The war was responsible for that; it made some men sexually mad.

"Expect to see a change in those women who have served; I don't think we can expect them to be the same after this four-year campaign. With a constant atmosphere of red tape and militarism, some of us have become hard-bitten, so I hope you will make allowances and help us get back quickly into civilian life."

Back on the ship, below decks, Lucy entered one of the holds converted into a ward.

"I've come to say goodbye."

A one-legged man got off his cot, and hopped like a crow over to a gramophone. He balanced himself and turned off the music. The young woman sat down on a canvas chair and smiled around.

"It won't be easy when you get back into civilian life," she said quietly. "Girls don't marry limbless men, or at least they didn't in peacetime. If you aren't careful, you could be doomed to remain in the trenches for the rest of your lives. Not trenches that have been attacked by the Huns, but trenches where self-pity will launch wave after wave of attacks on you. You must never be downhearted, do you hear? Never, never."

Lucy handed around some slips of paper. "This is my home address. If any of you have problems, write me a letter. Wherever I am, my parents will pass it on. My dear boys, I love you all."

After she had gone, it was generally agreed among the men that Miss Armitage was the finest soldier any of them had known.

The night nurse also came to say goodbye. A young man who had fallen in love with her during the crossing turned his back and lay in his bunk staring at the wall. After a few minutes of gentle coaxing she finally persuaded him to turn around and face her. She kissed him on the forehead, smiled, and held out her hands for him to hold. He looked up at her for a few moments, then reached out and placed his hands in hers. Without taking his eyes from the girl's face, he slowly twisted her wrists until he broke them both. The whole ward heard the cracks.

Three hours later, Lucy had got her ambulance ashore and parked in a shed with two hundred others. She had some food, then managed to find a ride going across the border down to Portland. She sat in a truck with four other ex-drivers, nobody feeling like talking. They gazed out the back, occasionally waving to lines of troops who were moving to the station, or climbing into motor convoys.

As they pulled out of town, Lucy went to the back, crouched down, pulled out a die, and dropped it on the floor. The cube vibrated, then a bump in the road threw it onto a new face. It shook but remained stable. "If it doesn't bounce over to snake eye, I'll make it," she said.

INSHROIN RETURNED TO AMERICA with the Drewstone crew on the troop ship *Trojan*. He disembarked in New York, visited a few friends, then caught the train for Hollywood. On the second day of the journey, the train stopped at Evansville, Kentucky, for half an hour to take on water. Inshroin was playing cards with five other passengers, and the drink was flowing. He had just dealt out a new hand when the group was distracted by a crash at the door. A man who had got on had fallen over one of the trunks. The new passenger got up, and walked down the compartment looking for a seat. He stopped by Inshroin and stared down at the players. They stared back at him. He was wearing a long flying coat, hide boots, and a leather wind-hat with the goggles pushed up onto his forehead. Two French army revolvers cased in canvas were belted to his waist. Seeing a space next to the actor, he sat down: As he did so, he scattered a great stream of spit on the floor.

"You revolting swine," said Inshroin. "Some of that went over my trousers."

"You don't say," said the man slowly. "And who do you think you are?"

"My name's my own business, and you can control your spitting habits in public."

"I should watch that mouth if I were you," said the newcomer. "You're speaking to John Farquharson, the flying ace. I brought down more Germans over France than anybody else in the Allied air forces."

"I happen to know that honor belongs to a Canadian," said Inshroin.

"Are you calling me a liar?"

"Yes, and an ill-mannered liar."

The intruder glanced around at the other players. He deliberately undid the flaps to his revolver cases. "I've got guns and knives," he said. "Will you step outside so this thing can be settled between us?"

Inshroin stood up. "Certainly, lead the way."

Everyone within hearing distance got to their feet and pushed toward the door. Farquharson, who was leading, took a few steps, turned, and held up his arms.

"It's just struck me," he said. "When I kill you, I'll have to pay a widow."

"Keep going," called Inshroin from the back of the group. "I'm not married."

"Good, but I'm not in the mood for killing today. I think I'll smash both your legs and leave it at that."

"Perfectly acceptable," said Inshroin. "Shall we proceed?"

The man didn't move. "I'll give you one more warning. At the Battle of the Somme, I jumped out of my plane and strangled fifty Germans with my bare hands . . . and I won't hurt you if you apologize."

"Never."

"That's what I wanted to hear. But I never fight in this leather coat, and I don't see a place to hang it."

"I'll hold it," someone volunteered.

"You puny rabbit-killer," said Inshroin.

"Another insult to be wiped out in blood!" said Farquharson. "I'll soon teach you a lesson in manners. Follow me!"

When he got to the door, Farquharson turned and once more held up his arms. "I would like to point out, gentlemen, it's a principle of mine *never* to fight beside a railroad track. I like a prairie where I have room to throw my opponent around."

"Suits me," said Inshroin. "Where's the nearest prairie? Lead the way."

Farquharson leaned against the car door. "It wouldn't be any good if we did find a prairie. I always hold a fifty-dollar bill between my teeth when I'm fighting on a prairie, and I haven't got one today. In fact, I'm dead broke."

A hand strained forward holding a fifty-dollar bill.

"Much obliged, but I never fight without painting my ears red for luck, and I haven't got any red paint with me today."

"Are you going to fight?" asked Inshroin.

"I gave a solemn oath to my dying father. I swore I'd never fight without painting my ears red for luck. You wouldn't want me to go back on a solemn oath, would you?"

"I think you're a coward, a liar, and a tadpole dressed up in shark's clothing," said Inshroin.

"I will give a thousand dollars for red paint! If I had red paint, we'd see some killing!"

The blowhard was lifted into the air and thrown down onto the tracks; the passengers then went back to their card playing. Inshroin was pouring out more Scotch from a flask when he caught sight of an apparition emerging from the nearby ticket office. He was holding a knife between his teeth, the hat was gone, and his ears were painted bright red. He walked down to Inshroin's window and knocked on the glass.

"Come outside if you dare, and prepare to meet your doom!"

Inshroin ran to the car door and started removing his jacket as he got off the train. The man retired slowly, backing up the platform. He stopped by the ticket office. "I'm just going to get my hair cut," he shouted. "I'll be back in fifteen seconds. I never fight without cutting my hair—I promised a dying mother!"

Inshroin got back onto the train. As the guard waved the green flag, Farquharson charged once more out of the ticket office. He ran down the platform after the moving train. His head was shaved, ears painted red; he was waving the knife in the air, and shouting at the top of his voice.

"Shell-shocked," said one of the card players.

"Is that what was wrong with him?" said Inshroin.

"Both of you," muttered the man.

PANORAMA

INSHROIN, LUCY, AND THE ARMY returned to a world that was starting to experience the second great social revolution of this century after Hollywood—the Bolshevik. Like the former, it blossomed quickly, and occurred in the presence of reporters taking acres of notes and filmmakers taking miles of celluloid footage.

Lenin had returned from exile to Russia in 1917 to lead the revolution, and made his first public address on April 3, 1917. Every word impelled action. He did not begin by saying, "Comrades, it gives me great pleasure to be with you on this momentous occasion." There was no mention of "I" in the whole speech; it was utterly selfless, and seemed to be the impersonal voice of unrelenting destiny:

"Comrades, workers, the world revolution is at hand; the bourgeoisie are about to be overthrown in all lands! Comrades, workers! Take the factories from your exploiters. Comrades, peasants! Take the land from your enemies the landowners. Comrades, soldiers! Stop the war, go home, make peace with the Germans, declare the fighting at an end. Poor wretches, you are starving, while all around you are plutocrats and bankers. Why don't you seize the wealth!? Steal what has been stolen! Destroy the whole capitalist society, down with it! Down with the war! Long live the class war, long live the dictatorship of the proletariat. Let our enemies tremble, no pity, no mercy for them! Summon all your hatred, destroy them once and forever!"

The Russians, in doing away with free enterprise, saying they were substituting nonownership for misownership, turned into the great source of American capitalism's unease. Because of events in the USSR, the world's Left became Russia, reaching out to lay a stranglehold grip on home, mother, and her household appliances.

This new Soviet, minus God and czar, was recorded most memorably in the films of Eisenstein. Apart from technical innovations, his portrait turned out to be mainly crowds, in which people were marked czarist (bad) or revolutionary (good).

L. J. Selznik, the producer, sent Czar Nicholas a cable:

When I was a poor boy in Kiev, some of your policemen were not kind to my people. I came to America and prospered. Now hear with regret you are out of a job. Feel no ill will over what your policemen did, so if you come to New York can give you a fine position acting in pictures. Salary no object. Reply my expense. Regards to you and your family.

He got no answer.

The Prince of Wales came to North America to present medals. He arrived at New Brunswick, and as a naval pinnace moved through the rain to Reid's Point, the guns of HMS *Dragon*, lying in the harbor of St. John, fired a royal salute.

Five minutes later, a slim, fair-haired boy in a sea captain's uniform stepped ashore. He tripped slightly, smiled, and shook hands with the duke of Devonshire, governor-general of Canada. The crowd stared. Shy, unspoiled, and good-looking, he appeared as a symbol of certainty, a resurrection, and a promise, as if in him were reborn the millions of dead buried in France. He had worn khaki, had visited at the front, and seemed to be all that remained of a sacrificed generation. All those present thought they might have met their dead husband, brother, son, or lover.

On the continent of North America, from Vancouver to New York, he would draw crowds surpassing those who had once come to see Abraham Lincoln or Rudolph Valentino at the height of their fame. Future leaders would sway masses by social and economic appeals to self-interest; he swayed them differently. He used no voice, had no radio or television, and urged no reason. He appeared, tripped, smiled shyly, and the legend of the Prince of Wales was born.

His first official function was in Vancouver, where he was to meet veterans and present medals. He came out of the station and walked into two hundred waiting reporters. The *Boston*

Globe representative wired down that a woman said she had lost a young husband and wanted just to lie in the prince's arms. An elderly man said he saw three killed sons resurrected. He turned to the person next to him: "He looks just like my—" Then he stopped as the vividness of memory deafened and defeated him.

The police pushed the crowd back, and the young man being questioned got out of the station, climbed into the front car of the cavalcade, and waved. One hundred thousand people had crowded themselves along the route to the saluting platform at the town hall.

As the procession started, people pushed forward into the road trying to touch him. A phalanx of motorcycle police attempted to clear a path, and with sirens wailing rode stutteringly into the wall of bodies, scything them down. Backing away, the mob tried to charge again and was swallowed up. The police panicked and hit out wildly with their truncheons. After an hour the procession was able to move again, but only because the crowd had fallen back exhausted.

On the last week of the Canadian tour, the prince's train was crossing the prairies from Vancouver to Montreal before going across the border to New York. A single farmhouse, the only building for a hundred miles, stood by the track at a place called Low's Point. As smoke appeared in the distance, a boy ran back from the rails shouting and waving his hat. As prearranged, a man in full uniform wearing a tin hat appeared at the door of the house. He was carrying a wreath of red poppies and a rifle with its bayonet fixed.

The man's wife came out and adjusted the soldier's tie, after which he slowly climbed up a ladder at the side of the building and stepped out onto the flat roof. He hung the wreath on top of the drainpipe and stood beside it. The train got closer, and swept past belching smoke and sparks. The man came to attention, put the rifle to his shoulder, and saluted. In the doorway below, his wife curtsied. The train faded away, and a guard in the rear box saw a flash as the soldier turned his head, and a ray of sunlight caught the sweat on his face. The prince didn't notice. He was talking to a man sitting next to him.

"When we get down to the USA," he said, "watch me rival Vernon Castle as a movie star."

Five days later at Grand Central Station, the crowd was bigger than the one that met him in New Brunswick.

His future wife was sailing with her parents in Maine.

> Are my buddies taken care of?
> Was their victory sweet?
> Is the big reward you promised
> Selling pencils on the street?
>
> Billy Rose

TWO YEARS AFTER THE WAR ENDED, a young British army chaplain, the Reverend David Railton, suggested that the body of an unidentified British soldier be buried in Westminster Abbey as a symbol of the nation's loss. The idea was taken up by other Allied countries, and on October 24, 1921, Sergeant Edward F. Younger of the American army entered the chapel in the French village of Châlons-sur-Marne. He carried a small bunch of flowers. Once inside, he stood undecided for a few seconds in front of four coffins. Finally he placed the flowers on one, saluted, and emerged into the autumn sunlight.

America's unknown soldier arrived in Washington on November 9 on the cruiser *Olympic*. As she came up the Potomac, fort by fort, post by post, guns fired a salute. Slowly she swung into her dock. Along the rails stood the crew in lines of dark blue.

The flag-covered casket containing the body was carried from the ship and placed on a horse-drawn, black-draped gun caisson. The route on the way to the final resting place was lined on either side of the road with marines at attention—behind them, the silent packed crowds.

At the Capitol, escort troops drew up in line facing the building with sabers at present. The unknown was lifted down and taken up the stairway to be placed on the catafalque in the dim rotunda.

There was the sound of sabers being drawn as the President and Mrs. Harding arrived. Lights were turned up so the press could photograph the scene. For a minute there was no other sound except that of cameras clicking. Mrs. Harding laid a white ribbon across the rain-sodden flag and some flowers picked in France. The President then pinned a silver shield of the United States to the ribbon, and put a great wreath of crimson roses on the casket. Vice-President Coolidge laid the tribute from Congress, as did Chief Justice Taft from the Supreme Court. For the American Indians, Chief Plenty Coos came and called upon the Great Spirit of the tribes to see that the dead had not died in vain. He took off his feathered war bonnet and laid it and the coupstick of tribal office on the casket.

The unknown was then left alone with the motionless guards who would be changed every few hours through the night. The body lay, his head facing east toward France and his feet pointing toward the lights of Washington. On either side of the doorway stood the statues of Lincoln and Grant, and as the lights were switched off, the dimmers on a few scattered electrics let shadows fall over the bier.

A huge monument to the Canadian dead was built at Vimy Ridge to commemorate the first great victory of the war. Standing on its outer wall, looking toward the Allied positions, is a massive shrouded female figure. Her body is hidden by a cowl that drops from her head to her feet without a single fold. The pose of death is eternal. She gazes across pale skies and a dead landscape. Thin stunted trees and shell-pitted fields spread around, a region where the storm has passed, a peaceful dwelling of quiet and resigned men. One of the founders of the Dada art movement wants to project a Chaplin film permanently on the vast wall of the monument. Charlie loaded with rifles and equipment, a look of mild surprise on his face, will stagger toward the German position on his flat, world-renowned feet forever.

> Poppy red, poppy red
> Dusky vivid among the dead
> In the trench that is my bed
> Poppy red, poppy red.

Hades Herald

He's sotch a dolink. Wot, one minute he makes you, you could die from leffing, und gredually in de next minute it becomes so sad, wot it could make you, you should cry.

Is werry appealing to de emulsions.

Milt Gross on Chaplin

IN 1922 CHARLIE CHAPLIN RETURNED TO LONDON for the opening of *The Kid*. He was accompanied by an army of reporters, and as the ship passed the Statue of Liberty, he refused a request to blow kisses. He said it was undignified. Standing there on the deck, his bottom seemed boy-sized, and he looked no higher than a dozen stacked eggs.

"Mr. Chaplin, why are you going to Europe?"

"To see some old friends."

"Do you want to play Hamlet?"

"I don't know."

"Why have you said you wanted to visit Russia?"

"Because I'm interested in new ideas."

"Are you a Bolshevik?"

"I'm an actor not a politician."

"What do you think of Lenin?"

"I think he's a very remarkable man."

"Why?"

"Because he's expressing a new idea."

When he arrived at his hotel in London, a letter was waiting for him from a member of the public. It contained some white feathers of cowardice, and the writer asked what he had done in the war.

Charlie visited the Star and Garter Hospital for disabled soldiers at Richmond. After 1918 dozens of extra wooden wards had been built behind the main buildings. Symmetrically laid out, with little roads between these huts, the whole area looked like a concentration camp from the next war. The VIP, with his predictable army of reporters, stepped out of his car and was taken into one of the new wards by a nurse. Once inside, everybody stopped and stared in a stunned silence. A group of about thirty maimed and crippled men stat around a long table and, as best they could, made artificial red poppies.

A doctor did the introducing. The first patient didn't have any arms and, before the arrival of the star, had been winding cotton around the stem of a flower with his teeth. The man next to him was blind, but said he was not unhappy because he could read in bed with a braille book under the sheets and not get his hands cold. Everybody laughed, and it eased the tension. At the end of the table, Charlie was about to turn away when a man he hadn't noticed slid forward on a little wooden board attached to skate wheels. His legs had been amputated at the thigh. He shook hands with the comic.

"Lame, ain't I? The lads call me their animated bust."

Photographers now wanted pictures of the actor with the ex-soldiers, and Charlie obliged. Camera bulbs flashed, and some of the shell-shock patients jumped noticeably.

"Sir! Can you put your left arm around Mr. Chaplin's shoulder?"

The man spoken to smiled and swung his body broadside to the lens. His left arm had been amputated above the elbow, and his left leg above the knee.

"Sorry," called the photographer.

A nurse said that the men had told her it would be a great honor if he could spare some time to do a few scenes from his films, and would he consider putting on a little performance.

When the request was first made, Charlie appeared shy and uncertain, but as the men looked expectantly toward him, he smiled, and said it would be his privilege to do so. Then he added, "But only if the reporters leave, they take up enough space for twenty."

There was an angry outburst from the press, but after they realized he was adamant, there was a rush to get a few more pictures. As they pushed forward, one of the men at the end of the bench was knocked onto the floor. He stayed there, sitting cross-legged and unsmiling. Blown from a ditch to the top of a tree, and from the tree to another ditch, he had had his fill of slapstick.

The table was moved out, and men from other wards came in, either being pushed in wheelchairs or walking and bringing their own seats. The doctor announced that Mr. Chaplin was to honor them with a sample of his marvelous acting, and he hoped everybody would enjoy themselves.

After the applause died down, Charlie stood in front of them for a few seconds. He noticed the row at the back was filled with men whose faces were completely covered with thick veils. They mesmerized him. He couldn't stop wondering what they looked like, how terrible the mutilation. Someone coughed and Charlie forced himself to look somewhere else in the room. Finally he drew himself together *and*

Straightened his shoulders
Tugged at the cuffs of his shirt
Gave a grimace
A wrinkle of his forehead
A curl of the moustache
And finally a wink.

He then began to perform cameos from his films. Soon the little man was talking without the slightest difficulty in the language of mime—the ability springing from a will to communicate with the ex-soldiers at all costs. The press outside could see nothing, but heard the roars of laughter.

Charlie worked for an hour, and in a scene where he hands a rose to a young woman and tells her of his love, he added some words to help the blind man he had spoken to when he first came in. He ended the performance by escorting an imaginary female victim away from the ogre of cities and police traps. Hand in hand they walked off down a long highway between the chairs, forever caught in a decreasing circle of spotlight.

When the performance was finished, a man came over holding a small wooden box.

"Mr. Chaplin, you made us laugh a lot when we were in the trenches, and we reckon that as you got nothing for doing what you did, we'd present you with some of the medals the lads got on active service. They'll commemorate your visit, and be a token of our appreciation."

For the second time that afternoon the actor hesitated and seemed at a loss for words, then he gave a little bow and accepted the case of medals. The men asked if they could all have his autograph, and Charlie said they could if he got theirs. Each man signed, including the patient without arms, who wrote with a pencil between his teeth. Charlie put the signatures in the medal box, and asked if there were a way he could leave without being noticed by the press. The men showed him a back door that opened onto an alley leading down to the road.

Outside, he walked slowly in the direction of his car, taking the long route behind three of the ward buildings. In smart civilian clothes he went unrecognized; he passed a nurse who thought perhaps he was a civil servant who dealt with veterans' pensions . . . When he finally got to his car, he climbed in the back and sank into one of the seats.

The chauffeur glanced expectantly in the mirror. The little tramp was looking at the medals and thinking about the blind man. During the performance, when he had offered the rose to the girl and told her of his undying love, he noticed the man's head was turned slightly to one side, and there were tears in his eyes. Charlie had never seen blind eyes brimming with tears before . . .

Charlie Chaplin was not the only comic of his era. During the 1920s the most popular comedy at the box office came from Mack Sennett's Custard College. His Keystone Cops made running a pleasure for lots of people around the world.

Michael Sinnot dropped his Irish name to avoid being called one of the S'nott family. As a boy he had loved the police, and had thought of joining the force until he learned it took a long time to make sergeant from patrolman.

On his film sets roads were so often opened up for joke repairs, his accountants suggested it might be cheaper to fit them with huge zippers. Many of his actors were noted for custard pies, which for photographic purposes were generally blackberry.

Chaplin got his big break with Sennett, but only after a lot of discussion and meetings. Sennett had a rule that every gag in one of his films had to be consummated in twenty feet of film; Charlie barely got started in the first hundred.

Dell Ruth, the playwright, worked with Sennett and said, "Your success lies mainly in your ability to write just up to the public's mental capacity; I think you are quite justified in continuing to do so." A sign appeared on the wall of Sennett's scenario department: REMEMBER THE EXTENT OF INTELLIGENCE OF THE AVERAGE PUBLIC MIND IS ELEVEN YEARS. MOVING PICTURES SHOULD BE MADE ACCORDINGLY.

Sennett had a Great Dane called Teddy that he wanted to

make a big pull. The animal earned forty dollars a week. Publicity men posed it for the camera with a pen in its paw, while Sennett looked over its shoulder at the contract Teddy was signing. One clause read: "He, Teddy, shall render his services in a conscientious, artistic and efficient manner, and to the best of his ability with regard to the careful, economic, and efficient production of motion pictures and photoplays. It being understood that the production of motion pictures is a matter of art and taste."

The first blow to Sennett's reputation was given by a comic who worked for him named Roscoe (Fatty) Arbuckle. Toward the end of 1921 the comic gave a party and invited a Miss Virginia Rappe. She disappeared into a bedroom with Fatty, and was later found naked and dying. A postmortem revealed she had died from hemorrhaging caused by an object like a bottle being pushed into her vagina.

In New York, Henry Lehrman, a director who announced he was Miss Rappe's fiancé, said: "That's what comes of taking vulgarians from the gutter, giving them enormous salaries, and making idols of them. Some people don't know how to get a kick out of life except in a beastly way. They are the ones who resort to cocaine and the opium needle, and who participate in orgies that surpass the orgies of degenerate Rome."

Mae Tauble, a friend of Arbuckle's, defended the comic. "I don't believe there was an attack on Miss Rappe as far as Roscoe was concerned. I have seen him frequently and he has always been a gentleman, and never told risqué stories in the presence of women."

Arbuckle was indicted and tried three times for manslaughter. The first two juries disagreed. The third acquitted him in three minutes. Outside the court he said: "This is the most solemn moment of my life. My innocence of the hideous charge preferred against me has been proved. For this vindication I am truly grateful to God and my fellow men and women. My life has been devoted to the production of clean pictures for the happiness of children. I shall try to enlarge my field of usefulness so that my art shall have a wider service."

Before the third jury verdict was given in April 1922, a second violent death occurred in Hollywood. W. D. Taylor, a chief director of Players Lasky Studios, was found in his home with a bullet through his heart. Charges and countercharges continued through the spring.

With its growing reputation of a city half-harlotry, half-banditry, Hollywood, it was decided, needed a commissar to keep an eye on its morals and its products. Will Hays was lured from his position as Postmaster to become the first president of the Motion Picture Producers and Distributors of America. Upon assuming his duties in 1923 he said: "I was down in the basement of Cyrus H. Curtis's new yacht the other day—the finest yacht afloat—and I saw a big bulb apparatus there that keeps the craft from tilting too far, what do you call it? A gyroscope—yes that's it—a gyroscope, a stabilizer. The motion picture is already the principal amusement of a great majority of people, it is the sole amusement of millions, it may well become the national stabilizer. The potential of motion pictures for moral influence and education is limitless. Therefore its integrity should be protected, as we protect the integrity of our children and our churches, and its quality developed as we develop the quality of our schools."

Hays remained the industry's official spokesman and arbiter of taste until his retirement in 1945.

Fatty Arbuckle never worked again. He was the best pie thrower in the business; he could even throw two at once, in opposite directions. He was a broken man. His great ambition had been to throw every variety of pie available in the cook book—he got stopped at C.

FINIS OF PANORAMA

THE CHIEF WATCHED THE ARBUCKLE TRIAL with great interest, but while it was in progress he was busily extending the boundaries of his empire. Day after day he was locked away in his office conducting interviews, while the main reception room was filled with girls, their mothers, and agents all milling noisily together.

Mrs. West, the Chief's secretary, sat watching them all: She said nothing, but enjoyed the atmosphere of nervous hopeful expectancy. She enjoyed even more the moment each one arrived and tried to make an appointment with her employer. She had joined the Drewstone Company while Inshroin was in France, and her reputation grew quickly. Film and gossip magazines billed her as the person the Chief relied on most, the power behind the throne who filtered potential stars for him. A well-built woman of forty-two, she had a small head with fine precise features, and had kept her health: full breasts, regular menstruation, and both ovaries intact. From severe straining, she had developed a small anal fissure and a hemorrhoid. Mrs. West relied on its twinges to give her the mood of the Hollywood market.

She was a widow with one daughter. When the mother was eighteen, her main ambition in life had been to marry, and push a husband toward achievement. The man she had married hadn't risen fast enough for her in the insurance business, and over the years her thin voice had beaten against his ears, slowly and persistently—a dull tone in the form of a constant complaint. She had enough character to be capable of strong dislike, and it flowed from her in a bitter, unceasing dribble of words that droned into the night. Her husband's hours became a hole of thin unremitting sound as he struggled to achieve wordly success.

Their daughter had been christened Olive, and during the early years of her life the parents argued so much that by the time she was two, as she lay in her crib, Olive looked the oldest of the three. When she was thirteen, her father got completely stuck in the mud, and under the tongue of his strident consort, ran up a white flag and died of a heart attack.

In 1917 Mrs. West brought her daughter to the studio, and Olive was "discovered."

The mother became the Chief's secretary, attached herself to his organization with the tenacity of a barnacle, and started to hack her way with a steely resolve to a generalship. She made a mental record of everybody who came into the office. She added her own interpretation to whatever they said, and passed the information on to others of importance whom she met. They themselves passed it on, and however unfounded the stories and details, Mrs. West's interpretations were so convincingly stated that everything she mentioned had the force of truth. People in Hollywood graded their actions and words according to what they thought Mrs. West's judgment of them might be. That was regal.

As she sat watching the girls in the Chief's office, one of the women got up and, holding her daughter by the sleeve, came over. Mrs. West recognized Tania Craig, and looked down at her writing pad as they approached her desk.

"We've been waiting for an hour, you know; we do have other people to see."

The secretary looked up, feigning surprise. "Mr. Drewstone is a very busy man. Sometimes interviews and auditions can go on for a long while over the appointed time. I know how long you've been here, but sometimes the biggest stars have to wait."

"That may be, but my daughter is well known; we've come to expect producers and directors to pay a little more attention."

"Let me see who's in there with him." Mrs. West flicked through her diary. "It's somebody from the Curtis Agency. I think there's a problem with contracts. Can't you wait just a little longer?"

The woman looked at her daughter, then shook her head. "No thank you. If he can't keep appointments, we won't."

Inside the office, the Chief lit a titanic cigar. He was sitting on a sofa talking with a girl.

"Tell me more about yourself personally," he said.

"Well I was born a Virgo, and raised in Salt Lake City in a very religious home. Mom sent me to charm school, where I learned modern ballet, tap, and singing. I took a leave of absence, and went to Tahiti, where I learned Hawaiian dancing. I then went back to Salt Lake City, and taught at the YWCA for six months. I was really depressed for a time. I tried to kill myself, you know?"

"No kidding, when?"

Almost imperceptibly, the girl pushed her leg against the Chief's. The hair stood up on the back of his neck.

"One morning when the world looked ickey. But I didn't go through with it. In the end I discovered it was me that was ickey, not the world. I decided I needed a complete change, so I moved down here, and added belly dancing to my repertoire."

"You sound like a real academic."

"I've never heard of 'real academic,' but then there are a lot of things I don't know. I simply know what's inside me, and want to fulfill myself to the best of my abilities."

"I'm really sure I can help you," said the Chief.

He undid his fly, and reaching out, took her hand and tucked it inside his pants. Without looking at him, she allowed herself to be led in.

"I worked in a bar once, and earned extra money for doing this." She gave him a squeeze. "Nothing intimate, mind you. I'm not one of *those* kind of girls. Poor things. Some of those guys really needed help, and they always gave me a good tip."

"You did it a lot of times?"

"Scads of times, but no intimacy. I'm saving that till I fall in love with the right boy."

"Have you ever done any striptease?"

She groped in a little further. "Only in a positive way. I've done some at private parties around Hollywood, in addition to my tap and belly."

"Would you do some for me sometime?"

"If you have a function, I'll come along. But it would only be for the extra pin money. I need it to tide me over until I'm in films proper."

"Have you got a special angle, something you've made your own personal style in the strip act?"

"I have if the request is a sincere one, but I prefer Hawaiian Islands dance in the traditional pre-missionary manner. It's so much more artistic than striptease."

The Chief suddenly sucked in his breath. She took her hand out of his pants.

"I'm being very naughty. I thought we were discussing my career?"

"Would you call yourself an artist?"

"It would be a privilege if I could. But I think you need luck to call yourself an artist."

"You don't need luck, you need opportunity, and I'm offering you yours now."

She gave him a coy, oh-you-are-a-liar look.

"No, I mean it." He got hold of her hand, and pushed it back into his pants. "Think of all that champagne and those orchids."

She worked on him harder.

"You angel," said the Chief.

"I don't think I'd like that much, angels have feathers that can prick and hurt, I want to be covered in silks and furs."

A few minutes later the Chief was showing her a standard chorus line contract.

"There's a lot of small print," she said.

The Chief shrugged. "They're all like that."

The girl flicked through to the last page and glanced at the dotted line along the bottom.

There was a tap at the door, not a knock, more a brush with the fingers. The girl looked up at the Chief as he said, "Come in."

The expectation of an immediate part in films and access to silks and furs was irresistible; she signed. The secretary ignored the girl and looked at her employer, then glanced at the desk, which was in a mess. "What are all those photos doing here. I filed them carefully yesterday."

The Chief ignored her and went on talking to the girl while she was putting her coat on. "Okay," she said. "I'll be there at six-thirty." The girl left.

There was a sudden stirring from the main reception area, and the secretary glanced over her shoulder. The door from the main hall had burst open, and a young woman walked in. She was wearing a crimson woolen suit, with a hat of red feathers that curled under her chin. A Pekinese dog was caught up under her arm—instant silence in the room. She stood appreciating everybody's word loss, then walked to the Chief's door, glanced at her mother, and stepped inside. Mrs. West waited a few seconds, smiled at her daughter, then left the room, closing the door behind her.

"Olive West," somebody breathed—there was a whistle, then the conversation started again. "Yeh, Olive West, you can see why she's a headliner, what a profile."

Inside, the Chief poured two Scotches as his star sat down.

Olive was beautiful in a fashionable way, but if you looked at her photos now, you'd wonder how it was possible for a face like that to launch a thousand scripts. The forehead was full of fine blue veins, and she had a soft pink complexion, like a handful of strawberries dropped into a jug, leaving the reddest one for her lips.* It was a delicate face, cut with precision, but too brittle to bend, and too finely carved to withstand blows.

She would never shatter completely, but suffer most through being forced to swim around on the surface of existence. She had cultivated a blasé look, and was fond of being bored. Her eyebrows were arched, and every strand of hair on her head was in its right slot. She ignored everything in life, unless, when she was at a party, everybody accidentally stopped talking at once. Then Olive, listening to silence, would panic and quickly restore the former talk.

Since her seventeenth birthday, Olive had been cloistered, petted, and sterilized by the Chief's company. Emotionally untampered with, she was self-contained and superficial. At twenty, these two traits were all she had of character.

Her most profound sexual experience had occurred when she was thirteen. At that age she had a great talent for singing. While performing at home for some of her mother's friends, she had become seized with a giddiness and an inability to carry on with the performance. She had run up to her bedroom, and was found weeping hysterically from vexation and a sense of shame at the failure. During the night she developed a fever, and early in the morning suffered from violent paroxysms that lasted until lunch. The doctor was called, and Olive was given a saline aperient that cleared the bowels of a large quantity of packed feces, and she soon appeared better. During the afternoon of the following day, the fits were repeated several times, and she complained of an aching in the hips and thighs, accompanied by a crushing-down feeling in the stomach. A croton oil liniment was applied to the loins by a doctor, and in the afternoon menses occurred for the first time.

*Olive's mouth was very small, a facial peculiarity not popular today. Grins have to be wide today. When a modern star smiles the head appears to split in half, as huge rows of gleaming teeth are exposed from ear to ear. Momentarily, the skull seems to be two independent sections held together only by a tiny hinge in the back of the neck.

Now, years later, she was fully trained to be motive power, with no feelings or imagination to hamper a loud progress. Like a poorly taken photo, Olive was overexposed and underdeveloped. Through the entire period of their association, the Chief would never manage to stop intelligence disappearing from Olive's face when he turned a camera in her direction.

"Well," she said to the Chief, "am I to be in *The Heart of Turbulence*?"

"I've always said the part was a possibility."

"I know."

"I asked your mother to get you here today because I think I can change possibility into something better."

"Do you mean probability?"

The Chief nodded.

Olive jumped up and kissed her employer on the cheek; as she did so, she stepped on the dog, which squealed loudly.

"We're having the charity party at my house tonight," said the Chief. "We'll announce it then."

"I was going out to dinner this evening; will it last for long?"

"Another movie magnate?" asked the Chief suspiciously.

"Nope."

"A cereal baron?"

"Nope."

"Who then?"

"A ketchup king."

"Which one?"

"John Sayer, Jr."

"Him? Isn't he the one who said the French national anthem was the *Mayonnaise*?"

"Who cares what he says. His dinners are always packed with European princes." Olive touched the lobe of her ear. "Because you're going to announce me in the film, I'll put him off for tonight. In any case, with such a big part, all the princes will be coming to me in six months."

In the reception room, Mrs. West was talking to Tania Craig and her mother, who had returned.

"We've come to apologize for our display of bad manners; we should never have walked off in a huff like that. But my daughter has been so busy recently, and we're running a bit short on temper."

Mrs. West gave a quick and sudden smile.

"It's all forgotten."

The woman shifted about nervously. "Is there a chance we can get another appointment for today?"

Mrs. West suddenly looked self-protective—a foot thick. "I'm afraid not. Mr. Drewstone is booked solid for the rest of the week. But what's the urgency, from what I've read your daughter is working regularly in most of the studios?"

"Yes, but she needs a firm commitment from one of them, and this is the biggest and the best; it offers the most security. Tania's been lucky up to now, but none of us knows how long that will last."

Mrs. West nodded slightly and looked down. The other woman went on: "Andrew Huskinson over at EUK told us how lucky we would be if Tania were given Mr. Drewstone's special treatment. He said . . ."

Mrs. West was a clever talker; now she decided to listen, allowing the other woman to relate the conversation. She sympathized, she appreciated, she tutted, nodded, and shook her head. Soon Tania's mother was confiding more intimate details and felt she was doing so to the most sympathetic listener she had ever met.

On the coastal side of his lot, the Chief had built a house. It was massive and looked like a hybrid of every architectural style known to man. The building had cost a fortune, but the bill had been so tactfully handled that the Chief's wife, Jean Drewstone, told her friends it seemed to have been presented on the back of a love poem.

For the evening the decor of the main room was blue velvet and silver lamé. A three-foot-wide silk frieze hung around the walls just below the ceiling, and painted on it were the notes of part of Wagner's *Ring* cycle.

Immediately at the back of the fortress was a large lawn containing a swimming pool, and around it that evening, three hundred guests drank, talked, and danced to the music of a white jazz band. Hanging over the pool was a canvas banner proclaiming A CENT FOR THE RENT OF THE WAR WIDOWS.

The Chief's wife was combining the announcement of Olive West's part in her husband's newest movie with the war widows' charity function. It was her first attempt to bring together every Hollywood notable, and so far everything seemed to be going well. Everybody who was anybody discovered she was the kind of hostess they could get on with. She was listlessly pleasant, because it cost her nothing and because she never surrounded herself with people compelling enough to upset her.

The highlight of the evening was to be a fashion show, with both models and dressmakers present in the house.

The woman friend she first approached with the idea was doubtful. She explained that everybody she knew expected dressmakers to come to the house of the person being fitted, and to be seen at no other time. When Mrs. Drewstone showed her an article that explained that all the best people in Paris and London were doing it, she had warmed to the idea.

When the guests started to arrive and found they were expected to mix with seamstresses, they were shocked. After a few drinks, however, they got used to the idea, and most of them felt very democratic and very daring.

Mrs. Drewstone toured the pool area to make sure everybody was enjoying themselves. More people arrived, and were greeted with varying degrees of effusiveness according to their income and social status. A complete stranger walking in might have thought everybody was drunk, when in fact they were merely in a state of Hollywood high spirits.

The men: "Haw, haw, haw."
The women: "Hee, hee, hee."

Dozens of waiters poured drinks, and twirled cocktail shakers as if they were drum major batons. Mrs. Drewstone went into the house to check that all the cigarette boxes were filled. She stood at the large main room, and pulled back a curtain that was drifting in the light breeze. Chairs were placed in a semicircle facing a raised stage, hidden by a drop curtain on which were embroidered the words: STEALING FRANCE'S FASHION THUNDER WHILE DEFENDING CIVILIZATION.

The Chief and Olive arrived, and his wife watched them walk into the room as journalists and photographers gathered like vultures around a dead camel. Olive sank into an armchair, and the Chief sat on the arm.

"Are you going to use Miss West in the movie?"

"She's going to be my star, and you boys are the first outside my office to know."

"How much will she be making in the deal?"

"I shall be paying her ten thousand a week on top of her normal salary."

"Isn't that excessive?"

"I don't think so. Olive only works three months a year, but in that time she works very hard, and makes a lot of pictures. So I think she's worth it."

"How much do you expect to make?"

"Now you're talking about something that's none of your damn business."

"Are you using a special staff story or is it from a book?"

"It's a staff story. As most of you boys know, it's not the story that matters with me, but the idea behind it. I have used very successfully a plot of twenty words written on the back of last year's calendar. This particular story was created by me from the adventures and romances of Phillip Inshroin and my film crew while they were serving our country in France. I've kept it on ice for a few years, but as the public is now starting to show an interest in the Great War and our American heroes, I decided to go ahead with the production."

"Miss West, are you pleased to be working in this picture?"

"I'm most gratified. This will be my twentieth essay before the lens, under the baton of the Chief, and I hope it will be my best."

"As it'll be a war story, do you feel you have had enough experience to handle the subject?"

"I know I didn't serve in the war, but I've thought about it so much I feel I could really live the part as if I had.

"I would have given a lot to be in the war, but my mother and the Chief convinced me that I could best serve my country by staying at home and giving our Allied forces the benefit of my services from the screen.

"It was a terrible disappointment that I couldn't serve with the nursing corps, but when a person has special gifts, he or she is both blessed and cursed at the same time. We have no choice but to put up with it, and do what our art demands we do unselfishly."

"So even though the role is a great challenge, you think you can handle it?"

"I'm positive I can. I know the public mostly sees my outer beauty, and though I'm grateful for the gift that makes it possible for me to give pleasure to so many, I have always felt unfulfilled. With this demanding part, I hope the mere beauty of my body will be a thin veil to cover a more meaningful spiritual beauty within."

"What do you feel about working with Phillip Inshroin? Is he here, by the way?"

The Chief glanced around. "I told him to be. He's probably been held up on the lot."

Olive leaned forward looking sincere. "Although we've never done a movie together, I watch him all the time and feel I know him better than any other human being. Nothing seems too big for him. He reflects the immensity of a sublime and ecstatic love.

"He is indifferent to pain, but cannot stand the sight of others suffering, especially women. It's destructive to his peace of mind; when he sees an unhappy woman, agonies of pity wrench his heart. As a consequence, his capacity to provide spiritual help is stupendous."

"Will you be earning more than him?"

"Only for the time being, it won't be more than he *can* earn."

"That's enough questions for the time being," said the Chief. "We should be getting on with this fashion show . . . Don't forget to mention that the royalties from the first performance of the picture will go to the war widows' charity."

There were more camera flash explosions as reporters turned toward the stage and fought with other guests for the best positions. The *Hollywood Courier* reporter smiled at his photographer as they sat down.

"Olive's getting to the divinity stage; she'll soon be in a position to sell her dung as holy relics."

Lights dimmed around the room, and the curtain on the stage lifted revealing two men standing at a lectern. One was the principal makeup man from the studio, and the other (everybody recognized with a gasp) was a famous tenor from the New York Opera.

As they turned over their announcement notes, the Chief went to the back of the stage, and pulled aside a flap. A dozen girls carrying stretchers and wearing nurse's uniforms appeared and walked across at the back. The Chief smiled at each one as she passed.

"Cold better, Mary?"

"It's okay today Chief."

"Having a good time?"

"A-one."

"Where are you living now?"

"In absolute clover, absolute clover."

The tenor turned to his co-announcer: "I disbelieve in the possibility of American creative design."

"I wager I can show you dresses of the first order."

"It's a go."

A mannequin appeared, walked across the stage, turned to the left, turned to the right, and walked across as the audience craned and commented. Their hands got instantly caught in a pandemonium.

"I just wish you could all be up here with me," said the makeup man. "It's such a shame perfume can't be recorded like moving pictures. All ladies should be able to smell like that gal. A Spartan splash of perfume makes all the difference, put it at the back of the knees, between your lovely bazooms, in all the most exciting places, all the pressure points, everywhere that's hot."

Another model came into view, and passed across the stage with a mean-all-thing-to-all-men walk.

"As the French say, she leaves me feeling un peu ga-ga. Top-of-the-milk personality, real cream. Did you notice how crisp the complexion is? Like fresh-cut lettuce. Superb skin, delicate and white like the finest porcelain."

"Or the inside of a toilet bowl," said a voice from somewhere behind him.

"Did someone say something?" asked the opera singer.

There was a pause, before the speaker went on. "I guess it was nothing but the wind," said the same voice.

The makeup man stuck his finger in the air. "Don't let your perspiration become a national disaster. I know the weather here is gorgeous, and winter is summer under pseudonym, but don't overdo things or you'll all start to have elephant hides. Treat your skins like house plants. If you don't, all the elastic fibers will rupture, and the oil channels will plug beyond belief."

Out in the garden by the pool, Olive's mother was talking to the Chief's wife. She never interfered when her daughter was being interviewed; in one thing at least she trusted her employer completely.

"This is certainly a big party," she said, "and big parties are a challenge, a responsibility, and a business investment."

"I'm glad Mrs. Miles could come," said the Chief's wife.

"Who?"

"Mrs. Miles, the wife of the director of the Bank of Hollywood, she's almost famous in her own right. She's a legend when it comes to laying foundation stones. When there's a big calamity in the world, her name is always at the top of the first charity list.

"I'm surprised she came now that she's working on her migrant fruit-picker canteen. She told me she hated seeing so many of them standing starving outside her front gates."

A black woman serving drinks appeared on the other side of the pool, and the Chief's wife called her over. "Mabel, I'll take another glass of champagne. How are you getting on? Good." She turned back to Mrs. West: "You know I had her working for me for years, then I had to release her six months ago. The succession of gals that followed was so unreliable I had to take her back. Do you know she was pregnant at every party I gave during the war, I can't remember a time when she wasn't in pod and pupping all over the place. She always seemed to have a fresh litter around her dugs."

"That reminds me," said Olive's mother. "Who was that girl you sent down to us last week; where did you find her?"

"Which one?"

"A red-haired girl with long silver earrings. She called herself Belle Hugent."

"Her—someone who was here for dinner introduced us."

"Is she top-drawer society?"

"She had a fine build, and wonderful eyes, pure violet, deeply, darkly violet."

"No, they were violet set in ivory," said Mrs. West.

"I didn't notice that."

"I'm Southern, it was the first thing I looked for."

"Southern, I've known you for all this time, and never guessed."

"Yes, as a Southerner, I saw there was no reflection of the eye's color in the surrounding white of the octoroon. It was a simple dead white to the line of the iris. That's the difference between the violet eyes of the octoroon and those of the caucasian—no reflection."

"Can you be absolutely sure?"

"If you want to be absolutely sure, try the nail test."

"The nail test?"

"When there is mixed blood, the base of the rosiest nails will be slightly discolored. Just the faintest tinge of yellow or brown is absolute proof."

Inshroin appeared from behind the hedge. He wore a single black body stocking with brown boots, and a gold leather belt around his waist.

"Mrs. West," he said, "I've been looking for you everywhere. I've just heard about something that might interest you. A young man has arrived in town who has a ghastly reputation for seducing older women, and using them for nothing but unusual sex practices until they're spent. Would you be interested in putting him up for the night?"

Mrs. West's nostrils struggled between a snap-shut of distaste and a sniff of contempt. She didn't like the actor for the same reason the Drewstone executives didn't like him.

"You were always rude," she said, "but recently you've become unbearable; sometimes I think you've gone quite mad."

"Just a touch of shell-shock," grinned Inshroin, remembering John Farquharson. The Chief's wife looked him up and down and smiled. "Inshroin, what on earth are you wearing?"

"I got my invitation cards mixed up. I wasn't sure if it was a come-as-you-are party, come-as-you-were-when-you-were-a-baby, or come-as-your-first-ambition party. I finally settled on first ambition, Hamlet."

"Did you know that the mother of your costar for the war picture is Southern?" asked Mrs. Drewstone.

"Is she? Then we'd better confine the conversation to assault, lynching, and castration. I've got an uncle who lives in the South; he runs a very exclusive hunting club down there."

"Really?"

"Yes, when it gets dark he takes parties into the black section of town, shines flashlight in the eyes of the locals, then holds them mesmerized while the visitors take a shot."

"Don't be flippant over something so serious," said Mrs. West.

"Serious?" replied Inshroin. "I've always taken it tragically."

The Chief's wife smiled. "Ordinary people wouldn't mind being a little less prejudiced, I'm sure, if they weren't so frightened of the colored people."

"We shouldn't make things complicated by talking about prejudice," said Inshroin. "Let's stick to something we can all understand and appreciate, like interracial sex."

The conversation was cut short, because the Chief caught sight of the actor, and with Olive and a dozen reporters in tow, came toward him, head down in the full-sleuth. More camera flashes popped.

"Hello, boss," said Inshroin. "I've been talking to Mrs. West about the colored problem, and she thinks it would be a good idea if Olive made a movie in which she marries a colored man and lives happily ever after. I agree; it would go a long way toward breaking down racial barriers in the world."

His employer's eyebrows became a single black bar, while Mrs. West's rose to the ceiling. Olive put her arms around Inshroin's neck, and as photographs were taken she stared up at him worshipingly. Her eyes grew bigger and bigger as if she were making them fill her face by a mere effort of will.

"How do you think working with Miss West will affect your career?" someone asked.

"Movies to me are nothing more than a form of pleasure extended into my normal working day; I don't call them a career."

Pencils poised, everybody looked at each other. Suddenly all the lights in the garden went out. From secret places a dozen men stepped out into the garden. They all carried long hunting horns, and were dressed in black boots, white leather jodhpurs, and red hunting jackets. They put the horns to their lips, and as the calls sounded, a spotlight was turned on at the corner of the pool. It revealed a mansize brown urn, and a spit-cooked buck hanging from a T-pole. Under the deer, waiters started handing out knives, forks, and plates. Guests cut their own meat from the carcass.

The Chief went over to the urn, and gave it a tap. The container wobbled for a while, then shattered, and the girl who had been with him in his office that afternoon staggered out. She looked nearly frozen to death, and was wearing a thin chiffon ballet skirt and shoes. Bowing jerkily, she went into a paroxysm of tap and belly as once again the audience got their hands caught in pandemonium.

A man came over and touched the Chief on the arm.

"I've got someone you might be interested in seeing."

"Who?"

"A little thing I found down at the Y. She really wants to get into moving pictures, she's working as a dancer at Mario's for the time being, and she's pretty good. You name it, that babe can do it, the fly-away, falling off a log, the Texas Tommy, everything. I had her down to my office, and when I asked to see her legs, she pulled her dress right up around her ears."

"Classy little shrimp," said the Chief.

"You'd really do her a favor, she's starting to slide, and we'd lose a big talent. It's the old story. She started sleeping with anybody hoping they were somebody, and ended up sleeping with everybody. The gal's had a strict upbringing, and it's beginning to tell on her nerves."

"What's she like to look at?"

"Great body. The face is a bit of a nuisance, and the titties could be pushed up a bit, but there's nothing the wardrobe department can't handle."

"Okay. Send her along, I'll see what I can do."

The Chief watched Inshroin walking away across the beach.

"I'll have to talk to him about that mouth of his."

Two days later, work on *The Heart of Turbulence* was under way.

In the first scene Olive is discovered swimming in the ocean. She emerges, walks out of the surf, and sits on the beach under an umbrella. (Black and white striped bathing suit.) She is reading a telegram that her young husband (Inshroin) has been killed in the battle on the Somme. (Flash of telegram, and fifteen seconds of troops advancing). A messenger arrives and tells her she is needed at once on a film set where a picture of hers is being made. (Flash of message.) An airplane is waiting at the aviation field. She decides to mount her favorite horse and ride to the plane. (Riding costume, she gallops off.)

In the next scene she is seen in flying gear, and sweeps off into the sky. Upon landing she gets out of the cockpit and then enters the studio in a beautifully tailored street costume. On the set she is seen embracing an actor. She looks despairingly into his eyes, then pushes him away.

After completing the film, she flies home. To show the domestic side of her nature, she is seen in a becoming apron, baking a pie.

It is now evening. Olive is next seen in her dining room in full evening dress. Guests are talking, and every time she pauses before a huge portrait of her husband, a handsome young man comes over and ogles her. She glances up at the picture, wipes a tear from her eye, and makes a valiant attempt at conversation. The butler enters (livery) carrying cocktails. Later, he announces dinner.

Long shot of dinner table. Olive sits in front of the picture of her husband (Inshroin), who looms over the gathering. Seen making valiant attempts at conversation. From their expressions the other guests fully understand her difficulty. Olive glances at portrait, puts hand to mouth, and slips to the floor in a faint.

Next scene Olive is recovering in her bedroom. She is sitting in front of a mirror, powdering her nose. Suddenly the door opens and her husband returns from the grave. He stands in the doorway and licks his lips. She parts hers, then throws her head back, and waits for his approach like a submissive cow. He comes to her like a python, their arms go around each other, her head goes back as he buries his mouth in hers—the woman's eyes close. They suddenly break apart like a couple caught fucking in a washroom at Grand Central Station.

(In all about forty seconds of war footage was used.)

The Heart of Turbulence was a huge success, and with the money he made from it, the Chief bought up more real estate around his lot, and acquired more actors and actresses.

As his fame, and that of the stars, became greater, privacy became a problem. The public would stand for hours around his house and sometimes even walk in the back door.

He would be having his dinner and suddenly become aware that somebody was staring at him through the window, and however hard the staff worked at moving them on, there were always others to replace them. At night when the curtains were drawn, he took to examining the folds to make sure they were fully closed.

He slowly came to realize that though he loved the idea of being stared at in public he hated being watched in the privacy of his own home. It was an aspect of intimacy over which he had no control. He decided he would build a castle on its own hill behind his main house. A castle surrounded by a high wall, to keep the public in its place, while at the same time adding to his stature and mystery.

One hundred and fifty thousand dollars were spent on landscaping, gardens were laid out and fountains placed. Sculptures were imported from Greece and Italy. The hill was built, terrace upon terrace, surrounded by a high iron and brick wall that went all around the estate. When visitors came in through the main gates at the bottom, they had to cross a marble bridge where ring doves cooed.

Right at the top, the castle rose up into the sky; it was surrounded by a moat, and when the bridge was drawn up, access could be had only by boat or swimming. It looked Bavarian, with its heavy masonry, buttresses, stone ramparts, and concrete parapets. A number of towers were placed in the same formation as Stonehenge. If the Chief stood on a parapet and looked back as the sun rose over them in the morning, rays would burst out fanlike, and shoot up to the middle of the sky.

Off the main hall at the center of the complex were twenty rooms. All had white walls, with baseboards and moldings painted black. Small square mirrors, framed in black, covered the inside of all the doors. The window drapes were green silk with a bead fringe, while the curtains were threaded glass crystal drops. The fireplaces in every room were of white marble. In the main hall above the bedrooms, the Chief's office opened onto a music balcony, with a rich embroidered gold brocade tapestry hanging over a Welsh harp. The walls of all the rooms had been covered with gold leaf, then smoked by candle flame to give character and to create the impression of age.

Tiffany's was commissioned to build the master bathroom's cut-glass tub, which cost $60,000. Casting it required as much precision as grinding the lens of an astronomical telescope.

Four extra hunting lodges were built on the other side of the moat for the staff or guests. Wooden beams were kept low enough for people to bang their heads and feel they were back in

Elizabethan England. Bars were placed in the windows, and aged by breaking or bending.

The estate shimmered in the California sun. Butterflies fluttered, bees droned and blundered. Flamingos stood stationary on single legs, and peacocks dragged fantails, eating nothing but sponge fingers soaked in freshly squeezed lemon juice. Fountains splashed, and deer wandered. In the rutting season, the bellowing males transported guests back to the insecurity of medieval Europe.

When heraldic flags cracked above the ramparts (sometimes alone, sometimes in unison), people could travel up and down the centuries on the estate.

One afternoon, a month after he moved in, the Chief was going over the profits for the year with his executives. Locked away for three hours, they purred over the figures. The job took as long as it did because returns were reckoned up in hieroglyphics so abstract that even the best of the company's accountants found them hard to understand.

When they finally emerged from the office, the Chief shook hands with each man; the grip was firm and long, as he gazed deeply into their eyes. "When I see Olive next time," he said, "I'll tell her I'd like to raise a stained glass window to her divinity, and it can be a church of her own choice."

The accountants turned to the drinks tray, slyly counting crushed fingers to make sure they were all still there.

In the music gallery, Mrs. Drewstone turned to some violinists and gave a signal. While servants dimmed the lights, the musicians began to play "Moonlight over the Ganges". Her husband smiled appreciatively to himself, wandered over to some french windows, and stepped out onto the balcony. He gazed down on his estate, then further beyond toward the studios that made it all possible.

His property was a city in itself, a state, the USA. Drewstone movie houses were a new power in the world. They provided potential immigrants with emotional reassurance. The downtrodden masses could walk into a movie house in most countries on the face of the earth, and despite the crumbling of so many European courts, see a place where monarchs still existed. It was a uniquely democratic royalty, one accessible to the humblest. Every man could become a king if he so chose.

As "Moonlight over the Ganges" reached a particularly poignant passage, the Chief felt a surge of joy and pride.

Olive and her mother were also having a new home built. During the war Mrs. West had purchased a large plot of land on the outskirts of Hollywood, and on the day of sale, workmen had moved in to start laying the foundation for a magnificent mansion. Each time Olive received payment for a film, the structure became a little higher and a little wider.

On the day following the Drewstone accountants' meeting, the builders informed her that the new home was ready for occupancy. Every antique shop in town was pillaged for furnishings by Mrs. West, and for two weeks convoys of trucks moved across the town carrying carpets, pictures, wall-hangings, and sculptures. When everything was finally installed to their satisfaction, mother and daughter left their downtown bungalow and settled into their new nest, cheeping contentedly. Because Olive couldn't spare the time from filming, they decided to put off a housewarming party till a later date.

The mansion was huge, and like the Chief's, set in its own grounds. It had a place where King Charles had hidden from Cromwell, a room where Queen Elizabeth I had given birth to a son, secret passages, priests' holes, and a corridor with a ghost that walked at midnight. Deep in a forest at the back, they placed an old priory shipped from Ireland. When Olive stood in front of it, she could actually *see* the monks sitting at their long refectory table.

The crowning touch was a walled bridge at the entrance. It stood there massive, foreboding, and giving a medieval sense of challenge to the outside world. The whole estate was a sanctum of solitude away from the jangling of the common people worrying about the number of hours they had to work, or the right to give their children a chance in life . . .

Almost simultaneous with the move, *Variety* announced that Inshroin had bought a disused tower on the outer, higher limits of the Drewstone lot, and builders were doing restoration work. When the place had first been offered to him by a real estate man, the actor hadn't been too enthusiastic; he didn't like the idea of living that close to the Drewstone factory. But as soon as he saw the tower, designed along the lines of a Victorian folly, Inshroin wanted it. The original owner had been a wealthy amateur astronomer and had built the place so that he could observe the sweep of the stars and planets.

From the top you could see for miles and miles. In one direction was the coast and Santa Monica, while in the other lay the line of the San Gabriel Mountains. Immediately at the foot of the tower, a winding road led down through rocks and scrub vegetation to the studio. When Inshroin looked toward the horizon, the surface of the earth seemed to melt and lose definition. It was almost as if his eyes became dreamy from gazing, causing things to drift and slacken their outline . . .

Inshroin had loved pigeons since boyhood, and instead of expensive furniture and accessories, the actor bought hundreds of the birds. They arrived in truckloads, and were transferred to large aviaries built around the base of the tower. On mornings before filming started, Inshroin stood among his pigeons. He held bits of worm in the palms of his hands and between his lips, and when he clicked his tongue they flew to him until he looked like an overworked tree. They stood on his head, they slid and fluttered up and down his arms, while others perched on his shoulders and rubbed their bodies against his cheeks. Within five minutes the whole upper part of his body was covered in long white streaks of droppings.

Olive's next movie was to be set in Hong Kong. She was to play the part of a rich American heiress who is kidnapped by opium addicts, and then rescued by a handsome white explorer.

The star sat through a morning's discussion of the film at the Drewstone castle, but by lunchtime she began to get bored and decided to go for a walk. After wandering around the Chief's lawns for a while, she found herself ascending a steep footpath somewhere at the rear of the estate.

Olive climbed further, following a brook that seemed to come out of the ground higher up. It wound down in a series of miniature cascades, over brown rocks, between mossy banks, and through the sun-shot dimness of transplanted oak trees.

She lay down in some moist ferns by a pool, and turned her head, hearing an extra loud patter on the leaves—a frog hopped away. She put her head down deeper into the green, and heard the din of insects crawling.

Sun and breeze, the smell of lilac pouring past in every direction. Buttercups, wind-beaten, staggered under a lopsided weight of bloom. Sheets of grass occasionally threw themselves down in the face of a wind. Bluebells hollowed and reflexed, showing deep tunnels of blue and white dimness. A bee entered one of the cups, and Olive, smiling, pinched the mouth of the flower together. A whirling noise, the blue tissue tears across like cigarette paper, and the bee is up and out. It sailed off, heavy, a dusky black with bright yellow garters.

Pollen drifted up from the ground like vapor and descended from the trees like smoke—billions of its specks bridging the distance of a foot between petals.

Over square miles around her, columns of air above each plant were packed tight with the dust. As a result Olive had an attack of hay fever. Nasal tissues discharged a thin clear fluid followed by a feeling of ants crawling behind her face skin.

Olive was bending over the pool discreetly trying to blow the contents of her nose into the water (she had forgotten her handkerchief) when she was startled by the Chief's voice behind her: "Books in the brooks," he said. "What are you reading?"

Olive quickly pulled off a long strand of mucus and stood up.

"It's not the brook I was looking at; I was trying to get the complete experience of this place. It's so full of mysteries, strange water secrets, and strange ancient water memories. Look! Can you see how that blue jay flutters in the water, and throws up sprays that cross the sunbeams? It's a delightful piece of nature that can attract all these lovely birds." She looked up the path ahead. "It's a beautiful waterfall. I wonder where it flows from?"

"A tap," said the Chief. "One of my gardeners turns it on from the house."

Olive looked shocked for a second, then changed her expression to one of awe. "You can sway the elements?"

The Chief shrugged. "I'm pleased you like it." He tapped his teeth and smiled. "I've got an even bigger surprise for you."

"What?"

"The Prince of Wales is back in America, and is staying on Long Island. Clarence MacKay, the millionaire, is giving him a party, and we've been invited down."

"Why didn't you tell me earlier?"

"I didn't know. I came up here with the telegram as soon as I got it. That's how big we've become; one of the richest men in the country has taken time to invite us to a party for the Prince of Wales."

"Who's been invited?"

"He's left that up to me, but I can bring four people. So I thought I'd make it you, me, Inshroin, and your mother."

Olive did a little dance on the spot, then arm in arm they started to walk back to the castle along a different path than the one Olive had climbed up. This one was a neatly cut, symmetrically cobbled road. A dove swept into view, swung in close and parted the hot air like a white fan. It then disappeared over the tree tops. They came to a little bridge with a stream pulsing underneath. A trellis frame arched over the stone structure, and from it hung vivid trembling blossoms. Two huge sunflowers cast disks of shadows, and velvet bees with soap-bubble wings staggered here and there.

Olive stopped for a moment in the center of the bridge and dropped a rose in the water. As she watched it swirling away, a breeze from the coast caught her skirt and blew it up, exposing suspendered and stockinged legs that started at her armpits.

"Did you see what that pesky wind did?" She giggled.

Her employer smiled appreciatively, then they resumed their journey. Past the bridge they stepped onto a different section of road, this part made of carefully spaced yellow bricks that wound up to the gates of his citadel.

"This is a real place of dreams for me," said the Chief. "Some parts of the estate are so private, not even the cops or mapmakers know they exist."

As they passed through the gates of the castle they nodded to a butler who was drawing up water from a deep rustic well. There was a shout from the top of one of the towers, and looking up the couple saw an executive making long sweeping motions with a can of film—he looked as if he was preparing to throw a discus. After a few swings, he put a megaphone to his lips. "Just seen the rushes of the new one Chief; it's a flier; it'll take off big."

Olive devoted a week to getting ready for the party, and spent hours with her hairdresser trying different styles. On the fourth day they arrived at a cut that suited the star's face. Mrs. West held her breath, there was a final snip, a little bit of abracadabra, and she was unveiled.

Work on the dress was reaching its climax, and from twelve midday to midnight on the evening before they left for New York, a dressmaker toiled.

The black seamstress knelt beside Olive trying to get pins into a fold at the back of the dress. She had lost her thimble, and as the star shifted sideways to get a better look in the mirror, she knocked the woman's elbow, causing her to stick a pin in her own finger; a little blob of blood spread on the silk. White tempers were running low: "Can't you be more careful," snapped Mrs. West. "Do you know how much all that material cost?"

"Everything here is so unbelievably intensely operatic," said Olive. She paused to pick up a slice of sugared pineapple, and took a sip of cognac and champagne, a drink that turned to velvet in her stomach. "This dress really makes me feel like a tyrant, it's gorgeous. I feel like, like, a deep blush. I feel like I'm looking out of a beautiful flower."

She spread her arms to suggest petals. Standing in that pose for a few seconds, she glanced in the mirror at the black woman. The seamstress was kneeling on the floor and looked very tired; one arm was taking the weight of her body, and her mouth was full of pins.

"You do look funny," giggled Olive. "Don't swallow any of the pins, you'll get indigestion."

The dressmaking went on until eleven-thirty, and then Mrs. West decided if it didn't work now it never would, and Olive should get a good night's sleep.

After a few more frantic adjustments, Olive was allowed to release the dress from her shoulders; it dropped to the ground, and she stepped away from its folds. Pausing in front of the mirror, she turned to profile, passed a hand under each breast, and propped them up in her palms. After she had posed like that for a while, her mother gave Olive her nightgown, and the star put it on and climbed into bed. The seamstress went into another room to continue working on the dress. Mrs. West kissed her daughter and sat down on the side of the bed.

"Just imagine what could happen if the heir to a throne fell in love with you? You'd make a beautiful addition to a royal household. You'd keep a record of your life in huge white leather-bound scrapbooks with gold crowns on the cover. You could play charades in coronation robes, reset the Crown Jewels, play dual bagpipes with your husband. You could do anything you liked."

The two women hugged each other, then Mrs. West kissed her daughter, got up and went to the light switch by the door. Before leaving, she turned on the threshold and smiled, then pressed the room into darkness, and quietly closed the door behind her. Under silk sheets her mother's words sang loudly once more to Olive as she fell asleep.

During the same year as the prince's visit Mary Pickford and Douglas Fairbanks went to Canada. They visited 211 University Avenue, where Pickford had been born. It was her first return to Toronto since she had left it as Gladys Smith. For years American tourists had regarded the house with the same awe they gave to the shrines of Washington.

On one afternoon they went to Christie Street military hospital. It was a quiet place filled with bedridden and crippled ex-soldiers. She stopped at a ward door, and said, "I want to thank you all personally for what you did for me in the war."

Fairbanks, who had been waiting downstairs, now bounded into the ward and chinned himself on a curtain awning around one of the beds, giving a whoop at the same time.

In the next ward Mary went into, she said, "I'm sorry I couldn't bring you happiness by giving each of you a package. Words are so inadequate when I see you all like this, but you make me proud to be a Canadian."

When the couple left, soldiers who had legs crowded at the windows, and those who didn't were lifted from wheelchairs so they could see. Douglas opened the door of the Rolls and, stretching his body out on the sidewalk, did some pushups from the running board. The ex-soldiers cheered louder, and those who had arms waved frantically . . .

"The Battle of Long Island" was the name given by the New York papers to the high society events centered around the Prince of Wales during the month he spent there in the autumn of 1924. The prince golfed, hunted, danced, dined, and played polo (constantly falling off his horse as everybody tried not to notice).

Clarence MacKay—cable, telegraph, and mining magnate—gave the future king the most magnificent party in US history at his Harbour Hill mansion near Roslyn. When the prince arrived at the estate, he traveled toward the house through six hundred of the most luxurious acres on the island. All along the route were festoons of electric lanterns, which flashed far beyond the range of army signal flares. One hundred thousand dollars' worth of electric candles in colored lanterns flashed among the trees. Placed three feet apart, they turned the grounds into a North American Versailles. On the terrace, in the blaze from twelve searchlights, splashed a fountain fifty feet high, a replica of the one in the Place de la Concorde. Rose arbors, bloom laden and heavy with scent, twinkled with lanterns. On each side of the house two great trees were so trickily electrified, they seemed to be burning.

A thousand guests attended. It was a mob scene—a gorgeous excessively refined mob scene. Food was served in a room of baronial proportions on plates made of silver that had been dug out of MacKay mines. Armor stood around the walls on which European tapestries hung. From the balconies drooped replicas of the banners of chivalry, to suggest that the MacKays were a medieval clan.

A month before, a family friend had mentioned to Mrs. MacKay that she had met a heraldry expert in New York who told her that the MacKays were entitled to bear a coat of arms, and his company could make up flags in time for the prince's visit. He had been invited to the house and asked to bring a picture of the family shield. After she had seen it, the hostess said it was a bit dull, but if she could have things from other family designs included, she would have some made.

The expert sold her $20,000 worth of MacKay pennants, adding some pretty blazonings borrowed from the Yorkshire and the Worcestershire Smiths.

Now in place, they fluttered gently to the sound of Paul Whiteman and his thirty-piece orchestra playing the latest white interpretations of jazz.

Among the guests were Vanderbilts, Astors, Biddles, Morgans, Harrimans, Roosevelts, and Marshall Fields. There were Lord and Lady Mountbatten, cousins of the prince, the Marchioness of Milford Haven, General John Pershing, Secretary of War John Weeks, and artists, actresses, and scientists without end.

The guests arrived in $2 million worth of cars. Flowers and

cut roses cost $20,000. Orange trees brought from Florida with the fruit on the bough stood in pots. The supper cost $30,000 to serve in a specially built salon—the salmon was so large that its cooking was a secret known only to the chefs.

Half an hour before the prince was due to arrive, you could feel people becoming tense. Inshroin and the Chief came early, and paraded around with Johnny Walker strides. The actor was feeling a little confused, and to compensate, a head of steam developed in his skull. He wanted to smile and have someone smile back to loosen the logjam in his mind. But he met no sympathetic face, and everybody looked serious.

"Her daughter married a Spanish prince."
"Life must be one continual European holiday."
"My daughter this, my daughter that."
"Do you remember?"
"Have you forgotten?"

Clearly a lot of guests had fallen on old times.

Olive entered the scene on her mother's arm, looking shy and restrained. Mrs. West had the same hairstyle as her daughter, but wore a hat, so as not to give the impression she was competing with Olive.

As was her custom, Olive paused, not to see what was happening but to give the crowd a chance to see her. As she looked around, men became unstrung and victimized and started to have trouble with their salivary glands. She walked forward, holding her body stiffly. Photographic representatives of the world's magazines trailed along behind taking pictures.

Her dress was a pearl-shot gauze, providing her with a spiritual atmosphere of spun thistledown. Color danced on her as it does on the scales of freshly caught trout. The mouth was a red bow and arrow, teeth white and perfectly even—coconut meat nestling in a rose. Olive was a perfumed, silk-lined jewel casket, and suspected that all guests thought her drenchingly beautiful.

A few women ran their eyes up and down her as though she had stolen something from them. But Olive paid no attention—she stared back, her eyes half closed, judging the danger of a hostile environment.

Once she got to the safety of the garden chair, Olive paid the gathering no further attention. She sat draped in an attitude that resembled a coma. Razor-sharp chins swiveled here and there, providing the room with perfect profiles.

Mary Porter from Rosco Films is there, her hair beautifully coiffured by Irving of New York. She has a flawless, well-dimpled smile that scatters starbursts into camera lenses. Everybody is strolling around like sprays of perfume, hearing a matronly voice say, "Everything is so divine and the essence of profundity."

Enter the prince attended. There is the sound of Handel's Royal Fireworks Music played by the Collegium Aureum on original instruments.

As the crowd packed in around him, waiters and detectives locked arms, and formed a barrier against attempts to break through to royal touchdown. It was twenty minutes before he could get a plate of food and start talking to the guests.

The prince recognized Inshroin from a film, and without any formal introduction started to chat. He said that he was also very fond of Olive West, and wondered if she was at the party, too?

Inshroin glanced around, and caught sight of Mrs. West waiting for a chance to move in. "Yes, Your Highness," he said, "she's here. I do hope you won't consider this forward of me, but if you get a chance, do ask her to give you one of her amazing farmyard imitations. To see her lay an egg is an experience not to be missed. Down on all fours she goes, and with a cock-a-doodle-do she cackles over what she's laid as enthusiastically as if it were her firstborn."

The prince thanked Inshroin, smiled wryly, and said if he got the chance he would certainly ask to see the act. He looked toward one of Mrs. MacKay's heraldic devices, and said, "They're very impressive designs, but I wonder why she has declared herself illegitimate?" Turning to pick up a drink from a table, he got separated from Inshroin for a second, and Olive's mother was on him like tar.

"I see Your Highness is eating salmon without the sauce, may I get you some? Sauce is the nobility of a regal dish." Dropping her eyes she curtsied low—knees cracking as she wobbled up. The prince handed her his plate. Mrs. West took it and gave a smile that made her look so much the milk of human kindness, she seemed to be waiting to be lapped up from a saucer.

"When I come back may I have the honor of introducing you to my daughter? She's been eating some, and I'm sure can give you a very complimentary account."

The prince looked across at Olive, and her eyes sank luxuriously into him. He took the stare, and they mixed themselves together across the lawn. Olive watched without expression, then sighed, and turned her attention to another part of the garden. In so doing she presented him with the nape of her neck. The prince was immediately interested. The common expectancy of monarchy is that it enters a room and at no time has a back turned on it. Here was an example of blatant post-colonial rebellion.

The heir to the British throne and the star from her stable were both products of similar high-pressure hothouses of privilege. Both had been pandered to from birth, and both kept away from opinions contrary to the best interests of those around them. Both had a smattering of social accomplishments, could ride a horse, and carry themselves without embarrassment at social functions. However, neither had been taxed to the extent of being made angry in argument, or even carried to a point in a conversation that demanded reassessment of opinion, or of feeling wrong about anything. The prince had one additional role, and it stemmed from the fact that it was his fate to be a living object lesson in applied genealogy. In each of his public appearances he had to play a living monument to the staying power of ancient ancestry—every mood, whim, expression, and mannerism traced back to a dim and distant past.

The prince went over to the couch, while Olive's mother was instantly surrounded by a group of women who chafed, fumed, seethed, and boiled.

Olive didn't get up as the prince bowed.

"I have been told by your mother that you have had some pleasant experiences with the fish sauce."

"That is true, O Monarch, and I can thoroughly recommend it."

"I'm not a monarch yet, just an heir." He smiled and looked at Olive a little closer.

"May I ask how old you are?"

"Twenty-two."

"You have a sophistication that makes you seem older."

"I'm older in mind. I've been through certain experiences, and they have had an effect on me."

"That's interesting. What kind of experiences?"

"They are hard to pin down and describe, Your Serenity. I have had some nasty disappointments with human nature. Things like that can age a woman."

"Would you care to dance?"

"I don't do it well, I'm afraid."

"You would do it as only you could."

"How is that, Your Reverence?"

"Well, of course."

Olive let go with a round of belly-shattering laughter that surprised the prince.

When she stopped, laughing, she said, "Do you think I like pretty things said to me?"

"Why not, if they're true."

Olive shrugged. The prince bowed and said, "Men will always find it possible to say nice things to you. Do you have such a poor opinion of yourself that you think all I say is flattery?"

"I suppose, so, Your Enormity; I sometimes think that I'm just four empty walls with nothing inside."

"What a delicious feeling that must be."

The band played, and Olive and the prince danced. Crowds stood watching. The Chief was with Inshroin and Mrs. Morgan, who was making an observation. "The good things in life are not only the cheapest in the long run, but the cheapest all the time, and good things are not as a rule more than moderately dear."

The Chief didn't hear. He was watching the dance with the absorbed concentration you can see in a boy pretending to be a locomotive. "A prince and an American commoner meeting at a great social function," he thought. "A movie based on the story of Cinderella." His interpretation wouldn't have much in common with the original, but then he had changed so many plots, what did it matter?

The original Cinderella had been found in a cellar performing her drudgery in a conscientious fashion. The prince of that story was allowed to fall in love with the kitchen maid because the author had a Protestant imagination, with its ethic of reward for hard work.

As Olive and the prince passed by, the Chief looked at them closely. He suspected neither (especially Olive) had ever been near a kitchen and wouldn't recognize one if they saw it. No, perhaps these two could adopt the style of another prince of legend, and be rescued from frogdom by Olive's siren call and kiss.

Back on the dance floor the prince suddenly stopped, and leaning forward said something to Olive. For a second she looked startled, then her eyes narrowed and threw sparks in Inshroin's direction—quickly her features disappeared under a great flow of blood. Inshroin smiled at Mrs. Morgan, then took a glass of champagne from a passing waiter.

"I'd prefer a glass of beer at the moment," he said. "It'd be cooler."

"You won't get beer here," said the Chief.

"Won't I? Olive's mother tells me the hostess used to serve nothing but beer. Has marriage to money changed her palate?"

His employer gave Inshroin a look full of asterisks. Mrs. Morgan pretended her attention was completely diverted by a magnificently dressed military man who had come up and saluted.

"Oh, my dear sir," she said, "that is the loveliest uniform I've seen all evening. What branch of the armed forces are you in? Oh heavens, you aren't someone from the royal party are you?"

"It's nothing, ma'am," said the man. "This is how we do things at Western Union, all the messengers have uniforms like mine. I'm here to deliver a cablegram from the President. The butler can't find Mr. MacKay and he told me you might help."

Mrs. Morgan opened the telegram.

"He can't come. He wishes to extend his apologies to His Highness, and says he'll see him when he gets to the White House."

Waving the telegram above her head, Mrs. Morgan began to force her way through to the prince.

"Excuse me please, excuse me please, excuse me please."

A reporter asked Inshroin how he was enjoying himself, and when he had noted the reply, said he was sorry that he had missed seeing Olive and the prince dancing.

"It was beautiful," said Inshroin. "At the end Olive curtsied so well, but I think she spoiled the effect by getting down on her knees and kissing his feet. When she returned to her seat, she stepped away from the prince without once turning her back on him, just like they do in England. Every ten feet she'd stop, curtsy, and say, 'The Prince of Wales by the Grace of God.'"

"Phew!" whistled the reporter. "That would have been something to see. My readers are gonna love that."

The prince came back to Inshroin.

"I asked Miss West about her chicken farmyard imitation, but she said she didn't know what I was talking about."

"No?" said Inshroin. "That's odd, she must have given up laying."

Olive sat silently staring straight ahead, and some of the other guests made attempts to talk to her. Although she was not completely unresponsive, the job was not easy. She listened to what they had to say, then gave a few quick replies with a mechanical smile.

The younger son of Mr. and Mrs. Vanderbilt came over and told her he was happy that she had come, because he loved all her films. He then said that although he didn't have her kind of talent, he was a success in his own modest way and was proud of what he was doing.

Olive allowed a smile of irony to play over her lips, which offended the young man. After that he made no effort to talk, but sat silently waiting for Olive to say something. Others came over and made conversational overtures. She answered languidly, condescendingly, making her voice deep and soulful. Occasionally she swept the garden with a glance, making sure the sweep caught every eye.

Olive had in fact met her social superiors with this group. Well-bred and secure with their status in life, they were at once too rich and too dull to be impressed by the presence of a celebrity from Hollywood, particularly when a future king was present. All they expected from Olive was a little gossip about the stars in California.

As the evening progressed, and the prince didn't come back to her, Olive became more and more short-tempered. She stopped speaking altogether and didn't reply to any remarks addressed to her. As a space formed around her and people turned their backs, she suddenly looked very despondent and sullen.

Olive opened her purse, took out a large white handkerchief, and flapped it open. Inshroin thought perhaps it was some kind of flage of surrender; the actress then patted moisture from her forehead. She fumbled some more, took out a cigarette and lit it. A manicured cough died away, and a woman's voice said, "Will you put that out, please? There are ladies present."

Without replying, Olive stood up and started to walk toward the house. Her mother blocked the way.

"Where are you going?"

"To lie down. I have a headache."

"You talk to her," Mrs. West said to the Chief.

Her employer sucked the memory of a Scotch off his teeth. "Did you have a good dance?"

"He seems very nice, but I think I'd like him better if he was older. If I was his wife, I'd be a loyal subject, but he wouldn't get me to bend the knee."

Mrs. West felt her hemorrhoid give a painful twinge.

In New York Inshroin decided that as the city was vast and anonymous, he would go to a movie house.

The Chief's movies were everywhere, and he ended up seeing *Adam and Eve*, which had someone else as leading man. It seemed that the apple of Eden and the orange of California had somehow got mixed up and were the same fruit.

The door at the back of the cinema occasionally opened, and people came and went bringing fugitive streaks of light with them. The silence was interrupted by the man next to the actor who was sucking oranges in a loud and slobbery fashion.

"You're not affected by the acting?" asked Inshroin.

"Why should I be. It isn't true, and if it was, it's nothing to me."

"You're a nice man to come to a theater and disturb people. Why can't you suck oranges at home—it'd be cheaper?"

"Look here." The man opened a handkerchief on his lap revealing a nest of ten oranges. "I shall suck this lot dry before I go: If you don't like it—leave."

"I will."

As Inshroin made his way to the exit there was a scuffle further down, and a woman forced her way to the aisle. She stood looking at the screen for a few seconds, then shook her fist at the picture.

"I deny that I am descended from those two!"

The Chief's star left with her, and as he emerged into the city light, he pulled up his collar and stuck his face down to the opening in the pay booth.

"Is Phillip Inshroin in this moving picture?"

"No sir; he's not included in the cast."

"I see. Well, please inform the management that the public is asking."

The following afternoon was the next great party for the prince while staying on Long Island. It was held at Meadow Brook, and organized around an international polo game between the USA and England.

The prince was the human centerpiece of the event. In a landscape of trees and pasture he sat in a box adorned with rugs, chairs, and tables on which cigars and refreshments were laid out as in a club.

When the prince gave the cup, he received a mobbing reminiscent of the scenes of 1919. He walked down to the crowds, which looked hot and helpless as they milled around demanding a speech. Eleanor Robson, wife of the president of the Westchester Racing Association, was so hot and crushed, her flame-colored frock was dripping wet from shoulders to the waist, and looked like a rugby jersey. State troopers and Pinkerton detectives with pistols drawn had to form a flying wedge to get the royal party back to the box. A photographer managed to climb up, and stationed himself behind the royal chair.

"Hey Eddie, look this way just a second wontcha!"

The prince refused to look, and before the man could call out again, he was pushed off the platform by a security guard.

"You and your damn empire!" he shouted.

"I do hope we won't have any more incidents like that," said Eleanor Robson.

That same afternoon Inshroin was sent an invitation to join the prince in the evening for cards.

At eight-thirty he was conducted by a butler to a pagodalike games room to the left of the mansion, but hidden from it by a high, thick hedge. It was full of wicker tables and chairs covered with purple blankets. A mass of ferns in pots partly obscured a dozen slot machines. Candles in huge silver holders flickered gently around the center table on which packs of cards had been arranged.

The prince hadn't arrived yet, but a dozen people were stationed strategically for a good view, and among them Inshroin recognized Vincent Erskine, the romantic lead from Coda Pictures.

"You been invited to play?" asked Inshroin.

"Yeah, he must like actors."

"Having a good time?"

"Not bad. Watcha think of him?"

"Nice, nice," replied Inshroin. "I prefer the Dane of Shakespeare, but we can't have everything."

Erskine lit a cigar. "It sure is funny how we threw out the monarchy, then mob them when they come to visit."

Inshroin ran his finger across a candle flame. "Everybody likes a bit of magic in their lives," he said. "We need a power behind the law, and something beyond what we elect."

The Coda man shrugged. "I don't know anything about politics, but I do know the MacKays are giving the guy the real red-carpet treatment."

Inshroin looked pensive. "I'd like to do a movie that brings out the significance of red in the carpet a king walks on, and in the robes he wears. The tradition goes back centuries and involves pagans and Christians. Red shows the blood of sacrifice is on a monarch and under him, while each bowed head salutes a victim."

Erskine gave Inshroin a long sideways look and was about to say something, when a young man came over and asked if there was a place where he could comb his hair. Erskine directed him to a clump of bushes just outside the rear door of the pagoda, then turned back flicking ash off his cigar.

"You stayed on the estate all the time?" he asked.

"I went downtown last night to see *Adam and Eve*. It's the only film the Chief's shot in three months without me."

"Good?"

"Terrible! Maybe Eve did climb the tree in the Garden but I betcha she never stood on a branch waving a G-string to attract his attention."

Erskine smiled. "My boss tells me your boss thinks it's a serious work of art."

"The only serious thing about it, is the price of admission. No there's only one solution, he's going to have to marry the widow."

"What widow?"

"The widow of the man who was watching the picture with me and died of embarrassment."

At nine o'clock the prince arrived with a party of men and women that included Mrs. MacKay. He smiled at those already in the games room, and sat down at the table. The two actors went over to join him, and on the way Inshroin stopped at one of the fruit machines. He put a coin in and pulled the arm. A correct combination of fruit sprang into view, and he won the jackpot. He began to feel lucky.

The game proceeded in silence for about twenty minutes, each of the participants looking as serious as the rent money. Suddenly there was a disturbance at the entrance to the pagoda, and the photographer who had tried to get the prince to pose at the polo game staggered in; he was very drunk. He went over to the table, and pulling up a spare chair flopped down, and threw his arm round the prince's neck.

"Hi! Remember me?"

"Your manner is familiar, but your name escapes me."

"Joe Davy from the *New York Daily*. I tried to get your picture at the polo game."

Shrugging slightly, the prince squirmed from under the man's arm.

"I won't spoil the game for you gentlemen," said the reporter. "I just came in, Prince, to ask if I could be included tomorrow in your yacht party?"

"That's impossible."

The reporter looked surprised. "Let me tell you now, sir, if you don't agree, I'll radio my employer to turn loose his minions on you, and believe me they can make life miserable for you."

The prince put down his cards and stood up; everybody at the table stood up.

"What in hell is that man doing?" murmured Mrs. MacKay. "What in hell . . ."

"I mean it, sir," the reporter rambled on. "This is a democratic country and my paper has one of the biggest circulations in New York. The readers have a right to know what you're doing each day. Now can I come or do you want trouble?"

During the conversation, the prince had started making gentle passes at an imaginary golf ball. When the last threat was made, he reacted by swinging the imaginary club backward around his shoulder as though he were going to drive off. Club in midair he stared for a full fifteen seconds, before the reporter swayed and sat down.

"You can tell your employer to do whatever he wants with his minions, and be goddamned." The prince also sat down and picked up his cards. "I'm sorry about this interruption, gentlemen," he said. "Shall we continue?"

A man from the group near the door came over, bent down, and whispered something to the principal guest.

"No, no, thank you for your concern. I don't want the rights of a member of the press intefered with. He is welcome to stay as long as he doesn't interrupt the game."

Champagne arrived, wires were removed, and corks left with their farewell pops. It was poured and served by a woman whose back showed to the bottom of her spine. The reporter accepted a glass, spilling some of the drink down his shirt—Mrs. MacKay watched him as if she were hypnotized. A butler appeared at the door, picked up two silver candle holders, and went out with them.

"We might need the extra light, Mrs. MacKay," said the prince. The hostess looked flustered.

"I expect my husband asked the man to check on them, Your Highness. They come from Versailles, and with such a huge crowd here, a thief could move around unnoticed."

"Surely your husband doesn't suspect me?"

"Not yet, Prince, not yet," said Inshroin.

As the prince laughed, everybody laughed, including the drunk reporter, who fumbled with a pack of cigarettes. He managed to pull one out and lit it. Between puffs he said, "Prince, I'm sorry for my display of bad manners. It's been a real hard day for me, will you accept my apology?"

"Your apology is accepted."

"Thank you, that's swell of you, you're a fine guy. I like you, everybody likes you. We're gonna separate tomorrow and maybe we'll never meet again, so I've got one question I'd like to ask you. Everybody wants an answer, and it would be a privilege if I could have an exclusive."

"What's the question?"

"What everybody wants to know, Prince, is why is it that whenever you play polo, you can't stay on the back of a horse for more than five minutes?"

The prince flushed, then turned pale. He put down his cards once more, and in the silence again stood up. He stared intently at Joe Davy.

"You can tell your readers that I'm never thrown from a horse. My horses have always fallen with me."

In the general applause that followed, the prince excused himself, saying that as he had an early start in the morning he had decided to go to bed. He smiled at Inshroin.

"A relative of mine, George III, once said to his wife, 'Remind me to forget to invite him to dinner.' As far as I'm concerned, the same applies to Mr. Davy. Please do go on with the game; is there anybody here who will take my hand?"

A man came over and sat down in the prince's seat; the game continued after he had left the pagoda. Mrs. MacKay went outside and brought back two butlers, who pulled the drunk reporter up from his chair and marched him off toward the house.

With the main attraction gone, most of the other guests wandered off too, leaving the four players around the table. Another butler appeared and replaced the remaining silver candle holders with brass ones; nobody noticed as play went on. Cigar smoke dense enough to knit with weaved around the flickering candle flames, while outside the moonlight blew across the sky in great waves . . .

There was a rustling on the path outside and Olive and her mother stopped by the window.

"You mustn't be silly," said Mrs. West. "The prince hasn't got any feelings against you; it's just that he hasn't any feeling for you—yet."

"I won't do it," replied Olive. "I've been insulted enough already."

"Good God, if you knew what I've gone through for you. When I was pregnant, and your father—"

"It must have given you a pretty belly."

"Listen to me, my girl."

"Listen yourself."

Mrs. West changed her tone, and now became all soft-spoken entreaty.

"Olive, the public is so fickle. At the moment you have admirers like a rat-catcher has terriers; how long do you think that can last? One bad movie and you'll disappear overnight. The country is packed with girls like you. If you don't marry soon, people will start to think you're old while you're still young. They'll say you're finished even if you are better looking than ever. The worst thing is that you'll begin to believe it. You are nothing as you are, so don't be fooled by success."

"Amen to that," said Inshroin.

The conversation outside stopped abruptly, and there was the sound of feet hurrying away.

Vincent Erskine suddenly gave a little gasp, and put his hand down to the small of his back.

"What's the matter?" asked Inshroin.

"Deal me out will you. After hearing the conversation, my old matrimonial wound is playing me up again."

One of the other players looked over the top of his cards.

"You shouldn't have any trouble married to one of the most beautiful heiresses in the country."

"Right. All the magazines call it the love story of the century."

"Don't talk to me about love. I married for money, not love."

"You married for money?"

"Don't blame money for buying me. Blame poverty for putting me up for sale."

"I'd love to be married to her, money or no money. She's one of the most beautiful women I've ever seen."

"She certainly is," said Erskine. "She's a goddess of the Greek variety, but packs a large amount of knuckle. When archeologists discover her missing arms they'll find she's wearing boxing gloves."

He tutted as he lost yet another hand.

"My old lady tells me I'm not much off the screen, but I'm sufficiently male not to believe her. She's got a hot tongue, and since I bought our new house, we've got a nagging overdraft, all ingredients for a very sweaty female curry. And my wife's temper is a very hot curry."

"She's living on top of the heap. A woman like that should thank her lucky stars, and keep her mouth shut."

"A girl like my wife raised by a woman like my mother-in-law couldn't. I'm lucky to be here at all this late. My wife tells me that when I'm out late, there's a lot of liquor drunk, a lot of unsightly behavior, and a very expensive brewery to be paid."

Ten minutes later he left and went into his room to bed. Inshroin and the other guests went on playing till four, when two more players decided they'd had enough.

"You're a nice bunch of boys," said Inshroin, "leaving a man to spend the rest of the evening drinking on his own."

After the others had left, Inshroin sat sipping Scotch till five, then went to bed.

He got up at two-thirty the following afternoon, washed, shaved, and had a light lunch. After that he went for a walk. Passing the entrance of the estate, he was held up by a line of Pinkerton detectives as the prince passed on his way to Washington. A patrol cop was locking the gates behind the disappearing cavalcade of cars when he recognized the star. The man touched the peak of his cap.

"Been up all night, have you, Mr. Inshroin? I should go to bed and get some sleep."

Olive never saw the prince again.

When the Drewstone party got back to Hollywood, the Chief read in the paper that MacKay had presented the prince with a silver dinner set. Not to be outdone, he had a reel of film clips made up of all his stars. He then had a solid gold container hand-molded in New York and asked Inshroin to find a nice quote from Shakespeare to engrave in silver on the side. After a couple of hours' research Inshroin arrived at the house with something suitable. The Chief read it over.

TO HIS ROYAL HIGHNESS
EDWARD PRINCE OF WALES
THIS REEL OF FILM
SHOWING CAMEOS OF DREWSTONE STARS
IS
WITH THE UTMOST JOY AND VENERATION

94

PRESENTED
TO HIS ROYAL HIGHNESS
BY HIS MOST DEVOTED AND SYCOPHANTIC FRIEND
MR. DREWSTONE (THE CHIEF)
OF THE DREWSTONE FILM EMPIRE
HOLLYWOOD.

"Very nice, what play's it from?"
"*King George X.*"
"Who says it?"
"King George X."
"Very nice, very nice." The Chief read it through again, "What does *sycop-hantic* mean?"

"It means someone who has great artistic vision, a man like Tolstoy or Leonardo da Vinci. In your own way you have some of their qualities; you create great stars."

The Chief smiled. "I particularly like the bit about my film empire, he's got his empire, I've got mine." He called the butler in, "Phone this down to the goldsmith in New York, and tell them to send the can of film to Buckingham Palace by special messenger."

In spite of the fact that they made the front page more often than a full stop, the next few years were a period of unremitting drudgery for the two stars. Their work in front of the camera was only occasionally relieved by parties or weekends away from the studio. Inshroin started drinking heavily, and Olive began to suffer from frequent periods of depression and moodiness. Neither, however, broke the principal rule of the Drewstone Empire: DON'T STOP SMILING.

The star's personal life provided her with no opportunities for maturing. Since her arrival at the studio during the war, her personality hadn't changed much, but to her limited range of emotional attributes she added cynicism.

Since her failure with the Prince of Wales, Mrs. West had intensified the search for a husband for her daughter, and Olive was encouraged to go out with a carefully screened selection of Hollywood notables. Initially every man seemed enthusiastic. Her quiet, virginal coyness had no accomplishments or warmth. Sexually she had gotten no further than heavy petting. When she got home, she relieved the excitement and tension by masturbating. Lying back on the bed, Olive would indulge in mild fantasies.

Sometimes turning on her face, she passes two fingers into the vagina, then to and fro—moving the body back and forth slowly, increasing the motion with violent pelvic thrusts. The duration of this active friction of the whole body on the hand lasts about twenty minutes. At the climax she grows red in the face and may cry out. Finally she drops down on her stomach feeling limp and exhausted . . .

Inshroin's ability was being eroded by the stipulations of the Drewstone contract, and the roles his studio chose for him. The Chief knew that all he needed was Inshroin kissing a lot of girls in close-up and he could make a million. As a consequence, story line was kept to a minimum . . .

Inshroin arrives on the set (a medieval period piece) and starts filming. Wearing a black velvet suit, he approaches Olive. Waves on waves of reedlike arms sway around them as they embrace. Soldiers with swords emerge from the smoke. Maidens in silk wisps try to defend their virginity as the troops pilage and rape. Olive is driven to the top of a tower, and to avoid being violated, throws herself from a high window. Prince Inshroin rides up on a white charger and catches her in his arms. He tells her he is looking for a soul into which he can sink his loneliness. Olive marries him and makes trips into the villages of his estate to distribute charity. As she walks among the peasants, she holds a basket filled with the fruit of human kindness, her eyes lowered to veil from sight the needs and hunger of those among whom she passes.

Inshroin had a few clandestine encounters with married women, who were keeping up the appearance of monogamy and virtue while their husbands spent long hours in the studio making money. Such an image was important in Hollywood (particularly since the Arbuckle case) with the world watching the colony for the slightest hint of immorality.

The price Inshroin paid for such encounters was an emptiness that made him drink more, and because they were brighter and more aware, he did so with writers. In that circle an extravagant consumption of booze was expected and admired. Liquor provided inspiration, and like a sensitive and soothing medicine it always seemed to touch the right spot. If minds were dry, a belt of Scotch was just the spark needed to fire creativity. Nobody at Drewstone's had any problems obtaining liquor. In an era of Prohibition, Hollywood could always bend a rule or two. By the middle of each day Inshroin found he always had an empty glass in his hand, and there was somebody standing close by ready to refill it. No stigma was attached to his condition. When he arrived on the set with a bad hangover, he was given a stiff-lipped smile of empathy, and one of the crew provided another shot to neutralize the effect of the previous day's drinking.

Because they had been on the MacKay party guest list, the Chief, Inshroin, Olive, and Mrs. West began to receive invitations to visit the best homes in California. Oscar Sisson, a newspaper millionaire, summoned the group down for a weekend at his ranch home in San Felipe.

"He's a great man," the Chief told Inshroin. "His presses fire as fast as machine guns, with one difference—they never miss. Everybody I know searches his paper's gossip columns to see if their careers are being built up or murdered."

The party left from the Hollywood main station for San Felipe on Friday afternoon. The platform was almost empty. Two middle-aged businessmen sat chatting, while a Mexican woman with a baby in her arms walked back and forth. When the train arrived, the Chief led the way into the first-class car. Porters struggled with a dozen suitcases and racks of clothes.

As the train pulled out, the two stars settled opposite each other in deep leather and brocade chairs. They pressed buttons, and lights sprang into existence in unexpected corners. Olive gave her chair a cunning push; it revolved backward and became a toilet with a screen around the bowl. She then righted the seat, pushed forward, and turned it into a beautiful metal basin with hot, cold, and ice water taps. Everywhere there were carved wood moldings covered with gold leaf.

"I've liked trains since I was a boy," said Inshroin. "Wheels mean escape, change, chance." He sat for the rest of the journey looking at the void of sand and sky where nothing moved . . .

The Chief and his party were the only people to get out at San Felipe, and the train was held up for ten minutes while their baggage was removed.

"Portah! Portah!" called Mrs. West. "God, where's a porter?"

A man in uniform came running out of an office further down the platform and, when he got to the group from Hollywood, began to pile their luggage on a trolley. He pulled it out onto the road, dropped the handle in the dust, and waved his hand in the air. A cavalcade of cars appeared as if they were attached to his fingers by string. When everybody was settled in, the convoy started off toward the ranch, drivers handing out great quantities of dust to anybody they passed on the road.

After half an hour, Mrs. West complained that she was thirsty, so the party drew up in a small white stone village that lurched at them out of the desert. They found a bar opposite the church and sat under a raffia awning drinking beer.

Outside the church a party of aquiline, coffee-colored people, covered in an aromatic cloud of cigar smoke, waited for a bus. Everybody had huge quantities of luggage. Pink or blue trunks. Heaps of bright, smashed-in cardboard boxes with yellow and green stripes on them, tied with dazzling ribbons. Rolls of grass matting filled with frying pans and kettles.

"Ten minutes everybody!" shouted one of the drivers.

Olive looked as if she were about to come over to Inshroin, and as he still didn't feel like talking, the actor got up and walked across the road to the church. He glanced at a car with Chicago plates parked close to the people waiting for the bus, and stepped into a bare rectangular room with an altar at the end—above it a small stained-glass window threw beams of orange light down onto the floor.

To the left, all along the wall, rows of glass cases were piled on top of each other. Toward the altar end, a young couple, holding hands, gazed intently into one of them.

Inshroin walked over and looked into the cases. Each contained a carved, life-size model of martyrdom that would have done credit to the best of modern realist sculptures. Christs with twisted limbs, agonized expressions, gaping wounds, lay in vast puddles of ersatz blood. Softly, Inshroin came up behind the couple, who still gaped into a case. He looked over their shoulders to see what held them so powerfully.

A female saint had conceived a child. She had not given birth, however, because someone had performed the crudest of Caesareans on her, and there she lay in the final stages of agony. The body had been ripped open from the pelvis to the neck, and the child bulged up, a sort of squashed pulp in a pool of blood that covered the whole lower part of the mother, and flowed along the bottom of the dusty case.

Inshroin studied the figure for about fifteen seconds, then glanced at the young man and woman, standing rigid, staring unblinkingly. Almost without realizing it, the actor uttered a low groan, followed by a short throaty sound suggestive of unspeakable pain. The couple suddenly twitched and came alive. Not noticing Inshroin, they both looked at each other and smiled, then turned away toward the exit hand in hand.

"Gee," said the girl under her breath. "Geee!"

Inshroin watched them leave, then looked back to the case. He stared at the distorted face, then quietly groaned again to himself. He understood why they had stayed so long and what had finally released them. All was perfectly lifelike in representation; however, *sound*, the culmination of experience, had been missing.

A car horn honked, and Inshroin went back out into the street. The Chief stuck his head out of a rear window. "Come on, we'll never get there. What have you been doing, getting religion?"

At the ranch, Oscar Sisson and his wife were waiting on the steps to greet the weekend guests. The owner shook hands especially warmly with the Chief.

"Business goin' well?" he asked.

"Couldn't be better," replied the Chief. "When I shoot a scene in my studios, it's a shot heard around the world."

"Would it be possible for me to talk to the woman who makes up the beds?" asked Mrs. West. "Olive likes to sleep in sheets and nightgowns that match, and we've brought our own."

Each of the visitors had separate houses, except Olive and her mother, who were put in together. Both women were very impressed with the boudoir where the star would sleep. The dressing table was covered from one end to the other with

Bohemian glass jars, and gold-stoppered bottles containing dozens of French perfumes. On a side table was a comb and brush case of solid silver, with the name "Sisson" studded on the lid in gold. The floor was covered with bootjacks and ivory whip stands, while in front of the empty grate, two huge tiger skins were draped across a set of brass fire-dogs. Above the mantel were a dozen or so crossed swords in all varieties of gilt, gold, silver, and ivory, each with a chiseled and embossed hilt. On the walls were a few French Impressionist pictures and some eighteenth-century animal portraits by English artists. The hangings that covered all the white walls were of rose-colored silk.

The rest of the house was made to look like an Austrian hunting lodge ready for a shoot. Box spurs, muzzle loaders, hunting flasks, white gloves, velvet and silk bags for bank notes, and a cluster of the latest English novels.

When Olive and her mother got back downstairs after the inspection, the maid asked them if they had noticed the bed. It was a huge four-poster that had been owned by Cardinal Richelieu, and his hat and initials were carved on the headboard. Olive said nothing, but wasn't sure it was right to sleep in a bed owned by the Bishop of New York.

Dinner was at eight in the main ranch, and as he arrived, Inshroin heard the Chief saying in a loud voice, "Risk is in the air. People used to buy bonds, they're buying common stock now, the public wants risk. Have you noticed the rise of the stock market?"

As everybody started on the soup, Sisson said, "I shall be going to Chicago next week to look into the affairs of one of my papers."

"A man must have a lot of responsibility and worry when his company is not right under his nose," said the Chief. "A lot can be gained by visiting your investment at the fountainhead, so to speak."

"That's very true." Sisson took a sip of soup. A silence fell.

"Do you have any particular paper that's a favorite at the moment?" asked Mrs. West.

"Generally the one making the most money."

"All the business you have," said Olive. "It must be a big worry?"

"Good business is always worry. The market is never stagnant; it never stops stirring."

They lapsed into silence, sipping quietly. The Chief's hands seemed to bother him. Between courses, he put them on the table in an uneasy imitation of Sisson's pose. Then he seemed to compare them and hid them back in his lap. From time to time they came up onto the table top, clasping and unclasping. The host turned to Olive and Inshroin.

"What does it feel like to be famous?"

Olive was suddenly tongue-tied, and blushed like a well-trained sunrise.

"You don't have to do much to be famous," said Inshroin. "Look at Goliath. Fame is a bit like a diamond. You need a market to give it a price. After that, the price of fame is what it costs you, and its worth is what you can get for it."

"I'm just pleased and proud that I can make so many people happy," said Olive.

Inshroin smiled at her. "That's because you happen to be one of those people who think pleasure is God's seal of approval.

"Being famous is a risky business. The longer the world of dreams goes on, the longer the void afterward. People go into a movie palace and see me in perfect roles, perfect parts, surrounded by the most perfect fantasy, satisfaction guaranteed from a lot of expensive sets and actors. We'll soon expect life to be like that. We'll ask for a little more, then a little more, and so it'll go on."

"I should stop complaining, if I were you," said Sisson. "It's given you more freedom than most."

"Nobody's free," replied Inshroin. "Because I'm earning a lot of money, I can choose from a wider selection of bonds. Everybody's a victim to a certain extent. If a man's married, he should carry insurance. If he doesn't, he's a bit of a fool, but if he does, he's a bit of a dupe. We should all make our choice quickly, and turn to brighter things."

Sisson smiled, as he extracted the spine from a grilled trout.

"You turned to brighter things quickly enough," said Mrs. Sisson. "My God, there's a million who would give a leg and an arm to be a star."

"I wanted to be a good actor and have a reputation as such. I didn't think about being a star. When I was on the stage in New York, the lights of Broadway became symbolic for something else, and I got sucked in. Each beam became an embarkation point for Hollywood, and Hollywood became an embarkation point for the rest of the world.

"I feel that quick money and easy fame are making me flabby. My grandfather was very poor; he spent a lifetime ordering things from a catalog. He'd say that as the goods were on approval and could be returned, he'd order them just to have a look. He was lucky; he always got them back on time; most of his neighbors didn't and ended up debtors. I hope I don't; I hope I know when to stop."

"You once told me," said Mrs. West, "that when I go to a dinner I should try to be different from the rest of the Hollywood crowd, and not monopolize the conversation."

The Chief gave a bleatlike laugh that had the impact of an indecent gesture. Inshroin stopped talking: His eyes chatted on for a while, but the mouth said nothing more. Mrs. Sisson supervised the coffee after the last of the dinner plates were taken away.

"Do you want some whipped cream with your coffee?" she asked Inshroin. "It's from our own cows, can you imagine?"

"I'm afraid I can't," replied the actor. "I've never been near one in its professional capacity."

Mrs. West pushed her cup forward. "Mr. Drewstone has a milking herd; he also produces his own honey."

Olive looked surprised. "I've never seen any hives on the estate."

"There are none," said Inshroin. "The Chief only has one bee, and it stalls with the cows. A single bee, but like its master, it is huge and prolific."

Mr. Sisson found that very funny because he smiled.

"How cruel dairymaids must be to whip such a rich substance as cream," said Olive. "But I suppose they are only cruel to be kind, cruel to the cream to be kind to us."

Sisson didn't find that funny, and stared blankly at Olive.

After dinner the men played cards while the women roamed the ranch looking at the furniture and accessories. At twelve-thirty Inshroin walked slowly back to his house. He passed Olive's house, and seeing her sitting out on the veranda, went over to say good-night. She was lost in the depths of a green silk-covered sofa, nursing an old tennis racket, and hugging a half-eaten orange to her chest.

"I thought I'd stop and say good-night," said the actor.

"Did you? My fingers are very sticky; can we just smile at each other and not touch?" asked Olive. Inshroin sat on the steps, lit a cigarette, and followed the girl's gaze upward.

"The sun has sunk and thrown up a beautiful splash of stars," sighed Olive. "Are they really separate planets, or angel eyes watching us like diamonds in the sky? When I look up on nights like this, my heart feels as if it could burst."

Inshroin drew on his cigarette. "The only diamonds and hearts that have affected me tonight are associated with aces and spades. I've just lost two hundred bucks."

"You can play cards with the night sky showing a hand like this? I could sit and watch them till there's nothing left of me. You're a funny guy. Why do you always have to be so rude? You really hurt the Chief's feelings at dinner."

"Hurt his feelings? He hasn't got any. All his emotions are just a collection of stumpy sensations. He's the kind of man who's affected by what happens to his property, not what happens to his feelings . . . Do you know the moon has no gassy atmosphere? It is completely noiseless except for the vibration transmitted if it's hit by meteors. Absolutely no sound at all. If you got up there and dynamited it, debris would fly apart silent as a dream . . ."

They were driven to the station the following morning in a Rolls-Royce. The glittering metal of the car fought for attention with the sheen of paintwork. The smartly dressed chauffeur had bright shining buttons that sparkled and twinkled in the sunlight. At the gate a group of men and women held out their hands for money. Inshroin wound down the window and threw out some coins.

"I don't know why you are doing that," said Mrs. West. "They are all fools. They don't want to work, so they are poor and can't get any food."

"I suppose food makes people good," said Olive. "There's a lot of talk about feasts in the Bible, feasts of this, feasts of that. But I'm sure all hungry people aren't fools."

"It's going to get worse," said the Chief. "The owner of Biographic was broken into last week by a bunch of out-of-work shipbuilders. Goddamn thieves, if any of them break into my place, I'll make sure they get the hot squat."

"I thought you believed in free enterprise," said Inshroin.

"Not that free."

"I get it, God helps those who help themselves, but God help anybody helping themselves at your expense."

"You've got it," said the Chief.

In the financial panic of 1929 Sennett lost out. When it was over, sound arrived and Mack disappeared, and his crown passed to the paintbrush. Sennett turned in his megaphone like a general surrendering his sword. Walt Disney plucked a Noah's ark from the inkwell, his characters worked for no salary, and never grew old.

Olive and Inshroin made a successful adaptation to sound. Drewstone's first production using voices was an epic. It contained his premier sound-screen kiss, which was a thrilling shock to the audience.

The two stars have discovered love, and Inshroin tries to present Olive with a mortgage while mixing his feelings as if he had sunstroke. He leans closer and glues his mouth on hers—the audience holds its breath. As they pull apart, the sound is like a cow dragging her hoof from a pile of dung.

On her return from France, Lucy Armitage had spent a month with her widowed father, then signed up with an agency and started touring, doing Ibsen, Strindberg, and Shaw. But things had begun to change, and audiences were drifting to the films. Managers now insisted that if the theaters weren't full three nights running, a production closed. Directors were told to leave out anything that asked questions or recalled problems at home. People didn't want to see by stagelight anything that reminded them of being out of work. Dance revues were being demanded more and more; theatrical productions started to look like films; and crowds of chorus girls began to appear in dressing rooms. Lucy's roles got smaller and smaller, and ended as nothing more than cameos squeezed between dance numbers. Managers started to encourage rivalry and jealousy among the girls, which was supposed to quicken drive and ambition. It worked with everybody but Lucy. She had her fair share of vanity, but was far too dignified to compete at that level. She began to get a reputation for snobbishness, and the other girls left her alone. They all talked of Hollywood for hours, each one growing more and more excited as the fumes of potential fame mounted to their brains.

Lucy went on with the work, gritting her teeth. She worked like a soldier in action, and what is required of a soldier in action is courage and stamina. She developed the quality of a bull who rams his head against a wall till he collapses, then gets up bloody but unbeaten. She moved from town to town for years, always staying in the cheapest, grubbiest apartments and hotels.

Early in the morning, the last moments of the melting dream. Awake, but with her eyes closed, she craved that unconsciousness would come again. But the interior landscapes always rolled away, and the things that had held her spellbound were gone. The stars she had roamed among were billions of miles away. Often without enough blankets, she shivered, then lay numbed at the idea of going out for breakfasts she could hardly afford. Assessing her career toward the end of the 1920s, she realized that she hadn't been in any serious production that had lasted longer than five months.

In her early thirties she was offered a part in a revue called *Return to Love*. The production was to be tried out in a small town in rural Illinois and, if it was a success, would be moved to Chicago. It was the story of life in Hollywood, and consisted of a gaudy confusion of mass whoopee and seduction on the part of a dozen couples trying to get into films. After a number of dramatic nervous breakdowns, everybody changed partners and returned to a life of mass whoopee and seduction, adding the extra diversions of motoring and swimming in large pools. Although she realized the play was nothing more than gross propaganda for flaunted wealth, she accepted. The production became very popular. Lucy began to go out with one of the men in the cast who seemed a little more interesting than the rest. He was funny and made her laugh, and after the years of drudgery, she wanted something bracing or stinging, someone to make her laugh or cry. She overlooked the weakness that was hinted in his face. He was handsome but showed no real character. His features had an odd sketchiness that was distinguished in some way, but they never fully expressed what they hinted at.

When he asked her to marry him, she accepted without hesitation, her whole self leaping forward to the act clean as a bullet, her body and mind leaping into that one desire to kill off the barren years. She also had a vague idea that it was part of her responsibility as a woman to help refill the ranks of depleted men. During the fourth month of her pregnancy, and before the miscarriage, she realized that he had no spontaneous feelings, not one emotion that wasn't contrived. In fact it seemed he only had two strong feelings, the first was a dislike of his name—Austin Dobson—and the second was an even stronger dislike for canned meat. The squabbles became more searing. Soon they weren't just arguing, but tearing elemental bits off each other—thwarted ambition, frustration, jealousy. Two weeks after the miscarriage, he disappeared on the same day one of the chorus girls vanished. They both left notes saying they were giving up the theater and going to Hollywood to get into films.

Lucy was forced to go on working to earn money. Things started to go wrong; she began to forget her lines. Sometimes in the middle of a scene she started thinking about the child that had been in her body. It floated gently before her eyes, tiny hands opening and closing like starfish in a void. After the show she became moody and silent. Some days a cool white light seemed to shine through her flesh; in her eyes was a strange unnatural glitter. She looked like a ghost on fire. At night her sleep would burst open, leaving her awake, her senses scattered. She could feel tears running down her cheeks, the working throat that swallowed nothing. Just before the production moved to Chicago she was fired. Without money she stayed on in Hampton, taking a job as a waitress in a restaurant, and a room at the withered end of town. It contained a bed, a chair, a cupboard, and a wall covered with an exquisite green map of damp and fungus.

Winter came on, and one cold November evening after work she wandered into the library for the warmth. Walking slowly between the shelves, a copy of the plays of Sir James Barrie caught her eye. She took down the volume and sat at one of the tables. Clipped to the front page of the book was a program from a recent Ottawa production of *Peter Pan*. Below the cast list, in an empty white space, was written by hand:

George Llewellyn Davies, the original Peter Pan, was killed in action on March 15, 1915. He was shot through the head while advancing toward the German lines, and died instantly. He had many powers undeveloped, no powers wasted.

On the back of the program was glued a cutting from the *New York Times* dated May 28, 1921.

It has recently been reported from London that Mr. Michael Llewellyn Davies, an Oxford undergraduate, was drowned while bathing at Sandford pool, Oxford. Mr. Davies was one of Sir James Barrie's adopted sons; the other, believed to be the original Peter Pan, was killed during the war.

Lucy stayed till closing time reading the play. As she was finally about to close the book, some more handwriting caught her eye on the inside of the back cover:

"One who has died is only a little ahead of a procession all moving in that direction. When we round the corner we'll see him again. We've only lost him for a moment because we fell behind, stopping to tie a shoelace." The early photos of Barrie show him impish. After Michael's death, they change. It is now impossible to tell if he is in the last stages of exhaustion or the first stages of rigor mortis.

When Lucy got into bed that night, she fell asleep quickly and instantly started to dream, and it was the most vivid dream she had experienced for years. She knew she was in the Llewellyn Davies boys' playroom overlooking Kensington Gardens. The room was a mass of toys and deserted hobbies, three chairs were thrown into a corner, they had something oddly human about them, suggesting a panic of ghosts. Lucy moved to the window and looked down into the park. Away in the distance she could see Barrie and what she knew was her child running in the direction of the round pond. Both were moving fast, arms to their sides, heads thrown back as if they were doing the hundred-yard dash. She looked up into the sky and saw that it was full of planes dropping bombs. One fell in front of the two running figures and exploded. As it did so Barrie and her child were jerked into the air, black against a sheet of flame, their severed arms and legs flying away in all directions. There was a great burst of applause from an unseen audience, a cumulative roar coming down from treble to base in eight distinct waves of sound. Then she heard a child's voice whisper to her, "A parent's heart bleeds more than an amputated limb, but we must put up with tears, they are not words, there is no reply to tears, but after the rain the grass is greener." The voice was oddly joyful and seemed to contain a hint of ambushed laughter. Barrie appeared in front of her and said, "two sons of mine killed." His eyes never left her face; they seemed to become immense like two large mirrors held up before an infinity of pain. Behind her, Lucy heard the sound of children laughing, and tried to turn to see who was there, but found she couldn't move. She strained harder and harder, then suddenly she was awake and staring up at the ceiling. As she became conscious of her surroundings the voices started to thin and evaporate into curling wisps of resonance above her head. The sounds seemed to hover for a few seconds then drifted into a faint vibrating hum. Lucy felt absolutely exhausted, exhausted but calm. In the morning she returned to the idea of work like a naked person returns to clothes. Her idea now was of becoming a different woman, a woman running on new lines till she ran out of the memory of her old self.

PART TWO

The social and artistic significance of motion pictures increasingly concerned critics of American life. Because an average weekly attendance of 75,000,000 gives the movies an influence equaled only by newspaper and radio, the Payre fund in 1929 financed surveys to estimate what that influence might be. The 115 films examined were found to portray a world where thirty-three percent of the heroines, thirty-four percent of the villains, and sixty-three percent of the sirens and villainesses were either wealthy or millionaires, only five percent of the characters were poor. If the people of the US were arranged as indicated in these films, "there would be no farming, no manufacturing, almost no industry, no vital statistics (except murder), no economic problems, and no economics," wrote Mr. Henry James Forman, analyzing the survey. It was pointed out that the pictures of the type studied portray a world unreal in fundamentals, yet so like the world outside the theater in superficial details, that moviegoers fail to distinguish clearly between the two, and carry home a sense of grievance at their similar but much more dreary lot.

The American Guide Series, California

For in the ferment of the stream
The dregs have worked up to the brim,
And by the rules of topsy-turvy
The scum stands foaming on the surface.
You've caused your pyramid t'ascend,
And set it on the little end.
Like Hudibras your empire's made
Whose crupper has o'ertopped its head.

John Trumbull

What was true of America in 1933 seemed even more true of California—unemployment, starvation, and death, creating despair with old leaders, and a desperate yearning for new ones. Thousands upon thousands of the nation's dispossessed had migrated west upon the premise that, "at least it was better not to have to worry about freezing as one starved to death." But once arrived, even the good weather could not make the squalor, misery, and terror of their lives appreciably more acceptable than what they had left behind.

Leon Harris
Upton Sinclair: American Rebel

THE DEPRESSION DECADE OPENED EVENTFULLY. On December 26, 1931, Ira and George Gershwin's musical *Of Thee I Sing* previewed. The production was a comedy that satirized the apparatus and people surrounding the election of an American president. The plot concerns John P. Wintergreen, who is elected to the nation's highest office on a platform of love. He is threatened with impeachment because he marries a girl he loves and not the winner of the Miss White House beauty contest. The nation forgives him, however, when his wife has twins. *Of Thee I Sing* led the way for a much more self-consciously left-wing (and even more popular) satire by Harold Rome called *Pins and Needles*, which would have 1,108 performances.

In Washington, Herbert Hoover began his campaign for presidential re-election in July 1932. His opponent was Franklin D. Roosevelt. By the middle of the month there were 20,000 unemployed men in Washington. For weeks the majority had lived in shelters they built on government-owned fields on the bank of the Anacostia River near the White House. Each day, groups paraded past the White House carrying banners that proclaimed BONUS TO BANKS—WHY NOT EX-SOLDIERS?

111

Hoover's campaign vanguard included four troops of cavalry, four companies of infantry, a mounted machine gun squadron, six whippet tanks, and three hundred city police. Among his immediate results were two veterans shot dead, and up to one thousand men, women, and children gassed. Troops with fixed bayonets moved through the camp of the unemployed and burned the shack village . . .

In Hollywood, Olive and Inshroin were making more movies than ever. Because the possibility of national collapse grew daily, the Chief became obsessive in his determination to wring every available coin from the public before it happened, and he worked his stars hard.

Long hours in front of the camera, reporters, and newsmen made the two major Drewstone money spinners feel like slot machine fruits. Their nerves pinged and snapped like rubber bands stretched beyond elastic limits; only a well-trained war correspondent would dare approach them.

The Chief, like the majority of Hollywood moguls, didn't understand the difference between entertaining the public by making them drink, and entertaining the public by making them drunk. Most of the stars were no better. They saw their parts as greater than the whole, and while they shone they didn't spread much light.

The Chief stuck to trite stories with Olive, and kept her roles youthful. Women who saw her films soaked up a simplistic world of romance, which had nothing to do with the complications of love and sex. Her roles consisted of respectable flouncings, proud virginal expectations of dream lovers, and a constant carping of "Do you respect me?" In her films, she either underdramatized or overdramatized without noticing it, and never developed any range.

There was a price to pay for keeping Olive youthful. Now older, she had to work consciously at keeping wrinkles at bay. To do so, modern science was brought in, and Olive was turned into a tinted and bleached walking chemical experiment. Her diet became viciously spartan, and on some days consisted of nothing but water and vitamin injections, a program that contributed toward persistent periods of depression.

The Chief's first sound production of the 1930s was a period drama set in fifteenth-century England. As usual the plot was sterilized and simple, but the settings were lusher and more extravagant than usual.

KING (Inshroin):	I'm glad we have a new princess in the family; let's call her Grace.
QUEEN (Olive):	I love that name.
KING:	I'm really glad we have another child; the only pity is that it isn't a boy.
OLIVE:	There'll be another time, sweetheart.
KING:	Do you want me to get you a drink?
QUEEN:	Certainly Sire; I'm very tired after the baby.
KING:	I know, my dear; you have a rest, and I'll get you some mead. Maid! A glass of mead for the Queen.
MAID:	Very good, Sire. (*It arrives.*)
KING:	Now my dear, don't gulp this down fast. Remember you're still weak, and this mead is very rich, and will make you put on weight.

On January 30, 1933, Olive awoke to the sound of music, got up, and stepped into her bath supplied by its multicolored fountain. The water was exactly the right temperature and perfectly perfumed, as she sat tubbing and making as much noise as a trained seal act. The tub floor, walls, and ceiling of the room were covered in baby blue tiles imported from Italy. Shifting in the luxurious water, Olive carefully and delicately passed wind, then watched the gas burst on the surface among the fragile soap bubbles.

She sighed contentedly, and gazed out of the window. A great frame edged with marble, it opened decisively and theatrically onto a long lawn here specially bred white blackbirds pecked among the flowers. Roses were everywhere, and hundreds of bees took signals from them, landed on the petals, and disappeared inside.

Soap drifts through Olive's drowned hair, as she draws her leg up to pick her big toe. Her private parts are toward us, and the nearest object of all is that staring orifice of the toilet bowl. The star's head is out of the picture in an ostrich-like display of modesty . . . Another half hour passes, then Olive steps from the suds. She envelopes herself in a monogrammed towel and

113

sits down before a mirror. With a soft blue pad of lambs' wool, she dabs a sweet-smelling powder over her body. After a few moments of this treatment, she opens a drawer below her mirror, and takes out a pair of stockings; they are the color of her skin, and extravagantly sheer. Olive puts them on, and fastens each to a garter, the straps of which are covered in little blue bows. She then calls a maid who brings a catalog of her wardrobe from which she chooses something to wear. After inspecting herself in the mirror, Olive quickly and silently leaves the house . . .

Downstairs her mother was completing some plans for an art show she was giving that evening. Mrs. West was justly proud of her achievement. Over the years, she had succeeded in making the fruit of her womb the envy of everybody. The egg she had laid was golden—and the price she had to pay for keeping it golden was vigilance.

Well-tuned ears heard the daughter leave. Mrs. West glanced at the clock, then went back to writing. She was sitting at a huge oak desk, and was wearing a white silk dressing gown bordered with white fur, held around the middle by a crimson cord. Although her face looked a little drawn, it was red from a luxurious bath. A towel was wrapped around her head.

Everything in the room was white: white carpets, white wallpaper, and white curtains. In the center of the room, near the desk, was a white piano. The french windows were open, and a little breeze lifted the bottom of the curtains and twisted them together.

At Mrs. West's feet was a group of dogs. They all sat at a foot-high table, at the center of which was a menu. The dish of fare included stewed liver, raw beef with a lemon sauce, and shredded dog biscuit. A yard of dachshund ate from expensive crockery, while a bulldog wearing a sailor hat straddled the table with a faultless bandiness, and watched its companion eat. Mrs. West glanced up as the gold Louis XV clock struck 9 A.M. with a delicate tinkle. A black maid entered.

"Where's Olive?" asked her mother.

"She said she was taking one of the dogs out for a walk, ma'am."

"You should have done that yourself; you know fan letters have to be answered in the mornings."

114

The maid said something about Olive having a headache and needing fresh air, but Mrs. West merely gazed ahead and made no reply. Then she changed the subject.

"You can paint my toenails now, and don't smudge them like last time. I think we'll do it on the veranda."

Mrs. West walked through the french windows onto the patio outside, sat down on a bamboo chair, and glanced down at the estate falling away beneath her feet. On the lawn was the marquee, filled with workmen bringing in sculptures for the evening's art show. To the left was a little orchard with dozens of apple trees. Fruit, ruddy to the point of apoplexy, hung from the branches.

The maid sat on a stool, took Mrs. West's foot in her lap, and painted the toenails, both women hemmed in by a clear blue sky. A hundred yards away was a small lake; in its middle, waltzing jets of water threw themselves as high as the chimneys of the house, while underneath the cascade, a swan turned its head on its stem and stared.

As Mrs. West leaned forward to inspect the toenail painting, Olive came through the french windows from the house and sat down in another bamboo chair. The mother noticed her daughter was flushed and was carrying a bunch of orchids. Mrs. West sat back in her chair. "You should be answering fan mail, not out walking the dog. Where did you get those flowers?"

Olive shrugged and put the orchids on the ground beside her. "An admirer gave them to me at the gate."

"Who?" Olive's mother asked, pushing the maid away and sitting up.

Again Olive shrugged. "Just someone who was passing."

"With a bunch of orchids?"

Olive began to look sulky, so the mother decided not to pursue the subject for the present.

"Now that you've decided to come back, we'll have a look at those new scripts."

"I don't want to."

Now it was Mrs. West's turn to look sulky. "How do you think this house gets paid for?" she snapped. "It eats money, and it's gotten worse since the crash, and that dreadful Russian revolution. I still don't understand how the Czar and God let it happen. We are lucky because the little amount of money people do have, they still spend at the pictures."

"Was my father affectionate?"

Mrs. West quickly dismissed the maid. Her eyes became suddenly impenetrable like clear glass frosted on the inside.

"How do you mean?"

"I mean sexually."

"I'm not the sort who bothers with things like that; besides my sexual side was never very important."

"Perhaps it was never properly brought out."

"Why are you asking me all these questions? Everywhere you look you can see the results of girls bothering with their sexual sides. They end up supporting families, living a life of drudgery, and losing their independence and freedom. It's your creative privilege to be separate from them, but it's also your responsibility to bring glamour into the lives of such people. That is your life's work."

"I know I have to work, and it's a responsibility," said Olive, "but don't I have any rights?"

"You can't talk about rights until you can buy them. Usually to be a success in life, a woman has to marry a man with money, then she can do what she likes. Motion pictures have changed all that: You're an independent woman in your own right because of your genius."

There was a pause . . . Olive sighed and asked, "How did you live before I became famous? Father wasn't wealthy, was he?"

"Your father could have been wealthy if I had met him early enough."

"So if a woman becomes independent, or finds a wealthy man, she can stop working?"

"Good God no! She has to work even harder. It's certainly easier if you're financially independent, but if a woman marries a wealthy man, she has to manage him well. She has to make sure she gets him, his money, and his position bound as tight as her shrewdness permits."

"Why do we have to do that?"

"Because a wise woman knows life is made up of love compromises. She can spend all her time looking for romance and never find it. If she uses her intelligence, ignores love, and gets a rich husband, the compromise is less of a burden. With money, a woman can get some wonderful things from society, and forget about love and sexuality."

"I know I've got money," said Olive, "but I'm not a wife."

"I never stop thinking about it, darling. You certainly have money, but I know you need the companionship of a financial equal. I've been thinking that perhaps we could take a vacation in Boston when your next film is finished. The best types the country has to offer live there. Rich, thoughtful people, all working hard at profound things to make them worthy. The kinds of people who are always going to lectures and taking life seriously."

Because Olive had been looking down while her mother talked, Mrs. West had managed to read the name on the card attached to the orchids.

"Who's Sage Lolland?" she asked.

"He's a man I met at the studio," said Olive with a flush, "somebody Mr Drewstone is using in a film. He was a soldier in the war, and tells me lots of interesting things about England and France. He thinks we should be married and have a family."

"Oh, I see. He's the one putting these ideas of stopping work into your head. Do be careful, darling; a sensitive person like you can so often be used by a lesser talent. You have no idea how easy it would be for someone to use your position to further his career."

Olive got up quickly. "I think I'll go inside and have a look at the scripts."

Mrs. West gave a warm smile of encouragement. The smile was still on her face as her daughter disappeared into the house, but she was planning hard. "Sage Lolland," she said to herself. "I'll make some inquiries. Drewstone probably knows something." She also got up, and went inside to finish the art exhibition preparations.

On that same day, thousands of miles away in Germany, an ageing President von Hindenburg had asked Adolf Hitler to form a new government. It was an event that would have a profound effect on Hollywood and the Drewstone Empire. Two weeks before, Hitler and Goebbels had seen the film *Der Rebell*, a blood-and-thunder drama of a young German patriot's fight against the French. They were very impressed. Hitler saw it four times.

The Germans as a whole are bemused by words. Anything that is barked, shouted, or bellowed with enough assurance impresses them as true. Their critical sense does not operate, and they are as a rule almost impervious to boredom. There is hardly a German book that would not be better from being relentlessly cut and pruned. One word leads to another.

A. H. Brodrick
Casual Change

ADOLF HITLER, the leader of the German people from 1933 to 1945, is a child of our machine age in terms of voltage, energy, discipline, and structure. Anything diminishing willpower and determination to succeed is abhorrent to him. Civilization's greatest Wagner enthusiast, he is the most hypnotizing speechmaker of the twentieth century. He is part romantic, part pirate, part butcher, and his ambitions are hitched to the stars. Hitler also has a bomb-proof conscience, and a world of self-confidence. "Let me be but one of fifteen men around a table and I will have my way," is his motto. In his career he will restore the pride of a defeated Germany, unite the country behind him, and embark on a program of world conquest using more military might than any other man in history. Coming from humble origins, he is the messiah of Teutonic nationalism.

To appreciate Hitler's determination to become leader of Germany, we have to understand his feelings when he returned from active service after the First World War. To start with, he loved Germany fanatically. If his joy would have been sublime in her victory, his grief was inconsolable in her defeat. When his adopted country lost, he was consumed with an apoplectic rage, and he began at once plotting to seize power in Germany, so that he could organize a return war.

In 1919 he nurtures and develops the current fantasy of a German army unbeaten in the field and adds his own obsession of how it was subverted at home by Jewish capitalists and communists. Hitler doesn't stop there. His obsession exalts the magnificence of the unbeaten army and turns it into the spearhead of a world-conquering master race that will be responsible for the rest of humankind.

118

He dreams this army will be so powerful, it will never be defeated again, a nobility of warriors led by an elite force of spartan SS knights. The SS will be the cream of battle units, the supermen and aristocrats of war; when they speak, no military dogs may bark. Fire a gun at these warriors, and the bullets flatten themselves. Hit them, and the hand that strikes the blow is turned to a bloody pulp. Out of this army will be forged a weapon that cuts the throats of what Hitler considers evil and impure. The SS will not shelter the poor and dispossessed in the lands that are conquered; instead they will hold an iron fist under the noses of such people, then annihilate them for being poor and dispossessed.

Hitler is convinced *absolutely* that destiny has chosen him to lead this master race, because since childhood he has hated impurity and loved the good. However, his good must be militant and pitiless if it is to impose itself between the source of all evil—Jewish/capitalist/communist subversion—and the vulnerability of the rest of humankind. He feels he can represent this good and can lead the world to a new peace—his peace. Before it comes about, there must be a cleansing violence, a washing-away of the old structures in society. His world will give birth to a new kind of baby, but it must have plenty of bloody, character-forming birth pangs.

During the 1920s, Hitler starts to prepare the country for the struggle and the war of revenge. He devises four rules of conduct from which he will never deviate:

1. The improbable always succeeds. The small propaganda lie is never believed by the masses—the big one always.
2. Always maintain the offensive; never be pushed into a defensive position.
3. Never be led into discussion if you want to get anywhere. If you decline discussion, an opponent gets nervous.
4. You can do anything with the stupidity and cowardice of the middle classes.

Hitler's objective is to fan the heat of German humiliation, then cool it to a tempered revolutionary fanaticism. His channels of mind-infiltration to achieve this end are a book and public oratory.

Mein Kampf is not literature any more than a grenade exploding in your face is literature. Like all great propaganda, it puts an end to doubt, closes open minds, and leads to action. Its pages thrust a political choice upon the German public as a matter of life and death. It separates them from the rest of the world by barriers as real as burning rivers; the Germans are on one side, the rest of the world is on the other. The book is a gigantic foundry of emotion, projecting a skyscraping enthusiasm for blood and sacrifice. It contains soaring diatribes in which the author tries to induce young Germans to drop Marxism and take extreme nationalism in its place. He pleads with them to become beasts of prey, men of hardness and courage, who shrink only from surrender, never from treachery or violence.

Hitler's public speaking complements the book, and consists of volatile speeches he gives first in beer halls. He speaks and behaves as if he has created Germany and it is his to play with. Ecstatic as a saint, he plunges deep into patriotism, and large numbers of those seeing the embrace are converted to his vision and believe it is reality. The speeches are full of scorn for the world that defeated Germany.

"The German people are betrayed! Those who perished in the trenches of Verdun perished in vain! Our rulers are a pack of criminals. Aliens devour our money. Since 1918 you trusted the world, you trusted Europe, you trusted in the world's decency and cast your honor away. And now, poor fools, the world has taken your last shirt as well! Communists and Jews lurk in every corner of government, and they have you by the throat. They have turned you into sheep with their talk of pacifism and humanity and other un-German words. Spurn the Jews! Spurn the communists! Spurn the whole world! We have never believed in its hypocritical decency. I tell you, I shriek it in your faces, Germany must be strong, Germany must have a sword again! Only then will Germany be respected, because it is by might and terror that people are swayed."

Because of his robust no-nonsense approach in an era of disillusionment, more and more people begin to accept him as the one realist who understands Germany and her problems. Facts do not stand in his way. His words come with a strong powerful rush, knock facts on the head, and cremate them at once. Appealing to raw emotion, his prestige and popularity grow. The beer hall speeches spill out into the streets and explode. His audiences, orchestrated by committed Nazis, begin a program of smashing Jews and communists to revenge German wartime humiliation and defeat.

In 1933 Hitler manipulates enough Germans into electing him democratically to the position of head of state; then he immediately does away with the democratic process. He turns his attention to students, because he is a nurseryman of genius and knows the value of pruning and feeding young plants to make them yield well. He convinces them that the path of national rebirth leads inward and that they must reject the outside world. With their approval and help, Jewish and foreign books are burned, while theaters, movie houses, and schools are strictly censored as to what they may say and teach—all principles that comply with the birth of any militant faith.

At huge parades under sweeping spotlights he offers his countrymen a future full of adventure in vast and strange epochs. He tells them he will create an industrial Germany of cogs, grease, and success, all wrapped in the memory of ancient Teutonic triumph and myth.

As Hitler pleads with the German people to accept him not merely as a leader but as their voice of destiny, he gives instructions to mass-produce a special cheap radio. With its help, Hitler weaves himself completely into the texture of German life, and begins to affect life beyond the nation's border. The performance is always the same and is repeated day after day. His scornful, contemptuous voice, sounding as if it has been half-choked by gas fumes from the trenches, rises above the roar of the Reichstag members and enters the homes of the British. His uncompromising battle cry starts to create a state of constant and unremitting anxiety in their daily lives.

The Chief had been at his office all day and was not looking forward to the art show Mrs. West had arranged for the evening. Now he was relaxing in his large boathouse overlooking the moat that surrounded his home. The wooden building was full of canoes, rowboats, buoys, lobster traps, and fishing nets. Three skiffs and a high-powered motorboat stood in the middle of the marble floor. Dozens of lifejackets, towels, picnic baskets and sets of oars were strewn everywhere. On each object in the boathouse were painted the words PROPERTY OF MR. DREWSTONE: HOLLYWOOD.

The Chief was reclining on his back in a sun chair, talking on the phone with Mrs. West about Sage Lolland. Sitting next to him was a beautiful girl called Fanny Locan. She had curly blond hair and was wearing a lime-green bathing suit, crimson high-heeled shoes, and a little white collar and bowtie around her neck.

The Chief was wearing a dark blue, double-breasted blazer, black tie, and white slacks. It was a uniform that at sea meant "Captain going ashore." He said nothing, but gazed placidly along the length of a fishing pole he had set up at his side and listened to Mrs. West. As he was in the habit of explaining, there were no fish in the moat as yet, but that certainly didn't stop *him* from fishing. The sun, an orange glow, cast long shadows that made him feel even more serene and harmonious.

The Chief finished his conversation, and put the phone back on its hook. He sighed, propped himself up on his elbow, and poured some Scotch over a handful of ice cubes in his glass. The girl leaned across, undid his fly, put her hand inside and tickled his testicles.

"Pleathe, pleathe, let me try for the part," she lisped.

"May-be, may-be," said the Chief drowsily. "I'm thinking about it. Keep your hand there, it's nice."

The girl stood up and undid Drewstone's pants completely. Then, bending forward from the waist and balancing delicately on her very high heels, she slowly brought on his erection with her right hand. For five minutes the Chief lay stretched out purring. He didn't come quickly, and the bending position the girl had assumed became tiring, so she tried to relieve the strain a little by pressing her free hand *hard* into the small of her back . . . She let go after he had ejaculated, stood up straight, put a hand on each hip and gave the tired spine a long straightening s-t-r-e-t-c-h-h-h. In the glass, the ice creaked loudly as its center of gravity shifted through melting.

"Pleathe, pleathe, let me try for the part," she lisped.

"I told you I'm thinking about it. I'll tell you later when we get back from Mrs. West's art show."

Mrs. West stood on the lawn in front of her pavilion, greeting her guests as they got out of their cars. Everybody was chattering excitedly, eager to see the one thing they had read about in the press, the sculptor's interpretation of Adam's genitals.

Mrs. West wiped her hand on her frock as the Scandinavian performer Greta Strindberg arrived in her Rolls. The star was wearing a black tube dress and an old fashioned priestlike hat. A slab of hair hung down from under its brim—and covered one side of her face, ashen under a groundwork of white powder. The lips were unnaturally red, and so thickly painted Mrs. West found it impossible to trace the real obliterated mouth. The eyes were brown, and glistened with salt and cool darkness—each one hung with a huge palisade of lashes. The whole look was still and melancholic, as though it had been frozen at a deathbed.

Greta glanced around, then glided forward, placing her feet delicately step by step in the manner of a mountain goat. She stopped in front of the hostess and stared, then, with the aid of a three-foot holder, distanced herself from a cigarette. The two women shook hands.

"I can't tell you how pleased I am that you could come," said the hostess. "I do admire your work so much."

There was a scraping sound from the Rolls, and Greta turned back to the car. As she did so, a chalk-white V sprang out from the back of the star's tube dress.

"Ah," she said, "here comes my friend and companion Frederick Milford." Frederick stopped for a second after the chauffeur had helped him down and stared at Olive's mother. He then walked slowly toward her on unsteady bowed legs, his tongue protruding from the left corner of his mouth. He stopped at Mrs. West's feet, and as the species will, asked a few persistent questions around her ankles.

"Mr. Milford seems to like you," said Greta.

"He's a lovely bull," said the hostess. "I'd never guess you were the owner."

"Why not?"

"The dog looks as if it should belong to a prizefighter."

"I like strong contrasts."

Olive's mother patted the animal's slobbering jowls.

"He's very handsome."

"He is," said Greta, "but he is also intensely selfish. But being a dog, he gets very little pleasure from the feeling."

Mrs. West sighed. "Why are dogs so much nicer than people?"

"Nearly all bad dogs are drowned, and all mad dogs are shot. The ones that are left have to be nice."

Mrs. West noticed the sculptor coming toward them. He was so gaunt that the planes of his skull were visible through greased-down hair. He was very excited and seemed to be removing his spiritual clothing, so that he might have a sauna in Greta's psyche. When his hand fell into hers, the grip felt like a pound of warm liver and above the hand was a pair of dopey adoring eyes. They made Greta think that she didn't often need a gun, but when she did, she needed one badly.

For a moment those eyes draped Miss Strindberg in velvet, then he said, "I have always loved and admired your work, I see such spiritual depths in your films, such is-ness, such was-ness, such pent-up sorrow. You remind me that death must be the most elegant woman in the world, because she considers nothing but herself. I see you . . ."

Mrs. West ushered them toward the tent. At the entrance, she stopped and glanced at the brochure pinned to the canvas wall, then peered closer. "I didn't know you were a Doctor of Divinity," she said. The sculptor dragged his eyes away from Greta.

"How is that?"

"It says here *DD* after your name."

"Oh that, no, I survived the 'twenties. I graduated with highest honors from the Dizzy Decade."

Greta looked at the young man and said, "I think you are a perfect imitation of a sentimental cream poof."

The young man smiled. "You mean cream puff."

"Yes, that is so, a sentimental cream poof."

Behind the rows of sculptures Mrs. West saw the Chief talking to William Wrigley★ and took Strindberg over to be

---

★William Wrigley began life as a drummer (traveling salesman) of hosiery. At that time, America was smitten with a fear of fires, so smoking was strictly prohibited in offices, workshops, and stores. Smokers found tobacco chewing the only narcotic substitute, but that was soon squashed by a fierce antispitting campaign. Wrigley thought he could capitalize on a new idea of salesmanship. When he called on drapers, he handed out a few strips of gum made for him by a man in Chicago. He used the sticks of gum as substitutes for introduced. The mint czar looked very grand in his handmade suit—the embodiment of force itself. The pockets bulged with so much money that they resembled cow's udders. The hair on his head was smooth, black, and shiny. The face was cut in something more durable than flesh. He was the bronze keeper-at-the-gate of American business—the very latest in its line of defense.

Mrs. West introduced her new guest to the two men. Although the Chief said, "Pleased to meet you," he looked indifferent. All film stars meant to him after so many years was a means of bringing money into the bank. Besides, she had already signed with another studio. Wrigley was a little more impressed and pulled nervously at his tie as he shook hands.

"Miss Strindberg," he said, "you show the world beauty on the screen; my humble offering is mastication. Thanks to me we have a nation of very strong jaws."

Greta drew on her cigarette, then closed one eye as smoke crawled up her face.

"What happens to the gum when people have finished with it?" she asked.

"Permanent mystery," said Wrigley with a shrug.

"When my manager sails on a ship, he tells me he has solved that problem, and also another of the world's great problems. How to get rid of used razor blades. He wraps the blades in the gum, and throws them both out of the porthole."

"It sounds like a clever idea," said Wrigley, "but do you think I can afford to supply all my chewers with portholes?" He fiddled with his tie again. "I'm sorry if I seem nervous, but meeting you like this has confused me. In the roles you play, you seem so real; I keep thinking you're performing now."

Greta drew on her cigarette. "You feel unreality now and reality on the screen?"

---

a calling card, and became known throughout his territories as the "gum drummer." He became the world's dandiest chew salesman. Wrigley quickly gingered up the "can't-see-you" and the "nuthin' doin'," till they turned into the glad hand: "expectin' you," and "dee-lighted you've come." As the habit spread among retailers, Wrigley's stock of gum got bigger and bigger. One day he decided there was more money in gum than in hosiery. He went in fifty-fifty with the Chicago man producing his supply. By 1935 the entire chewing gum industry would be worth $9,100,000.

"Yes, but as this is a real party, I think it must mean that when you act so naturally on the screen, you're simply being yourself."

"That is so. I thought perhaps I would be no good in America, because people here like hot peppers, and I am not a hot pepper."

"Well, that shows how wrong you can be. Us Americans know great things are quiet and deep. Is that how you manage to act as you do, because you are quiet and deep?"

"No, I act as I do because I cannot do otherwise. I often do things on the screen I shall never do in real life. For example, I often sacrifice my good name to save the reputation of a dear dead one."

"I've always admired the way you do that," said Wrigley.

"Why? Why does a living woman have to lose her reputation for the sake of a dead one?"

"The dead one might be a long-suffering husband?"

"So, what of that? Men take care of themselves. Believe me, unselfishness is wasted on them."

Mrs. West drew Greta aside so they could look at the sculpture alone. Standing in front of the first man, Olive's mother assumed an expression of absolute indifference and snatched her first glance at his genitals. She did some quick thinking. Adam was featured in the Bible, so he must be religious and respectable enough for a lady to look at. But how was it possible for someone to have something so enormous? She leaned forward to read the descriptive card.

A man babe of giant strength, squat and unrefined. The father of a teeming race as yet unborn, his genitals swung to his tread, as does the kilt to the music of the pipes.

"What do you think?" the sculptor asked his patroness.

Mrs. West screwed up her eyes and stood back a step or two: "The first thing that comes to mind is that it has a great spiritual depth and profundity about it. It's up and down, in and out, here there and everywhere in enormous yet distinguishable complexity. How did you so aptly describe Miss Strindberg? Such is-ness, such was-ness, such pent-up sorrow . . . A perfect description don't you think, Greta?"

The star seemed unmoved. She drew on her cigarette, and

with an almost Islamic standard of modesty, obscured her face behind a cloud of tobacco smoke.

"Are you married?" she asked Mrs. West.

"I was once."

"So I can assume you are a woman with experiences?"

"You could say that."

"I was married once," said Greta, "but I am now divorced."

"I see."

"Yes, it was a joke."

"A joke?"

"A joke. But is that the word, I speak so bad. Joke is a word, I think."

"Do you mean you married in fun?" suggested the sculptor.

"That is so, just in fun."

They stood in silence for a few seconds, then Greta said, "I was expecting to meet your daughter. Is she here?"

Mrs. West looked around. "She should be."

The Scandinavian actress studied Olive's mother through her cigarette smoke: "It must be strange for you to be a star's mother."

"How nice of you to consider my daughter a star," said Mrs. West. "But I don't see why you should say that; I'm fiercely ambitious for her and her art."

"But you always attend the triumph of another. How can the 'me' in you stand it?"

"I like to think I'm somebody, I assure you, even though I'm Olive's mother."

"I can't see it," said Greta, "she's the face, and you're the face's mother." There was another pause.

"Have you never wanted children?" asked Mrs. West.

"Children? No. A daughter would be a rival, and a son a bother. Keeping children requires a different knowledge of diseases than those of dogs. I keep dogs, I pay for their licenses, which I cancel when I wish. They are also reliable and faithful. A boy would be around my neck until he found a softer neck to sleep on. Then where would I be?"

Mr. Milford decided to wander over. He stopped at his owner's feet and showed some yellow around his bulging eyes. A fly ran over his head and stopped by his left ear. He wrinkled his flexible skin, and the fly flew away. After that he sighed and flopped down on his belly.

Suddenly Mrs. West went rigid; her eyes became cold and hard, as if that part of her body had died. Olive had just come in on the arm of a man. She was looking up into his face and smiling brightly. Her mother left Greta without saying a word and marched toward the new arrivals with the precision of a Roman legion.

Olive's escort was offering the star advice: "We must try for a different type of makeup. When you laugh, you're still lovely, but you look like a newspaper advertisement, all bold type on white. Perhaps we can change the face powder; with your black eyes, you could use a little rouge."

Mrs. West made her presence known. "I disagree," she said. "And besides her eyes aren't black. It makes me think of jet, like a colored person's, all shiny surface. If you must comment on my daughter's eyes, look before you speak . . . they're brown. Who is this young man, Olive?"

Her daughter introduced Sage Lolland.

"I hear you served with our forces in the war?" said Mrs. West. It was impossible to judge the effect of the question on Olive's friend, because at this stage his face was just one vast grin.

"Yes," he replied. "I'm thirty-four now, and I was a boy soldier then; I just got in at the end. I had a real thing going between me and my buddies. We went through the worst kind of hell. I played my part when the bullets were flying around, and I kept going till the final curtain."

"What exactly did you do?" asked Mrs. West.

Sage's features became a little more set and defined, although the smile didn't completely disappear—it hung there, a single quivering particle. Putting on a silly voice, he replied, "I'm sorry, Mom told me never to speak to ladies who speak to me first."

Some of the listeners were taken aback, a few sniggered, then everybody laughed. Mrs. West smiled politely. "I only asked because I'd heard from a friend that you had lived all through the war in Paris with a Major John Smith; you're not the same Sage Lolland, I expect?

The young man flushed crimson; he was so caught off guard he didn't have the presence of mind to deny it.

"How do you know about him?" he asked. "He's a relative of mine."

"Oh, I see," said Mrs. West. "No, it's just that this friend of mine told me he was a homosexual." She gave him a dazzling smile. "Did you know he was a homosexual?"

There was a long sweeping hus-h-h-h-h-h-h. The dazzling smile disappeared from Mrs. West's face, and it took on the expression of a closed door after it has snapped somebody's fingers off. "Are you a homosexual?" she asked. "One of those men who prefer romance with one of their own sex?"

Sage protested loudly, stuttering and blushing, a fear of ridicule overriding a fear of her. People looked away from the scene, and he knew he was getting no support. His defiance wilted to unease—unease to helplessness, finally he gave up with a giggle of pure nervousness, and looked pleadingly at Olive. He got no help there. Her mouth had fallen open, as she looked up at him in blank amazement, her eyes sticking out like a shaved dog's testicles . . . The assault had started at five past seven without a preliminary barrage, and was all over with complete victory to the hostess two minutes later.

The Chief, who had never been interested in art, strolled outside to look at the house. He wanted to see how it compared with his, and whether there was anything he could add to his own, to maintain the lead in grandeur. He was gazing up at the roof when he felt a tap on his arm, and he was joined by Wrigley.

"Lots of stars here this evening," said the mint czar. "My assets aren't so noticeable."

"How did you manage to get so big in such a short time?" asked the Chief.

"I cornered mint in the Great War, and now at my plant, I have rows of tanks containing the stuff. I've got enough to keep the world supplied for five years. Now everybody has to come to me. My agents are everywhere watching mint crops, and I never tie myself to one grower." He spoke in short urgent sentences, his eyes holding the listener like a vise as he drilled him full of holes. "If one crop is indifferent, I buy elsewhere. I can work like that because my agents watch mint like other agents watch cotton. I bet you didn't know I even supply my competitors?"

The Chief looked puzzled. "Why do you supply your competitors?"

The mint czar smiled. "I'm a good American businessman,

so I believe in competition, but I believe in keeping competition where I can see it. At every counter where Wrigley's is sold, you'll always find one or two other brands. I like Wrigley's chewers to have a change now and again—I know they like a change, because as American citizens they are a curious people. When they've tried other gums, they always come back to Wrigley's. The public's fancy is a peculiar thing. If it was deprived of the democratic right to change from one gum to another, it might go off gum altogether, and that would be fatal."

A butler came over at this point and told the Chief that a call had come through for him from his home, and would he take it out on the veranda. The Chief excused himself, walked across the lawn to a small wicker table, and picked up the phone.

"Yes, what is it?"

One of his house servants was on the other end of the line. "I'm sorry to report, sir, that Miss Locan has returned to the house. She is up in the master bedroom, and has asked me, a member of your staff, to join her in drinking a magnum of champagne. In fact, sir, she is as drunk as a lord."

Drewstone, fearing the untimely return of his wife, left immediately for his home. When he arrived he ran up the stairs and burst into the bedroom. He didn't see the girl at first, but heard a giggle from the other side of the bed. He went around and saw she had crumpled some pages of a script, tucked it under the quilt, and was building a campfire. She saw Drewstone and swayed as she tried to focus on him.

"Baby's just in time for a weenie roast," she said, holding out a box of matches. "Itsy me's dweadfully tired, lover will have to cook supper."

The Chief lifted her up and laid her out on the bed. He stroked her forehead and said, "Soon be fine for Daddy's tired tired baby. Close your eyes now."

He kissed her on the shoulders, moving down her body until he was kissing her stomach.

The girl giggled. "Daddy should get his head down a ickle lower, and put that kiss where it's supposed to go."

The Chief fumbled with her skirt . . . "No, no," she said, "dirlie will show daddy. Dirlie will give daddy yum-yums, 'cause daddy's most wunerfullest man in the world. Dirlie loves daddy."

She pulled the Chief down on the edge of the bed, then slid to the floor between his legs. She groped at his pants, pulled them down around his ankles, took them off over his shoes, and spread his legs.

He hears her spitting loudly into the palm of her hand, and then finds himself moistened, and being drawn up with a firm kneading grip, as if she were shaping clay on a potter's wheel, squeezing, and controlling the wobble as he strains up larger.

Collecting a little extra globule of saliva in the center of her tongue, she valleyed it into a U-shape and drew him through the center as though she were licking ice cream. Closing her lips around the head (looking up and gleaming a smile with her eyes), she held him between her teeth, spilling air out of the sides of her mouth. Miss Locan then rolled her tongue delicately up and down the shaft several times. Squeezing it hard around the middle she lifted his leg, pushed the knee against his chin, ran her lips along the ends of his anal hair, then probed him quickly with her tongue. After that treatment, she nipped his testicles like a cat about to lift kittens.

The girl stood up, smiled, then swooped down, and went back to sucking him, occasionally snorting as he touched the back of her throat. Hearing him moan, she put her hands on his knee and bounced her head up and down, working her mouth over him hard. As she did so, her hair ran truant: Curls, half-curls, and wisps of silk cascaded and rippled all over her skull. A few seconds later she stood up, and reeled a little as spermatozoa died a lingering death on her lisps and larynx.

"Didn't dirlie give daddy lovely yum-yums? Pleathe, pleathe let dirlie try for the part."

Olive sat in her bedroom sobbing helplessly, leaning forward, her face in her hands. Slowly the sobbing began to subside, then it stopped altogether, and she sat silently gazing out of the window. Her mother came into the room, walked quietly across, and put an arm around her daughter's shoulder.

"I'm sorry if I appear cold and heartless, but I had to make you see what kind of person he was. I knew that if I confronted him in that way, he wouldn't have time to think up a lie."

"You were so cruel to me," said Olive, "so very cruel. Why did you have to show me up like that?"

"My child, I was only being cruel to be kind. In speaking like that, I felt a deep concern for your welfare."

131

"But I feel so alone."

"You have me. What would he have given you? Can't you see how he would have used you, without ever giving true love? The man only wanted to latch onto your soaring star; he couldn't possibly have any interest in you as a woman." Mrs. West sat down beside her daughter. "Darling, you must face up to your destiny as a great actress, and sometimes part of the destiny of greatness is to be alone. If the burden ever seems too heavy, I hope I shall always be here for you to lean on."

Mrs. West watched her daughter nervously, but Olive merely bit her lip and continued to stare out of the window. She sat in silence, feeling a deep emotion over which she had no control or understanding.

Tucked away in the corner of a Drewstone props department, a bar had been set up. A dozen or so bottles of liquor and some cases of beer had been brought in, and Inshroin and the film crew were starting to wind down after the day's shooting.

"Have you got something to soothe an attack of double dyspepsia?" asked Inshroin.

"Double?"

"I'm a big star. I've had double pneumonia, a double hernia, and double vision. Do you think a man in my position could have single dyspepsia?"

"I've got just the thing," said the man. He dropped some chipped ice into a glass, whirled it around in the cocktail shaker, then poured the contents into a glass and gave the murky green liquid to the actor.

"Try that: You'll feel like a million dollars." Inshroin drank the absinthe.

"Not bad, now I'll have a cocktail."

"Martini?"

"Too dry."

"Manhattan?"

"Too strong."

"A Sidecar?"

"Too rapid. No I'll have a good old contradiction."

"That's a new one on me."

"Never heard of a good old American contradiction? Whisky to make it strong, water to make it weak, sugar to make it sweet, lemon to make it sour. It's called Hot Stuff, but you put ice in it."

"A Whisky Sour is what you mean."

"I suppose it is . . . Don't worry about a cocktail, just make it whisky. All drink would be Scotch if it could."

A writer sitting next to Inshroin drained a glass of beer at one gulp.

"Are you voting?" he asked the actor.

"I usually don't bother," said Inshroin. "I just read the densely packed pages of the *Times* and feel I've done something for my country. This time I'm going to put my X on Roosevelt."

A hot argument sprang up between three of the drinkers, as to the possibility of balancing the human body in the same way Eros balances on the fountain at Piccadilly Circus—on one foot with the body thrown forward. One of the men was trying to prove it possible by standing atop a bottle of beer on one foot.

"Yes," repeated Inshroin, looking toward the performance. "I'm putting my X on Roosevelt."

"I feel an outbreak of oratory coming on," said the writer.

"Good, that means a thirst," replied Inshroin. "Barkeep! More beers, and I'll have a treble Scotch to accentuate the positive."

"Yeh," said the man, taking a sip of his fresh beer, "Roosevelt is easygoing outwardly, every aspect of his personality spells confidence, but does that confidence run all through him? As sound as he seems in the upper part of his body, he can't stand up, so I wonder if he'll be able to stand up to all the political chicanery in Washington.

"He's a magnificent actor, but does he know deep down he's acting when he makes all his promises? I think his mind tends to skirt the fundamentals; my guess is that he shrugs them off. He's no radical or revolutionary, whatever the Hearst press says; he prefers to patch rather than to replace. He's a juggler of imperfections, but he makes promises on such an epic scale, the voters think something is really going to happen. He's always talking about the rise of the common man, but I bet that won't go very far. I bet he'd like to see the common man under an uncommon man like him."

"I'm going to take that chance," said Inshroin. "The country needs something new. Roosevelt says prosperity is just around the corner, and he's around that corner after it. He wants to put the cards of a new deal face-up on the table, and I think I'd like to see what kind of hand he comes up with."

The standing-on-bottles-to-emulate-Eros-at-Piccadilly infection was spreading. Lots of drinkers were doing it, calling to everybody to look, and just as they did so, down toppled the person doing the demonstration. "I'm voting for Hoover," said the writer, raising his voice above the noise around him. "I've always felt more secure with a Republican in power, no matter how bad his reputation."

"Hoover!" shouted Inshroin. "He has some knowledge about a lot of things. As far as I'm concerned, if he knew something about politics, he'd know a little bit about everything. And why do you want security? We produce monster flicks for a purpose, you know? It's to show the public that amidst all the fun of life, a menacing howl can rip the air, causing everybody to pause in their search for happiness, and be reminded of the sordidness and uncertainty of existence."

The balancing act had become an epidemic, and somebody challenged Inshroin to do it while drinking a bottle of rum.

"Give me that pirate's elixir," said Inshroin. "It may kill me, but everybody in America has the right and privilege to be his own executioner!"

He held the liquor up in the air, balanced on a bottle, and called for silence: "Gentlemen!

> "Oh you demon rum, you foul destroyer
> You curse of society, and its annoyer,
> What have you done, let me think?
> You've caused most harm, you nasty drink."

After he had concluded the toast, the actor drank the rum in twenty or so determined gulps. He tossed the empty bottle over into a corner, and stepped down unsteadily to tremendous applause. He smiled a ghastly smile as the drink claimed him—then asserted itself. Inshroin threw up his hands and started to slip toward the floor. As he did so, he accidentally knocked over a plate of oysters somebody had put on a beer case, and a dozen were redistributed. One lay on his shirt front, another took refuge in his left eye, the remainder rested in his hair. Inshroin rolled over, lay face down, burped, and brought up some of the demon rum. He found it impossible to rise but managed to lift his head, and with a cunning smile said, "This must be a very disreputable place."

Then he dropped his face into the vomit, and the subsequent proceedings interested him no more. A man stopped on his way out, patted the actor on the head, and said a kind word, seeing his forlorn condition.

IT WAS NOW EARLY EVENING. Inshroin regained consciousness and found himself lying on a pile of buccaneer costumes. A hat with a skull and crossbones painted on the front was resting across his forehead. He took it off and sat up. A stagehand who was clearing up the mess smiled down at him. "We tried to make you as comfortable as we could; you've been unconscious for three hours."

The actor got unsteadily to his feet. "Have I? Well, I needed the rest."

He blinked and ran his fingers through his hair. "I'd better get back to the tower, and clean up."

It was cold outside, and as Inshroin stood in the doorway of the building, a strong wind came in from the coast, blustered into studio fronts and whimpered in alleys. By the time it had reorganized itself and reached the Drewstone lot, nothing seemed to be able to stand in its way, and there was nobody around who cared whether anything could or not . . . or so it seemed. Inshroin felt a quick light tap on his shoulder and looked around. A one-legged man in a Long John Silver outfit emerged from the shadows, touched his hat, and bent forward, leaning on a crutch.

"Axin' yer pardon, Mr. Inshroin," he said in a hoarse whisper, "might you be a gen'leman wot also enj'ys 'is grub, an' a bit o' terbacker? Leastways, if I'm wrong, I 'ope as 'ow you won't say nothin' to get a poor man into trouble."

A parrot with some previous experience of his conversational manner shifted apprehensively on his shoulder. Inshroin pressed a few healing coins into the hero's hand. Long John coughed loudly.

"Nasty cough," said Inshroin, stepping back into the doorway to avoid the wind. The other man hopped after him.

"Cough! I've got a cavity in the apex of my right lung the size of a hen's egg, but, thank God," he said raising his voice, "the left lung is as good as ever!"

"You should see a doctor," said Inshroin.

"Is Hippocrates available?"

"He died a couple of thousand years ago."

"Then I must decline. A modern doctor will increase my symptoms, add to the pain, and get me ready for an expensive scalpel. The entire medical profession is a vast empire with a never ending desire to revenge itself on health for existing at all."

"That's true," said Inshroin. "I once had dinner with my lawyer and my doctor. They spent the whole evening winking at each other."

The parrot took to biting the pirate's ear, and Long John gave back a blow so original, it deserved a patent. The bird retaliated with a flurry of woodpecker drillings, and arms and wings went into a violent blur, accompanied by squawks and screams. Finally the two of them settled down again.

"I get so hungry sometimes, I swear I'll eat the damn thing. In Hollywood, if you're lucky enough, you'll make more money than the President. If not, nobody will interfere with your starving to death."

"So you haven't been working lately."

"I arrived from Britain three years ago. My first and longest engagement was sweeping the floors at the Trent Studios until they closed down. For the last two years, my salary has been around five hundred dollars per annum. In future it'll be a little more precarious, as the man I borrow the money from has just died. These days I do my best acting glancing meaningfully at people who might give me some dough."

From the first the two men liked each other. It had been a click of billiards balls, the impact of solids.

"Do you know," said Inshroin, "the idea of getting out of Drewstone City for a few hours seems as exhilarating to me as a prison break. Do you want to go downtown and have a meal?"

"You won't take back any of the money you've given me?"

"No."

"Suppose I had a wife?"

136

"Get a wife-sitter; it'll be difficult for me as well. I don't go out much these days. It's a real problem when I'm followed everywhere by ten million fans."

"As it so happens," said Long John, "I don't have a wife, and I'd be delighted to accept your offer. Where do you want to eat?"

"Somewhere quiet, away from the public thoroughfare, so if there's a riot, traffic won't get held up."

"The Royal Lodge?"

"Sounds good, not many of the big stars go there, so no one will bother us. I want to go back to my place and have a bath and change. I'll reserve a table, and meet you there at ten? By the way," Inshroin said, "it's not usual to make a reservation under the name of Long John Silver."

"No," said the pirate. "Andrew Aitlee, at your service."

At a quarter to ten Inshroin was driven in a Drewstone car into downtown Hollywood. He got out a block from the Royal Lodge and told the driver to park as close as he could to the restaurant. He then walked the final hundred yards, so as not to attract attention when he arrived. He passed an apartment building whose front door was surrounded by a circle of palm trees. Under the watchful eye of a doorman, a boy and a girl in a man's pajama top were fighting each other in their eagerness to pick up what appeared to be pearls strewn all over the sidewalk. As they scrambled, argued, bit, and scratched, the sound of a wailing saxophone drifted down from an open window on the third floor.

As he got closer to the restaurant, Inshroin stopped and looked around. There seemed to be no fans waiting outside. Cars slid up to the front door, deposited their occupants, then slid away. A huge neon sign scribbled the name Royal Lodge, erased it, then scribbled again. Each time it happened, people and the street were turned into a Picasso painting.

Inshroin walked quickly to the door, which was held open for him by a man in a gold and blue uniform. Once inside, he peered through the candle-lit room looking for Andrew. The coat-check girl sat watching an army of moving jaws, then shifted on her stool and began ogling Inshroin as soon as she recognized him.

A steady trickle of Puccini came from a corner, where a

bushy-haired Russian swayed with his violin and helped increase the din made by fashionable and civilized people when they nourish their bodies.

The headwaiter came across. "Mr. Inshroin, it's an honor to have you with us here tonight. The other gentleman has arrived. If you follow me, I'll show you to your table." The actor fell in step behind, as the two of them wove their way across the floor to a darker corner, slightly away from the rest of the diners. Andrew, now in a dark suit, looked up from a menu.

"So you got here before me," said Inshroin, as he sat down. "I was wondering if you'd be in your Long John outfit. You look thinner."

"Thin! I'm nothing but skin and bone. If it wasn't for my Adam's apple, I'd have no shape at all." Andrew stood up. "Go ahead," he said, "look me over and catch your breath. I can hold on."

Inshroin looked him up and down. "I see what you mean. You remind me of a Southern slave driver who has gone to New York for a shave."

Andrew sat down. "Does that mean I look hungry?"

"It sure does. The sooner we get some food in you the better."

The host for the evening glanced at his menu. "Don't go away," he said to the waiter, "we'd like to order now."

"I don't usually take the orders, sir, but with you . . ."

He stood pen poised over his pad expectantly.

"Lots of good things listed for tonight," said Inshroin.

"We have the best of everything here, sir."

"Good, the best of everything is good enough for me. I'll start with the turtle soup, and then get straight into John the Baptist's head on a silver platter."

"How would you like it done, sir?"

"Heaving and bubbling from the heat of the oven and handsomely scored with the charred stripes from the grill."

"Vegetables, sir?"

"New boiled Murphies in their sweaters, and white buttered beans à la orchestra."

Andrew looked up from the menu he was going over, and said, "I wonder why he was called John the Baptist?"

The waiter gave him a withering look of contempt. "We all have a nickname of some kind, sir."

138

"I think I'll change my meat order," said Inshroin. "I'll have fresh lobster, something plain and simple."

"Very good sir," the waiter turned to Andrew; "and you, sir, are you ready to order?"

"It's the same old problem," said Andrew, "there are so many good things to choose from, I can't decide. I'll have to resort to the usual solution."

He took a pen out of his pocket, and closing his eyes tight, whirled it over his head. After a few seconds he brought it down onto the menu. "Some ice cream to begin with."

A whirl of the pen and another plunge: "Followed by New Zealand lamb, and make sure it *is* lamb, I don't want any of your small sheep." A third whirl: "Then some oysters. I hate oysters, but they've been chosen for me. That should be enough to go on with."

The waiter picked up the menu and went off toward the kitchen.

"I've usually been lucky with the hazard of a whirling pen," said Andrew. "I went to Texas for a holiday by doing it over a map. I ended up being very grateful, I would never have realized what a godforsaken spot Texas is."

The waiter appeared with the oysters, and they were the biggest that Andrew had ever seen. He chewed one slowly.

"Good?" asked Inshroin.

"I feel like I've swallowed a newborn baby."

A magnificent specimen of lobster arrived and was placed before the host in a pile of potatoes. Inshroin sat back and looked at the plate.

"Anything wrong, sir?"

"No, I'm just contemplating the utter destruction of this food. Here I sit with a lobster. All of us together, me and the food. When I've demolished this lot I'll need gallons of cold water to wash out all the corners in preparation for fresh chunks of lobster. What an enchanting idea. If someone put it to music it would captivate the whole world. A symphony on food with a lobster solo!"

The meal proceeded.

"How long have you been resting?" Inshroin asked.

"Rest," said Andrew. "There's nothing more deadening for an actor. Change the vowel and you have rust. I've hardly had any work for two years. In fact I've had the longest relax in history, a siesta that's turned into a sabbatical. I had the possibility of one small job last month, then lost it to a man who couldn't act and was about as handsome as a Scotsman's tip. But I have my health, and I'm able to mix well with all the races in California. Would you believe I know five languages? A man as successful as you probably doesn't need one."

"Why did you learn so many?"

"I couldn't borrow any more money in my own. But I persevere because as long as I can believe I'll be acting one day, I can put up with a lack of cash for the moment. Anyway, I don't care too much for money."

"You don't believe in money?" asked Inshroin. "The world wouldn't get on without it."

"I don't agree," said Andrew. "The only capital in the world is the energy and intelligence of people. Money is just purchasing power and bookkeeping entries. Capitalism only survives by a succession of disguised bankruptcies called devaluation, or ceaseless expansion that leads to war and disintegration."

"Then why the hell am I always being told money is the great power in the world?"

"How should I know," shrugged Andrew. "Anyway, the people who tell you that are wrong. Words are the real power in the world, you're an actor, you should know that. With a few well-chosen words, a handful of fanatic nomads brought down the Roman Empire, and the Russians did the same under Lenin."

"Do you approve of communism?" asked Inshroin. Andrew put down his knife and fork, folded his arms across his chest, and leaned back in his chair.

"I couldn't be a communist," he said. "I lack the religious temperament. Besides, Marx is just a German-Jewish fanatic with the temperament of a nonconformist missionary. I respect Western civilization, so how can I embrace a cockeyed creed based on envy and destruction—a plan to destroy the elite of the world in the alleged interests of a submerged proletariat. There was a similar revolution in Sixth Dynasty Egypt, and the pyramid texts show the comrades pinched everything they could lay their hands on. Men will always be self-seeking and treacherous, whatever political or economic system they choose."

140

"I agree," said Inshroin, "but communists are the people who would take away my money."

"Why not? I bet you've got too much. If communists don't, capitalists will lose it for you by devaluation or war."

Inshroin smiled. "From the way you're eating, I see you enjoy the good life, and one needs money for that."

"I know, but I'm not greedy. I like money, it's a guarantee of safety and respectability. With a modest amount I'd be able to freeze all the enemies of my life at one swoop."

Inshroin took a bite of lobster, and stared at Andrew. "I think you're probably right. I suspect that money and capital are only a tiny episode in the human flux. Where did you learn so much about politics anyway?"

Andrew shrugged. "My father was in the game. I had to convince him and myself that I could be an actor. You've got no idea how difficult that can be with a family that has been involved with politics since the Mayflower."

The headwaiter came back to the table. "How are you gentlemen enjoying the food?"

"It's very good," said Inshroin.

"I know it's good sir, we wouldn't serve it here if it wasn't good. How did you find the lobster?"

"I found the lobster by moving a pea."

"These are trying times, Mr. Inshroin. Everything is smaller than it used to be in the old days."

"I notice your prices aren't."

> "We came for a change and a rest.
> The waiters took the change
> And the owner took the rest."

There was a scream from the door of the restaurant, and before either of the men had time to look around, a blur of girl was on Inshroin. She made a dive at him, and for a second he thought he was being attacked by a wild lion. She secured a stranglehold grip and screamed, "Darling!" Inshroin tried desperately to claw her off and put a hand firmly into the center of a plate of food. Finally the girl quieted down and got off Inshroin, leaving his face covered in lipstick. She pulled up a chair and threw herself down between the two actors.

"Phillip Inshroin, is it really you! *Really* you I mean, not someone pretending to be you? I'm just the happiest girl in America! In the whole world! And it's meeting you that makes me so. I saw your movie *The Love of a Huge Heart* ten times. I've been doing some courses in time-thinking, and now I'm trying to think in time as well as in space. I'm getting on pretty well at it, but I'm not perfect yet, and oh my, it's making a new girl of me. I'm so fulfilled, Phillip, I can create happiness everywhere I go, and gosh I love happiness, and I'm happiest when everybody around me is happy and fulfilling themselves. I've got these amazing selves that make up my new personality: gentle, dreamy, loving, thinking selves—gosh, I've got them *all*! I've got them because of time-thinking, and you will call me Susie, won't you? To think I should be talking to you now, I'm just thrilled, it's simply fine. I'm from Texas, it's the bulliest state in the union. The climate puts kicks in you all day and every day!"

Suddenly she stopped talking, raised her foot, rested it on the right knee, and inspected her sole as if she had stepped in something nasty. Then she put her foot down, and resumed her monologue.

"When I was a kid all the boys wanted me and I mean *all* of them. Then I found out they only wanted me for my shape, not myself or my kind, and *boy* was I depressed when I discovered that, not that I mind being attractive, we've all got to be attractive, Phillip. After that I started dance classes and searching for a cancer cure, because every American girl has to make one *big* discovery and have an achievement that is all her own that nobody else can take. Then I met this boy I loved, and it started all over again when I found out he didn't want me for my mind. I tried all the time to get him to talk about my search for the *big* cancer cure, but he wouldn't listen, he only wanted to kiss and paw me. Then I got angry and lost my time-thinking self-esteem because he wanted me to marry him and become his little woman. But I knew I could never be held by any man because of a *real* inner refusal my whole being had developed in its self-discovery. I *knew* my time-controlled inner happiness must never be restricted. I'll never be anybody's little woman, Phillip, because I love politics, medicine, interior design, and all my other work. So I left that boy, and after a year of *really* hard work I mastered all my problems and finished up optimistic and enthusiastic, everything time-controlled, and

142

gosh Phillip that was a real ordeal even though I still have a beautiful body.

"I'm really happy now, I've never been happier. I'm still dancing though I've given up searching for the *big* cancer cure, a girl can't do everything. I work in this lovely apartment a super boy gave me, and if you saw it, Phillip, you'd adore it!! Oh I'd love to be down here in Hollywood all the time, but I'm only visiting. I'd love to be trained for the talkies, but I'm not going to be. When I was at college I got a prize for an oration on the Constitution. Tell me what you think of my pronunciation? How do I compare with the way English girls speak—I mean, the educated ones? Why only six months ago this man from Hollywood offered me a job. He was the third in six months. I said, 'Yes, if I can choose the parts.' I'm not going to act in *those* scenes with the men! You know the scenes I mean, the ones they have to drop the curtain on. I'm really a kind of pioneer, experimenting every minute of the day. I'd have loved to come out with the pioneers like my grandmother. You'd love my grandmother and mom and dad, too. They're just lovely, yes, sir! And I'm a hunter, too. Yes, sir, I can *hunt*. But my axe and rifle are my soul- and time-controlled inner consciousness, that's why I've got standards and ideals. And, boy, didn't I let that man from Hollywood know it!!!"

Inshroin looked thoughtful. He leaned some toothpicks up against the side of his water glass—they were cruel staves with points as sharp as needles.

"Don't ever catch laryngitis," he said.

"Oh, why, Phillip?"

"Because your lovely voice would be reduced to a bellow."

"Gee, wait till I tell the girls how you're interested in my health. But don't worry, I've never had a day's illness in my life. I'll always go on seeing your movies. Will you just hang on a second, Phillip, I've got some friends outside, and I'd love you to meet them. Gee, they'll be so happy!"

When she got up and rushed back onto the street, Inshroin and Andrew beat a retreat to the back of the restaurant. The headwaiter came across with the bill. "I'm sorry about that, Mr. Inshroin; the doorman didn't see her come in, and I didn't want to create a scene by having her removed."

"We understand," said Inshroin. "I've got my car parked

143

out front, could you send someone to tell the driver to collect us at the back?"

The headwaiter nodded, clicked his fingers to call another employee over, and passed on the instructions.

While they waited, a man at a table close by was talking about the courses as if they were revolvers. "The soup repeated, the steak repeated, the cheese and biscuits repeated." He pulled out of his pocket a beautiful heliotrope pill and swallowed it. "This should help," he said, "until the depression's over, and we can get some better food."

Judging that the car should have arrived, Inshroin paid the bill, pressed a note into the headwaiter's hand, and left with Andrew by the back door. The man unfolded the paper and read:

A LIST OF GRIEVANCES FOR THE OWNER'S CONSIDERATION.
Cold soup.
Fish not done.
Vegetables old and cold.
Lobster tough rancid and high.
Floor covered with cigar ends, bread and butter.
Dirty dishes piled everywhere.
Small spoons instead of large ones for gravy.
Someone to the rescue. AMEN.

When they got to the car at the back of the restaurant, the waiter who had gone to fetch it held the door open for the two men. He saluted when Inshroin gave him a tip, and made a great show of helping them to get confortable in the back. He then closed the door, saluted again, and stood rigidly at attention until the vehicle had moved off out of sight.

On the drive back to the tower, they passed houses and eating places of every possible shape and variety, each positioned at the center of a lawn or parking lot. There were fairy-tale castles, tumble-down horror houses, vast flop-eared puppies, ice cream cones sixty feet high, and huge fish. Above it all, the sky was clear and cloudless, with moonlight blowing across in vast waves. Young people were everywhere, all of them dressed in silk pajama suits that were every color of the rainbow.

When the car finally arrived at the Drewstone gates, they

stopped to let a beautiful girl cross the road in front of them. She was dressed in a blue pajama suit and carried a brass parrot cage stuffed full of narrow lemon-colored shoes.

"I like the message," said Inshroin.

"What message?" asked Andrew.

Inshroin pointed out of the window at the wall. Scrawled across the bricks in white paint were the words ART FOR GOD'S SAKE!

"The guy who wrote that was illiterate," said the driver. "The expression is, 'Art for Art's Sake.'"

"Yeh," said Inshroin.

As soon as the girl had passed, a night watchman opened the gates, and waved the car in.

Once they got past the studios, they began to climb a winding road that soon became so steep it was like driving up a map nailed to the wall. Their route was bordered on one side by the ocean and on the other by a vista of sand dunes filled with clumps of poppies. The ocean was calm. Water didn't even run up the beach, but kept at a distance, forming cutting little waves that fluttered permanent white handkerchiefs. A few white gulls bobbed on the surface, occasionally disappearing into a hollow.

"Great view," said the driver turning his head, "clear as day, miles and miles of open ocean."

Inshroin grunted. "I've never seen anything less open. The sea is forever slamming down trapdoors of surf and covering the treasures of the deep. Isn't that right, Long John?"

Andrew nodded. "True enough, Jim lad."

The driver raised his eyebrows and glanced at the two men in his mirror.

When the car pulled up outside Inshroin's house, the actor didn't wait for the door to be opened.

Inshroin led the way up to the tower, which at close quarters seemed to hang over the surrounding area like a huge ancestral eyebrow. As they passed between rows of aviaries, Andrew paused to look into one.

"I've kept mainly pigeons up to now," Inshroin said, "but I'm starting to keep some more exotic varieties. Those you're looking at are beautiful singers, but they only seem to perform first thing in the morning."

"A few have legs missing," said Andrew.

"They fight a lot, but it doesn't matter. They're singers, not dancers."

"Is the collection big?"

Inshroin nodded. "You can't see much at this time of night, but I've got hundreds of specially built boxes all over the place. I had them made for the local birds who find the few trees around here overcrowded, and want a place to live."

At the foot of the tower was the entrance, lit by a single spotlight hanging from the wall. The door itself was made from polished mahogany and seemed strangely contemporary and out of place among the aged stone that surrounded it.

"The tower seems old, but the door looks very modern," said Andrew.

"It is. I hooked it one day when I was out fishing. It comes from an expensive yacht that sank off the coast last year."

"Keep it!" said Andrew. "If I catch the yacht next time I go fishing, I'll make my own door."

Inside, it was pitch dark, and there was a deep musty smell in the air. The owner felt along the wall and flicked a switch that turned a light on in a small elevator. The two men got in, and when Inshroin pushed a button they started to rise quickly and silently. After a few seconds, it stopped without a jolt, and Andrew looked out onto a square, discreetly lit room. The damp musty smell was strongest here. With the exception of a desk and three leather chairs, the place was stuffed with books—thousands of them. They were on shelves that lined the walls, and piled in great heaps on the floor. Any space left over was filled with tennis rackets. All were broken, the strings hanging down from the frames like long strands of spaghetti. Inshroin picked a couple up off a chair so his guest could sit down.

"I play a lot of tennis," he said, "but as I always miss the balls, I make sure I give the net posts a damn good thrashing."

As Andrew sat down in the cleared chair, he suddenly became aware of a pair of eyes gleaming out at him from a dark corner of the bookshelf.

"Have you got a cat?" he asked.

"A monkey. It's called Lester Harding. Lester!"

There was a rustling sound, and a small furry bundle jumped from the shelf, landed on Inshroin's shoulder, and carefully wrapped its tail around his neck.

146

The actor bent down and picked up an uncooked egg from behind a pile of books. When it was offered to him, the monkey took it and bit off the top of the shell, put the little cup to his lips, and drank the contents. Lester then unwrapped his tail, jumped down onto the floor, and disappeared behind a pile of books. For the next twenty minutes, a brown wrinkled face could be seen peering around corners and from behind books, the eyes never still.

Inshroin went over to the desk, opened one of the drawers, and took out a bottle of Scotch and two glasses.

"The real thing," he said. "I get it from over the border." He poured two huge drinks, gave one to Andrew, and drained his at a gulp. He then went back to the desk and refilled his glass.

"Jesus!" said Andrew, "not so fast, you'll burst your liver."

"That dinner was too solid and heavy for me," said Inshroin. "It's made me feel dull, overloaded, and way above the Plimsoll line. This booze will swell the stomach, lighten the load, and put me back on an even keel."

"Is this place still on Drewstone property?" asked Andrew.

"Yeh, but the area covered by the tower is mine. I bought it."

"What's Drewstone like?"

Inshroin took another mouthful of Scotch, and sat down at the desk.

"His astrological charts apparently show he possesses the virtues of a gangster, combined with the domestic constancy of a dove. He is in fact half-hooligan, and half-messiah. The men who work for him on a big salary say he's a genius, those who don't call him a fool. Women under contract making a fortune call him a swine, women who hope for both call him the Almighty.

"I've witnessed that both sexes will climb into his toilet and pull the chain on themselves for an appearance in one of his films and their names stenciled on the back of a canvas chair.

"He has a motto sewn into all his clothes—*Rather a coward for ten minutes than dead for the rest of your life*—and he once thought of joining the Spanish Foreign Legion because of its motto, *Death to intelligence, long live death.*"

Andrew gave a laugh that filled the whole tower. If a drum could laugh, it would have made that sound.

"Drewstone may be all of those things," he said, "but the man's made you famous."

"He's made fame a monster to me. I don't remember when things started to go sour. When I first came to Hollywood I was young and inexperienced, so I copied the styles and habits of those who were already famous. One day I discovered I was completely like them, and I began to hate them like they hated each other. All the bad feeling is caused by the vicious competition for the big roles. In the end I became hateful of myself.

"If Hollywood is America, then the rest of the country that I know is definitely not America. After appearing in about twenty movies, I feel like I'm walking close to nothing. I feel that if I were given a slight nudge, I'd fall into a void, leaving nothing but a surrounding tumult and America's problems to testify I once existed. When I get into that kind of mood, I drink to avoid self-contempt. Sometimes days follow days and each one is a pisser, so I have a lot of nips to burn off the scum of the bad feelings."

"How much do you drink?"

"Hard to tell, and it also depends on how much I can get in from Canada. Sometimes I have a bottle for breakfast, sometimes two, then on other mornings I drink a lot."

"How much did you drink this morning?"

"Double the usual quantity."

"If you're so frustrated," said Andrew, "why don't you go back on the stage? I read somewhere you worked on Broadway for six years."

"Terrified of how I'd be in front of a live audience after all this time. If you were ever on the stage, go back before it's too late. Once you get dragged in here, however talented you may be, you either become artistically flabby, or wildly resentful." He took another swallow of Scotch. "If things are bad with me and I'm a success, how do you manage?"

"I did a lot of my early training on the English stage, and I picked up the British attitude. People over there aren't pelted with success stories as a way of life. They can make terms with life on whatever scale it happens to present itself. That's how I cope with my frustrations. But I shouldn't worry about the stage: It's like riding a bike; once you've done it, you never forget. That's what a man called Sid Namen once told me when

I was working with him in pantomime years ago in London. Great act Sid had."

Andrew got up, knelt on the floor, put one hand on his chest, and threw the other one out wide.

> "Don't 'ang my 'Arry, for e's my only son.
> Don't 'ang my 'Arry, for a murder wot 'e never done.
> Don't 'ang my 'Arry, we could never bear to part,
> W'en you're snappin' the poor bleeder's neck
> You're breakin' an old muvver's 'eart."

"One of the old actors in my latest film performed in a great vaudeville show once, called *Do You Love a Gentile?*" said Inshroin. It was now his turn to throw his arms wide.

Do You Love a Gentile?, an episode of eighteen minutes, the hit of New York. So far the production has been very popular, there is such a long lineup, the manager wishes his hall were elastic. This is *not* a gentile of fiction, but a living, breathing gentile, as he lives and works! Incorporated with high seriousness will be the latest in fun and frolics! THE NEWER NONSENSE. THE LARGER LUNACY. THE GREATER GOOFINESS. THE ULTIMATE A LA LUNE. THE COMPLETELY DIPPY IN THE DREAMBOX! In the story, a Jewish gent makes the money, a gentile gent takes as much from him as he can, then they both get outvoted by the Methodists.

> "For the world is his birthright
> The world is his throne
> The glory of ages
> Is ever his own.
> So God save the Hebrew
> His glory enhance
> But God think of us too—
> Give Gentiles a chance."

Inshroin lurched back against the wall. As he did so, Andrew finished his drink and stood up. "I'm going to have to leave. I've got a screen test early tomorrow for a part as a butler. I'll walk down to Drewstone's and get a cab from the gate." He looked around, "Can I take a souvenir?"

"What would you like? I've got some monogrammed handkerchiefs."

"I'll take one, it'll look nice in the top pocket." Inshroin was shocked. "One! I'll give you a hundred to start you off on the right track. All of a star's possessions belong to the public because of the money they pay at the box office. Our business is *always* to get from the public as much as we can."

He pulled some paper and a pen from the top of the desk. "Give me your phone number, and if anything comes up, I'll call you."

"Do you think there's a chance?" Andrew asked.

"Maybe. If you looked at my mother in the same pleading was you're looking at me, you'd be able to do anything you wanted with her."

Andrew said nothing, but sank to his knees and reverently kissed the bottom of the star's jacket.

At the door Inshroin asked, "What do you think of the place?"

Andrew winked. "It looks as if it's been cut out of history with the single stroke of a sword blade. I call it Oklahoma Byzantine."

"Do you like Oklahoma Byzantine?"

"Not much."

When he'd got a way down the road, Andrew looked back. Under a vast lasso of stars, Inshroin was standing on a rock beside the tower. He was sipping a drink with one hand, and fluttering a white handkerchief in the air with the other. Andrew waved back.

At the Drewstone gate Andrew found the driver and car that had brought them back from the restaurant.

"Was Mr. Inshroin drunk when you left?" asked the chauffeur.

"He'd had a lot."

"It'll get him into big trouble soon. Some mornings when I collect him, he's coughing up blood. If he goes on like that much longer, the next thing we'll be pouring is him—into an urn."

If the Prince of Wales's visit to America in 1919 caused a sensation, Winston Churchill's lecture tour caused a lesser reaction. Churchill was in the political doldrums in 1933 and was visiting the United States to give some lectures, and to visit

Hollywood, to see if he could sell one of his novels to a movie company.

One Sunday afternoon when he was in New York, he decided to visit a friend, Bernard Baruch, who lived on Fifth Avenue. He wasn't quite sure of the street number but thought he would recognize the house, so he took a cab.

When he arrived in the vicinity, he decided to get out on the west side of the avenue by Central Park. He started to cross, and in the British tradition looked in the wrong direction. The car tricked him, and before Churchill knew what was happening, a group of pedestrians were trying to remove him from its bumper.

He lay in the road, blood trickling from his mouth. A woman, thinking blood looked more in place on something white and hygienic, dabbed the trickle with a white handkerchief.

A policeman leaned over the body with a notebook in his hand. "What's your name?"

"Winston Churchill."

"How old are you?"

"Fifty-nine—what happened to me?"

"You got hit by a car, but don't worry, we've got the vehicle and the driver."

Churchill was lifted into a taxi, and his hands, white and covered with blood, were placed across his chest. He tried to move his hands and his toes, but nothing happened. The thought "crippled for life" passed through his mind. As the cab moved through the streets, to Churchill's great relief, he began to experience violent pins and needles in his upper arms; his fingers began to move, with accompanying spasms up and down his body.

In the hospital, his wife and Bernard Baruch visited. When the politician saw his friend, he smiled and said, "What's the number of your house?"

"Ten fifty-five."

"How near was I to it when I was smashed up?"

"About ten blocks."

Churchill wrote a feature on the accident for the *North American Newspaper Alliance*. He concluded the piece: "Such in short were my experiences. I certainly suffered every pang, mental and physical, that a street accident can produce. None is

151

unendurable. There is neither time nor fear. For the rest, live dangerously. Take things as they come! Dread naught! All will be well!''

While he was recuperating, Churchill went to Hollywood. At nine o'clock one midweek evening, the politician was on the miniature section of a large golf course in Hollywood.

It was an absolutely still night, the clear sky containing nothing but stars and a few clenched clouds—all of them motionless for the moment, as if they had nothing to do. Behind the group of players Churchill was with (including Inshroin) was a long line of men firing off retrievable fluorescent balls down the fairway. The politician watched them, and leaned against a tiny windmill. A Coda Brothers executive also leaned against the windmill in the same pose as Churchill. The film man's wife, wearing a low-cut frock, stood at his side. Huge silver chains hung around her neck, while the wrist jewelry was big enough to be a national monument. A few feet away stood a bridge, and a six-foot plaster-of-paris tree bending slightly away in the direction of her stare.

Churchill lit a "half-hour-in-Havana" cigar, held it out in front of him, and seemed intent on making sure nothing happened to the ash. He smoked one end of the cigar and chewed the other. When he took it out of his mouth, it was covered in teeth marks. His breast pocket contained six fresh ones in a row. Side by side, they looked like Cossack cartridges.

Churchill's figure was rotund and dumpy: slight arms and legs, narrow in the shoulders, mostly stomach, chest, and head; pink and white cheeks, light blue eyes, and no neck. He moved as though he didn't have any joints, all of a piece, slowly, unhurriedly.

A man with a slight Scots accent had started talking to the Coda man, and from the way his conversation went it seemed he was a doctor. "The nation is still full of shell-shocked and self-shocked men," he was saying. "It's worse in Europe, Mr. Churchill can confirm that. I did the best I could at the veteran's hospital when I worked there, but however much I tried to patch up those mutilated bodies, I knew a time would come when they'd ask for a mirror. That was the worst part of the job. I used to catch them looking at the back of a spoon before they took that final big step."

"Fascinating," said the Coda man's wife. "Speaking of operations, last week I was taken in the middle of the night with a pain in my stomach, a violent stabbing pain which—"

"Listen, woman," the doctor caught her arm and spoke gently and patiently, "I've had a hard day, and I'm not interested in hearing how you had your womb stitched up."

The executive's wife sucked air in through her teeth and seemed to shudder like a horse flicking away flies. As she breathed in, two crescents of moon pushed into sight above the horizon of her frock—a slipped crucifix wedged between them. Churchill gazed at the orbs and thought of billiard balls.

"I expect a little more respect and interest," said the woman, "when my husband is paying you so much money for his operation."

The doctor shrugged. "If he was poor, I'd only charge him the occasional kind thought."

Churchill brought the conversation back to the game. "The Scots were the first to decide that golf could be played on Sunday," he said, "because golf is less of a sport than a test of fortitude. They reasoned that it was the secular equivalent to Knoxian theology, a stern communion with solitude. I've played in Scotland with original hand-hammered gutta-percha balls, which often broke when you hit them. The rule was, you put a new ball on the place where the largest fragment fell."

He tapped a ball along a little gully as Inshroin joined him.

"It's a pleasure to meet you," said the actor. "I've been reading your pieces on Hitler and the new Germany."

"I hope you found them int-e-e-r-esting?" There was a slight stutter. The eyes of the two men hardly met, and it wasn't Inshroin's fault.

"Very."

The politician seemed on the verge of saying something, then stopped.

"I'm not sure if Germany and Hitler are intent on war though," said Inshroin.

"What do you mean?"

"I mean it may just be a figment of the British imagination. A lot of people I know think it's just you and the press stirring up trouble. Take the Irish Catholics. They hate the British for what seems a good reason to them. Take our German element, which is also large; they hate the Anglo-Saxons because of an old rivalry for empire. Why, most of this country grows up anti-British; we don't like your imperialism, and nobody can make us; we're the friends of the underdog."

"Rubbish," snapped Churchill. "You're a rich and successful film star, you know nothing of the underdog. Besides, we have to forget about the underdog for a while. With the pressures of Nazism and communism building up, we are fast approaching an either-or situation in the world." He drew on his cigar. "And as much as you dislike the idea, with all its faults and flaws, the British Empire, including your neighbor Canada, is the best stabilizer in the world today."

"Maybe," said Inshroin, "but you won't find many people in America who believe in this either-or business. We Americans are a strong middle-of-the-road people, and it won't work to wave the flags of Joe Stalin Terror and Hitler Menace at us."

Churchill again drew on his cigar. "Then later on in this century, America will end by falling between two stools," he said.

The woman who had talked with the doctor passed by, tapping her ball along the grass border. Inshroin smiled at her and leaned on his club.

"How's that charity work you're doing down at the YWCA getting on?" he asked.

"Depressing is the word I'd use," she replied. "I'm working with a lot of girls who are having nervous breakdowns while they wait for a starring role. I find it impossible to get them to externalize themselves, project their imaginations, to come to grips with individual problems. The only method I know to get them to achieve objectivity is to appeal to what they know best—the movies. I tell them to close their eyes and look at their domestic problems as if they were looking at a movie called *What's the Matter with Susie and Her Folks?* It's a trick that tickles their fancy and gets them to objectify without noticing it."

She made a drive with her club, and her neck chains and wrist jewelry swung to and fro in wide arcs. "Apart from that, the only thing they take an interest in is the names of stars and the names of their nearest relatives or friends. If anything happens to them, they want to be buried right."

Inshroin looked around to see what had happened to Churchill. He was standing by the gate, backed against the fence. His chubby face looked hard and rigid, the right arm hung straight down by his side. He was encased in a great cloud of smoke. Behind him the fluorescent golf balls curved in the air like tracer bullets.

On December 1, 1933, Hitler declared state and party one unit: *Partei und Staat sind eins.* Four days later, the streets of the United States were suddenly lit with signs that read IT'S HERE AGAIN! Within hours, speakeasies vanished, and magnificently dressed doormen appeared outside night clubs to take the place of disembodied eyes peering through chinks in a door.

The methods used in defeating Upton Sinclair for the Governorship of California were perhaps unprecedented in terms of sheer wickedness and villainy. Every crime known to man was shamelessly resorted to. Falsehood, forgery, libel, slander, and character assassination all played their part.

Unity, Chicago, June 26, 1934

IN 1934, CANDIDATES FOR THE GOVERNORSHIP OF CALIFORNIA were the Republican Frank Merriam and the Democrat Upton Sinclair. Suddenly, California, which hadn't had a Democrat governor for thirty-five years, might elect a socialist reformer who attacked big business, was dedicated to "production for use, not profit," and was the apostle of a program built around the slogan END POVERTY IN CALIFORNIA (EPIC).*

*Upton Sinclair's wife was named Craig, and she had a sister named Dolly. One day in 1931 Dolly came into the house, and said, "There's an old man walking up and down the street outside, and he keeps looking at the house." Dolly went back out to find out who it was, and returned with Albert Einstein. He had written to Sinclair:

EPIC was based on twelve principles described in Sinclair's pamphlet "*I, Governor of California, and How I Ended Poverty, A True Story of the Future.*"

Point one stated: "God created the natural wealth of the earth for the use of all men, not the few." And point twelve concluded: "This change can be brought about by the action of a majority of the people, and this is the American way."

Sinclair talked all over California. He told his audiences it was far more important for them to understand the causes of the depression than to elect him governor. His opponents didn't know how to handle him. He answered every question from the audiences that came to hear him and advised people to question the other candidates closely. Rival Republicans stopped denouncing one another and took to telling their audiences how absurd and un-American, anarchistic, and atheistic was the promise to end poverty in California.

On the day Sinclair won the Democratic nomination by the biggest vote in California history, the Chief's office was all activity. Auditioning hopefuls, managers, writers, stockbrokers, investors, and two dogs sat around a table, all making their points at once, the animals barking furiously. There was a lot of heel clicking as these rubber stamps busied themselves, everybody looking as confident as Soviet revolutionary wall posters.

———————

To the most beautiful joys of my life belongs your wicked tongue.
Who does the dirtiest pot not attack?
Who hits the world on the hollow tooth?
Who spurns the now, and swears by the morrow?
Who takes no care about being undignified?
Sinclair is the valiant man,
If anyone, then I can attest it.

In heartiness
Albert Einstein.

A swanky restaurant was engaged at the Town House in L.A., so Einstein could meet Upton's friends. The author was in the dining room when the scientist arrived. He did not take off his coat and hat in the foyer. He took them off upstairs, folded the coat carefully, and laid it on the floor in the corner. He then took off his hat, and laid it on top of the coat, he was ready to eat. When the meal was finished, Einstein said, "Now I would like to meet Charlie Chaplin."

Mr. Drewstone's new secretary Miss Paxton was young, very beautiful, and wore a beret. She frequently removed the little hat and allowed a golden avalanche to tumble down around her shoulders, then gave it a wish by shaking her head, and sent it flying away in all directions. Presently she engaged in the task of rebuilding her crown, but within a few seconds the beret was off again, and the hair was cascading down once more.

A middle-aged woman was standing to the left of the scene, waiting for her daughter, a nine-year-old with soft curly hair, to be made up for an audition. A man was putting body makeup on the child, and had stood her on a table. He worked up her legs with a soft brush, then dusted carefully around the crotch. "What a beautiful little girl you are," he kept saying.

The man had a cigar between his lips, and each time he stroked the girl's legs he rolled the cigar from one side of his mouth to the other, then clamped it still between his front teeth. He powdered the top of the girl's legs again: "A real beautiful little girl." As the meeting proceeded, the Chief's lunch arrived, and he talked and ate at the same time. Now and again he stopped chewing and pointed with his fork to accentuate a point.

"I should try and show a little more leg in the opening shot."

Turning to somebody else he said, "If you wear that dress, what happens to the drapes? It's much too bright."

One of the dogs shifted in its seat and barked furiously. The Chief turned and shook a fork at Rex. "You'll get a raise all in good time." Bim Bim barked furiously in support of his colleague. A manager arrived. "I think we're getting into deep water with the *Moon over the Kremlin* story, Chief. Two of the characters are lesbians."

The Chief looked puzzled. "I've heard of has-beens, but what are lez-beens?"

"They're . . . ," here the manager leaned forward and whispered into Drewstone's ear.

"Well, make 'em Albanians. I've spent a lot of money on that story, and I intend to make it." His face lit up when he saw another man walk into the room. "Clem, are you settling in okay? You must have seen all my movies now. What do you think of them?"

"Well, Chief, it seems to me they're all the same. You change a plot very slightly here and there, but essentially you use the same story over and over again."

The Chief smiled. "You've got it right the first time. Our motto here is, *Never experiment, never provide a message*. Leave messages to Western Union." A woman came over and whispered something in the Chief's ear. "The kid's ready, is she? Okay, bring her on and let's see what she can do."

The little girl who had been body-painted walked nervously into the center of the office, and her mother took up a place at the Chief's side.

"Give her a light!"

As the single spot went on, the child was blinded and frightened. She started to cry and call for her mother.

"No good," said the Chief. "We'll try again in a minute."

The mother walked over to her daughter and slapped her hard on the face. "Pull yourself together, and show the gentleman what you do at home." The child stopped crying and sniffed. "Come on now, do it for Mommy and the nice gentleman." The girl sniffed again, then did a little tap dance and sang a song. When this was finished, she sank to her knees, put her hands together, and gazed up toward the ceiling. "Pleathe God, make all the bad people good, and all the good people nithe."

"I think we can use that," said the Chief.

He looked over to the far side of the room and stared at a row of seated girls, ranging in age from eighteen to about twenty-three. All were wrapped in fur coats and represented not only steps in age, but an increasing scale of expenditure upon their persons. Platinum rings adorned every finger. Each had a left leg crossed over the right, making a formidable array of youth, vigor, and brave drapery.

From the center of this group, a girl wobbled up and started to walk toward the Chief. He sat and stared transfixed. She had blond hair down to her shoulders, and a fur coat down to the ground. She stopped two feet away from Drewstone, threw open the coat, and put a hand on each hip: Her blouse was loaded to the point of explosion.

An agent's face peered around from behind the huge torso.

"Mr. Drewstone, I'd like you to meet a girl I represent, June East."

The Chief nodded, then noticed some strange markings on her throat.

"What's that on your neck?" he asked.

"Love bites, big boy."

"Give the gentleman a few of those lines, June," said the agent.

The girl relaxed on her pelvis, stuck out her chest a little more and said, "Kiss me quick, kid, I'm gonna eat garlic. Get your feet off the table and give the cheese a chance. Anybody can go to bed, it takes a man to get up."

The Chief felt a surge of excitement. "What's your bust measurement?" he asked.

"Why?" asked June. "Who wants numbers?"

"Eh?"

"Don't worry 'bout no tape measure, just feel the shape . . . That's enough, creepy, paws off, I don't want no groping."

"Great pair, eh?" said the agent. "They'd look swell in a tighter sweater."

The Chief coughed and tried to appear indifferent. "I'm not sure," he said. "A big girl in a little sweater would slow down production, because the crew would spend all day staring. Mind you," he added quickly, "a little girl in a big sweater would be an industrial hazard. It would catch in everything."

"Sure, sure," said the agent. "Walk up and down, June, and give us some of your conversational lines."

The girl turned and wiggled across the floor. She stopped by a sofa and stared down at a handsome, muscular man sitting next to a thin male dancer. "Mind yer feet, Tarzan, I don't want to step on yer brains. I'm going to the kitchen, shall I bring you back a banana?"

The man squealed with delight, and held on tight to the dancer's arm.

"I'll give her a screen test in the morning, ten o'clock sharp."

As the girl and the agent left, the Chief watched her carefully, in the same way a shipbuilder looks at his new liner as she plows down into the sea at launching.

Another man was already at the Chief's side and talking urgently.

"*What!* Is that true!"

"Just come through, Chief. Sinclair won the Democratic nomination by the biggest vote in the state's history."

"How's the betting going on him making governor?"

"Hard to tell. Everybody suspects the worst. Stocks on six companies have already dropped sixty million dollars."

The Chief sat back and lit a cigar. "We'll have to organize something to stop him. What's everyone else doing?"

"Louis Mayer is getting something set up at his studio, and Bill Hearst is coming back from Europe, 'cause he's just finished his interview with Hitler. Trouble is, he won't be able to get into action straight away; seems a lot of his staff are Sinclair supporters and he'll have to get rid of them. You'll love this one, Chief. A New Yorker asked Sinclair what he'd do with unemployed motion picture people, and he said, the State of California should rent out a few of the idle studios and let the unemployed actors make movies of their own."

Just as the phone started to ring, Inshroin walked into the room. "*Hello customers!*" he said. "*Slap! Bang!* Here we are again!" He picked up the phone as the Chief started to stretch his arm forward.

"Who?" asked the actor, sitting down on the side of his employer's desk. "Mr. Hearst, Mr. Randolph Hearst? You're what? Oh, I see, phoning from Europe. No, you may not speak to Mr. Drewstone. I'll tell you why not, my inquisitive friend. He's right here beside me in bed and won't be disturbed for even a second, and furthermore—"

The Chief wrenched the phone from Inshroin's hand. "Just a bad joke from one of my actors, Mr. Hearst. What can I do for you?" He listened intently for a while. "Yes, I had intended going to see Sisson. No, I agree the news is terrible, we'll have to drop all the old rivalries and pull together."

He stopped speaking again. Curls of cigar smoke rose around his head and made him look like a man-o'-war. "I'm sure we can. I had already arranged to see Sisson. I'm sure we can come up with something to disrupt the campaign. I'm going to San Francisco this evening and as soon as we come up with a plan I'll call you back. When are you leaving Germany? Tonight?"

There were a few further exchanges, then Drewstone put down the phone. Everybody waited. "Damn Upton Sinclair! Give the fool some money, and it seems he wants to put it in another man's pocket. He's absolutely without business sense. I'll make sure he doesn't get his hand in mine."

160

He turned to his new secretary. "Get me Sisson's office in San Francisco, and I'll take the call in the other room."

Inshroin watched him go next door, then smiled at the secretary. "See that scowl? What a lot the Chief has on his mind! Makes me realize that, like war, making money is hell. But he's doing his best. He sails the good ship American business and the course is reckless and onward." Everybody in the room watched him without saying a word. A few minutes later, the Chief came back in from his other office.

"Miss Paxton," he said to his new secretary, "I'm just going home to pack a suitcase. Arrange a compartment for me on the next train to San Francisco and make sure it's first class."

"Why?" asked Inshroin, "they've always been against you."

In spite of the fact that the Chief's head was full of stupendous schemes for defeating Upton Sinclair, he didn't forget the day-to-day running of his empire.

"You've missed an early morning studio call twice this week. How long do you expect to carry on like that?"

"That's why I came over, Chief," said Inshroin. "I thought you needed an explanation. I've had a very nasty attack of laryngitis."

"Have you? I heard you were drunk in one of those bars your friends are always setting up."

"That's where I got the laryngitis, Chief, but I knew you wouldn't believe me, so I got this note from Father."

Dear Chief
I am sorry Mr. Phillip Inshroin was not at work yesterday, but he had an atack of ~~larin laroon~~ laryngitis.

> Yours sincerely,
> MR. INSHROIN (Senior)

After he read the note, Drewstone put it down on the desk, stared at Inshroin for a second, then turned, walked across the office and pushed open the door. It pressed back hard on its hinges, then shut finally and deliberately, and the Chief was gone.

The secretary picked up the note and read it. As she did so, she again pulled off the beret and let the golden locks cascade around her shoulders. She smiled and looked up at the actor.

161

"You'll go too far with him one day. I don't know why you seem to have such a low opinion of him. He's a real gentleman."

"That shows how badly you misunderstand me," said Inshroin. "I've got a higher opinion of him than most people . . . low though it is."

Two hours later, Mrs. Drewstone was seeing her husband off at the station. To her left a porter was loading up his dolly. No other human being could have shown as much contempt for people's property. He tossed bags, kicked boxes, crushed "fragile" cartons and finally smashed everything down to make it fit. Mrs. Drewstone watched him for a few seconds, then turned her attention back to the Chief. She noticed his hair was sticking up at the back. She tapped on the glass and called out: "Can't you do something about your hair?"

Her husband didn't hear properly and tried to open the window.

"What did you say?" he mouthed.

"Your hair's sticking up. Can't you do something about it?"

Still the Chief didn't hear and cupped a hand over his ear.

"It doesn't matter!" shouted Mrs. Drewstone. The Chief got up and walked down toward the door at the end of the car, his wife keeping up with him as the train began to move. At the end of the car he opened a window, and leaned out.

"What did you say?"

"I said your hair's sticking up on end. Can't you do something about it?"

"I suppose I could water it down."

"You won't brilliantine it?"

"No, that stuff's too sticky."

The interconnecting door opened and a waiter appeared carrying a tray with a coffee decanter and a meringue pie on it.

The train lurched and the Chief lost his balance. He fell sideway and stuck his face squarely and firmly into the middle of the pie. The cars gathered themselves together, and Mrs. Drewstone watched as her husband regained his balance, only to be thrown back against the toilet door by another lurch. There he stood transfixed, his face and shirt front covered in pie crust, lemon filling, and meringue.

When he arrived at the Sisson office in San Francisco, the Chief

162

was taken through the composing room to the editor's office. The place was bedlam. Clattering typewriters, clicking telegraph instruments, and ringing telephones.

As the Chief came into the office, Sisson turned around from his desk, shook hands, and said, "Things are moving ahead well." Then he waved his arm in the direction of a group of women sitting around a book-littered table at the side of the room. "These ladies are picking out interesting quotes from Sinclair's books and putting them back together in unusual combinations to show the man is atheistic, communistic, and sexually perverted. All the ladies are volunteers, determined to go to any length to bring the dangers of Sinclair's program to the attention of the public. This room is solid American womanhood with all the stops pulled out. If my regular staff worked like them, my papers would be selling on Mars."

"Mr. Sisson! What should I do about this passage?"

The newspaper owner stepped across to the woman's side, whipped out a pencil, and made a few quick strokes. "There," he said, "that should make it clearer."

He handed the results of his work to the Chief. "You'll like these. When the readers open up the paper, they'll find similar quotations on the top of every page. Whatever story they're reading, people aren't going to be allowed to forget the Sinclair campaign." He smoothed some hair back from his forehead. "We've got something special for the front page. It's being brought up to the office now."

"What's that?"

"One of my reporters has found someone who'll swear he was paid by a Russian agent to support Sinclair."

"Expensive?"

"We only had to pay him five hundred." Sisson picked up a pile of photographs. "Which one of these do you like?"

The Chief flicked through and pulled out one of Sinclair in his pajamas. The EPIC leader was running toward the man taking the picture, his hair standing on end, arms waving in the air.

"I like this one best. By God, he looks mad!"

Sisson glanced over Drewstone's shoulder. "So would you. I've got a hundred photographers standing around his house night and day. They all have instructions to make things as difficult as possible for him. That one we got by directing

163

headlights into his bedroom and emptying garbage cans on his front lawn at three in the morning."

He was handed an envelope, which he quickly opened. "This is it . . . Boy! Go upstairs and tell everybody that the front page material has come in."

He looked down at the "signed communist confession," picked up his pencil, and made some notes on a pad. In a few seconds the story was furrowed, harrowed, manured, and top-dressed by the master. The two pieces of paper were given to another boy. "Tell them the headlines are to be four inches deep." He then spoke down a brass tube. "Make sure the inserts are ready. We go to bed in five minutes."

"What inserts are they?" asked the Chief.

"Some people I know acquired a box of EPIC notepaper. They wrote a letter on it to the Russian Embassy saying all was going well, and signed Sinclair's name at the bottom."

"Suppose he sues?"

"I'll claim immunity, and say I can't disclose my sources."

"How many are you distributing?"

"About five million."

Another woman at the table stood up. "How does this sound, Mr. Sisson? 'Revolutionaries massing at California border . . . ready to cross and take over key installations in main counties . . . women being threatened by their advance . . . reports of extensive looting . . .' "

"Very good," said Sisson. "We'll use it for the main story in the morning edition."

The Chief threw out his chest. "I intend starting a program similar to MGM's. Tomorrow I post notices telling everybody that if they vote for Sinclair they get the sack, no matter who they are. Every employee earning over a hundred dollars a week will contribute a day's pay to a defeat-Sinclair-campaign. I shall also expect stenographers, technicians, writers, everybody and anybody, to put something in the kitty.★

"I shall make and distribute free a lot of five-minute news

★A very small number of movie people were able to stand up and oppose the studios. Among them, Charlie Chaplin, Dorothy Parker, Nunnally Johnson, Jean Harlow, James Cagney, and Morrie Ryskind. A court action was begun in an effort to stop the coercion, but EPIC didn't have the time or the money to sustain the legal battle.

clips on the dangers of voting for Sinclair, *and* I'll make a point of using unemployed actors. That should show who has their best interests at heart."

Sisson nodded. "There's one thing I forgot to mention. We've managed to raise about a million for billboards. Can you put something in?"

"Who's we, and what billboards?"

"Some Californian editors and businessmen are buying billboard space all over the state. When we've finished, nobody will be able to arrive or leave a town in California without knowing something about the dangers of voting for Sinclair. Since you left your studio, I've already got a dozen up in downtown Hollywood."

"Put me down for a hundred thousand," said Drewstone. All the women applauded.

The scene: the beach a few hundred yards from the Chief's home, ten o'clock in the morning. Some fishing boats from the Drewstone collection had been placed upside down in the sand and actors dressed as Spanish fishermen were standing around talking. Umbrellas, canvas chairs, cameras, and sun shields were being set up by another group of men, everybody working silently and efficiently.

Drewstone arrived in a chauffeur-driven car, pulling a small caravan. With him were Inshroin and Olive, who had come to watch. Behind them was a truck containing fifty or so bearded and scruffy men. As soon as the convoy appeared, activity on the set increased. Performers mumbled their lines, electricians fiddled with their wires, and camera crews adjusted their lenses. The Chief got out of the car and disappeared into the caravan. A young man of about twenty-five, wearing a pair of horn-rimmed glasses, busied himself organizing the newly arrived actors. He got them to stand in a tight circle around the hood of the truck, making sure the scruffiest and most heavily bearded were at the front.

The Chief emerged from his caravan, walked over to one of the canvas chairs, and sat down. Inshroin and Olive joined him and sat in two other chairs that had been placed on either side of their employer.

The Chief blew a whistle and all fell silent. The man with the horn-rimmed glasses stepped in front of a camera that was pointing at the fishing boats. He held up a small blackboard with chalked cabalistic signs all over it.

"Action!"

The fishermen started to mend their nets and paint the hulls of the boats. They were approached by a man holding a microphone. "Good morning, gentlemen, may I ask who you voted for in the primary?"

"We all registered Democrat and voted for Seenclair [the Chief's idea of a Spanish-American accent], but we'll vote for Merriam in the finals."

"Why is that?" asked the reporter.

"You don't know what Seenclair has said about the Catholic Church? Eef we vote for Seenclair, the Virgin Mary weel be angry."

"Cut!" said the Chief. "We'll go on to the next story."

The camera now turned on four well-dressed men who were standing holding a map between them. One of the men made a sweep with his arm.

"It's wonderful that Florida is going to let the movie industry relocate here tax free. This space will be great for Mr. Drewstone. He's moving his business from California if Sinclair makes Governor."

"Are you really planning to move?" Inshroin asked the Chief.

"Don't be stupid! Do you know what the mosquito problem is like down there? One bite on the nose of a star, and production would be held up for days. If I tell the public that's what will happen if they vote for Sinclair, enough will believe me to make a difference at the polls."

"You hope."

"I know. Okay, now we'll do 'revolutionaries massing at the border.' "

The camera was focused again, and the reporter from the first film went over to talk to the bearded men standing around the truck.

"Why do you gentlemen support Upton Sinclair?"

"His system vurked well in Russia. Vy can't it vork here?"

"Are you gentlemen residents of the State of California?"

"None of us are. But ven Mr. Seenclair becomes governor he is going to let all the poor of America live tax free in the

Sunshine State. Ve are just waiting here at the border so ve can get the best houses ven he vins."

On the fringe of the group, some of the men suddenly drew aside, exposing a man wearing a Long John Silver outfit and leaning forward on a crutch. He screwed up his face, leered into the camera, and said, "Ah! Jim lad," two or three times. Then he was lost from view in a seething crowd of extras.

The Chief opened his eyes wide and ran a hand through his hair.

"Did you see anything strange then?" he asked Inshroin.

The actor shook his head, "Perfect take, Chief, why?"

"I thought I saw something strange."

"I'm not surprised. Everything looks strange today. Have you ever thought of growing a beard? No? I thought not. Most bosses don't. It gives a man something to hang onto until the salary he's been promised is paid. Did you see anything strange, Olive?"

The actress shook her head. "I wasn't watching."

The Chief still looked puzzled and was about to call a technician over, when Inshroin surreptitiously knocked the scripts onto the ground from the arm of his employer's chair. The Chief got out of his seat, and as he bent down to pick them up, the actor slapped his behind. "I should stay sitting if I were you boss, when you bend over like that, I can see the shadow of your piles."

The Chief gasped, put his hands up to cover his backside and stood up in time to see Inshroin wandering off. He was about to shout something in reply when he noticed a limousine pull up and a tall, well-dressed man get out. Surrounded by a press gang of assorted aides, he advanced toward the Chief.

Drewstone tapped Olive on the knee. "Here's somebody you'll enjoy meeting."

As the newcomer passed among the actors and technicians, everybody instinctively drew aside. Conversation ceased . . . the silence of ordinary birds in the presence of a hawk.

The Chief introduced the newcomer to Olive. "This is Bob Kent. He's a friend of Mr. Sisson's, and he'll be working with us for a while to keep an eye open for Sinclair and union support in my company."

Bob didn't smile or change his expression; he merely extended his hand to Olive, lifting it from the shoulder as if it

167

were coming back into use after a cramp, and let it fall in hers. Then he lifted his gaze and gave her the full voltage from a pair of browns. The skin crawled up Olive's back, then crawled down again.

"It's a privilege to be able to help," Bob said. "The country's being undermined by unions. Nine times out of ten the heads of unions don't know nothing 'bout trades; it's just a racket. Anyway, if a man is really interested in the union, he's a communist, and he's a communist because he was born on the wrong side of the tracks. Those kinda guys undermine America, and I don't like a place where there ain't no free enterprise. I believe what the Republicans believe, and I vote for them, even though I don't follow politics much. That's why I'm down here with your boss. I want to help stop unions because the free man in this country shouldn't worry 'bout no union. You can't make any money unless you've got a few guys working under you, and if a guy is willing to work under another guy, all the stiff is good for is drivin' a nail."

Bob was a very successful gambling and prostitution boss from Los Angeles. He had grown up in Chicago, and received a gangland education in blood transfusions and last rites. He hadn't learned to read or write until he was nineteen, when he discovered that ignorance of the alphabet constituted twenty-six barriers to real success, so he mastered it in eight weeks.

His first killing assignment had been a knifing. A local Italian restaurant owner hadn't paid some protection money, so Bob broke into his home late one night and got him out of bed. He told him, "There's an old man downstairs with a beard and a scythe. He says your time has come to meet him, seems you got lotza pasta but no future." He took the man from behind and, holding him over the mouth, drove his blade into the spine. He could feel the victim writhing, and it made Bob feel powerful.

He took to killing in a very fastidious fashion—never gluttonous, savoring every morsel. He allowed the restaurant owner two gasps of air, just enough for him to think he was saved, then he drove the rest of the long blade home. His spine was so tender it was like slicing through mashed potatoes.

After that he adopted a gun, and for the next ten years it created an arrogance in him that prison had blunted but never broken.

Bob pulled at the lapels of his suit and stared at Olive.

"How about a cigarette?" he asked.

"Lovely," giggled Olive.

He pulled out a deck of Luckies and threw one at Olive, which she just managed to catch.

"Thank you," she said. "Much obliged."

His eyes burned down the front of the star's blouse, and she smiled nervously.

"What are you looking for," Olive asked, "buried treasure?"

Once more he gave her the voltage from the browns, and once more the skin crawled up and down her back.

"Why dontcha show me around?" Bob said.

Olive looked at the Chief, who nodded.

"You couldn't have a better guide," he said.

"You look after me, I'll look after you," said the Chief's new assistant. "A dame needs protection these days. I bet you got no idea of the sexual perversion you'll find in this country. I try to live up to my mom's ideal of treating a woman as the most perfect thing in the world. I was at one of your movies last month, and these negroes at the front were watching you, and one of 'em said, 'Look at that babe!' I sent a couple of the boys down to tell 'em to shut up. Damn niggers should have a season for their heat, we shouldn't let 'em into movie houses at all."

Olive listened with an expression on her face that alternated between affected surprise and gratification.

The Chief kept nodding, but his attention had been drawn away to a girl who was lying out in the sand. When she saw him looking, she sat up and pretended to be bored. She yawned, put a hand up to her mouth, patted it, and said, "Ooh, la, la." Realizing she had uncrossed her legs in the process, she crossed them again, leaned back on her elbows, and looked around.

"You show our guest the set," murmured the Chief, speaking to Olive but looking at the girl.

Bob noticed something on his shoes.

"Christ," he said, "some goddam swine stepped on my new leathers. They're ruined, and I got 'em sent over from Italy. I'd have preferred a smack in the kisser to this. A bruise disappears, but a scratch on my shoes is gonna be permanent." Olive took hold of his arm, and led him away, making sympathetic comments about the condition of his footwear.

After they'd gone, the Chief wandered over to the girl lying in the sand.

"Hello," he said. "I haven't seen you before."

The girl put her arm up to shield her eyes from the sun.

"No sir, my boyfriend is in this movie, and I came down to watch."

"It's a pity there aren't any parts for women in it, you look as if you'd be pretty good."

The girl giggled and smiled up from behind a fringe of hair that had been cut as precisely as a privet hedge.

"I'd love to be in the movies, Mr. Drewstone. I go to acting classes all the time, every spare minute I've got."

"Step into the caravan for a minute," said the Chief. "I'll see what you can do."

When they were inside, the Chief went over to a cupboard, took out a bottle of Pepsi, then sat down in the only chair.

"Give me a few lines from something."

"Ooh, la, la," said the girl. She began to speak, and instantly got caught up in a rush of words that didn't form complete sentences. There was a pause, then another rush of words even more incomprehensible than the first. She tried again, but this time the performance began with a stutter, then dribbled off into a silence that lasted.

"Great," said the Chief. "You've got a real talent there; it just needs to be brought out. What was it from?"

"Alfred Lord Tennyson's 'The Revenge,' a ballad of the British fleet fighting the Spanish."

"Well, I've never heard it done like that before. There's only one problem, you breathe with your stomach. I'll show you what I mean. Come here and unbutton your skirt."

"Ooh, la, la," said the girl.

"Don't be shy, this is the way I train all my best girls. Come on, unbutton your skirt and I'll explain the breathing."

She did so coyly. The Chief put his hand inside and placed it on her stomach.

"Now breathe."

She drew in her breath.

"Harder."

She pulled in harder.

The Chief took his hand out. "Now you've got it. Whenever you do a performance, you must breathe like that. Breathing is the secret of acting success because it helps you relax. Always remember relaxation is good for the body, and it's good for the

170

morals. Did you know morals are a real drag on a girl who might be a big star? They ruin her face and figure."

"I see what you mean, Mr. Drewstone," said the girl. "If I had someone like you to teach me, I'd be a star in no time."

She looked down and began to button her skirt up. As she did so, the Chief unbuttoned his fly.

"Now," he said, "give me your hand."

"Ooh, la, la," said the girl.

That evening Bob and Olive went out to dinner. Later they took a sightseeing drive, then went back to Olive's house for a nightcap.

As the Rolls purred along Cherokee Avenue, the star pointed to a high brick wall. "Mr. Drewstone's illusions man lives in there. The house is absolutely beautiful, and straight out of fairyland. It's made of papier-mâché, and the window glass is spun sugar candy. He's got stones on the lawn made of wood and tarpaper. He can even change the seasons. When it's snowing in other parts of the country, he piles bleached cornflakes all over his grounds. The effect is incredible."

Bob shifted in his seat. "Don't you ever take an interest in what's going on around the world?"

Olive had an oysterlike interest in passing events, and said, "If you read the papers you only hear nasty things about poverty. Then there's that man Hitler in Germany who hates the Jews."

"See, that just shows how wrong you are. Hitler ain't against the Jews; he's using them as a scapegoat. He really wants to get all the different classes together to fight the one big thing we all have to fight, communism. And we've got to have somebody strong at the helm to do that."

"So he's not against Jewish people?"

"Naw, naw, this guy Hitler believes they got a right to exist as long as they don't overstep the rights of others. All this stuff about the Jewish problem. Ain't no such thing as the Jewish problem, they're all too smart to have problems. You talk to a Jewish kid, and he knows what he wants in ten years. That shows Hitler does have a problem facing the domineering type of Jew. He should segregate them like we do the niggers, and set certain standards for them to live by, 'cause at the moment they live off a guy and overcompensate. I knew a Jewish kid once who was tops in everything. See, he was overcompensating, made the rest of us nervous."

"Perhaps he was just clever," suggested Olive.

"Naw, overcompensating. Do you know how—?"

"Don't let's talk politics tonight," said Olive. "Look, we've arrived somewhere very special I want to show you." She leaned forward, tapped on the dividing glass, and told the driver to pull over. As soon as the Rolls stopped, the two passengers climbed out, and with the hostess for the evening leading the way, they walked toward some gates into a park.

The chauffeur glanced in their direction, then took out a newspaper, and began to read. Olive tried to hold Bob's arm, but he got embarrassed and started slapping her in the small of the back and pushing her ahead of him.

"Don't do that," said Olive.

"Why not?"

"Let me just hold your arm, that's what I want. There, good, that's better. Now, where is it?"

The couple strolled down gravel footpaths and through landscaped lawns and bamboo palms. Suddenly, the clouds broke up, and the moon swam out in a romance above their heads. In the light provided, the film star saw what she was looking for. A bronze statue by Roger Noble Burnham. It was a memorial to Rudolph Valentino called "Aspiration," a nude male figure surmounting a globe. Behind it was a billboard:

HE OR SHE
That hesitates is lost!
This axiom holds good in
Real Estate as well as in
Affairs of the heart.
SELAH!!!!!!!!!

Olive sighed and held Bob closer. "I often try and come here at night," she said. "I'd like to come during the day, but wouldn't be able to get away from the fans. Isn't it beautiful?"

Bob nodded and felt around Olive's waist, as if he was examining a link of sausage. There was a rustling in the bushes, and as Bob put his hand quickly into his coat pocket a veiled woman loomed out of the darkness and stopped in front of the memorial. "Oh I'm sorry," she said. "I hope I haven't disturbed you?"

"No," said Olive drawing back. "We're having a stroll and stopped to admire the statue."

The woman raised her head up toward the figure and the globe. "It is beautiful. An inspiring memorial to a sensitive artist. I saw every one of his pictures at least a dozen times. I'm a busy woman, but when I get to California, I always try to look at anything to do with Rudolph. I live in New York, and I go back in the morning."

"Did you come all the way here to see a memorial to Rudolph Valentino?" Olive asked.

"That, and to settle about the final grave. The plot belonged to my husband's family for eighteen years; now I've bought it for another eighteen."

The star relaxed. Through a combination of the darkness and her heavy veil, the woman didn't seem to recognize Olive. "That's good of you," she said. "Your family can sleep peacefully for another eighteen years now."

"Oh well, I can afford it since my husband died. I just had a big stone put over his grave made of real marble that high! I got it during the Wall Street crash for fifteen dollars. You couldn't buy a slab of stone like that today for under three hundred. I brought my husband from New York, but I'll never do it again. I'll use cremation next time. You ought to see how a corpse moves on a train, you'd think it was trying to get out of the box!"

The woman ran her hand around the base of the sculpture. "I love everything in human nature that casts a spell, and Rudolph could do it beautifully. I loved him so much. Every time I saw him on the screen my feelings were so intense I wondered how I survived. Even now the thought of those evenings leave me exhausted. I suppose it's the price I have to pay for being sensitive."

Bob stifled a yawn, which caused his jaw to crack and made his ears ring.

"It's your privilege as an American to feel above the average," said Olive.

"I know, but sometimes I'm so lonely. I've never felt the same since he died. They don't make movies like they used to.

Most of the plots are up in the air, but then we're all air-mad these days."

There was a silence, and Olive took hold of Bob's arm and guided him away.

"I think we should leave her alone," she whispered. "Doesn't it touch you deeply to think that fans are so loyal?"

"Yeh," said Bob.

They drove back along streets girdled by a fortification of huge billboards and cascading neon tubes. Between two nightclubs, a forty-foot Fatima lolled, smoking the world's sexiest cigarette. Somewhere else, a monstrous babe called for its favorite food.

Soon they were driving through the commercial section of town. In thousands of empty offices sheets covered millions of silent typewriters. When Prince Charming entered the palace of the Sleeping Beauty, he met with the same suspended animation.

They passed another billboard sixty feet by twenty, lit by a cluster of searchlights.

WHO IS EATING INTO THE HEART OF AMERICA?
MAGGOTLIKE HOARDS OF REDS WHO HAVE
SCUTTLED TO UPTON SINCLAIR'S SUPPORT.

Bob gave his companion a nudge, and directed her attention to the other side of the street. "See the sheikh over there? The guy with the cigar? It's a cinch he'd look swell in skirts."

Olive sighed, and snuggled up close to Bob, as the car approached her estate. Within two minutes they were through the covered bridge, and zipping along the curliest road ever invented. On and on, until they finally drew up at the house.

Bob got out of the car first and stood staring at the Wests' mansion. He knew nothing about architecture but was lost in admiration for the sheer opulence of the place. He tried to adopt a cool, indifferent attitude as he gazed around at the magnificence. Inside, he followed his hostess down what seemed miles and miles of corridor.

"It's very classy."

Olive looked over her shoulder. "Mom and me are nuts on refinement."

"Is your mother in?" asked Bob.

"No, she's visiting Mrs. Sisson in Mexico. I expect she'll be there for another three days."

At the foot of a Jacobean staircase, Olive turned to the right, opened an oak door, and ushered her guest into a satin-lined room filled with a jungle of potted ferns and ivory figures. Bob walked over to a silk couch and slid its whole length before he came to rest.

As Olive poured drinks, Bob looked around. The rugs were so thick and deep he could have stood on a chair and dived in. He drew his pants into a comfortable fold above the knees, then suddenly remembering the gun in his pocket, pulled it out.

"Watcha think of this—a beauty, ain't it?"

It was now Olive's turn to appear indifferent. "Peachy," she said.

Bob put the gun back into his pocket and took out a silver cigarette holder. When Olive brought over the champagne and brandy mix, he was in the process of lighting up. He took a deep draw, then held it out to Olive.

"Do you smoke?" he asked.

"Now and again, but I'm not a slave. What is it?"

"A special something I get from one of the boys. Try a pull."

Olive took a tentative draw on the marijuana, then wrinkled her nose.

"Suck it down hard, or you won't get the benefit. Got any music in the place?"

Then Olive put on a record and went over to his arms to dance, Bob proceeded to push her around the room like someone moving furniture. For all his stylish appearance, he had no coordination. To prevent his treading on her toes, Olive stopped, took another draw on the dope, and another sip of champagne and brandy.

"Mmm, it's a divine drink; it goes with the other things I love: oysters, caviar, and kisses."

Again she drew on the marijuana and sucked the smoke deep into her lungs. She looked out of the window at the cloudy night sky, swaying gently to the sound of music . . . Suddenly, the trees on the horizon curled across the lawn and folded into her body. Spray on spray of flowers washed along the ground toward her and furrowed up into her brain. The foamy commotion swirled through her veins and became multicolored waves that lifted her backward . . . She stuck her knee through

175

the slit in the front of her dress, tossed her hair back, and took another draw on the marijuana.

"It's a great leg," said Bob. "Can I see the other one?"

"What do you mean?"

"I want to see them together from top to bottom."

Olive undid the silk wisp she was wrapped in, threw it aside, and did a complete turn on tiptoe.

Bob sat down on the sofa, held the star around the waist with one hand and zigzagged her panties down to the ankles with the other. As he did so, a button on his cuff knocked off one of the little bows on the suspenders. It dropped silently into the carpet.

"Don't be rough, Bob. I've never undressed before to let the boys touch me."

He said nothing, but yanked open the lips of her vagina with his free hand, as if he were about to examine a horse's teeth. Olive winced.

"Be gentle, darling; make it a marvelous moment for me. I can hear a waterfall. I can hear a waltz. It's 'The Blue Danube.' It's blending with the waterfall, and they're mixing like a cocktail; it's the grandest cocktail in the world, darling."

Bob ignored her remarks and conducted a private conversation with Olive's genitals.

"You're a cute little thing ain't ya," he said. "I bet you've given a lot of pleasure to the boys, eh?" He looked up. "Didja wash this thing last time you went to the bathroom?"

"Sweetheart!"

"Didja?"

"Of course, I did."

He pushed his finger in as if he were testing the temperature of water in a bath . . . Suddenly Olive's labia burst into a huge grin, and the filmstar got so excited, she could have ridden the surf in her bloodstream. A thousand violins began to play, and the noise was deafening. When Garbo nestles into the leading man's arms, *A-h-h-h-h!* The moment Phillip Inshroin puts a headlock on a girl of his dreams. *Wow!* When Olive glides into a half nelson with the handsome army officer. *Wham!* Clark Gable gets a stranglehold on a jungle Jane in a tropical love scene. *Zam!* That's the *real thing! The real! Vital! Pulsing! Action-packed thing!!!!!!*

Bob took his finger out of Olive's vagina, sniffed it, then

pulled her down on the sofa, got up, and crouched on the floor in front of her.

"Pull your knees up against your chin. That's it, dammit—stop jumping around! Just keep your ass still, keep your whole body still, I want to do all the work. Now you're gonna get a few of those little kissing treats I've been keeping on ice for the right girl."

He bent forward and pressed his tongue against her clitoris, which instantly caused Olive to dry-shampoo Bob's head violently. As she did so, an image of her mother suddenly floated up above her lover's head. It was rigid as it hovered close to his hair—then Mrs. West trailed off into transparent ribbons . . .

"Oh Bob, do you love me?"

He didn't look up. "Provin' it, ain't I?" Suddenly he was on his feet and undoing his fly. Olive sat up promptly.

"Not for a while, darling; it'll spoil everything. I don't want that, sweetheart. Can't I just be your slave like in my last picture? I'll be your loyal and humble slave, and you can be my master who caresses me day and night. We can sit on silk cushions and—"

"You'll be my loyal and humble slave, will you?" Bob interrupted.

"Oh yes, darling, yes."

"Yeh, it's a great idea. I'll make you a loyal and humble slave."

Bob sat down beside Olive, chucked her under the chin, then held her jaw, rubbing the check with his little finger.

"Open your mouth."

She did so coyly.

Bob leaned forward, and spat down her throat. Olive was unable to move or say anything, as her jaw was still being tightly held. The star's eyes opened wider and wider, and her glands gave off a blast of fear that could have knocked ten men into the next state. Doglike, Bob noticed the smell. Olive moved her head back, trying to swallow without gagging. Finally she managed to get free from his grip and struggled up. "What the hell are you doing?" she screamed, and slapped his face. Bob stood up quickly, gave vent to a string of profanities, and punched her under the right cheekbone. As she reeled back, he grabbed her by the throat and ring-whipped her so hard he slapped the taste of champagne and brandy right out of her mouth. Then he knocked her to the floor, where she lay in the fetal position saying "Oh" and "Ah" as he began kicking her.

As Olive tried to crawl toward the next room (decorated by Illings and Webb before they became so completely commercial), Bob slipped off his belt and began hitting her over the back as hard as he could. The attack took Olive so by surprise she didn't scream, which made him wilder. At last she gave one long moan and he stopped the beating.

Bob leaned back against the wall and looked down at her. After a couple of minutes, Olive started to show signs of life, and he lit a cigarette. "Where I come from," he said, "that's how we break in a bad horse. Now we'll start again. Go get some of your sweetest smelling oil, then I want you kneeling on the couch with your ass pushed up in the air . . ."

Outside, the sky cleared completely, and millions of stars flowered and dripped into the darkness. A tiny cloud over the full moon made it look like a medallion floating down on a parachute. Deep in Olive's forest a nightingale awoke and, thinking night had been turned into day, soared up raining song.

While Bob and Olive were out eating, the Chief had invited the caravan girl and her boyfriend back for dinner. After brandy Mrs. Drewstone chatted with the man while her husband took the girl for a stroll to discuss business. They walked two hundred yards to a small wood and stood looking back at the castle. It stood on the brow of the hill blazing with light. Behind the structure, a slope stretched upward to a crest of wind-torn beeches. That evening the trees were still, while their branches seemed as unsusceptible to any motion as a toy landscape.

An owl hooted, and the Chief was just about to put his arm around the girl's waist when he heard the sound of an advancing horse. He listened harder. The clopping of the hooves got louder and closer, then suddenly a man dressed in a cowboy suit and riding a white mare came into view. He reined up as soon as he saw the Chief and the girl, then spurred the horse over to where they were standing. As he drew alongside, he pulled a gun from a holster at his side, and pointed it in their direction. A handkerchief covered the lower half of his face, just like a movie outlaw.

"Get up to the house," he said.

"Who the hell are you?" asked the Chief, "and where did you get that horse? It's one of mine."

"I know, I got it from the stable. Did you expect me to walk around the place looking for you?"

The Chief was about to say something else, when he noticed the man was now pointing the gun directly at him. The thought passed through his head that he should say dramatically, "Put away that revolver!" but he didn't. The three started back, the two walkers in front, the man on the horse staying about ten yards behind.

They passed an apple tree, and the Chief turned just as the man reached up from the saddle and pulled a Granny Smith from a bough.

"Don't touch that," said the owner. "It's not your property."

"I have the right to touch what I want," said the man. He lifted the bottom of his mask and took a bite from the apple.

When the group arrived at the front door, the man dismounted and led them inside at gunpoint. In the main room the Chief saw that his wife, the girl's boyfriend, and three of the servants were tied to chairs, and three other masked men in cowboy outfits were going through drawers and cupboards. The one giving the orders was wearing a sheriff's badge. The Chief and the girl were also tied to chairs.

"Ooh, la, la," she said as a knot was adjusted, "how exciting. Why are you all wearing those masks?"

"To keep our faces warm," said one of the men without looking at her.

The Chief looked at his wife. "A goddamn break-in. Why didn't you keep your eyes open, and shut all the doors?" Mrs. Drewstone merely shook her head and seemed on the verge of tears.

"I've worked hard for all this," said the Chief, "and now some punks think they can help themselves to it."

"We know you worked hard for it. If we were mean enough, we might be the owners."

The Chief sneered. "I suppose you're part of America's great unemployed, are you?"

"We are, and at the end of our rope."

"There's no reason why anybody should be unemployed in

this country if they want to work. When I started in this business, I had nothing but the suit I stood up in; look at me now."

The sheriff came over and looked at the Chief's rumpled state, then readjusted the tie that had worked itself around to the back of Drewstone's neck.

"Okay, I believe you, but most of us aren't lucky enough to look as funny as you in a suit."

"If you'd been disciplined a bit, you'd be more respectful."

"Yeh, and if you'd been kicked, you'd be more of a man."

The girl moved her wrists to stop the rope from cutting, and said, "Are you well known in your trade?"

"We will be tomorrow when we get our names in the paper; we also robbed Joan Newsom's house tonight."

The girl opened her eyes wide. "Did you go there? Isn't she beautiful?"

"We never saw the dame," said the sheriff. "We don't usually ask to see the lady of the house when we visit."

He picked up a framed Victorian photograph and glanced at it. A woman in a long skirt was standing behind a seated and incredibly stupid-looking young man. His hair was parted down the middle, and in a high white and starched collar he looked like a horse peering over a gate. Behind the couple was a studio backdrop, on which were painted gables and towers of medieval splendor.

"Leave that, at least," said the Chief. "That's a photo of my mother and father." The sheriff put it back.

After another half an hour the thieves had collected as much as they could carry. The man who had ridden out to find the Chief said, "We'll call the gate and get someone to come up and free you when we're well away." Then they were gone.

There was a distant sound of a car starting. It moved over the bridge onto the yellow brick road, and finally faded into the distance. The Chief bit his lip. "Did you see that they knew where to look? Somebody must have tipped them off." He shook his head. "I don't understand it."

"A man as rich as you has probably got a lot of enemies," said the girl's boyfriend.

"Impossible. I pay everybody a fortune to be a friend whether they like it or not," said the Chief.

.   .   .

Inshroin was standing outside the Drewstone pay office. He hid behind a pillar and every now and again cast furtive glances at the people who came and went. Inside, Long John was cashing a check for his last bit part.

"Ah, the golden bars that separate the princess from the herd," he said to the girl behind the grille. "I'm off to New York tomorrow, and have come to claim some wages for a cinematic gem I have been working on."

The girl looked at the check. "Do you want all this cashed?"

"I do. If you remember the Wall Street crash, you will know that in spite of its iron and steel bravery, banks were unable to protect the public's hard-earned cash. Give me the lot with your brightest notes; I want them to match the color of my suit."

"What denomination?"

"Which are the most fashionable now? I don't want to appear out of the swim of things."

The girl stared at him and pursed her lips. "Will you stop wasting my time and tell me what denomination you want them in?"

"Make them all tens."

The girl counted out five hundred dollars and pushed it under the grille.

Long John flicked through. "Are you sure these are freshly picked? You see, I may not be cooking them all at once." He scratched his head. "I suppose I could use the stale ones for shoulder padding."

Long John smiled at the girl, "What have you been doing all your life, my dear?"

"Improving myself."

"Well you can give up now, you're perfect." He stood back, put a hand on his chest, and said in a deep voice: "Sweet maiden, how I adore thee. Ere yonder sun sinks to its rest you *shall* be mine!"

Inshroin's head appeared around the door. "Will you hurry up!"

The girl's face brightened. "Mr. Inshroin! Mrs. West's butler dropped this note off for you; she's apparently been looking everywhere for you."

Inshroin screwed up his face. "Has she? Probably bad news then." He didn't open the note, but put it into his pocket. The two men walked out of the office.

"God you took your time. How many people do you owe money to?"

"Six," said Andrew.

"Well, I swear nobody followed us, so they can't be onto the fact that you've got some cash."

"Good enough. I'll have enough to give a hundred to the EPIC campaign with plenty left over for the fare to New York."

"Is this theater job definite? It seems so risky packing up and leaving. The theater isn't actually at the center of today's acting profession. It's a kind of wandering off onto the grass on either side of a well-beaten track to Hollywood."

"Its the best offer I've had in months. I can't afford to sit here waiting and hoping. Are you coming down to hear Sinclair's speech?"

"Where is it?"

"The Regal Cinema. EPIC has rented it for the day. You won't be out of place, there's going to be at least ten big stars there in support."

One day a Jewish leader in our party said to me, "When Hitler comes to power I hope he'll persecute the Jews." I protested, but he explained quite seriously that after many centuries of existence, the Jewish race, despite its fecundity, could count only 16,000,000. Why? Because of the tendency of the Jews to become assimilated. "We thrive on persecution. As soon as it ceases English Jews become English, and American Jews become American. That is why we disappear. Our religion no longer holds us together: the Jews are sceptics. Therefore we need the revival of race consciousness, and race consciousness is revived by persecution."

Sisley Huddleston
In My Time

AROUND THE ENTRANCE OF THE REGAL was a densely packed crowd of people held back by a line of police. Most looked fed and employed, but they were in a dirty mood after a long day under an employer's thumb. Some carried large photos of Sinclair, while others held up placards that read: KEEP THIS A CHRISTIAN COUNTRY. REMEMBER SINCLAIR IS A COMMUNIST AND COMMUNISM IS THE RUSSIAN CANCER. They all wore swastika armbands. Their leader occasionally stepped out, and goose-stepped up and down in front of the others, causing everybody to cheer and shout "*Sieg Heil.*" A reporter with a microphone walked down the line, and people leaned forward over the linked arms of the police, so they could say something to the nation.

"I'm against Roosevelt and Sinclair, I'm for totalitarianism. I don't like to call it nationalism, because that's what they call it in Germany and Italy. I call it 'Yankeeism.' Our motto is to restore the Republic. A democracy pulls things down to the same level, and that makes it communistic. We don't want the mob rule of democracy, we don't want to be part of a zoo-ocracy. It gives the same rights and privileges to the drunk and the heroic person, and that's bad for the country. I think we're losing the old ideal that it's a privilege to have a handicap, it gives people drive."

"So what do you want?"

"We want to see everything swept away, and a Yankee aristocratic rule imposed on the country. That would stop the depression."

A dozen others gave the Nazi salute. "Yankee aristocratic rule!"

"See the way we do it? It's a purely American salute. The German Nazis use the right arm, we use the left."

"So you would like to see an American Hitler?"

"Sure. A champion of the people, a mystic like Hitler. A man the people can look up to but not touch. A man who has come from the people, who has reached so high no one dare call him their own."

"Hitler uses violence to get what he wants."

"So? Don't you go to the cowboy movies? Hitler took over Germany in the way the boys take over a ranch. He used a shotgun to move a fence instead of doing it legal with a surveyor."

The reporter noticed the woman next to the speaker had a small white eagle on her blouse.

"What's that?"

"It's our symbol. I think it's great, 'cause it's the German emblem too. There's one big difference. Our eagle has its head up, the German eagle is crouching."

"I gather you don't support Sinclair?"

"Sinclair? Him and Roosevelt are communists. All they preach is 'Give, give, give,' which isn't human. Everybody has to take sometimes. Us Americans are born to have enough of everything if we work for it. It's a big world we live in, and we own part of it. All we got to do is stand up for our rights, and things will improve. See, we need *will*. Sinclair and Roosevelt don't have will, and they support the Internationalists who oppose Hitler. He's *the* man with will today."

"Don't say 'Internationalists,' sister, say 'Jews.' Don't be afraid to say it."

"Okay then, 'Jews.' When we get in, we'll dig those bloodsuckers from under their rocks. Us Nazis are the salt of American nationalism. There aren't many of us yet, but just a pinch of salt in your coffee, and no matter how much sugar you put in, you still taste the salt. We're the salt, and we're here to sour this American zoo-ocracy."

The girl suddenly started waving her arm in the air. "Look, there's Phillip Inshroin! *Phillip Inshroin, why are you going in? Are you for Sinclair and communism?*"

At the entrance Inshroin turned and cupped his hands around his mouth. "*I oppose rheumatism, and will help in any way I can to fight it!*"

"Very funny!" The girl pulled the reporter's microphone closer. "Hello America. Phillip Inshroin is going into a Sinclair meeting. He's a dirty red!"

All the seats inside the movie house had been taken, so the spillover sat at the back on stools. Among them was a middle-aged man reading a paper, and drinking some coffee from a flask. On the floor beside him were two placards; one read:

> HOW DO I SPEND MY LIFE
> RATHER THAN MY MONEY?
> THE PEOPLE DON'T WANT TO BE SUBDUED.
> THEY WANT TO BE COOPERATED WITH.

The other:

> IN 1776 THE PEOPLE DIDN'T
> HAVE A RAG TO THEIR NAMES.
> TODAY THEY'RE COVERED IN THEM.
> DON'T PUT YOUR X ON MERRIAM
> AND VOTE PROGRESS DRY.

Inshroin and Andrew looked over the packed crowd and leaned on the small dividing wall that separated the last row of seats from the foyer. Inshroin glanced at the man on the stool. "How do," he said.

The man looked up, said nothing, then went back to reading his paper.

Inshroin tried again. "Do you think Sinclair will win?"

The man looked up, then he sighed, and folded up his newspaper.

"No, he'll lose. The concentration of power against him is too strong. In American politics a man isn't elected by friends and supporters, he's elected by his opponents' enemies. Sinclair has been so honest he's frightened everybody in both parties, so none of his opponents have enemies."

He paused and ran his hand over a lot of forehead before reaching hair.

"Upton's idea is wonderful, and why can't we dream? We're in the world's dream capital. I'm a bit of a dream myself," he smiled quickly, "though I haven't slept much recently."

He looked sharply at Inshroin. "I believe Hollywood has a lot to answer for. I think the film moguls are responsible for communism. By going to the movies, the world's poor see a large class of people who spend their time in dancing, having sex, and swallowing a lot of champagne. They think that's Western civilization. Those visions have created two desires in the communists. First to stamp out the champagne drinkers, then become champagne drinkers themselves."

"That's an interesting thought," said Andrew.

The man smiled at him. "You English?"

Andrew nodded.

"Fine king you've got over there. I saw him when he was Prince of Wales. Only two big shots in the world today."

"Who?"

"Him and Roosevelt."

"Roosevelt seems popular."

"Not with the bankers he isn't. He's for the working classes like Sinclair. Get the king and Roosevelt together, and between them they could settle the peace of the world. There's going to be big trouble soon."

Inshroin pulled out some money from his pocket. "Here's a few bucks for you."

The man shook his head. "No thanks, I've never accepted charity the four years I've been out of work. The wealthy like charity because they can merely tip the dispossessed with a fraction of their gains. I'm a socialist and I want to see a legitimate redistribution of wealth."

He took a sip from his coffee. "I should try to find a seat if I were you. Sinclair comes on in a couple of minutes."

As Inshroin moved around him, the man touched the actor's arm. "Before you go, can I have your autograph?"

"Sure."

"Thanks. When I can afford it, I never miss a movie. I haven't quite succeeded in immunizing myself against Drewstone dreams. Use my pen please—green ink."

"Green?"

"It's a little artistic fad of mine."

When Sinclair appeared on the stage in front of the screen, there was no shouting, but a steady and sustained applause that lasted for two or three minutes.

Everybody rose and sang "The Star Spangled Banner." The flag, with a spotlight turned on it, was raised to answer the charge that Sinclair was a communist. Somebody then read the Twenty-third Psalm to answer the charge that he was an atheist.

Sinclair then began his speech:

"Thank you, it's a pleasure to be here in Hollywood, the center of the film business, and what a hornet's nest we've stirred up! The establishment must be on the run! Sisson's papers have been publishing millions of dollars worth of lies about us, but we can ignore them because the world has never seen an honest newspaper since the Garden of Eden. EPIC has tried to get Sisson to retract the lies, but we can't afford to get through the wall of laywers he's put up around himself. Don't worry; heaven isn't crowded with lawyers. Some of course will get in to keep an eye on the angels, but the majority will find some excuse to stand outside to see if the Pearly Gates are closed with a simple latch key or a combination lock.

"I know most of the film moguls are against EPIC, but they've always opposed the people. Over the years they've given us hot, extravagant dishes basted with money. If that didn't tempt our palates, the moguls turned it into a custard pie and threw it in our faces. We're being treated to a dose of that successful formula. We have to wipe off the custard and forge ahead! When we get into the White House we'll make some fundamental changes." (Sustained applause.)

"As you know, I've told the President that a few of his efforts are sound, the majority futile. Around the world, the profit system is crumbling, and there are only two alternatives. They are social ownership and operation of the industrial plant, or else fascism, which is nothing more than capitalism plus murder. The real culprits of the depression are the stock-and-bond owning classes. They've got hold of the means of production by watering stocks and bonds, then manipulating the markets. EPIC will get them back by watering the currency.

"When you vote, remember, it's 'End poverty in California' today; tomorrow, it's 'End poverty in the world'!!!" (Sustained applause.)

After it had died down, Sinclair went on quietly. "When you see people who have come in from other states and who are out of food and a place to sleep, help out as best you can. Don't tell them the Lord will provide, because he won't. He doesn't provide provisions for that kind of market. Get right down deep into your pockets, and give all you can spare. If heaven does anything further, that's extra. Jesus never sermonized. The blind man's vision was simply restored. He was not told it was sinful to be anxious about his sight when he had a soul to save, nor was a tract thrown in his face the moment his eyes were opened. Left to show his own gratitude, he followed Jesus."

Inshroin started twitching badly, and when Andrew looked at him, sweat was trickling down his face. "Are you all right?"

"Fine. It's an amazing speech. Mark Twain and Lincoln couldn't have done better. I'd like to step out and toast him in something."

"You want a drink?"

"Just a nip."

They got outside and crossed the road unobserved, as a fight had broken out between the police and the Nazis. They walked down fifty yards and found a bar. It was very dark and smoky inside, and heavy glasses weighed down tables and the countertop.

A car door slammed in the street, throwing a flash of light through the window and into the eyes of a drinker. He turned his head, then wheezed and belched over his shoulder. A lazy flicker of cigar smoke, then he pushed his glasses further up his nose and focused on the two newcomers.

"Phillip Inshroin!" he said. "Phillip Inshroin walking in places frequented by Upton Sinclair. You'll get yourself into trouble."

The actor attracted the attention of the barman. "I won't care when I get a few drinks down me. What'll you have?"

The man had some friends with him, and Inshroin ended up buying for a dozen. When he pulled out some money from his pocket, he also pulled out the note Mrs. West had sent him. He read it through.

"Anything interesting?" asked Andrew.

"Seems she wants me to call her, and it's urgent. I'll have a drink first."

When everybody was served, he said. "I'd like to drink a toast to Upton Sinclair, Roosevelt, and my theatrical friend Andrew Aitlee. The last-mentioned is about to resume a career on the stage in New York, and I wish him every . . ." Inshroin glanced down at his drink. "*Barman!!* I want to drink a toast to three of my friends, and there's not enough liquor in this glass to float a letter of the alphabet, let alone a complete name. Fill it up!"

The man wearing the spectacles drained his drink at one gulp, then smacked his lips. A dozen Nazis ran by outside. "Look at them nuts," he said. "These sure are nutty times. There are more nuts running around free than you could ever imagine. My wife seems to have joined 'em. She follows every new craze that comes along. Last week she woke up around three in the morning and said, 'Knock, knock!' I knew she was trying to get me to say, 'Who's there?' so I ignored her. Then she starts in on those threesome jokes.

One Russian = a genius
Two Russians = two fools

Three Russians = anarchy.

One Canadian = one Canadian
Two Canadians = two Canadians
Three Canadians = three Canadians.

"You know them?"
"Sure," said Inshroin, "it's the latest craze down at the studio."

One American = a millionaire
Two Americans = a cocktail party
Three Americans = prohibition.

One German = a professor
Two Germans = a beer hall
Three Germans = the goose step.

"You've got it," said the man. "Anyway the jokes go on, and the 'knock-knocking' goes on. So finally I picked up a Scotch bottle I had by the bed, and I hit her over the head with it."

He raised his glasses and rested them on his forehead. The man then wiped his eyes. After that, with a quick upward jerk of his eyebrows he replaced the glasses on his nose.

"That was a week ago. I thought I'd cured her. No such luck. Last night she started to wiggle her fingers and stick out her tongue. I asked her what the matter was, and she said, 'Don't you get it? I'm a cash register.' I picked up that bottle and gave her another good one. I told her I was too old for all that kind of kid stuff. Beats me why she wants to be like a kid with every advertiser in the country trying to steal her money."

Inshroin quenched a smirk, then made his way over to a phone booth. Mrs. West answered the phone.

"Thank God you've called, Phillip. Olive has disappeared. She's been gone for three days, and I'm going out of my mind. I can't imagine what's wrong. If she's ever been unhappy before, she's turned to me. Do you know anything about a man called Bob Kent?"

"Only the fact that he's working for the Chief."

"Well, all this moodiness started when he appeared on the scene. Things seemed to come to a head last week when *Screen*

Story printed a review of Olive's latest movie. Did you see it?"

"No."

As Inshroin listened, he picked at the edges of a sticker that had been plastered onto the booth wall:

PEOPLE OF CALIFORNIA, IF YOU VOTE SINCLAIR EVERY BUM IN AMERICA WILL COME TO THE STATE AND COMPETE FOR YOUR JOB.

"I've never read anything like it," said Mrs. West. "Damn critics ought not to be allowed into theaters. He was vicious. He compared her to that New York snob girl, Lucy Armitage."

"Lucy Armitage?"

"Yes."

"That's amazing, I met her in the war. She always wanted to go on the stage."

"Probably not good enough for the screen. She does a lot of highbrow stuff. It doesn't pay very well."

"What highbrow stuff?"

"I can't remember. She appeared on Broadway once in a play by some Swede or Finn or something, Ibstein or some such name. It's called *The Gabbler* or something like that. She also does that kid's thing, *Peter Pan*. Believe me it's nothing; this highbrow stuff is all bluff. Anyway, I wrote to the editor and said we'd sue, and he wrote us a letter I still don't understand. Have you got a minute?"

"Sure."

There was the sound of paper rustling. "Listen, this is the worst part."

Dear Mrs. West:

We asked our theater critic to write something on the movies for a change, and we asked him to write on Olive West's latest film in a good-natured and friendly way. I'm sorry he should have allowed his fancy to run riot and become so abusive. But, dear Mrs. West, that is the fault of all magazine writers. I understand the passage causing most offense says, "Her enemies say she cannot act and is a charlatan. I defend her from such a charge by saying she is merely a vain fool."

Mrs. West, I never reprimand my writers once they are in print. By your daughter's popularity, she is open to such attacks, and where would she be if she wasn't being constantly maligned. Sue if you must, but if you try and brush away the filth I publish, you will only dirty your own hands.

Mrs. West sighed, "Can you imagine the nerve of those damn dime-a-liners? I should like to hang the lot of them with piano wire and drag their corpses to the river. Would they be missed? Not one of them. They're all vicious, jealous, and nasty, and I happen to know they all support that communist Upton Sinclair."

A curved melancholic smile appeared on Inshroin's face.

"Maybe they are everything you say, but have you thought that being jealous, vicious, and nasty makes them tell the truth?"

"Phillip, I don't want to start arguing. I need some help. We've never gotten along, but I feel I can trust you. I've heard from a friend that Olive's staying with a religious group called the Kismet Foredoomists. They have a center on Well's Road. Will you go down and see if she's there and talk to her?"

"I suppose I could go down there and see."

"I'd be really grateful. You don't know what it means to a mother to have her only daughter run away from home."

Inshroin stopped himself from commenting on Olive's age. He concentrated on getting the last inch of the sticker off the wall.

"Oh yes, I nearly forgot," said Mrs. West. "Mr. Drewstone wanted me to ask you to call right away."

Inshroin put the phone back on the hook, and before dialing again, he opened the booth door and called for another round of drinks, then he phoned the Chief.

As he came out of the booth five minutes later, a man tapped him on the shoulder.

"Mr. Inshroin!"

The actor turned and gave him a distant, aloof, have-we-been introduced? look. Then his eyes glazed over as if he hadn't noticed, or was even aware of the man's presence.

"Mr. Inshroin I . . ."

The actor now looked at the floor, "Have you a warrant for my arrest?" he asked.

The other man was getting nervous, and said no very emphatically. Inshroin gave an affected start.

"Have you brought the handcuffs?"

"What for?"

"No? Good, I'll come quietly." He turned, slipped into the center of the group he was drinking with, and disappeared from view. There was a whispered conversation, then Andrew came over to the man. "I'm afraid Mr. Inshroin wants an apology, he said you were very loud and pushy and reminded him of the police."

"I'm a reporter, I only wanted to—"

From the center of the group where the actor had taken refuge, a loud voice proclaimed, "*Upon compulsion never!!*"

"I say, sir," said Andrew anxiously, "you haven't come to ask for money have you? I just ask, sir, because Mr. Inshroin is approached by a lot of charity people for money. He's a good sort, is Mr. Inshroin. But I tell you he's really hard-up and he wants all his money for himself."

"Sorry if I was rude," said the reporter. "It seemed a great opportunity, me here at the same time as Mr. Inshroin."

Andrew went back to the bar, and there was some more whispered conversation, then Inshroin reappeared and walked over. He nuzzled the edge of a glass gingerly, as if he couldn't be sure whether it contained liquor or dynamite. "So," he said, "you're a journalist. Well, train the camera on me. Here I am, the man of the moment. I hope you ignore the garbage they write about me in the *Enquirer*. What paper do you support?"

"The *New York Times*."

"Could be worse," said Inshroin.

"Yeh, I work for the *Enquirer*, but I read only the *Times*."

"Very funny," said Inshroin. "When I first heard that joke, I nearly kicked my playpen to bits."

"I'm glad you thought it was funny."

"I'm not sure that I did. Can you leave it with me for the week? But you're just in time for the big news exclusive: Drewstone has given me the push."

"Why?"

"Thanks to the American broadcasting system, he got to know that I was at a Sinclair meeting; he's been threatening to sack anybody seen at one, so I suppose he feels he has to set an example."

"Do you support Sinclair?"

"I can't remember. I had my head blown off in the First

World War, and the medics sewed on an Australian's. It's the head of a younger man, and he urges me into adventures in which the rest of my body is not particularly interested."

"So what are you going to do now?"

Inshroin rolled up his sleeve and bent the arm at the elbow. "See this?" He flexed the muscle. "Much brain power gives much blows. My whole body is a steel whiplash with a guiding brain." He put his arm down. "I should get by, but it'll be difficult. Over the last ten years I've made money faster than I ever will again; I'm thus emotionally barred from all even-paced competition."

"This is certainly a big news-story day," said the reporter. "Vincent Erskine from Coda died of pneumonia this morning."

Inshroin sat down quickly. "Are you sure?"

"Positive. I'm replacing our gossip columnist from today. He got badly beaten up when he went down to the Erskine house for some pictures of the family."

"Another talent taken from our ranks," said Inshroin. "The last time I saw him, we were together at a party for the Prince of Wales. It only seems like yesterday."

In among the drinks the barman turned up his radio.

"When the picture business gets aroused, it becomes *aroused*, and, boy, now they can do it!! This campaign against Upton Sinclair has been, and is, *dynamite!!* It's the most effective piece of political humdingery that has ever been effected, and that is said in full recognition of the antics of that master that used to be Tammany Hall. All this activity may reach further than the ultimate defeat of Mr. Sinclair. It will undoubtedly give the bigwigs in Washington and politicians all over the country an idea of the real power that is in the hands of the picture industry. Before Louis Mayer, Irving Thalberg, Charles Pettijohn, Carey Wilson, and Mr. Drewstone stepped into this political battle here, the whole Republican party seemed to be sunk by the insane promises of Sinclair. With this group in the war, and it is a war, things are different."

Inshroin took a taxi to the headquarters of the Kismet Foredoomists. Driving through the slums, they passed a large tenement building. As the cab slid past a group of drunks, one got up from the sidewalk. He pulled a bright object out of his pocket and put it to his mouth. A little cloud of yellowish-blue smoke exploded from the neck and blew him backward stiffly. As he fell, the eyes gazed up, looking surprised and startled.

"I think someone has just shot himself back there," said Inshroin, taking a swig from the Scotch.

"Happens all the time around here," said the driver. He looked over his shoulder and grinned. "If that's the way America treats its poor, she doesn't deserve to have any, eh?"

The streets changed dramatically as they entered a white suburb of neatly laid-out houses. They were all one-story stucco bungalows, white, green, red, yellow, pink, or blue, and all roofed over with tiles. A lawn and a garden in front and rear, with a side driveway leading to the back, and a two-car garage. A palm tree grew on the front lawn, and a pepper tree was planted in the strip between the sidewalk and the curb.

The taxi purred further west on Sunset Boulevard and passed the Trocadero and other night spots. Soon they were in the film production part of town proper, where the atmosphere became one of the efficiency of the modern factory combined with the irrationality of the theater. The daylight had faded quickly; the sky's color had fallen from blue through red to gray, from gray to lavender. Now it turned a dead alkaline white . . . Civilization quickly disappeared, and the high-sounding names turned out to be simply high-sounding names. Signposts pointed across areas of brown grass and tufts of red poppies. They stopped at one, but found it wasn't a name but directions. It pointed down a sand-filled gully, and read THE ROAD ENDS AT THE CEMETERY.

"Are you sure we're in the right direction for Well's Road?" asked Inshroin.

"As certain as I can be; let's try over the next hill."

Well's Road started immediately alongside a billboard showing a huge pair of hands. The caption read:

> HE LOST HIS HEART ON THE SWEETHEART SHIFT
> TO THESE HANDS.
> WORK WELL AT YOUR JOB GIRLS
> BUT DON'T HARM THE CHARM.

The headquarters of the Kismet Foredoomists was on the brow of the next hill. A low dark structure sticking up out of the earth, it looked like a blimp hangar. The only decoration was

194

the name of the organization over the small entrance door, and a neon sign announcing, A SPECIAL LAYING ON OF HANDS BY AIMEE MCPHERSON. Lined up down the side of the building was a row of ambulances with big red crosses painted on the side.

"Do you want me to wait?" asked the driver.

Inshroin shook his head, and as the cab drove away, he looked at the Hollywood skyline. In the dusk the town was a think neon strip of white light. An effervescence of popping bulbs cascaded over it . . .

Once he was inside the meeting hall, the thing that struck Inshroin was how crowded it was. There were very few cars outside, and all these people couldn't have come in the ambulances. He slipped unobserved into the back row of fold-up benches and sat next to a woman in white gloves, who had her eyes riveted on a curtained stage at the end of the building.

A small wooden box, full of leaflets, was nailed to the back of the bench in front of him. He pulled one out and read it.

"Your church and its expenses."

Underneath were listed alphabetically the costs of running the establishment. He put it back in the box, and glanced at the woman sitting next to him. She was chewing gum loudly. Apart from the jaw movement, she sat perfectly still, cotton-gloved hands crossed in her lap.

"What's going on?" whispered Inshroin.

"Aimee should be here in—" The woman turned in his direction, and her eyes opened wide. "Phillip Inshroin!"

Everybody in the row leaned forward to see him.

The woman gave a sigh. "Phillip! Phillip! This is a miracle. I've been praying for you ever since I read those dreadful lies in the paper about you supporting Upton Sinclair. Now I feel as if my prayers have been answered, because I really am one of your greatest fans."

"The place is packed," whispered Inshroin. "How did you all get here?"

"We walked. There's very few people here who can afford transport. It was wonderful; lines of people walking to this cathedral of love in the desert, just like in the Bible."

Inshroin was about to ask her what the ambulances were doing outside, when she went on, "Do you like my white gloves? I got them from a man in Los Angeles. They were made to shake hands with the Prince of Wales when he toured our part of America last time he visited. The route was changed at the last minute and they've never been worn."

Inshroin looked around the mausoleum, and at the silent waiting crowd. "It's a bit like the Mormon Church in Salt Lake City," he said. "I went down there once for a service. After it was finished, the congregation went to a special theater performance."

"I didn't know the Mormons like the theater in their city?"

"This was a very religious production. We all sat around a bed that was sixty feet long, and watched Brigham Young's forty-five wives fight for the best position."

During the prolonged silence that followed his comment the stage curtain drew back, revealing a crowd of men and women dressed as angels, complete with wings. A band at the front struck up. The heavenly host stood in a semicircle around a wooden throne, behind which were three empty crosses. Three huge nails had been driven into the central and bigger cross, with red daubs of paint around them.

On the wall behind was a mural. Rats labeled THE SUPPORTERS OF COMMUNISM burrowed under the Washington Capitol, while to the left of the picture Jesus was shown hanging on the cross. He was being given vinegar by a man labeled EARLY MARXIST AND FRIEND OF UPTON SINCLAIR.

Aimee, the evangelist, appeared from the wings and walked to the throne. She stood in front of it, turned with her arms in the air, and shouted: "God bless you all!" The cloak fell from her shoulders, and the sequins on the dress sparkled and cascaded.

"Praise the Lord! Praise the Lord!" came the acknowledgment from around the hall.

Aimee raised her face to the ceiling and crossed her hands over her chest.

"I'm here to drive the devil out of the city of Hollywood, so I might as well give you people hell to start with."

"I bet we catch it now!" called a man from the front.

"You said it brother!" said Aimee. "Everywhere I turn I see people drinking, joining unions, and falling into the hands of the communists. The roads are littered with their corpses! Speed-speed-speed! On you fly over the highway of sin, flirting with the crumbling edges of the chasm of despair . . . *Ha!* that was close. Come, my people who are God's traffic wardens, let us go after them on our motorcycles of mercy. God has spoken to us time and time again through my traffic wardens of example. Oh people stop at the cross tonight, pull over and refuel at the Cross of Calvary!"

"We will! We will!"

Sister Aimee remained standing, waiting for the noise to die down. When all was silent she said, "Beloved people of my congregation, your pastor is greatly in need of a fur coat. The nights are cold, and you wouldn't want me to freeze to death, would you!?"

"No!"

"Well now's the time to save her."

A man came down the aisle from the back pulling a white rope behind him. He got to the stage and hooked it up beneath the preacher's feet. It cleaved the temple, stretching the full length of the aisle, taut and steady.

"Beloved brothers and sisters, you may wonder what the rope is for. It's to hang your money on." (There was no room for coins; only dollar bills, bent to an inverted V and hung over, would stay put). Within two minutes the rope was covered from end to end, and a man with a bucket came along and swept the plunder away. The rope was removed, and Aimee thanked them for what she called their "love offering."

"Before we go any further, I'd like to bring on Father Hobbes, a truly spiritual man, to give you his message."

To great applause Father Hobbes was spotlighted to the center of the stage.

"Folks, why grope in darkness? There are definite instructions in God's words on how to become and stay rich in times of depression. God's financial plan applies to widows, workers, kings, and princes. Light and wealth is for the asking. I'm a metaphysical practitioner to whom this message has been revealed, and you can come to me and talk about it. Your consultation will be strictly confidential, and for the ladies, there is always a maid in attendance. I've treated theatrical, political, business, and motion picture people. You've heard me on the radio—"

"We sure have!"

"And now you can come and see me in the flesh. I'm the true psychic master born with the gift."

Aimee applauded Hobbes as he walked off the stage, then turned back to the crowd. "After that important message, my children, I will now come among you while we sing the hymn 'I am the Rock.' My traffic wardens of mercy will hand out the word sheets autographed by me, and they are only thirty cents a sheet."

Aimee came down from the stage and wandered down the aisle handing out flowers as people began to purchase song sheets from the army of ushers. Working her way down toward the entrance at the back, Aimee came upon Inshroin and was about to say something to him, when she noticed a man standing at the entrance smoking a cigar.

"What are you doing with that thing in your hand?" she asked.

"I'm just looking after it for Brother James. He stepped outside for a minute and asked me to hold it for him."

"Did he? Throw it on the floor and stomp on it."

"Yes ma'am!"

The usher threw down his cigar and stubbed it with his toe.

"Harder! I said stomp on it!"

The man stubbed the butt a little harder.

"More, more! Jump up and down on it. I want the devil in that cigar chased until it's exhausted!"

The man pounded and stamped on the cigar as if he were doing an Indian war dance. Shreds of tobacco flew off in all directions.

"That's better," said Aimee. "I don't want any nicotine to sully fingers or lungs. Your body is a temple, not a furnace."

"Yes ma'am! Yes ma'am!" said the abashed follower.

Aimee now turned to Inshroin. She held up her arms and everybody fell silent.

"Brothers and sisters, it's a privilege to see that we have one of the greats from the film industry with us here today. He must want us to pluck him from the hands of the sinners he has fallen among. Phillip Inshroin!"

As the people applauded, Inshroin noticed that someone on one of the stretchers on the stage sat bolt upright, and looked in his direction.

Inshroin said, "I'm reminded of the shortest sentence in the English language."

"And what's that, brother?"

"Jesus wept."

"A very great sentence, brother," said Aimee. "I'm glad you know the words of the Lord." She smiled a dazzling smile. "Do you pray regularly, brother?"

"As often as I can, but with my popularity I'm forced to do it in private these days. It's a pleasure to be in a congregation again. Before I came here I stepped into the privacy of *another* public toilet and was locked away in a closet praying. Suddenly the door flew open and the washroom attendant burst in. He had been checking under the doors to see if there was more than one man in each cubicle and saw my feet facing the wrong way. He thought I was on my knees trying to commit suicide by putting my head down the pan."

Amy's eyes glinted as the people within hearing distance gasped. Then she fell on her knees and started praying. "Phillip Inshroin, may you be saved from the sin of pride. Go to Jesus for consolation. The only way to be beautiful is to go into the Lord's great consulting room. There he will put you under his great white light. He is the surgeon who can take a life, no matter how mutilated it is, and mold a new and more beautiful life. He sees a bit of pride in you, so he takes his knife, cuts it out and puts love there. He works on you until you are just like the chart he has pinned up on his surgery wall." Aimee got to her feet and swept toward the stage to the sound of applause and the crash of the band.

Once back under the spotlight, Aimee started to walk along the line of people laid out on stretchers. Beside each person she knelt down and put a hand on their heads. "Arise and walk, sister. Arise and walk, brother." Each time she finished the blessing, the recipient threw back the covering sheets and stood up, to screams from the congregation and dramatic chords from the band.

"As you can see, my congregation are all wearing evening clothes. So great was their faith, they knew they would be cured and are ready to go out and enjoy the wonders of the Hollywood nightlife."

When she got to the end of the line, Aimee pointed down dramatically at the person under the sheet.

"Friends, here is a *true* believer from the movie kingdom who wishes to be blessed. Healthy in body, she is sore pressed in mind. Ladies and gentlemen, Olive *West!!!*"

Everybody stood up and strained forward. "Brothers and sisters, do you know what she has asked the Lord for?"

A voice said, "To give her an ounce of acting ability?"

"Did someone say something?" asked Aimee. There was no reply, so she turned her attention back to Olive.

"I guess it was nothing but the wind," said the same voice.

Without warning, Inshroin was standing beside the evangelist. He shouted,

> "The angel blew his trumpet,
> The heralds shouted come,
> The pearly gates swung open,
> And in walked Olive's mum."

Aimee's temper went off like a hand-grenade, and she spat in Inshroin's face. He took a handkerchief out of his pocket and dabbed it against his wet cheek, gently, as if he was sopping up blood from a wound.

Three ushers came across and, holding the actor's arms, pushed him toward a door to the left of the stage. As he was being led away, Inshroin looked over his shoulder and said, "Crow away, you consumptive old rooster, it won't get you into Heaven!" Then he was standing on the road outside. The ambulance drivers watched him curiously, but nobody attempted to speak to him.

A few more minutes passed, then Olive came through the back door and made a sign to one of the ambulance drivers, who drove over.

"Did you catch my performance?" Inshroin asked. "Not a titter of appreciation. I could have been lecturing on differential calculus to a bunch of loonies. Why are you wearing sunglasses?"

"The sun hurts my eyes."

"It's evening."

"I know but I don't want anything from the evening air to get into my eyes."

"Your mother has been very worried about you," said Inshroin.

Olive shrugged. "Has she? She won't need to anymore, I'm going straight home now."

"In an ambulance?"

200

"Yes."

"Do you want me to come with you?"

Olive shook her head.

"Your mother mentioned something to me about a Bob Kent, is there any problem? Because if there is you should tell someone about it.

"Best to inform your mother,
Won't she be angry—rather!
Tell her the truth,
Mention the youth,
Nothing conceal,
Inform your mother."

Olive sighed, "Joke, joke, joke. Do you think you can go through life without taking anything profoundly? I've just had a wonderful healing experience in there, and all you can do, after you've made me look a complete fool, is joke. I don't know what would have happened to me if Aimee hadn't accepted my offer of a car and let me keep my membership in the church."

As Olive was about to step into the ambulance, Inshroin grabbed her arm. "Don't leave this and allow the blood that boils in my veins to ooze through cavities of unrestrained passion and trickle down to drench me with its crimson hues! Surely you aren't going off without giving me your usual salute?"

"What's that?"

Inshroin bent Olive back over his arm. "Your lips, madam, if you please, *your lips!*" He kissed her, then lifted her glasses to see the eyes. They were bloodshot, glazed, and looked into the distance like desperation staring at a white hospital wall. After she had gone, Inshroin drained his flask and began to return home bit by bit, along a very obstinate but talkative road:

SINCLAIR PLANS TO TAKE TOTS FROM MOTHERS.
WOMEN OF CALIFORNIA! SINCLAIR IS A FREE LOVER
AND RUSSIA WANTS HIM ELECTED.

FLITZ THE BEER THAT MADE TEXAS FAMOUS
BLITZ THE BEER THAT MADE TEXAS ENVIOUS

201

Inshroin was sitting on the grass border taking a rest, when another of the ambulances pulled up beside him. The driver leaned across grinning like a Halloween pumpkin. "Can I give you a lift, Mr. Inshroin? We Sinclair supporters have to stick together!"

Once Inshroin was laid out on a stretcher, the driver pulled away. He glanced over his shoulder. "Comfortable?" Without waiting for a reply, he went on. "You should be, I drove one of these things in the war and never bumped a soul! Now that was a *real* job. When men got hit, you had to get them away quickly for their own peace of mind, and the peace of mind of their buddies. If you couldn't move them to a safe spot, you just moved them a few feet."

"It would have been better to leave us where we fell," mumbled Inshroin.

"No, the place they got struck down in becomes unlucky. You'd often see an ambulance going around in tight little circles. The wounded thought they were being moved to safety, and in that way they relaxed." The driver laughed. "Fooled 'em every time, because there never was a safe spot. A front-line dressing station isn't a safe place, but the wounded always thought it was. When they were being unloaded and saw nurses, their first thought was that they must be safe, otherwise there wouldn't be women around . . .

"Funny when you think of it, me getting this job driving for the Kismet Foredoomists. I gave up praying during the war. See, I might have been meeting the Lord at any time, so I didn't need to telephone him, then feel slighted if he didn't answer me as soon as I dialed. I put my prayers in my work. My body was nothing because it could have been smashed to a pulp in a second. My job was to get through with the wounded."

The driver changed gear, and as they surged toward a sharp turn in the road, he began to sing:

> "Hushed and happy whiteness,
> Miles and miles of cots,
> Wards of contented brightness,
> Where the sunlight falls in spots."

As soon as they got around the bend, a renewed and determined barrage suddenly came down on them without warning:

UPTON SINCLAIR CALLS FOR THE ABOLITION OF CHRISTIANITY,
THE NATIONALIZATION OF OUR VIRGINS,
AND THE EXECUTION OF THOSE WHO DON'T SUPPORT EPIC.

Inshroin was driven back to his tower, where he slept until eight. As evening came on, he came out of his front door and walked down to the back of the studio. The gates had been locked, and everybody had gone home. He found an open window, climbed in, walked through several corridors, and let himself into Drewstone's office. Picking up the Chief's phone, he spent a patient hour going through agents and theaters, trying to locate Lucy. He tracked her down to a hotel in Waslend, Illinois, and put through a call.

When Lucy heard his voice she instantly recognized it. In the sky above Inshroin's head three stars twinkled, backed into Heaven, seemed about to leave, then leaped forward with a start. They went through the preliminaries.

"There's not much point in going on about how I intended to get in touch, but never found the time," he said.

"I'd have to make the same excuse."

"It seems like a lifetime."

"Things have changed." Her voice seemed hesitant, guarded.

"And how's your dream coming along?" Inshroin asked. "I hear you're doing very well."

"Not for years I didn't. I used to spend months wandering the country looking for the best suicide spots. I'd just decided on jumping off the Empire State Building when I got a job."

Inshroin laughed. "I'd go for booze. Oblivion not mutilation for me."

Lucy went on: "Now I just about make ends meet, and spend a lot of time trying to keep my own personality and feelings intact."

Inshroin shook his head. "I don't go too deeply into my feelings. Feelings are like chemicals, the more you analyse them, the more they stink."

As they talked, the past flowed back to him like a half-forgotten dream. He remembered their meeting, could see her, smell her, half sad to remember, because to remember is to have forgotten.

"Movies did better than you thought," he said.

"I still don't think much of them," her voice quickened. "Half the stuff they put on the screen would have been jeered off the stage before the war. But audiences have changed and I haven't, I've got a prewar mind. What's your latest movie?"

"*Mabel Saw It Coming*. It's the story of a wife who loses her husband, me, to another woman."

"What happens to the wife?"

"She wins me back, of course. Do you want an unhappy ending?"

"A logical one might be unusual, something different."

"Drewstone doesn't like anything unusual or different. A logical ending isn't good box office, and that's what we all have to think about. You can't send people away from the theater unhappy."

"Does the wife win you back by getting new clothes, visiting the beauty specialist, and wearing gorgeous bathing suits, which makes you realize for the first time that she is actually a lot lovelier than the other woman?"

"That's the story in a nutshell."

"I thought it might be; you've got another winner."

"You sound as critical as ever," said Inshroin. "In Hollywood, that's a crime; 'Buy and Be Blind' is the motto."

"And you sound a bit defensive."

"I have to be. I'm supposed to be a success, but I don't feel it. I've got a hunch I confuse happiness with pleasure, cost not quality, we all do down here . . . Are you married?" he asked.

"I was for a while, to an actor," she hesitated, then stopped speaking. The line crackled.

"Lucy, are you still there?"

"Sorry, I was just thinking, yes, for a while, no children, you?"

"I've nearly been married three times, but each time we announced the engagement, their relatives appeared from all over the world and carried them off . . . Have you been back to France?"

"No, somebody I work with went for a vacation, and tells me everything has changed. Where we were is a sightseeing attraction these days, the sandbags are whitewashed, and the trenches are swept every morning. I wouldn't like to see it now."

Inshroin accidentally knocked a paperweight onto the floor, and the room jumped back into focus. He realized his immediate surroundings had grown hazy and indistinct while they talked. For a few moments, time was humbled; a clock on the wall had ticked without emphasis.

"What's your next blockbuster going to be?" Lucy asked.

"I won't be doing one. I was caught helping out in the Sinclair campaign and got fired. Drewstone says he'll miss me, but missed I must be."

"So, you're useful as well as ornamental. If I were out there, I'd vote for him. Any other plans?"

"Artists don't make plans, they seize an occasion. I've been thinking about the theater again, but I'm rusty. I can just hear that long sustained burst of enthusiastic silence as I forget my lines. I've decided to travel for a while, escape my reality, or get as far away from it as money will take me."

"I suppose you've got pots of that?"

"It oozes out of my ears if I don't watch it, but I spend a lot, I find that money kept longer than three days starts to go rancid. Maybe we should meet before I leave?"

"Sounds nice, but I'm going up to Canada at the end of the week. I don't know where I'm staying yet."

The operator cut in to tell them their time was up.

"What did you say earlier about keeping your feelings intact?"

The operator came on again, and Lucy raised her voice to speak over the girl. "It's easy; when you're a success, everybody likes you including those who have to pretend to; just make sure you know the difference."

Inshroin sat on the top floor of his tower looking at the moon, the sky filled with its light. Absolute silence, and he would not have appreciated the whole depth of the universal muteness except for the ticking of his bedside clock. The power of the enveloping solitude struck him with great force for the first time. At each tick the silent shining disk moved a thousand yards through space, carrying him along through reality as if it were a dream. Millions of years before it had shone down on empty waters, while humanity waited its slow unfolding in the limbo of future possibilities. And one day, a poor enfeebled lamp, it would shine down on a cemetery of ice. There would be no more clocks to measure the hours, no human beings to count them.

Something moved in the empty air of the tower. Nothing specific, a vague unrest, a gentle fluttering, a sigh. Inshroin concentrated, but what was there would not affect his five senses. It evaded them, gliding through or under them, only touching at their roots and prompting half-forgotten impulses he could not define, but felt belonged to his childhood. Then the motion ceased, and although Inshroin sat quietly for half an hour, was not repeated. What was there was waiting. He went to bed without having a drink.

A T A LOCAL RADIO STATION one single flicker of support for Upton Sinclair pumped out its weak signal. A journalist was on the air attacking the Sisson press and the Drewstone movie empire. The microphone became the man's cobra, and he treated it as if he were a snake charmer. He smiled, scowled, ogled, and grinned. He bullied it, he confided in it, and he insulted it—then he changed completely and looked at the microphone as if he were about to make love to it.

"The newspaper business is certainly a great one. When this country was founded, the writing and editorial function was the highest in the land. Its business was to acquire facts and give out information, because facts and information are the bricks and masonry of honest social responsibility. But Sisson has done away with such principles. He uses his papers to blow on the flames of discord so that we can boil his own pot, and if you or I swallowed the monstrous lumps of fudge he ends up cooking, we would develop a strong desire to go out and do something criminal.

"When he had made a million dollars in the gutter, he decided he wanted to be President, so he went vote hunting. Do you remember him in '25? He stumped the country looking as happy as a lunatic having his straitjacket removed. He said, 'When I stand at the wheel of the Ship of State it will look like it has an extra funnel.' You, the voters, turned him over, looked at him from all sides, and came to the conclusion that nature had never intended that he should stand as the nation's watchdog. You the people stripped away his camouflage and the camouflage of his rich supporters, saw them for what they really were, and decided you wanted nothing to do with them.

"If a pig is clothed in silk, it is still a pig. Put a collar of gold around its neck, and the bristles will protrude through the finery. And Mrs. Pig? Clothe her in satin, hang her ears with diamonds, cover her teats with lace, and yet between the words she utters, you will hear the grunts of her gorging and guzzling at the elite swill tubs.

"After his defeat Sisson retired for a while into seclusion and tried to pretend he was a holiday pensioner rather than a drummed-out Presidential candidate. But behold there has been a rebirth! The old reprobate has returned to captain his newspaper and do battle with Upton Sinclair. There he stands at the wheel, worn and thin, his skin flapping about him in loose folds like his principles. His editorials on the EPIC campaign are so poisoned, he must have used a typewriter ribbon made of cobra skin. He is floundering in his venomous ink. Can you see the waves of words tumbling over his shoulders and delighting to feel the place where rests his chip?

"Led by the Drewstone empire, Hollywood is building up the terror. One day's pay has been taken from everybody in the studio and put in a fighting fund. If you ask the California press what is happening, they are so silent you could hear a mouse tiptoeing across the roof of the Empire State Building. Upton Sinclair had to buy a copy of the British *News Chronicle* to learn that Jean Harlow and James Cagney are among the protesters of such action. Katharine Hepburn has been told she'll be dismissed if she supports Sinclair. Phillip Inshroin already has . . ."

The day after Andrew left for New York, Inshroin went to Vincent Erskine's funeral. The car he was traveling in had collected him at 12:20 and at 12:35 pulled out of the Drewstone driveway and added itself to a line of vehicles that stretched to the horizon. A mist that had lain over Hollywood since early morning thinned and shredded away in long ragged clouds, which trailed off the edge of the buildings. As the mist parted the sun broke through. It gleamed and shimmered on hoods and bumpers of a vast body of cars. Rank after rank, they choked the streets, while fans weaved in and out, giving a constant motion to the shimmering mass of steel.

As the car edged along, faces peered in as people tried to see if the occupants were anybody they recognized.

"Goddamn morons," said the man sitting next to Inshroin.

Nobody talked. That morning Inshroin's headache stuck out like a pair of antlers. He took a nip from a hip flask, which he then held above his head. "A war-time toast, gents.

> "Hold your glasses steady.
> Drink to your comrade's eyes.
> Here's a toast to the dead already.
> Here's to the next man that dies."

Inshroin took another sip, then passed the flask around.

"He was a good actor," one of the Coda men said.

"You think so?" said his companion. "He was a man who had a lot of lucky breaks. As a star he wasn't an actor, he was nothing more than the sandwich-board man of the privileged classes. He captured the whole nation without struggle, and got his picture in every paper except the *Daily Worker*. While the majority of the country was underdressed and standing on soapboxes complaining about it, he was overdressed and stood drunk on champagne buckets.

"I remember telling him once that he should put a little money aside for a rainy day. He told me he couldn't be bothered, because if a rainy day didn't come along, he'd be stuck with all that cash.

"It's said he died from being out in the rain and catching pneumonia, I know he died from an explosion caused by receiving more hero worship than the human frame could stand."

"He gave a lot of money to the Republicans," said the first Coda man.

"He wasn't interested in politics, he supported the party that said it would maintain his way of life. To him, 'left' meant the little bit of caviar he didn't quite finish. His great guiding principle in life was self, self, self. I bet I know what happened when he died."

"What?" asked Inshroin, taking another sip from the flask.

"His ghost rose up to Heaven. St. Peter introduced him to the Eternal Father, but Erskine stood by silently brooding. The Madonna then offered him flowers, which he ignored. The Holy Dove landed on his arm, but he accepted the homage without comment. Jesus came over and said, 'Poor creatures that we are in this family, what do you desire?' and Erskine said, 'The photographers, where are the photographers?'"

"Did you know that Coda films has got the Reverend Archibald Scott, Archbishop of L.A., to perform last rites? The man's close friends call him Archy Bishop. He's burying a comic next week who has the epitaph LET HER RIP! carved on his stone."

The car shook and vibrated with mirth . . .

When they arrived at the cemetery, squads of police had to hold back the weeping crowds so that the principal mourners could drive in.

The small preburial chapel was packed to suffocation as everybody stood around the bronze-and-steel coffin allegedly worth thirty thousand dollars. The casket was covered in so many wreaths and flowers, it caused one man to ask if the deceased had decided at the last moment to go into the vegetable business.

The service started with the sign of the cross, accompanied by the sound of police dogs barking. More fans tried to climb through the windows, and fell on those inside.

"For Christ's sake, stop pushing!"

Uproar arose: scuffling, shoving, and shouting. Through it all, the immediate family stood around the coffin, their shoulders heaving. Archy Bishop preached a short sermon, and from what Inshroin could hear above the din, it was about sin, and the speaker was against it.

The service over, the bearers tried to get the body out to the grave. People closed in screaming, trampling over other graves, and climbing into the few trees to get a better view.

The police made a path for the flowers and the body, but no sooner had they passed than the space was filled and Erskine's family was cut off. They stood in a self-protective circle, the women veiled and weeping, the men hitting and kicking anybody that tried to get in close. Because the crowd was getting uncontrollable, there was no further ceremony at the graveside. The coffin was lowered, and the excavated earth shoveled back into the hole. One or two women tried to jump in as it was being refilled, but they were dragged back by the police. It was all over in five minutes.

Suddenly the hysteria was diverted. All along the grass border of the path leading to the chapel, small fires had been started, and the flames were spreading. Inshroin, who had been hiding behind Erskine's mother-in-law, took a swig from his flask, then noticed the Chief's doctor standing about ten feet away.

"Hello," he called, "what are you doing here? Looking up some of your old customers?"

"I came down to do some autopsies! I didn't know he'd died!"

"Well he has. You think this is a rehearsal!"

"Phillip Inshroin, we still love you!!!"

The horde of fans came at Inshroin screaming. They swarmed like bees from a hive, and he was the flower.

ZZZZZZZ
ZZZZZ
ZZZ
ZZ

Inshroin made a dash for the car, but it was too late. Three girls in advance of the others reached out for him like they were Noah's family receiving the returning dove. In trying to avoid them, the actor tripped, dropped to his knees, and a mass of bodies fell on him, licking and kissing till he was whiter than a washerwoman's thumb.

Inshroin panicked, and by punching in all directions, managed to get to his feet. Then he threw out his arms, spewing off clouds of fans in all directions. Some fell on top of their companions, others crashed into parked cars, and one girl on the outskirts was knocked into a patch of the burning grass. As her dress caught fire, police and friends rolled her back and forth trying to beat out the flames.

Part of the crowd now started to get angry, and began clawing at the star's face. With arms and feet flailing, Inshroin began to back toward the car. The ensuing fight was as vicious and heroic as anything seen in the ring at Madison Square Garden.

Inshroin finally managed to get to the door and was dragged

inside. He lay on the floor, breathless and wiping blood from cuts and scratches on his face.

"Revolting and disgusting," he said.

"Never mind that," said a rescuer. "That feeling is like seasickness, you get over it."

Inshroin sat up and, taking the barometer that registered interior temperature from the back of the driver's seat, placed it against his stomach. The actor looked down and watched the needle. "It's swung around to very dry," he said. "I think it's time to flop my lip over a few drinks."

"We'll join you," said the two Coda men.

Slim Whitelaw, Drewstone's singing cowboy, swung easily down from his spirited horse. Every muscle in his supple body rippled rhythmically as he carefully tethered the animal to the saloon rail. His bearing spoke of courage, a firm belief in the final triumph of virtue, purity, and clean living. In the half-light provided from the window of the bar, the strong angular lines of his tanned face gave him an almost spiritual look.

He wore a silk tartan shirt with white pants that were tucked into silver boots. A gun was slung on his right hip, and the belt buckle was made of mother-of-pearl with the initial *S* in the middle. He was twenty-five years old, tall, and long-faced like Gary Cooper; his eyes peered through creased lids weathered by a lot of hard riding in the blazing Texas sun.

As Slim walked into the bar, conversation stopped and fifty pairs of eyes scrutinized him closely. Realizing he was the center of attention, the singing cowboy opened his eyes wide in an effort to make the crow's-feet disappear from the corners, and sauntered across to the bar.

The walk was upright, a slow stride that never faltered. Arms bent slightly, palms of the hands near his gun butt, eyes fixed on something in the middle distance. The barman watched him, but continued wiping a glass with his dishcloth.

"Howdy, Slim."

"Howdy, Bartholomew."

"Usual?"

The new arrival nodded.

When the fresh fruit cocktail arrived, Slim put his foot on the bar rail, and sucked at his drink through a waxed straw. A phone next to the cash register rang.

"A dozen wranglers wanted at Studio B. Studio C is looking for a bullwhip man!"

Everyone at the bar sat on stools made of real cowhide, while the footrests were stirrups with spurs attached. One of the drinkers took a sip from his glass, turned to Slim and said, "Didn't see you last night, where were you?"

"I was in the mountains exploring," replied Slim. "I couldn't sleep."

"I've never understood why you don't take sleeping pills like the rest of us."

"So that's why you've got spots all over your face: Sleeping pills are bad for the complexion."

"You can talk, sonny. You've got bags on bags under your eyes."

An older man in the group pulled himself up from the glass of Scotch he was drooping over.

"Ker-rist," he said, "can't we act like proper cowboys? Slim, for God's sake, stop getting your dick in a wringer!"

Slim was about to make another observation, when he noticed two men who had just staggered into the bar. His eyes opened wider and wider.

"Look, it's Phillip Inshroin, and is he drunk! What's the matter with his face? He must have been in a terrible fight!"

Inshroin and companion pounded on the bartop.

"Barkeep!"

Bartholomew wandered across cleaning another glass.

"Ah," said the actor, focusing with great difficulty, "a bartender, the only psychiatrist who works in an apron."

"What's your pleasure, gents?"

"Women are our pleasure, but we are here to drink. Two large Scotches."

Bartholomew leaned over his counter and pointed at another man who had crawled in on all fours. "Is he with you?"

"He is," said Inshroin, "but don't serve him, he's driving."

He looked around. "What bar is this?"

"Greg's Place on the Drewstone lot."

"Never mind the details, what city?"

The third man pulled himself onto a stool, dropped his head on top of some glasses, and fell asleep.

Slim wandered across and propped himself up beside Inshroin. "Hello Phillip, if this isn't an absolutely private party, can I wish myself in on it? I saw your last flick, and it's great."

"What flick?" asked Inshroin.

"She Went All the Way."

"Get lost, little boy, there was no such movie, no such actor."

Slim flushed and glanced at his friends, who were giggling. He poked out his tongue then turned back.

"I'm sorry you find it necessary to be so rude, Phillip. I know you're having a hard time, but you only have yourself to blame if you support communists like Upton Sinclair."

"Are you talking to me?" asked Inshroin.

Slim smiled. "There's nobody else standing in front of me."

Chairs skidded across the floor as everybody ran for cover. A silence fell. Men could be seen blinking from different corners of the room, each pair of eyes as bright as a cat's shining out of a barrel on a dark night.

Inshroin lurched a bit, scratched his chin, and said, "Have you ever heard Hamlet's great speech recited properly?"

The room strained its ears to catch the reply.

"Can't say that I have."

"Well, most actors miss the correct spirit of the thing. I'll show you how it's done." He began, " 'To be or not to be,' " then dropped his voice so low, the cowboy couldn't hear. As he leaned forward to catch the words, Inshroin grabbed Slim's gun from the holster and put it against his own forehead.

"Shall I end it all then, shall I?" he shouted. "Shall I end it with you here in the bar and perhaps responsible for my suicide?"

Slim jumped back with his hands in the air. "Ker-rist! Are you touched? Put the goddamn thing down!"

Inshroin affected a very angry expression and dropped the gun to his side.

"So," he said, "you're a philistine, are you. I can see you don't appreciate great tragedy. No doubt a gay blade like you enjoys comedy. I expect you see life as one big laugh!" He pointed the gun at Slim. "Right, take off your shirt and dance. *Come on! Take off your shirt and dance, or you're dead!!!*"

Inshroin's eyes were blazing with fury, and Slim, transfixed with fear, undid his shirt, took it off, and did a little shuffle on the spot.

"Not like that!!" roared Inshroin. "That's not funny, nor is it

tragic. Take your pants off. Don't stop dancing, *hop!* Good, that's it, keep going, peel the pants off over the footwear. I want you to keep your boots on. Now the shorts. *Keep hopping, damn you!!*" Inshroin fired two shots between Slim's feet. "Now do it faster!!!"

Slim took to running violently on the spot, wearing nothing but his silver boots.

"For God's sake, let me go," he gasped.

"Not yet, not yet, one false move and you're dead!! Keep dancing, you're a comedian. Let's try some ballet. Do a turn on tiptoe like Nijinsky. Hands up over your head, fingers making a point, now t-u-r-n. Good! Now do a Keystone Cop, go cross-eyed, and stick your teeth out like a little rabbit's."

Everybody in the bar had come out from their corners and were standing around the two men laughing. Inshroin watched his victim for another minute, then dropped the gun to his side.

"Okay, that's enough. Get out of town, and don't let me see you back here again."

Slim picked up his clothes and pulled on pants and shirt as he made for the door.

Outside he sat down on the bar steps and put his face between his hands. Cowboys riding horses, with golf bags and clubs hanging from the saddle, rode by and stared curiously. The sounds of glasses clinking and men laughing increased to a crescendo from the bar. Then there was a *crash*, and everything fell silent.

Five minutes went by, and Slim was about to get to his feet when an ambulance and a police car arrived. A cop and two men with a stretcher went inside. They reemerged carrying Inshroin, who was as white as a sheet.

The actor smiled at Slim. "There was a funeral right there at the bar," he said. Then he held out a glass to the cowboy. "Hold this coffin handle for me, will you? I'll be back as soon as I can."

The cop leaned over the stretcher.

"You look familiar. What's your name?"

"Cock Robin."

"Wise guy."

"No, Cock Robin."

"Okay, next of kin, are you married?"

"No, I'm suffering a great deal of pain, which is why I look as if I might be. Leave my two friends alone, they can drive the car back."

"Those two are in no condition to drive."

"They're in no condition to walk. A good driver who is drunk has one golden rule, my friend. Never lose your head and obey all the traffic signals!"

As he was lifted into the ambulance, Inshroin sat up and shouted, "My teeth hurt, get me a gum architect!" Then he fell on his back.

Slim watched the two vehicles drive off, spat, and threw the glass into the street. The bar door swung open, and his three companions came out. They stopped at his side, giggled, then crossed to where their horses were tethered. Everybody mounted and rode away. At the corner the group swung around in the saddle, removed their hats, held them up in adieu, then cantered off toward the hills. Slim stood up and leaned across his saddle weeping with rage.

"Fuck!" he said. The horse turned its head and snorted in sympathy. To Slim it seemed like another giggle of derision. He pulled out his knife and sliced off the animal's left ear. The horse bit back instantly, laying open the man's scalp into a fringe of flapping skin that hung down in his eyes. They silently stared at each other, breathing hard, blood trickling down their foreheads.

At the hospital Inshroin swam in and out of consciousness as he was taken to the operating room. He strained his ears and heard the clanging of elevator doors, and a whirl of cables and spools. He opened his eyes.

"I've always wanted to descend into the valley of the shadow to be snatched back by a great surgeon, and now here I am being wheeled along to the guillotine."

In the operating room he looked around.

"Which one of you boys is going to cut me up?"

A head loomed over him. "I am."

"Ever done it before?"

"Wish I could count the times. Burst stomach ulcers are my specialty." He prodded Inshroin's stomach.

"Drink?"

"Lots."

"Cocktails?"

"Scotch."

"Hurts?"

"Incredibly."

"Stomach?"

"Pride."

"Mortified?"

"Mostly." Inshroin sighed. "But I'm a grand and clever man if you catch me sober. Actually, Doc, there is a physical pain, but it doesn't seem to have a favorite spot; it's scattered. Please remember it takes a lot of chloroform to put me out; I lap it up. I love the buzzing, swimming feeling, the dreams that solve everything."

When the mask was put over his face, he took in great gulps, and his head began to swim. "Who are all these white-sheeted people?" he murmured. "Prophets, Trappist monks, the Ku Klux Klan? Humpty Dumpty had a great fall, and had to put himself together. We all do after a bad fall."

The last words he remembered hearing from the operating room were, "He *does* lap it up!"

Inshroin began to dream. He was in a place that looked like a theater dressing room. The air was sticky with the smell of greasepaint. A light bulb hung from a cord in the ceiling and illuminated the place brilliantly. In the middle of the floor, a woman who had her back toward Inshroin was standing between the legs of a seated man.

The actor couldn't see the person in the chair, but knew it was a man from the breathing. The sound suggested he was suffering a great and unspeakable pain. Inshroin then saw the man's hands resting on his knees. Each had a hole driven through the center and blood from the wounds dripped down his legs, joining a stream that flowed from two similar holes in his feet. The bottom of the woman's dress was wet because the material sopped up blood from the pool that had collected on the floor.

It was Aimee McPherson, and she was standing between the legs of Christ making him up with a long brush—the eyes were already caked with mascara. A crown of thorns was on his head, and as the blood trickled down, the evangelist smeared it to make the effect more dramatic. She had come to the lips, and dipped her brush into a pot of crimson. The door of the room opened, and an usher came in. "Is he ready yet?" Inshroin now heard a vast crowd outside that was wailing and sobbing. Standing back for a last look at her work, Aimee nodded, then she helped Christ from his chair and allowed him to fall to his knees. After he had settled behind the door, she laid a huge cross over his shoulder.

"Now crawl along the passage, out into the middle of the stage, and don't stop until you get right into the center of the spotlight."

As Christ crawled past, Aimee bent down and forced the crown of thorns a little firmer onto his skull. "Just a minute!" Aimee opened a penknife, and made the wound in his side an inch longer. "There, that's more dramatic."

After he had gone the woman stood in the doorway, a hand on each hip, and watched his progress. Suddenly the mob fell silent; Aimee held her breath. There was a deep and satisfied sigh, then the hysterical screaming reached a new level of intensity. Above the din, individual voices could be heard praying to him brazenly and loudly for cars and houses, all demanding instant and efficient service. Aimee grinned and grinned.

EPIC lost the race. The final vote was Merriam 1,138,800, Sinclair 879,000, and Haight 302,000. After the result had been announced, Sinclair received a note.

Dear Upton Sinclair:

My son, when he was about five years old, attempted to split wood with my razor. You can be sure it was less bad for the wood than the razor. I remembered that story when I heard from you that you had got yourself into this rude business. As I read that the cup has passed from you, I rejoiced even though it has not gone exactly according to your wish. In economic affairs the logic of facts will work itself out somewhat slowly. You have contributed more than any other person. The direct action you can with good conscience turn over to men with tougher hands and nerves.

To you and your wife, the hearty greetings of your

A. Einstein

After the defeat, as it turned out, Sinclair was the least unhappy person. He began to think, "I can drive my own car again, I can sleep with the windows open." But he kept a calm exterior, because if he smiled at the funeral, what would the mourners think? He decided to go straight back to writing his books. They needed replacing; Hitler had burned a lot of them.

At the moment Sinclair started to plan his next story, the Chief stood on his lawn watching a man operating a crane from the back of a truck. A huge and heavy box covered in silk bows and silver paper was being delivered. Machinery squealed and strained as the massive weight hung in the air, then it descended quickly and settled six inches into the grass, crushing a rosebush.

The operator jumped down and came over. "Gee, what a weight! Must be a coupla tons!" He held out the invoice. "Five thousand dollars to pay."

"I've got to pay five thousand dollars?"

"That's what it says. The party who phoned us to collect it from the station, said it was a gift from Mr. Sisson."

The Chief paid in cash.

After the truck had gone, the recipient walked around the huge monument twice. Finally he stripped away the decorative paper, exposing the wooden container. Some members of the staff were called over to get it open. When the last splinter fell away, everybody stepped back to see what had been revealed. The gift was a vast slab of marble. Across the front, carved in intricate tombstone lettering, was the epitaph.

> THIS WEIGHT
> HAS BEEN TAKEN
> OFF MY MIND
> SINCE YOU KISSED
> ME GOODBYE.
> P. INSHROIN

In later centuries when one will have a true measure for things as they are today, it will be said, Christ was great but Adolf Hitler was greater. The question of the divinity of Christ is ridiculous. A new authority, Adolf Hitler, has arisen as to what Christ and Christianity really are.

District leader Becker, in L. D. Weatherhead
This is the Victory

Thy bones are marrowless, thy blood is cold:
Thou hast no speculation in those eyes
Which thou dost glare with.

I float on the midnight waters
With my deathly demon head;
My skin is an iron armour
Which flattens the hunter's lead;
And my eyes are a living terror
Glassy as those of the dead.

Midnight deeds have I witnessed
But never shuddered to see.
Tremble not you murderer pale
Go and leave the corpse to me,
And not a hair or whiten'd bone
I'll leave to speak of thee.

A. R. Wallace

ADOLF HITLER IS GIVING A PERFORMANCE IN BERLIN. We catch him in the final act, just before the curtain. The audience is completely bewitched by the sound of his voice. Everybody has been drawn out of him or herself and is floating in a fog of mystical enchantment. The listeners are held enthralled by an unmovable "will" strong enough to break down all opposition and resistance, then subdue and dominate everything. Each person is conscious of only one desire, to be enwrapped and lost in that mighty single will emanating from the stage.

219

As Hitler speaks, he flashes his jawbone around, churning the language as if he were a pile driver in a heavy sea. His mouth becomes an instrument, an accordion spread, a trombone growl, a trumpet shriek. His motifs are recurring, like those of Wagner, always rising to a hoarse scream, then dropping down to a tearful wrenching sob. It is a blend of the pompous with the nebulous, the brutal with the innocent. After each sentence he clamps his teeth into the final word like an untamed tiger, pushes back a lock of hair from his forehead, and folds his arms across his chest:

"*We are awake!* We are gathered together to demand that Germany be returned to the German people. We demand retribution for the life that has been stolen from us. We demand retribution for the death and suffering of our sons and husbands. We have had enough of suffering, we have had enough of resignation. *We are awake!!*"

"*Heil!*" The hall seeths and glitters with an ecstasy that can be felt. The audience throbs and quivers to the rush of words; it almost swoons.

"Before us we have a task appointed by Heaven. We are brought here to bring a higher civilization to the world. The greatness of Germany was never brought about by her merchants, diplomats, scientific men, or artists; the mailed fist established our greatness. Let us drop our miserable attempts to apologize for German history; we have nothing to apologize for. Let us abolish unripe and false shame; we have nothing to be ashamed of. A whole generation must voluntarily sacrifice its freedom in order to save Germany. The new German will not die for a program he understands; he will die for a belief he loves. There lies our tragedy and our happiness. Our might will create a new law in Europe!"

"*Heil! Heil! Heil!*"

"To achieve this end Germany must hate, because hate gives strength. We must organize hatred, educate a desire for hatred against those who have stolen Germany from us. To us from today is given faith, hope, and hatred, and the greatest of these is hatred. Do not talk of suffering, talk of glory. We have found ourselves, resurrection has come!"

"*Heil! Heil! Heilllll!*"

Hitler stands motionless on the platform. He stands like God on the mountaintop. A spotlight picks out a heavily decorated officer standing at the front of the hall. He raises an arm in salute.

"Fellow Germans, the other nations buried their unknown soldier; in Germany he has arisen."

The roar that follows sounds like the roof of the hall collapsing.

In the evening Hitler goes to a Wagner performance. It is a very moving experience for the Führer. As the closing chords die away they seem like stones being rolled across cemetery vaults for the last time.

As he leaves the theater, Hitler turns to Goebbels and says, "The opening A note of the *Rienzi* overture is blown on the trumpet. That note tells us Wagner is an original, creative artist. At the same time it is of great significance that the trumpet call in question should also be a summons to freedom. The sound reminds me of a fat sausage. It contains all the beefy force of my Third Reich.

"The trumpeter who has to sound that note must be inwardly conscious of what he is blowing when he does it. He must be penetrated through and through with the knowledge that the note *is* German liberty. Should the trumpeter only understand that A note as a musician understands it, simply confining himself to sounding it correctly—that is, exactly as it is written—I do not want him to play at my funeral."

Before he steps into his car, Hitler goes over to a group of swastika-waving children.

"And what are you doing?" he asks.

A small boy says, "We are waiting to see our Führer."

"Well then, my little person," says Hitler, "you must gaze upon me, for I am your Führer."

The child beams radiantly, then balances on the edge of a good cry.

From the theater Hitler goes straight to a private party. After eating supper, he talks with some guests about palm reading. (He thinks his own right is probably the finest thing God put on a human arm.) When he has exhausted the subject, Hitler walks around, chatting, smiling, and shaking hands. It causes a lot of people to note that in friendly encounters he is addicted to the two-palm grip.

At twelve o'clock he starts to talk of the early days before his rise to supreme power. The voice drops to a whisper and the throat becomes choked with emotion.

It is time to return to the affairs of state. Before he leaves the room, Hitler turns, places his right hand on his hip and submits to the photographers. The camera flashes make the room look like a silent-film version of an artillery bombardment.

PART THREE

Whether Hollywood intends it or not, the movies are painting our picture for posterity. It won't be too accurate a portrait. We are going to be prettified and sillified. There will be little of the restless spirit of our times in it, scant mention of the depression, of hunger, unemployment, and industrial unrest. Future generations will see 1939 on the screen and wonder if this truly had been the age of rebellion and war, of the test of strength between dictatorship and democracy, of the intense scrutiny to which all the rules and laws of the twentieth century civilization had been subjected.

D. Churchill
We Saw It Happen

"Ah, Madame Melba, you should be happy. You have been able to express every emotion. You have laughed in the *Barber of Seville*. You have wept in *Otello*. But suppose you had never been allowed to weep? Suppose like myself you had always been forced to laugh." His expression changed abruptly, "I would give my soul to play Hamlet."

Charlie Chaplin, in Nellie Melba
Melodies and Memories

ACCORDING TO THE HEARST PRESS, by 1936 Roosevelt was spending money left and right, mostly left. The paper asked, "O debt where is thy sting? This new deal croupier realizes that a game has been invented where the banker pays all the time. He needs a first class juggler, not a man to balance the budget."

In Germany, Goebbels wasn't happy with the Reich's film industry. In 1936 it reached its lowest creative level in many years. He made a speech on the situation and praised the success of American films. "The supposed public taste has no rigid standards, but is influenced by the taste of the artist. One only need look at such American movies as *Lives of the Bengal Lancers*, and *It Happened One Night* to be convinced that art in the film is attained through depiction of life in the most natural manner possible."

In New York City, near Broadway, Andrew Aitlee was outside a theater listening to a black woman. She was standing on a box, lecturing to a group of thirty or so people who were lined up waiting to go inside and audition.

"Now you've all heard about this man Hitler," she said, "and he's doing all right in Germany. Hitler is right about the purity of race. So copy like he does, and remember there isn't such a thing as social equality. Don't believe no such thing about brotherhood; there isn't no brotherhood for the colored man

225

except among his own kind. The Jews are the people that brought us here, and Jews are all communists. We owe nothing to the Jews, and we owe nothing to America. This isn't my home; my home and culture are African. I'm a foreigner here, and I'm persecuted and hated. Don't believe the white man when he says we should be against Nazism; that's just white racist talk.

"Between Nazism and democracy, I'd choose Nazism, because it can make the colored person proud like the German and Italian people are proud. Nazism is only another word for anti-Jewish nationalism, and what's wrong with that? If the colored people turn against Nazism and Fascism, we'll be supporting the Jewish imperialist conspiracy.

"The colored person is crying out for revenge, and the salvation of my race is my religion, like it is to Hitler. What Hitler says about the nobility of the Aryan race also applies to the nobility of the colored person. If it comes to war, we colored people of America must stay out of the fight; let the white man kill his brother white man. It'll leave fewer whites for us to bother with later when we step in to get justice for ourselves."

A chain of nudges and mutterings shuddered from one end of the line to the other as the people's marginal attention shifted from the black racist to a striking figure who strode toward them.

He was wearing a monk's habit with the cowl down. His graying hair hung to his shoulders, and his beard looked like the thicket that trapped Abraham's sacrificial lamb. On his feet were a pair of leather sandals, and he carried a six-foot staff. As he passed the theater front, Andrew gasped, "Inshroin!"

The man stopped and glanced back. "Long John Silver."

"My God, what on earth are you doing here?" asked Andrew.

Inshroin fumbled in the folds of his cloak then pulled out a card. "Here, this should explain." The card read:

> THE ROYAL BANK OF PLEASURE
> I promise to pay the bearer
> a billion laughs and dramatic
> moments.
> P. Inshroin

"I've been abroad for a few years; the day after I got home I saw the ad for the audition. I thought I'd come along and see what's happening."

"How long have you been back?" asked Andrew.

"Two days."

"Are you staying in New York?"

"I've got a small room in the Bowery."

"Comfortable?"

"A bed, and hot and cold running water."

"Doesn't sound bad."

"Down the walls?"

"Let's see if we can change your luck; come in and meet the director. I've just finished a job, and he's taken me on." The two men went into the theater arm in arm.

"I wrote as soon as I read you'd been fired," said Andrew. "Why didn't you write back?"

"I didn't get the letter. I left the country pretty quickly. It must have arrived after I'd gone. I was very ill: exhaustion and drink. I went to Africa first, and for weeks I kept looking over my shoulder expecting to see the old looming wall of hangers-on, but they'd all gone. How have you been getting on?"

"I'm a success. I was in a show for three years—it was in Manhattan but not on Broadway."

"No wonder you look pale."

"You'd look pale if you went to bed at five every morning, and were never quite sure who with."

They stopped at the back of the foyer.

"What kinds of things is the Federal Theatre looking for?" asked Inshroin.

"Everything and anything. The Federal Theatre Project has been given a million dollars to produce shows all over the country; we're doing classics, plays by new people, musicals, you name it, we're trying it. Got some big names involved. Lucy Armitage has offered her services and she's auditioning."

"I know," said Inshroin. "I read it in the paper; we met in France during the war. Is she good?"

"Good? She's so damn dramatic, she can't take a potato off the stove without stabbing it. When she's finished with a part, it's like a well-sucked orange, there's not a bit left for anybody else."

"Have you worked with her?" asked Inshroin.

"Not yet. We've spoken at parties, but that's about it. Shall we go down to the stage?"

Inshroin looked nervous. "I'd like to say hello to Lucy in private first. Can you go in and give her this note?" He pulled a piece of folded paper from a pocket in his cloak.

Andrew went into the main auditorium and found Lucy standing with a group of other women beside a coffee urn. He gave her the note, which she opened.

Have just returned from the goldfields of Australia. Will you meet me outside town after dark. Please bring shoes, socks, underwear, shirt and suit. Have own hat. P. Inshroin.

"Where is he?" she asked.

"Out in the foyer."

When Inshroin saw her come through the door, he instantly got caught in a memory that took him back years. The walls of the trenches seemed to grow up around him again; he could smell the smells and hear the sound of gunfire. She still looked much the same, but the features were tighter; the expression fitted the voice he had heard over the phone, and was more guarded.

"My God," said Inshroin, "you're a sight for sore eyes."

"I'm sorry to hear your eyes are sore, my dear," she said quietly.

After she kissed him, he saw that she shifted her eyes quickly. The arched eyebrows and slightly wrinkled forehead gave him the feeling that she felt a vague doubt, it was almost a look of startled fear. Then the expression passed, and her face settled into a languor of patient sadness.

"It's hard to remember what you look like now you've grown your hair and beard, but your eyes are still nice." She showed no surprise at his appearance, didn't seem to notice it. They went over to an alcove and sat down.

"I've only been back a couple of days," Inshroin said.

"You've been away ever since you phoned me?"

"Yes."

"Did it help?"

"I visited about twenty countries. Do you know there are millions all over the world who don't know who I am?"

228

"Truly amazing." She sounded sarcastic.

He nodded. "At first I expected a fanfare to sound every time I entered a new country. It took me a long time getting used to it not happening. I was very popular with the insects in New Guinea. I was bitten from head to foot in every village I visited. If there had only been one mosquito in the whole country, I know it would have met me at the border."

"I'm sure the fans here have remembered you."

"You're wrong. I haven't been noticed much since I got back. Seems they adjusted to my absence pretty quickly. Fame is as fickle as a kiss, and lasts as long. Nothing's a dream until you wake up."

"I don't think that's such a bad thing," said Lucy. "It's a fresh start, a clean slate."

"Which is why I thought I should see if I could get back into the theater. I feel I can cope now that I've had time to sort things out. It came to me one morning in Spain. I realized I was depressed because I'd spent years making a bunch of bad movies that bred like rabbits. The depression got to the bar stool stage, and I fell into my liquid lunch. It was the right thing to do, getting out. I don't want to end up like my ancestors, who were all alcoholics. Most of them died from the exertion of chasing imaginary rats up imaginary walls." He leaned forward and touched her knee.

"You still have the same style and poise I remember."

"Poise will be poise." They both laughed.

"I've never completely given up the theater," said Inshroin. "I played Hamlet every day when I was with Drewstone."

"That figures. When you left, I read you were known as the mad Dane of the studios."

Inshroin looked surprised. "Hamlet wasn't mad. A reverential awe was paid to the insane during his time. He knew the fool was the safest man in court."

"Hamlet probably had a lot in common with Peter Pan."

"Who, as you know, emerged at eighty into his full powers after a long and painful adolescence. No, I'm fit again and looking for work in the theater." He stood up and took hold of her hands. "I know I'll get it. I can *smell* the overtime. Now I'm here, don't even try to stop me getting a job, *don't do it.* I'm desperate to work myself to death."

"I'm sure you are."

"*Don't stop me.*"

"I won't."

"And whatever you do, don't lend me fifty dollars if I ask; it won't do me any good. I need a job not a loan. *Don't do it.*"

"Are you off the booze?" asked Lucy.

"Not staunchly, but these days I try not to drink anything younger than me. I don't worry about it though, I've got my father's iron constitution. When he died, they had to cut out his heart and beat it to death with clubs."

"Shall we go in?"

"Before I see a producer, I'd like to have a haircut and a shave."

"Our makeup man can handle that."

Inshroin followed Lucy up the stairs, behind the curtain, and into a little alcove above the wings. A man was sitting on one of two chairs reading a newspaper.

"Can you give this gentleman a shave and haircut?" Lucy asked.

The man lowered the paper and stared at Inshroin. "I've got no water, it'll have to be a dry shave."

"That's okay."

Lucy disappeared to prepare for her audition.

The man walked around Inshroin slowly a couple of times.

"A shave and a haircut, is it, sir?"

"It is. If you think I'm a poet you're mistaken."

"I didn't think you were a poet for one minute, sir; I knew at once you were more of a poem than a poet; we get lots of poems in here these days. Before I start, I'd better warn you, sir, it's a bad day for me. I was up late last night on the booze and the old hand isn't too steady."

"I know the feeling," said Inshroin. "If you hold the brush I'll wiggle my chin against it."

The makeup man picked up a pair of scissors and began cutting the beard. When it had all been removed, Inshroin got up and looked in a small mirror that was nailed to the wall. He rubbed his chin.

"The face is getting older. There are a lot more bristles that will be harder to get out of deeper wrinkles."

He peered closer into the mirror.

"I don't need to put any makeup on for the audition, do I?

I've developed a bit of acne over the last couple of years, and it takes a long time to dig the stuff out of the crevices."

"You must be the first actor in here to worry about full pits, sir. I wouldn't bother. Mr. Willis, the director, likes to see all his people in their natural state; then he can know where to place them."

Inshroin changed into a suit that had been hanging in the corner then, holding the cloak over his arm, walked out onto the stage.

He stopped by the coffee urn and filled a cup. Then he looked around. On the other side of the machine a girl was sitting on a stool. Her face was perfectly still and looked almost nunlike except for the moving jaws as she chewed gum. As Lucy passed along the front row of seats, the girl did an amazing thing; it was totally natural, and something Inshroin knew she would never be able to repeat in a performance. She looked Lucy up and down, eyes flashing, with long piercing glances mixed with curiosity and blistering envy. Then the look vanished as quickly as it had come, and the face resumed its expression of nunlike passivity.

Lucy came up through the wings, walked across the stage, and put her hand in Inshroin's arm.

"As handsome as ever," she said.

"That won't help me much. Now I'm up here I'm very nervous. My mind was under the influence of booze for a long time, and the old memory may be damaged. In that state you can hardly bunch a few words together, let alone form complete sentences, and there are a lot of sentences in Shakespeare."

"I shouldn't worry about it. Acting is like riding a bike. You never forget once you've learned."

Inshroin stared at her. The possibility of failure hovered over his head for a second, then spiraled down like a shell and vanished in a splash of craters. He remembered sitting outside the officers' mess when the German barrage started, and for the first time since the war felt a rush of panic.

There was the sound of a bell ringing.

"The producer's coming back. He'll want the stage cleared. We'll have a drink after the audition. Now that you've come back, don't expect a twenty-one gun salute from anybody, and don't think of yourself as a failure. If there's a problem, I'll snap you along for a while."

Inshroin saw Andrew sitting in the fourth row and went down to join him.

"Now I recognize you," Andrew said. "I've talked to the producer, and he remembers you from the Drewstone days; he says he'll give you a tryout."

Inshroin sat down.

"Where did you go after you left Hollywood?" Andrew asked.

"I traveled all over the world. I've dined off monkey, and drunk ant beer. I've ridden through India on a horse and lived with gurus. But the most amazing place I discovered was Texas. It was just as you once described it to me. Americanism isn't recognized in a quiet way down there. You have to shout about it and roar like a bull. In Austin I couldn't walk down the street unless I was wearing the star-spangled banner, and slapping it in the face of everybody I met."

"It's very important to be patriotic these days," said Andrew.

"I agree, but you don't need to shoot off a whole battery of guns to call your dog when a whistle will do just as well. Drewstone was always excessive like that. Have you heard anything about him recently?"

"I read in *Variety* he's producing a lot of novelty films with colored actors," said Andrew. "Apparently it's a very lucrative market these days."

The director appeared on the stage, and after shooing away the dancing girls, he pulled up a chair and sat down.

"Okay," said the director to the first hopeful, "what can you do?"

"Play the violin."

"What are you doing at the moment?"

"Playing the violin at a restaurant."

"What do you want to do with us?"

"Play the violin."

"What salary do you want?"

"Anything."

"What do you mean?"

"I mean I want to play the violin, and I'll take any salary you want to give me."

"Okay, I'll arrange for you to see our musical director. *Next!*"

A girl walked into the center of the stage, and said, "I'm absolutely and profoundly stagestruck. If you give me a chance you'll be signing up the finest girl on God's planet."

"Will I? And if you wanted to be a journalist, would you say you were paragraph-struck? Would you say you were court-struck if you wanted to become a lawyer?"

"No sir."

"Well, don't use a silly expression like stagestruck. Any experience?"

"Not acting on the stage. But I have a beautifully decorated home, and all my friends tell me I'm so artistic I should try to go on the stage. I'd like to sing a song for you."

The director sighed. "Go on then."

"I was going to sing 'A Little Jappy Soldier,' then I thought I'd do 'How ya feelin'?' but I've finally decided on 'Oh Blackbird.' She gave a discreet little cough, and began:

> "Oh blackbird, what a boy you are,
> How you do go it!
> Blowing you bugle to that one sweet star
> How you do blow it!"

When she reached the final high note, the girl went up on tiptoe and squawked loudly.

"Incredible," said the director. "Would you mind doing me a small favor, dear?"

"Anything."

"Speak the words of the song."

The girl did so.

"Yes, that's better. Now just one more time, please, and do it a little slower." She did so, wondering.

"Fine," said the director. "Now you've had your moment of glory. Get off the stage, and don't bring your silly voice back here again. *Next!*"

Two men carried an enormous dog kennel onto the stage, put it down, and walked off. The director got up and walked around it slowly. There was a creaking noise, then a little door opened in the roof, and a long white arm shot out, holding an apple. The director took it and began munching. The front door opened, and a girl's face peeped out.

"I'm Pert Onslow," she said. "Can I come out, hmmmmm-mmmm? May I please, hmmmmmmmmmmmmmm?"

"Show me what you do."

As she stood in front of the kennel, she presented a letter of recommendation from an agent. The director read it, then glanced back at the girl.

"You're a singer are you? Okay, sing."

> "I'm a girl who's far too wise
> To form those—"

"Stop!"

The director went over to the girl and undid the top button of her shirt. "How do you expect to sing trussed up like that?"

She began again:

> "I'm a girl who's far too wise
> To form those long term ties,
> I'll dance and laugh forever
> And suffer propriety—never."

The song went on and was about marriage passing away. Apparently it would first leave the church, then drop into the crypt, and finally be swept into the abyss.

"We'll use you," said the director. "Novelty number. Keep this letter of recommendation as a souvenir. It tells me not to bother with you. The agent only sent you along because you were nagging him for a job. *Next!*"

A man walked on with a music stand and a trombone. He set things up, opened his sheet at the first page, put the trombone to his lips . . . and made a noise like a foghorn. The noise was repeated and sounded like a distress signal from a ship lost at sea.

"Just a minute," said the director. "Before you cram that pipe down your throat again, what do you think you're doing?"

The man grinned sheepishly. "Auditioning for a band. You will be having one?"

"I may be, but why are you making that din? Don't you like what you're playing?"

"It's not that. I just don't like music."

"Then why waste my time? *Next.*"

"Does that mean I can't play in the band?"

"Not if you're going to play like that."

"Not ever?"

"No, not with me you can't. No! *Next!*"

"Don't repeat yourself," said the man fiddling with his valves.

"I will if you won't listen to me. No you can't play in the band. Do I make myself clear? *No! Next!*"

The man smiled. "By the time you've said the last no, I've forgotten what the first no was all about."

"Have you? Then I'll give you one big *no* to cover all the others. No you can't play in the band. *No! No! No!*"

The trombone player pulled a handkerchief of crimson silk out of a pocket and blew his nose loudly. He then looked at the contents of the silk as if it were a threatening letter, glanced back at the director and said, "No what?" Then he swayed slightly.

"Are you drunk?" asked the director.

"I had a few beers before I arrived."

"Perhaps that's what affected your playing?"

"Nope, I always play like that."

"Well, if you ever decide to audition again, though God knows why you should want to, sober up. It might make a difference."

"Sober up? It's easy for rich people like you to talk that way. Do you have any idea how much it cost me to get like this? I won't be able to afford to get this drunk again for years. I want it to last."

The man was led away by the two men who had carried the kennel on.

The director came to the footlights and peered out into the theater.

"Mr. Inshroin, do you want to come up and do something?"

Inshroin stood up.

"Now?"

"Now."

"God, I feel paralyzed, do . . ."

"Body?"

"Emotions."

"All right, we'll try Miss Armitage. Miss Armitage."

When Lucy arrived on stage, the director got up and shook hands.

"It's very good of you to offer your services like this, Miss

Armitage. The work will be hard, and the money is a pittance, but it's probably the most exciting thing that's ever happened to the American stage."

"That's why I want to be part of it."

"What do you want to do for us?"

"I thought I'd do something from *Romeo and Juliet*, and then *Peter Pan*."

Lucy began to perform. As the scene developed, her eyes sank back and ringed themselves with darkness; the skull sharpened. She looked like a woman at bay, her fingers cut through the air like claws. When she had completed the Shakespeare, she turned to the Barrie.

"I'll teach you Wendy. I'll show you how to jump on the wind's back, and then away we go—and if there are more winds than one they toss you about in the sky—they fling you miles and miles—but you always fall soft onto another wind—and sometimes you go crashing through the tops of trees, scaring the owls—and if you meet a boy's kite in the air, you shove your feet through it. The stars are giving a party tonight. Oh Wendy, when you are sleeping in your silly bed, you might be flying about with me saying funny things to the stars. What was that? That was the west wind whistling to me. It is waiting outside to take me back."

When she finished, everybody applauded.

"Now you, Mr. Inshroin."

The actor came up on stage and shook hands with the director.

"Forgive me," he said, "I haven't been on stage for a long time, and suddenly feel very shy."

"Don't be stupid," said Lucy. "Shyness is just ego multiplied by itself."

The director looked nervously from one to the other. "Lucy Armitage, this is Phillip Inshroin."

"We know each other from a long way back," said Lucy.

Inshroin drew himself together, walked to center stage, and bowed.

"Good morning, ladies and gentlemen. My name is Phillip Inshroin. I'm an actor. Yes I can describe myself as such. One day I'm Othello, then later a Latin lover in Rome or Paris. I'm everybody, anybody, nobody. I command, I obey, I starve, I

236

feast, I love. A mortal man, a glutton for ale and wenches. My personality is made up from a jumble of contradictions—a puffball of talent, a rock of stability in a sea of trouble."

"Okay, now give us something from Hamlet."

"Why don't you relax into it," called Andrew. "You haven't had any time for a rehearsal. Tell us something about Mr. Drewstone."

Inshroin felt on firmer ground at once.

"What can I say about that genius Mr. Drewstone? He has a build and carriage that come across as something between a cowboy and a US marine. Long and lean, yet tough and soldierly. He is often photographed, like Herr Hitler, with his hands crossed over his groin. This is because his testicles have wings and might take flight in front of the camera.

"There is nothing chichi about the fella, he just wades in and takes pics. The man's a steam engine in pants. He swears a lot in public though seldom in the presence of ladies. This is because in his very depths he's as sensitive as a great violinist.

"An interesting thing that most people don't know is that Mr. Drewstone has hypersensitive skin, and he can't stand being touched. If someone walks up and pats his bottom in a friendly way, that person will get a smack in the kisser. The Chief can't help his quicksilver reflexes; he's swinging before he knows what he's doing. Touch the genius and *socko!* . . . Good, that feels better, now I'll do something from *Hamlet*. Could I have a spotlight please, and will you ask the operator to concentrate on my hands?"

Lucy laughed. "Which finger?" she asked.

Inshroin glowered at her.

When the spot came on, and the actor was settled into the middle of the pool of light, he began: " 'To be or not to be, that is . . .' "

His performance was interrupted by the sound of crashing buckets and screams of laughter from the back of the theater.

"Ladies!" called Inshroin.

There was no reply. Seats were lifted and thrown down.

"Cleaning ladies!"

There was immediate dead silence, and all the women looked toward the actor.

"Are you talking to us?" one of them asked.

"I have that honor. Will you ladies do me a great favor?"

"What?"

"Will you put down your cleaning implements, each take a seat, put your mops across your knees, and listen to me recite a speech from *Hamlet?*"

When all the women were seated, Inshroin said, "Thank you, ladies, and if my performance moves you, please don't restrain the tears."

After he'd finished, nobody said anything at first.

"What do you ladies think?" Inshroin called.

"Terrible!"

"I see, and what do you know about acting, may I ask?"

"Nothing. We don't lay eggs either, but we know the difference between a good and a bad one."

"And what does the director think?"

"I can hear that you knew how to do it once."

Lucy came over holding out a pencil and sheet of paper. "Will you give me your autograph?"

Inshroin signed.

Lucy looked at it closely, turned it upside down, then back the right way. "Oh, yes you can," she said.

"Can what?"

"I watched you act, and wondered if you could write."

"Are you prepared to do a lot of rehearsing?" asked the director.

"Day and night."

"You'd probably be a big crowd draw. I should think you still have fans. What salary do you want?"

"What will you offer?"

"Hundred a week."

"That's an insult. I could borrow more than that."

"Hundred and fifty."

"You got me. There must be a four-sided something in the house on which we can sign a contract. Bring it out and I'll sign up."

"I do signings at midday. I hope you realize you are joining a *theater* group. I don't like any individual stars in this organization, and the government isn't going to sponsor a star system. Our function is to bring theater to the people. If I see or hear of a head trying to push in front of the others, I'll give it a crack. Remember, Rembrandt never thought his work would be improved by putting the names of the models on his canvas."

Inshroin, Andrew, and Lucy went across the road to a bar after the contract signing. Outside, the line of people had dwindled, and the black woman orator had gone. Lucy stopped to sign an autograph, but nobody seemed to recognize Inshroin.

"Out of the public eye for a few years, and they forget you," he said.

Next door to the bar was a book shop and its window was full of popular psychology books. Inshroin stopped to look at the titles. On the left was a pile called, *Are You Considering Psychiatry?* On the other side was another pile entitled, *What Psychiatry Can Do For You.* In the middle of the display was an avalanche of *Neurotic Personalities of Our Time.* A sign taped to the window declared:

> Everybody in America wants to improve their lives, but only too often, the social system being what it is, people will never have the faintest chance of attaining that goal. The result will be a personal neurosis. Come in and buy a book on how to handle it. AMBITION MINUS REALITY = NEUROSIS.

Inside the bar there was so much smoke that Inshroin couldn't see for a moment. Newspaper readers were bent into the pages trying to see the print. Some of the men and women who had been auditioning were also sitting drinking and chatting.

"I haven't been in a place like this for years," said Inshroin, looking around and sniffing. "It brings back old memories. I used to swing on those bar stools with the assurance of a Chinese emperor."

The three of them sat down in a cubicle vacated by a man who went out muttering, "The booze in this joint is liquid poison ivy, liquipois'nivy, liquipois'nivy." A waitress came over to take the order.

"Maud!" said Lucy. "You've changed bars, it's nice to see you."

"Hello, Miss Armitage. It's got more class than that other old dump. I can wear what I want, and I haven't been told off once about my hairstyle. See, I became Jean Harlow last week."

"What are you going to have?" asked Andrew.

"I'll have a Manhattan," said Lucy.

"And I'll have a Scotch," said Inshroin.

"After your show in there, I don't think you deserve one," said Lucy.

"After the performance I put on in there I deserve a dozen, but I'll start with one, Miss."

The waitress glanced at Inshroin as she wrote down the order. For an instant there was a flicker of recognition on her face, then it vanished.

While they waited for the drinks, Inshroin glanced around the bar, then out the window. Across the street at the theater, a large old-fashioned convertible pulled up. It was chauffeur-driven and contained three passengers, a middle-aged man and woman, and a large stuffed gorilla smartly dressed in a man's tweed suit. Inshroin watched the two humans climb out, and disappear into the theater carrying the ape between them.

The drinks arrived, and as he sipped, Inshroin looked at Lucy over the top of his glass.

"Why have you offered your services to the project?" he asked. "You're certainly not out of work."

Lucy smiled. "I need a real change in my life at the moment. I've been playing the same roles for too long, and it's affecting me personally. Every day I'm getting bitchier and more petty. I'm starting to forget that as a woman I'm supposed to possess a finer perception of life's subtleties. I thought a turn on the road would buck me up."

A column of men passed outside carrying placards. Lucy sighed and shook her head. "Thousands of men who didn't die in the trenches are now dying in the gutter, and after all the promises they were given. The way of the world seems to be depression, boom, crisis after crisis, then war."

"I suppose that's why some people think there should be a revolution," said Inshroin.

"You have to forget how to think in a revolution," Lucy said.

A man staggered into the bar and knocked against a girl who was sitting talking to a middle-aged man.

"Sorry," he murmured.

The girl glanced over her shoulder. "That's all right, sweetie-pie. Will you buy me a glass of champagne; there'll be something nice in it for you?"

"I will, I will," replied the man hicupping. "I *will*."

The girl shrugged her shoulders. "Yes, I've heard that one before, darling."

The man leaned across the girl's lap and spoke to the barman, who listened then nodded. The newcomer lurched across and sat at a table near Lucy. He remained silent for a few seconds, and then, because Inshroin grinned at him, leaned over and said, "I'm waiting for a phone call. I'm going to kill a man in a few minutes."

Inshroin raised his eyebrows. "Are you?"

"Nothing to worry about, though," said the man glancing at this watch. "I'm a judge, and I've just condemned a man to death; pretty soon he'll be taking his last walk. I've spent the whole morning walking around and wondering if I made the right decision. I'm not God. Waiting for that phone call fills me with dread. The bastards make me responsible right up to the moment when they throw the goddamn switch, and the kid takes the hot squat. I have to call them wherever I am and leave a number where I can be got hold of. Jesus, I hate this part of the job."

The waitress brought over a dry martini and put it in front of him. He sat twiddling his thumbs, with his head drooping down onto his chest.

A spotlight came on, picking out a girl in a tight-fitting silver dress who was leaning on a piano. There was a spattering of applause, which she acknowledged with a nod of her head. Her accompanist, a man with huge shoulders and a cigarette in the corner of his mouth, began to pick out a tune, and after three or four bars, the singer sucked in her breath. Her dress followed the contractions and expansions of her body. It became so tight, the rigging that held her head to the mast of her body could be traced. A windpipe resting in a cat's cradle of veins, tendons, and backbones. She gave a clear ringing upper note, dropped down a bit, then cushioned off into a spiritual treble. The note lifted and stretched out into a thin wail as crystal as a thread of boiling sugar. It was a long coaxing sound, strong enough to pull the moon above the tops of the skyscrapers.

The waitress came over and tapped the judge on the shoulder.

He woke with a start. "Ladies and gentlemen of the jury, it is up to you to decide. If you believe the evidence presented by the prosecution, you must come to the conclusion . . ."

He quickly recovered, thanked the waitress, then threaded his way through the smoke to a phone. The singer reached out for him as he passed.

"I think we should get back over the road, and see what's been planned for us," said Andrew.

The street was now completely deserted of auditioners. As the trio crossed the road, the door of the theater was violently thrown open, and the man who had helped carry the stuffed ape appeared at the door. He looked distraught. The woman was nowhere in sight, but the man was still holding the ape. He ran down the steps, tossed the animal into the back of his car, then ran over to the bookstore. He looked at the selection of titles in the window, then disappeared inside. A bell tinkled gently, then died away.

Inshroin was scheduled to be sent to Arkansas with a troupe that included Lucy, who was put in charge. Andrew was sent to Chicago. The renewal of the two actors' acquaintanceship had lasted three hours.

Sinclair Lewis's anti-Fascist play, *It Can't Happen Here*, opened simultaneously in twenty-one theaters in seventeen cities on the night of October 27, 1936. Up to opening night the newspapers of America had given 78,000 lines of pro and con comment to the play.

The *Hollywood Citizen News* said:

> Where the motion picture feared to tread, the Federal Theatre tomorrow night will step boldly to the limelight of a controversial issue . . . The project has been the target of criticism from sources holding that the play will antagonize sympathizers of the Hitler and Mussolini regimes.

Three hours after the performance telegrams were still coming in from all over the country.

Bridgeport: RECEPTION SPLENDID. Cleveland: RESPONSIVE AUDIENCE. APPLAUSE AFTER FIRST ACT TREMENDOUS. Miami: AUDIENCE DEEPLY INTERESTED. ENTHUSIASTIC AT CURTAIN. Detroit: AUDIENCE ENTHUSIASM MOUNTING. Tacoma: RECORD

CROWD TAKES PERFORMANCE BIG. Boston: RECEPTION MAGNIFI-
CENT PLAY WILL BE POPULAR SUCCESS.

In English, Yiddish, and Spanish, in cities, towns, and villages, before audiences of every conceivable type, *It Can't Happen Here* played with the Federal Theatre for 260 weeks, or the equivalent of five years.

When John Houseman and Orson Welles took a black company into Harlem, drums beat and people clogged the streets. They followed the scarlet and gold banners, each of which bore the device MACBETH BY WM. SHAKESPEARE. Flash of police holding back the crowds. Flash of newsmen grinding their cameras. African drumming follows Lady Macbeth walking down the center of the street to the theater. Flash of headlines in the press. EMPEROR JONES GONE BEAUTIFULLY MAD! BLACK MALE WITCHES STRIPPED TO THE WAIST AGAINST THE WORLD'S LARGEST SKELETON ARCH! A TRAGEDY OF BLACK AMBITION IN A GREEN JUNGLE SHOT WITH SUCH LIGHTS FROM BOTH HEAVEN AND HELL AS NO OTHER STAGE HAS SEEN! BLACK ACTORS SUPERB!

After the first night in New York, the production went on tour to one hundred thousand people in Hartford, Chicago, Detroit, Indianapolis, Cleveland.

In Dallas, when the mayor met the manager of the town's main theater after the show, he said, "You've got a ten-foot high picture of a bald guy out in the foyer, who is it?"

"It's Shakespeare."

"Shake-hell, what's he done for this town? Take him down and put me up!"

We appear to be in a tree-filled glade somewhere in the deep South. Under the bough of a weeping willow is a beautiful ivy-covered cottage, around which white Union soldiers are happily building a veranda. Three little black girls are playing in a pumpkin patch. Their hair has been lacquered, combed up straight and stiff from their heads, then tied with white bows. A middle-aged black man is standing at the wicker gate of this little property. He is being questioned by a Northern cavalry officer on horseback. In the background fifty or so black people are picking cotton and singing plaintively.

The scene is being filmed. The Chief is sitting in a canvas-backed chair with a megaphone on his knees. To his left is a camp table with a huge box of chocolates and a bottle of champagne on it. Mrs. West is sitting at one side of the table, and a woman reporter at the other.

"Take two!" called Drewstone through the megaphone. "And don't forget, John Boy, look scared, keeping rolling your eyes!"

The Northern cavalry officer steadied his horse, then said to the black man, "How many men did the captain have with him when he left?"

"Niggers mars'r?"

"No, the general number, black and white."

"'Bout sixty hundred t'housand million, I 'spec's."

"What! Are you sure you aren't mistaken?"

"Y's mars'r."

"*Keep rolling your eyes!*" called the Chief to the black man. "*Look scared!*"

"How long were you a slave here?" asked the cavalry officer.

"Oh t'ree, two, sixty days."

"You mean years, don't you?"

"Y's mars'r."

"Did the captain treat you with great cruelty?"

"Oh yas sah! Cap'an treat men fust rate!"

"He's perfect for the role," said Mrs. West to the reporter. "I picked him out of a line of fifty; I recognized his talent the moment I heard him speaking." She bit into a chocolate. "Read back what we've written so far."

The other woman turned the sheets of her pad back three pages. "Drewstone Films is in the lead for providing drama and comedy with colored actors. Their plaintive crooning and natural humor, wide smiles, and brisk tapping provide unique opportunities for film novelty. Colored actors perform with verve and abandon and take it all very seriously. The Drewstone Company has found that an all-colored cast is acceptable in any locality. Only when the casts are mixed (unless the role played by the negro is a servant or a comic figure) is prejudice aroused. What does movie success do to them? Plenty! They take it large, Ah says they does! The ebony heroes swagger around talking with grandiloquent vagueness about this high white world they're 'cottonin' up to.' Mrs. West is the prime mover behind the Drewstone drive to employ colored actors, and ebony films are proving to be immensely popular at the box office. Mrs. West says, 'My Southern background makes it easy for me to get on "wid de down home folks." I notice a difference in attitude the moment I open my mouth. They say with a broad grin, "Oh, you's a Suthun lady, yassum!" But I know they wonder why their own colored help is more deferential to me than to themselves. Down in cotton land all the colored people are loyal with a love that no white domestic seems capable of giving. It is interesting that . . .' "

The reporter glanced up then stopped reading. "Look, John Boy has finished his scene. Could I ask him a couple of questions?"

Mrs. West waved her arm in the air, "John Boy, will you come here a minute."

The black man walked over and stood between the two women, grinning, rolling his eyes, and twisting a cap between his fingers.

"John Boy, this is a reporter from *Hollywood Bandbox*. She's writing an article on colored actors, and she'd like to ask you some questions."

"Y'sm."

"How do you do," said the reporter. "I've got most of the information I need, but I was wondering if you think all the money you're earning will have a bad effect on you?"

"No ma'am. God kin tak care o' me. Ah don't worry 'bout nuthin'. I'm jes' natchully tired. Mah feet hurts fierce."

"Do you have any trouble learning the parts? I suppose you can read?"

"I kin jist, as long as de words ain't too big. We cullud folk goes bad whin we go high-falutin' wid de big words—I stays clear o' de big words. But I knows drama, mah life ain't nuthin' else but!"

"Charming, absolutely charming. What were you doing before you became a star, Mr. Boy?"

"Fust I was in France wid de marines, den I come home an' wukked in a hospital for rich white soljahs dat had shot deselves in de toenail to git out o' goin' to de war."

Inshroin was sitting in the empty bar at Grand Central Station. It was eleven o'clock in the morning.

The rest of Inshroin's troupe had gone on ahead, while he remained in New York to sort out the back taxes that hadn't been paid when he left the country. For two days he had struggled with a problem that the Drewstone accountants had always dealt with before. Finally he had added together his income over five years, divided by ten (his lucky number), completed everything with a couple of financial somersaults of his own invention, and then wrote out a check. He sent a note with the money:

> Please find enclosed a check for back taxes. As a loyal American I shall pay this time, but in future the Government must not look upon me as a permanent source of income.

A waitress wandered over to Inshroin's table. "Good morning," he said. "It's a lovely day."

"Yes it is, and it was the same yesterday. My name is Mary and I know I'm a little peach and have pretty blue eyes, and I've been here quite a while, and yes, I do like the job, and I don't think I'm too nice a girl to be working in a place like this. My wages with tips are pretty good, and I don't know if there's a show or movie on in town, and I don't want to go to Hollywood to become a star."

"Neither do I, and I used to work there."

"What as?"

"An actor with Drewstone Films."

"I don't recognize you."

"It's been six years."

"That's before my time."

"How old are you?"

"Eighteen."

"Yes, it would be; the turnover is pretty fast. I'll have a triple Scotch on the rocks."

When the girl returned with the drink, she watched him taking his first sip. "What are you doing now?" she asked.

"I've been abroad for a while, but I've just gone on the road with the Federal Theatre."

A train whistled loudly, and he looked up with a start.

"What's the matter?" asked the waitress. "You've gone as white as a sheet."

"It's nothing. I thought I heard *Variety* give a hysterical scream of laughter at one of my performances." He drained his glass and asked for another.

The waitress put her hand on her hip. "You really like the stuff, don't you?"

"I do, that's because I'm a professional alcoholic. Do you know what alcoholism is? I'll tell you. It's either a physical allergy coupled with a mental obsession or a physical idiosyncrasy coupled with a psychological compulsion, and I can't remember which one applies to me."

"Whatever it is," said the waitress, "it adds up to loser."

Inshroin glanced at his watch.

"Time for my train."

He paid for his drink and walked over to the platform his train was leaving from. He made his way through the groups of passengers, found an open door, threw his bag up, and climbed in after it. Steam poured out from under his feet, as the porter waved a flag in the air.

"Arl-a-board," he called. "Arl-a-board."

Inshroin leaned against the window trying to catch his breath. Sweat trickled down his forehead, and his back ached. The conductor appeared, touched his cap and said, "Can I have your ticket please, sir?"

Inshroin sighed. "I suppose so, but I fail to understand why an employee of the railroad cannot travel free."

"Very funny," said the conductor. He clipped the little square of cardboard, then glanced down.

"Where's the ticket for the bag?"

Inshroin also looked down. "What bag?"

"The bag between your legs."

"I didn't get one."

"It's extra; you'll have to pay me now."

"How much?"

"Six dollars."

"Daylight robbery," said Inshroin. "I wouldn't give you ten cents."

"If you don't pay for it, I'll have to put it over the side."

"I'm not paying six dollars."

The conductor opened the door and dropped the bag out onto the platform, then he looked up at Inshroin and smirked.

"Now what are you going to do?"

"Nothing."

"I put your bag off and you do nothing?"

"It wasn't my bag; mine's over there."

247

"Why in hell didn't you say?"

"You didn't ask."

As the train began to pull away, a huge man appeared and demanded to know what had happened to his bag. People on the platform watched the train shudder to a halt about a hundred yards up the line. The conductor climbed down, walked back to the bag, lifted it up and staggered to the rear of the train with it. Inshroin and the owner leaned out of the window watching his progress.

Inshroin stepped down from the train at a small Southern station and looked around. He wore a thin brown overcoat, and a trilby hat was pulled low over his eyes. The train left, enveloping the newcomer in a cloud of steam. Within a minute all was silent once again. At the end of the platform, the stationmaster was on top of a ladder fixing an overhanging light. He fiddled with the bulb but all the time kept an eye on Inshroin. The actor approached and stopped at the foot of the ladder.

"Can you tell me what stop this is? I'm not sure I got off where I was supposed to."

The man didn't look down but continued fiddling with the fixture.

"Don't know anything about it," he said.

"You don't know what town this is?"

"Can't you tell I'm busy."

"Do you happen to know what country this is?"

"Never had the time to find out."

"You're the very man I've been looking for for a year."

"Why?"

"We need you to come to Washington, and run for President. A man of your intellect should do very well."

The man at the top of the ladder sighed, gave the bulb a tap, then slowly climbed down to the ground. When he got to the bottom, he turned to Inshroin, and looked him up and down.

"Young man, let me say at once, if you have come down here to embroil me in the corruption of Washington, I have to say, 'No sir! go elsewhere.' Go to the sycophants who surround those in power; they want the job, I do not. I wish to remain happy and content, a citizen aloof from the corruption rampant in the nation's capital. You say you have been looking for me for a long time; well, you have found me, and all I can say is, 'Go away sir, I am not your man.' " He then indulged in a strange quirk of shutting his eyes very tight, then opening them very wide.

Inshroin laughed. "Good, very good, and I'm not a political agent, I'm supposed to be in Huntsville for a theatrical engagement; I fell asleep on the train."

"I don't mind a little deception," said the stationmaster. "I've indulged in a little deception myself. I'm not really an employee of the railroad. I run the theater in town. Miss Armitage told me you were coming in on the train, and I wanted to look at you in the raw, so to speak. Bob Ganster's the name."

"How do you do. Has everybody else arrived?"

"Everything down to the performing fleas. Nothing like this has happened to Huntsville for fifteen years, the town's on fire with anticipation. We've also got a rival."

"What's a rival?"

"This is cotton country, and all the sharecroppers, black and white, are on strike for a minimum wage. That communist evangelist Claude Williams is leading it, and he's due in town to speak to the sharecroppers."

"So, the people's theater is straight in the front line, is it?"

"We stay out of politics," said the theater owner. "The government's mandate is to bring theater not politics to the people. Come on, I'll walk you part of the way to the hotel. I'm due at the theater in twenty minutes. We're having trouble with the electrics."

The two men walked out of the station straight into a typical southern town. The whole community, top crust, middle, and bottom, contained about three thousand people.

There were stores, a flour mill, three churches, the theater, the doctor's house, an ancient brick courthouse, a school, a jail, and some hotels. In the better part of town, on the outskirts, were large brick and frame houses under big trees. The trees themselves were hung with Spanish moss and surrounded by sunflowers. Somewhere to the east a river wound by and gave some good fishing. Cotton grew strong because the earth was still rich, and the surrounding area once contained big plantations, all closed now, the land divided up and sold.

The street Inshroin looked into was strangely quiet; everything was still except for the movement of a red and white barber's pole. It rotated like a demented peppermint stick, all the stripes going around and around, up and down in an uncanny silence. Some music trickled across to Inshroin from a radio in an upstairs room.

Inshroin and Ganster walked past the bank, which was boarded up, and stopped at the next crossroad.

"I go this way, you go that. Keep going straight, and you'll hit three hotels. Two may be full, but there's another just off the road, about a hundred yards outside town. Lucy and your people are in the first one, the Beacon Arms."

When he was alone, Inshroin stood listening for a few seconds. Above the hardware store a curtain was pulled back, but nobody looked out.

As he walked down the street, it became a little more populated. Men and women, children and dogs, sat on small verandas and watched him go by. Once or twice the actor spoke to someone, but he didn't get a reply. Inshroin stopped outside the Beacon Arms and peered through the window. Inside people sat around in deep leather chairs, reading, the men smoking. Inshroin was about to enter when he felt a tap on his shoulder. He turned around and looked into the large red face of a man in a police uniform with a sheriff's badge. Under his blue shirt a stomach swayed like a large balloon on the end of a string, and seemed to have a life and motion independent of the rest of the body.

"Yes?" said Inshroin.

"Good day, sir. You mustn't think me intrusive by stopping you like this" (his voice was so deep it sounded as if he had swallowed God), "it's just the pleasure we Southerners take in being hospitable and attentive to strangers. Our feelings are in keeping with our state pride and extreme sense of honor, which forbids meanness. My name is Jones, Police Chief Jim Jones, but please be free with me. Just imagine yourself perfectly at home, and I'll show you what hospitality is. In this part of the world we don't go by the system of Mr. So-and-So, so just call me Jim, y'understand me?"

"Thank you, chief, yes I'll remember that."

"Good, now I s'pose you're one of those theater fellas who are down here to put on some drama for us?"

"I am, chief."

"Jim."

"I am, Jim."

"Fine. Now as you've just arrived, I'll take the opportunity to ask you to keep clear of any public gatherings you see. I've told all of your friends the same thing. We're having a spot of trouble with the plantation hands, and there's such an infernal imperfect state of things going on in the world today, I have to be vigilant all the time. I just worry that radical outsiders might come in under whatever guise and cause a stirabout with our own radicals, and we do have a few down here, sir. My job is to see everybody respects Southern traditions, and don't cause any breakdowns in our institutions." He nodded toward the hotel. "I've just been talking to the owner in here sir, and he tells me he's crammed to the rafters, couldn't squeeze another soul in."

Inshroin nudged him in the ribs.

"Can you suggest anywhere else? From the size of your belly, I should say there are some excellent hostelries in town."

The smile disappeared from the sheriff's face, and he stuck his head to within an inch of the actor's.

"Do you think you're good in the theater?"

"Passable."

"Well, just remember this is a star town. Pavlova danced here. She came all the way in a boat from Russia. Our streets were filled with flowers; my predecessor made sure of that when Pavlova came to town."

"We've got some good things worked out. By the time we've finished I expect you'll want to strew flowers in front of us."

The smile reappeared on the sheriff's face. "Good, I'm looking forward to it. Now sir, if you continue further down the road, you'll come to a field. Just beyond the field, set back a bit is Tom Davies's place, he'll be the boy to show you the varieties of Southern hospitality."

"Straight down this road?"

"Straight down."

When Inshroin had walked to the last house before the field, a dog emerged from the alley, sniffed the air, then trotted off in the direction Inshroin was heading. The animal's body was tattered and frayed. It still had ears, but they were serrated like the fronds of a fern. Its tail was cut to half its natural length, while the nose was twisted to an odd angle and hung onto the muzzle by a thread of gristle. The flanks and shoulders were crisscrossed with scars.

Inshroin glanced back to see if the sheriff was still there. He was and had been joined by a man in a black suit. Both of them stood watching Inshroin. "Keep going," called the sheriff, "beyond the field."

Inshroin trudged on. A car passed him throwing up a cloud of dust and disappeared beyond a bend in the road. When he got past the field Inshroin turned left at a sign saying HOTEL that pointed toward a wooded area fifty yards from the road. The actor walked along a brown dirt path surrounded by high yellow grass, until he came to a wall of high trees. At the foot of the one nearest the path was a boulder. On it was written in faded lettering:

> DR. PEPPER'S MEDICINE:
> THAT GUARANTEED
> EFFICIENT CURE
> FOR THE SECRET DISEASE.
> ONE DOLLAR A BOTTLE.

Immediately behind the trees was a three-story dilapidated clapboard building.

The only colors in the area were shades of brown that were thick, light, or textured. The clearing at the back was bordered by the trunks of more trees, all standing, but leafless and dead. Years had passed since they had been cut, and boughs had fallen and were rotting amid a deep carpet of damp vegetation. Beyond them and higher up were younger, growing trees, and a distant view of mountains. An occasional rush of wind swept around the building followed by a dead calm. Inshroin stopped in front of the hotel and stared at a man who was sleeping in a chair on the veranda with a newspaper over his face. A chicken was squatting in the doorway just behind the sleeper.

Inshroin put down his bag and wiped his forehead. "Good evening, my friend."

"Who's yer friend?" said the man without removing the paper. "'Pears to me we've never met before."

"Just a figure of speech," said Inshroin. "I was told by the sheriff that you'd have a room. All the other places are full," he added.

252

The man pulled the paper off his face, and looked at the actor. "You with this the-ater group that's come to town?"

"From your tone, I gather you don't like the theater?"

"Can't say, don't know enough about it, but I reckon it's a damn queer way of earnin' a livin'."

"Of course it's damn queer," said Inshroin. "It's a damn queer world we live in. It's two-thirds water, and we humans are animals born without gills."

The owner got up, folded the newspaper, and put it on his chair. "I've got a room which is the best in the county. It's just gone vacant; I'll show you."

As the man got to the front door, he kicked out at the chicken, which fluttered away with a squawk.

"Shoo, you pesterin' torment. May the eggs o' your breed be destroyed. I'll make sure the room's cleared out," said the owner. "Why don't you go into the bar and have a drink?"

"Good idea," said Inshroin. "I think it's about time I took an underjawful of a fighting something."

He went into the bar through a swing door as the owner disappeared upstairs. After he'd rung the bell twice, a tall gangly youth appeared through a small opening between the shelves and stood grinning at the actor.

"What'll it be?" he asked.

"Everything and anything you put in front of me. Got any good Scotch?"

"Nope."

"Rum?"

"Nope."

"Gin?"

"Nope."

"Beer?"

"Golly blue, we will soon! Our long-lost ice wagon has just arrived, and the beer's coolin' now."

"Then give me a glass of water; I suppose you've got plenty of that on tap?"

"We do, but you said you wanted a good Scotch. I've got some local brewed whusky."

"I'll try anything once. What's your name, by the way?"

"Hess."

"Well, Hess, give me a double."

Inshroin took a sip, then put down the glass with a grimace.

"Jesus, it tastes like raw sewage. Give me that glass of water, I need it to put out the fire!"

Hess gave Inshroin the water and watched him as he drank it.

"You with this theater group?" he asked.

"I won't be for long if I drink any more of this stuff. Yes, I am for the time being. You like the theater?"

"Naw, I reckon if I'd studied it since I was born I might, but I reckon it's too late now. I like flickers."

"I do too, but that doesn't stop me liking the theater. You must come along and try us out." He drained his glass, put it down on the bartop, and asked where the bathroom was.

"Follow me," said Hess.

He led the way out of the bar, around into the dining room. They went through another door, and walked along a dimly lit passage to a door at the back. Hess opened it, and stood aside to let the actor through. Inshroin gazed out into the tree-filled landscape and a fringe of mountains beyond.

"Where's the toilet?" he asked.

Hess gave a wide sweep of his arm. "Anywhere between me and them thar hills."

Inshroin walked over to a clump of bushes and urinated. As he was doing up his fly, a window was opened on the first floor and the owner leaned out.

"Mister, why don't you come upstairs an' I'll show you yer room."

When he got upstairs, Inshroin was shown into a room twelve feet by eight, which contained a single bed, a bedside table, a chair, and a bare light hanging from a cord in the middle of the ceiling. Over the bed were two embroidered homilies in wooden frames:

ALL OUR ROOMS ARE BULLET PROOF.

NO SWEARING IN BED.
IT'S BAD MANNERS.
NUFF SAID? GOOD.

"All the bedlinen's been changed," said the owner, "and dinner is at eight. Be on time if you want to eat."

After a dinner of ham and eggs Inshroin took a bottle of Hess's Scotch up to his bedroom, slowly undressed, and got into bed. He lay gazing up at the ceiling for half an hour without moving. Suddenly he threw back the blankets, swung his legs over the side, and sat up. He should have put in an appearance at the theater; he should have gone down. Inshroin took a drink from the bottle, and as he put it down on the table, he noticed a Bible sticking out from under the bed. He picked it up and, laying the volume across his knees, opened the cover.

THIS SACRED WORK IS THE PROPERTY OF THE KISMET FOREDOOMISTS. NOTE TO SALESMEN:

Enter town and call at the corner store. Make a small purchase, and engage the owner in conversation, thus getting into his confidence. Wait until children arrive, then as they are choosing their candy, open the Bible as if by accident at the picture showing our Lord blessing the children.

By the time Inshroin fell asleep, the bottle of whisky was empty.

Inshroin woke up around eight the following morning to find a girl and a boy in the room. The girl was standing in front of the mirror combing her hair, while the boy (of excruciating ugliness) sat at the foot of the bed grimly excavating his left nostril. The two males stared at each other for a few seconds, then Inshroin said: "Need any help?"

"Nope, I 'spect yur finger's too small."

"Didn't you know it's rude to pick your nose?"

"I'll put it back fur a dime."

Inshroin directed his attention to the girl and smiled. She stared back at him from the mirror.

"Have a good sleep?" she asked.

"A vast quantity. I suppose I should get up."

"Jist as you please."

"Is it late?"

"'Pends what you call late."

"Is everybody up?"

"Nope, you ain't." She turned around. "Are you a star?"

"Depends what you call a star."

"Anybody I've heard of."

"I'm Phillip Inshroin."

The girl stopped the combing, turned and peered closer.

"You ain't what I expected."

"But you won't stop seeing my films and shows?"

The owner appeared in the doorway.

"How do you do," said Inshroin.

"Pert, yourself?"

"Fine."

"Sleep well?"

"To a point. Have you got a corkscrew?"

"It's a bit early for drinks."

"That's not it. I want to dig out a piece of your very hard pillow that's worked its way into my ear."

The owner said, "I see you've met my son and Mrs. Kincaide's daughter. She wants to get into the moving pictures."

"I met Mrs. Kincaide last night," said Inshroin. "She was serving me dinner."

The owner gazed fondly at his son.

"My wife would've been proud o' him."

"Where is she?"

"In the cemetery." He tapped the boy on the head, causing him to jab his finger farther up his nostril and make his eyes water. "This child has more bright points than a new saw; everything he does he does well."

"Except pick his nose," said Inshroin. "He does that with a kind of vulgar ostentation."

The owner suddenly grabbed his son by the chin, turned his head from side to side, and glanced open-mouthed between the boy and Inshroin. "Why," he said, "I should say the child is the spittin' image of you!"

"How do you make that out?" asked Inshroin. "Does my nose look like a boiled lobster claw? Do my eyes resemble the head of a screw? Does my scalp come right down to the bridge of my nose, and my upper jaw rest on my shoulders? Of course not."

The owner sighed. "Then you wouldn't consider taking him in fur the theater?"

"I wouldn't advise it; it's a chancy trade."

"I had been plannin' on 'prenticin' the boy out fur the law."

"Much safer, but he's a bit young, isn't he," said Inshroin. "He can't be more than eight."

"Seven years, six months, but he'll be very fitted fur the law. When he were five he'd lie like all of creation. When he got to be six he was as sassy as any critter could be. And this year I discovered he'd steal anythin' he could lay his hands on."

"Should go far."

"You say-ed it, stranger!" The man scratched his chin, then abruptly changed the subject.

"Would you let yer daughter marry a niggrah?" he asked.

"I haven't got one."

"Well, that just goes to show. I believe the niggrah is a very respectable race of people, and don't want to come into our houses as equals. There'll be plenty of time fur equality when we go to Heaven. God didn't intend that we should have equality here on earth. When Jesus talked about coming into our houses, he didn't mean our material house, he meant our hearts. There's a lot of communist talk goin' on about sharin' and givin' things away to yer brothers. If everything in this world were free, what could we look forward to in the next?"

"You should be in the legal profession, not your son," said Inshroin as he started to get out of bed. As soon as his legs appeared from under the sheets, the girl disappeared from the room. "By the way," he said, "after I turned the lights off last night, a lot of animals, large animals, started jumping around on the floor."

"You don't like animals, mister?"

"In their proper place."

"I like to think yer room is their proper place. They come every night, but they're perfectly harmless."

"That's good to know. What are they?"

"Rats."

"Rats?"

"Rats from the fields."

"I see," said Inshroin. "There are also some big leggy things that climbed up the walls."

"They're stinkbugs."

"Can't you kill them?"

"If we killed them they'd stink, that's why they're called stinkbugs."

"I really need a dog with me at night, don't I?"

The owner shook his head slowly. "A dog wouldn't help much. The rats are real fast and vicious, and the stinkbugs fly."

FROM ITS INCEPTION UNTIL THE OUTBREAK OF THE SECOND WORLD WAR, Hollywood will be a passionate propagandist for the inferiority of the black race. Scores of films will be produced in which blacks are depicted as cowardly fools whose hair stands on end or turns white whenever they suspect danger. The formula never varies: one haunted house, one black person, and a white hero and heroine. The black characters are always stupid, and often verging on the bestial. They are afraid of the dark, of thunderstorms, firearms, animals, and the police.

The most successful film of this type is D. W. Griffith's *The Birth of a Nation*. The film's justification of the Ku Klux Klan will be one factor that enables that organization to enter upon its period of greatest expansion, reaching a total membership of five million by 1937.

THE DINING ROOM WAS EMPTY WHEN INSHROIN WALKED IN. But a smell of fried bacon hung in the air. He walked over to a table by the window and sat down. After a few seconds the swinging doors at the back opened, and Mrs. Kincaide appeared wiping her hands on her apron. She wandered over to Inshroin's table.

"Good morning," said the actor.

Mrs. Kincaide nodded.

"I'll start with some orange juice, then—"

"You're an actor. You'll start with prune juice."

"Yes I see, then I'll have an omelet, and coffee without cream."

Mrs. Kincaide wrote down the order on a pad, then went back into the kitchen. There followed the sound of food being cooked and coffee poured.

Inshroin opened *The Complete Works of William Shakespeare* and went over the first act of *Hamlet*. He was starting on the second act when Mrs. Kincaide returned with breakfast. She put a plate down in front of the actor and stood back as if waiting for a comment.

258

"This is eggs and bacon," said Inshroin. "I asked for an omelet."

"I couldn't spell omelet, but I know how to spell eggs 'n' bacon. Yur also going to be disappointed with the coffee. We don't have coffee without cream, so yur gettin' coffee without milk."

Inshroin picked at the eggs with his fork. "Couldn't you do something about this egg; it's raw and it looks like Jell-O floating in the middle of the bacon."

"I ain't got the time. Treat it lak an ornament and eat around it."

Inshroin concentrated on the rolls and ate in an absent-minded fashion. He sat pulling off little tidbits, crispy corners, flaky bottoms, until they took on the appearance of dismantled wrecks. Twenty minutes passed; he began to feel that he could procrastinate no longer and made up his mind to go down to the theater for his first rehearsal.

He passed Mrs. Kincaide on the way out. "Excellent coffee," he said. "I'll give you a tip that should make it even better. If you want to add the final touch to your perfect beverage, put in the other half of the tweed jacket you used and add a pair of soiled boots diced into pieces an inch square. I think that should help the taste a lot, but won't cut back on the smell of the stuff. Good morning."

"Good fur-nothing," said Mrs. Kincaide.

Inshroin stood in the street looking up at the theater: a small dingy building set between a garage and a bar. A pay booth jutted out into the sidewalk, above which was a sign that read THE LIMIT.

Inshroin walked to the front door and shook it, but it was locked. He was about to walk down the side alley, when he heard footsteps somewhere inside, so he knocked. The footsteps stopped instantly, and he knocked harder. There was the sound of a bolt being drawn back, the door opened six inches on a chain, and a small elderly woman looked up at him.

"Good day," said Inshroin.

"Git."

"Pardon?"

"Git."

"I was wondering if the owner's in?"

"Meander."

"Do what?"

"Meander."

"I'd like to see the owner, is he in?"

"He is. He's in. I'm in. You're out. Vamoose."

"I'm sorry, my old sweetheart," said Inshroin, "but I've come all the way from New York, and I'm supposed to be in a production you're going to put on here."

The door was slammed shut, there was the sound of the bolt being drawn back, then the door opened completely.

"Why didn't you say who you were? I have to keep the door locked, 'cause all the town troublemakers try to break in. I thought I was in for a quiet few years since the place went bust, now this. Nothin' will come of it. I told Mr. Ganster the theater is on the bum. It ain't his fault, he's done his darnedest. He put on a grim upper lip and made a hard fight. But the show is over, and the gold brick of theater is now residin' in the soup." She sighed: "Follow me."

Inshroin followed the woman up some velvet-carpeted stairs, past a Gothic fountain with some dead goldfish floating on the surface of dank green water, through the swinging doors and into the main theater auditorium. The stage was bedlam. A chorus line was dancing, and other small groups were rehearsing their own particular specialty. Sitting in the front row was the owner, who presided over all the chaos. Inshroin walked down to him and was greeted effusively. "It took me a while to find the place," said Inshroin. "It's a funny name to give a theater, 'The Limit.' "

"My father gave it that name," said Ganster. "Years ago when performers traveled all over the South, they used to arrive in town, spend an hour buying up all the insect repellent they could find, then come to pa's office, and stand around shaking their fists in his face and say, 'This place is the limit.' "

Inshroin saw the slogan WE KNOW THE THEATER'S LOUSY, HOW'S THE SHOW? painted on the arch over the stage.

"It's wonderful to have the live theater back again," said the owner trying to talk above the din. "I ran the vaudeville for fifteen years before the flickers came. The gold brick of theater seemed to have gone as far as it could travel and was residing in the soup, until today."

"Your doorkeeper just told me the same thing; let's hope we can revive the live theater."

Ganster smiled and nodded. "Let's hope so. When I closed down I took to the projection business. Thanks to me, you and Olive West came over at the right speed. For a dime folks could sit beside some nice person in the dark and delight in variety. We often watched Mary Pickford in a short frock being wooed in a garden by a huge man with a square jaw and an air of unnecessary determination. Other times we saw Charlie Chaplin being seasick in a scissor chair off Atlantic City."

"Did you close down the movies as well?"

"Had to. The big boys with the Rialto moved in."

Lucy came over smiling. "So you've decided to come to a rehearsal, have you?"

"I'm only looking in to see what the place is like. I don't need to rehearse, it's all come back to me now. I know my part backward."

"From what I saw of you in New York, that's the only way you do know it."

Inshroin looked around. "I should do pretty well here. It's not the best, but it's beautiful in comparison to some places I've worked in."

"Come up on stage," said Lucy. "We'll try something from *Macbeth*."

As soon as Inshroin and Lucy climbed the stairs at the side of the stage, everybody stopped what they were doing and moved to the side to watch.

The opening scene of Act One began, but the lines didn't flow; paralysis descended upon him, making his voice crack and stiffening his movements.

"You're not reflecting the part very well, are you?" said Lucy.

"I'm acting," replied Inshroin; "a back of a spoon reflects."

"Does it? I think I could put on a better performance in my toilet."

"Maybe, but you couldn't squeeze enough people in there to make it a paying proposition."

"Try again."

Inshroin did it again with the same results.

"Can you hear that noise?" asked Lucy.

"What noise?"

"That whirling sound. It must be Shakespeare turning over and over in his grave. Do you know we're on in eight hours, and there are people from all over coming to see us?"

Inshroin went for a train ride. The 12:30 for Tunsala was already in the station when he arrived, and by the time he got a ticket it was beginning to pull away. Inshroin scrambled into the last compartment, dusted himself off, and dropped into a seat. He glanced up, and found himself gazing into the eyes of untempted, Southern, Victorian virtue.

Two women in their mid-sixties sat opposite him. They were suspicion and disapproval personified. Skin tight as a drum was drawn over high cheekbones. Their thin lips were partly hidden by velvety moustaches.

"I love train rides," said Inshroin. "Whenever I'm upset, I always get on a train. Trains mean escape, adventure, and change."

There was a pause: "Did you know this compartment is for ladies?"

"So am I, madam."

All three watched the landscape in silence for a while, then Inshroin took a cigar and lit it.

They entered a tunnel, and the two women shrank into their corner. It became pitch dark, no lights were turned on. A minute passed, then another. There was the sound of a body shifting, a catch of breath, and a sigh. This was followed by a loud sucking, slurping noise, which ended in a long sensuous moan. It was repeated several times. The train burst out of the darkness into the light. The two women were pressed against the window, sitting so close together they seemed to have become one. Inshroin was lying back in his seat, legs stretched out straight in front of him. His trousers were pulled down completely and lay in a bunched up heap around his ankles. He looked across and sighed.

"I don't know which one of you ladies was responsible for that," he said, "but I've never had it done better in my life."

At the next station the two women got out. They shut the door and stood frozen on the platform looking up at Inshroin. Their eyes slowly grew bigger and bigger with horror until they seemed to fill the whole horizon.

.   .   .

262

That evening, backstage, Inshroin peered through the curtain. Rows and rows of faces seemed to leap out of the auditorium and stare at him. He noticed that a lot of people were carrying thick bound volumes of what looked like Bibles.

"Why have people got those books?" he asked Bob Ganster.

"They're family Shakespeares. The people are going to follow along as you do the speeches."

"Oh my God!" said Inshroin. "They'll pick up every mistake I make."

"Will you be making any? The people out there don't expect you will, I hope you're not going to let them down."

Inshroin held onto the curtain and looked down. He felt sick to his stomach.

"Do you have somewhere private I can sit down for a few minutes. I need to collect my thoughts, so I can work myself into the feel of the part."

"You can use my office," said the owner.

Inshroin was just about to enter Ganster's room when he heard voices inside. For a second he hesitated then pushed open the door. Inside a man was trying to pull a pair of pants up around his waist. A woman was standing behind him pulling on them, too, as the man cursed and swore at her. Both stopped when they saw Inshroin.

"Who are you?" asked the man.

"I'm one of the performers, and I just need to be quiet for a few minutes before I go on."

"Do you?" shouted the man. "Well, get out. This room is not a goddamn footpath; we're using it for a changing room."

"I will not," said Inshroin. "I have been given permission to use it by the owner. We'll have to share."

"Come here!" roared the man. Inshroin walked over to the couple. The man put his hands on his hips and stared at Inshroin intently. After a few seconds of this scrutiny, he suddenly shouted, "Dammit, put it there!" He held out his hand. "You're the first person who's had the guts to talk to me like that in weeks. If we work together again, feel free to use my room as a footpath any time you like. Now if you'll excuse me, I have to finish dressing. My name's Bill King, and this is my wife Phyllis."

He continued wrestling with his pants, then looked down between his legs. "Where's the suspenders?"

"You had them attached to the pants last time I saw them."

"Oh yes of course I did," said Bill. "It was me, I did something with them. I sent them off to Hollywood to star in a big movie."

"If you hold on for a minute," said Mrs. King, "I'll fix them so you won't need suspenders."

"That's it," roared her husband, "you've got it, fix them so I don't need suspenders. We'll go on stage with you walking behind holding them up! Perhaps you could ask President Roosevelt to come down and help. Perhaps you could pull them up and button them around my neck. Shall I put them on upside down, so if they fall off they'll fall up?!"

He looked at Inshroin. "Will you come and pull them from behind?"

"Sure. Have you got anything to drink?"

"I brought a bottle down from the hotel. Help yourself."

Inshroin went over, picked up the bottle, and took half a dozen deep gulps, then turned to help with the pants. They had fallen to the floor, and when Mrs. King tried to pull them up she pulled aside Mr. King's shirt. His balls were hanging out of the vent in his underwear. Inshroin opened his eyes wide; he'd never seen a pair like them. God Almighty, they hung down to his knees! Mr. King puffed and pulled the trousers up.

Inshroin gulped. "My God, right down to his knees!"

"Come and pull them at the front will you, while my wife holds them at the back."

Inshroin took another couple of drinks, then went over, wiping his mouth on the back of his hand.

Mrs. King and Inshroin pulled and tugged while Mr. King packed his genitals firmly down inside. "Whoooh!" he said when his wife gave a particularly hard tug. "Drop anchor, that hurt."

Inshroin leaned back against the wall sweating. "My God," he thought, "I'm about to go on stage for the first time in years, and I'm standing here playing ping-pong with another actor's balls!!"

When Bill had finished his act, Lucy (who seemed to have adopted the role of mistress of ceremonies) announced that Phillip Inshroin would do some passages from Shakespeare. Everybody waited . . . there was a rustling from the wings, and Inshroin appeared. He stood stock-still as if he had wandered

264

into a room full of people he didn't know. "Good dear Lord," he said in a loud voice, "I am ready to begin." He staggered to the center of the stage, and said, "I am dead drunk, ladies and gentlemen." If he expected to get a laugh, he was mistaken; the mood of the audience was almost Biblical. In the ensuing silence Inshroin tried to collect his thoughts and added, "I'm dead drunk with pleasure at being here with you tonight."

It was too late; the audience sat gaping up at him swaying in the center of the stage. Inshroin's lips moved silently as his face whitened. Then he bowed gravely, or rather he flopped down from the waist, legs straight, his knuckles scraping the ground. He hung in that position for a few seconds, and seemed on the verge of pitching forward, when Lucy walked in front of him and pushed him up by the shoulders. He stood there flushed and swaying.

A murmur ran around the theater, then there was silence again. Inshroin turned his face away from the audience. It was the same instinctive move that causes an Indian to pull a blanket over his face when he is dying. His eyes were dull and sunken; every muscle in his face seemed to quiver. In the silence he stared into Lucy's face, breathing loudly and irregularly.

"Keep it up, ham," she whispered. "This is a very meaty performance."

Inshroin clenched his fists, hunched his shoulders, steadied himself, turned back, and took on the burden of the play. He started off with something from *Lear* in a heavy slurred voice. He faltered, stopped, then started again.

"Oh my God, you son of a bitch," said Lucy, "You son of a bitch."

The audience was growing restive again, and there was a buzz of voices from the back rows. Lucy thought she'd better do something herself. She took a deep breath, opened her mouth to speak . . . and Inshroin put his hand over it.

"Stay, madam, I have things to say." Inshroin then gave a brief description of the Chicago stockyards and recited his favorite recipe for roast chicken. When he had finished he sighed and said, "Now leave me; I am weary."

Lucy gasped and tried to collect her thoughts.

"My Lord," she said, "I cannot leave you; I have matters of great import and moment to impart."

Inshroin shook his head. "I will not be disturbed by such a

foul churl as you. Your tidings can wait until I am better disposed to hear them. Meanwhile since you will not leave me, I will leave you." Inshroin bowed, lurched, and walked off the stage . . . Lucy stood staring down at the rows of gaping and silent faces. She turned and ran off the stage and almost tripped over Inshroin, who lay in the passage that led down to the changing room.

Lucy smoothed her hair, wiped the sweat off the palms of her hands with a cloth, and walked back onto the stage. As soon as she appeared, people began hissing. A man stood up in the balcony and called down: "We want our money back!"

"Money back!"

Lucy said nothing, but stood staring into the crowd of faces. After a few seconds, the place fell silent. She sighed and said, "Ladies and gentlemen, what *exactly* do you want? I presume from the pigsty noises you're making, you want something?"

Several voices shouted, "You said it! We want our money back!"

Lucy frowned and, with great gravity, said, "I don't understand. There are too many of you shouting at once. Ladies and gentlemen, what exactly is the problem, and *please* one at a time!"

The man in the balcony stood up again, and said, "We can't hear you up here. Speak up, talk louder," then as an afterthought he added, "louder *and* funnier."

"Now, we're getting somewhere," said Lucy. "Thank you, sir, I'll speak up, I'll try to be as funny as I can, and I'll deal with you first."

"Who, me?" asked the man, looking around.

Lucy pointed directly at him. "Yes sir, you, the bum in the balcony waving a mouthful of very noisy buckteeth in the air, I'm starting with you. Now tell me *exactly* what you want?"

The man became bashful and sat down blushing. "We want our money back. The show's rotten."

Lucy pretended to be shocked.

"You want your money back?"

"Money back, money back!" the chant began.

Lucy held up her arms. "Please, *please* give me a chance to explain. Let me explain things to *that* gentleman who is calling the loudest for his money back."

266

Again everybody fell silent.

"What is your name, sir?"

"Jamie Hules."

"Well, Jamie, I know the show isn't all it should be, but surely a man like you, a man of obvious insight and intelligence, doesn't need to be reminded that the chances and changes of life are dependent upon circumstances and not upon ourselves?"

Everybody looked at everybody else, and Jamie said, "S'pose not."

"I see, you suppose not," said Lucy with withering contempt. "I know Mr. Inshroin is drunk, but do you have the *faintest* idea why he is?"

Jamie pulled at his tie. "Why?"

"Because he has been slaving day and night to bring you the best performance he could. Do you know what pressures that can place on a great actor? Of course you don't. While you're sitting there shouting imperiously for your money back, Mr. Inshroin might at this very moment be lying in the wings surrounded by his weeping family, a family whose very existence depends upon the money he brings home at the end of the week."

Lucy now turned her attention back to the rest of the audience.

"Surely some of you gentlemen here tonight are fathers? Surely you understand the responsibility and sacred trust of fatherhood? Is it so difficult for you to imagine the suffering Mr. Inshroin is going through at the moment, knowing as he does that he has failed the government, you, *and* his family?"

Lucy gave a sigh, and again pointed at Jamie. "And while Mrs. Inshroin suffers, *that* gentleman sits there demanding his money back!"

A female voice was heard to shout "*Shame!*" which was picked up by others.

"You are right, ladies and gentlemen, it is a shame, it is a shame and cruel. Such a man as that Jamie Hules, standing there, concerned with nothing but his present amusement, and calling for his money back. Sir, do you know that money could feed a starving family for a week? Are you a father, are you a husband?"

"Throw him out, throw him out," was now the cry. Lucy pretended to receive the suggestion as though it were a question directed at her personally. She spread her arms and shrugged her shoulders.

"You appear to be an audience that knows what it wants," she said. "Who am I to argue, ladies and gentlemen? If that's what you want, *throw him out!*"

The man disappeared in a seething mass of bodies, his arms swinging wildly in the air.

"Put me down, put me down!"

He was finally lifted bodily over the heads of the people in the balcony, and passed horizontally along the row. Before he was hurled through the door, his red face turned toward the stage: "Get them to put me down," he screamed. "Get them to put me down!"

Lucy cupped a hand over her ear. "Louder," she said, *"Louder and funnier!"*

After Jamie had been removed, the rest of the audience gave Lucy a standing ovation.

"Thank you, thank you, ladies and gentlemen. Now, in spite of the minor setbacks we've had this evening, I can assure you there are a dozen performers just *itching* to come on stage for your entertainment."

A row of dancing girls, arm in arm, high-kicked out onto the stage. In the wings Inshroin sat propped up in the arms of the owner.

"How is he?" asked Lucy as she came off.

"Hard to tell. He's recovered consciousness anyway."

Inshroin got slowly to his feet and leaned against the wall behind him. He looked around at the staring faces. "When a man gets a slice of luck, nobody says anything," he said. "If he gets a kick in the pride, a crowd of mutes appear to see him go overboard, then watch his face until he's swallowed by the sea."

He lurched toward the side door, pulled it open, and disappeared into the alley at the side.

At ten o'clock that evening, Hess was wiping off the table after the last of the diners had left. Mrs. Kincaide took the final pile of dirty plates into the kitchen and began to wash them up. The owner came from downstairs and walked over to his employee.

"Hev you heard anything since he got back?"

"Nope, he didn't come down to eat, and my daughter has already taken up a bottle of whisky."

There was the sound of a door opening upstairs, and Inshroin shouted, "Hess, bring me up another bottle!"

Hess looked at his boss, who nodded: "Tell him this'll be the last one."

Hess collected a bottle from the shelf behind his bar, put it on a tray, and took it upstairs. When he got to the actor's room, the door was open, and he could see Inshroin sitting on the side of the bed, looking at an empty bottle that was standing on the copy of the Kismet Foredoomist Bible.

Hess tiptoed in and stood waiting by the bed.

"Leave the bottle," said Inshroin.

"Okay, anything else?"

"The room." The actor looked up: "No wait, can I give you some advice?"

"Uh-huh."

"If one day you ever think of going on the stage, you should always remain sober, industrious, and never allow bad company to be the ruin of your youth."

"No, sir."

"Will you sit down and keep me company for a while?"

Hess shrugged and sat down next to Inshroin, who smiled at him.

"You may have heard that I was drunk tonight at the theater, but I wasn't. I was busy thinking up new ways of expressing emotion in the works of Shakespeare, and I think I've hit on some new things. What's this, for example; what do you think I'm trying to express now?"

Inshroin twisted his face into an unrecognizable distortion.

Hess looked puzzled. "Er, it's very hard, Mr. Inshroin; I can't make it out."

The actor ran a hand through his hair. "I'll do it again. There . . . what was that?"

"I can't tell, it seems t'be very deep."

"Give a guess."

"It's very, very good."

"I know it's very good; what was it?"

"Anger?"

"Anger! You goddamn fool, it was love. Now what's this?"

Another face was pulled.

"Jealousy?"

"Jealousy! You know nothing about acting, and you have no

imagination. Now you won't mistake this one." He gave a sidelong leer, causing Hess to scratch his head. "Revenge?"

"Revenge! Revenge, good God, it was fear. I'm going to need another bottle after this!"

Inshroin went to the door and opened it. "Landlord, bring me up another bottle!" As he stood listening for a reply, Hess tried to slip by.

"No, you don't," said Inshroin grabbing him by the jacket. "You stay where you are; if you try and get away, you're a dead man; I've got a gun in my jacket pocket. Landlord!"

Inshroin dropped down on his knees and addressed the room below through the ceiling. "Bring me up another bottle!"

Mrs. Kincaide's voice floated up.

"Git t'bed you drunken slob. There's no more liquor comin' up them stairs."

Inshroin reached for the empty bottle and broke it.

"Can you hear that, you old bitch?"

"Bet yer life I can!"

Inshroin stood up and started throwing chairs and cupboards into the middle of the floor. "*And that?*"

"Git t'bed. I'm not coming' up."

Hess made another attempt for the door, but Inshroin was too quick for him, and dragged him back to the bed.

"Oh God," said Hess, "I've got to leave." He twisted around and kneed Inshroin in the groin, then made a dash for the door, wrenched it open, and bolted out into the hall.

Inshroin followed him, picking up the bedside lamp as he did so.

As Hess fell down the stairs, Inshroin leaned over the banister and threw the lamp after him. "If you must leave, don't say I sent you out without any light!" Inshroin dropped down on the top stair and put his face between his hands. He sat like that for ten minutes in complete silence; the rest of the house stayed as quiet as the grave.

Inshroin slowly got to his feet and walked downstairs. He made it to the front door when Mrs Kincaide appeared in the doorway behind him.

"You tarnation fool, you ain't goin' out on a night like this, it's rainin' cats n' dogs, you'll catch new-monya!"

"I don't mind rain," said Inshroin. "I ignore anything that ignores me."

My heart went open like an apple sliced
I saw my Saviour and I saw my Christ
Says, "We'll walk together, and we'll both be fed."
Says, "I will give you the other bread."
Oh the bread he gave and without money
Oh Drink, oh fire, oh burning honey.

L. Ridge

I got a new frock wid-out a single thing a-missin'
You heap a-grudgin' 'cause it looks a little bettuh'n dis 'un,
Lawd, Lawd, das de way things be.
Das de reason we's an unprotected nigguh nation,
All time begrudgin' one anothuh out dey situation.
Lawd, Lawd, I wonduh wat make it be?

R. E. Kennedy
Mellows

INSHROIN OPENED HIS EYES . . . AND GAZED UP INTO A HAZY MORNING SKY. He was lying under a tree, and in front of him was a solid wall of men, black and white. They all had their backs to him and were ringed around a man who was talking to them from the back of a hay cart. The actor got up and looked around. He realized he was in the field opposite his hotel, as he could see the roof over the top of a long line of beat-up old trucks that filled the road in front of the building.

The man on the cart was Claude Williams—the patron saint of Southern agricultural labor, a white minister the church had dismissed because he was a Christian communist. He was the first man in Southern history to get poor blacks and whites to strike together. He explained to poor whites that their poverty had nothing to do with the blacks but was caused by the planter bosses. He advised poor blacks not to go north, but to stay and grow with the South. He said the North had ground the colored man into the dirt just as badly as the South.

"North says the Lord intended you to be free, damn you; South says the Lord intended you to be a slave, bless you."

271

As Inshroin got to his feet behind the big crowd, Williams was already speaking.

"Good Jesus above, I see a mix of faces before me, black and white together, and both colors look hungry!"

"We sure are!"

"Since this strike started, the first in the country where poor black and white are solid together, I notice the white boss planter hasn't rushed in to help his own color. The boss planter is very democratic that way, he's letting black and white starve together—there's only one race for him where profit and loss is concerned!"

"Jist one race!"

"Now a lot of you people know who I am."

"We sure do!"

"Now, you people know I'm a clergyman and a communist, and I know most of you aren't, but you all know I can help you organize a union, and a union puts food into the bellies of your families. I'll tell you why I'm red, working for the union, and a Christian. I grew up poor on a Tennessee dirt farm. My father told me a damn Republican was just a damn nigger-loving Tory, and damn niggers weren't human, they were like animals because they had no souls, and the proof of that was in the Bible.

"He told me, 'The Bible says, "Thou shalt not kill," but it doesn't say "Thou shalt not kill a damn nigger," ' and niggers needed to be killed once in a while to keep them in their place.

"Now I often passed people of mixed race when I traveled about, and I remember my pa telling me a white person had a soul and a colored person didn't. But as much as I searched the Bible I couldn't find any mention of a people who might have a fraction of a soul because they were part white. I asked my pa about it, who told me a damn nigger was a damn nigger.

"Years later, when I qualified as a preacher, I visited a black church for the first time, and listened to the congregation singing. When they lifted up their voices I felt my soul was mounting to glory! I could feel myself standing in line robed in heaven's clothes, with my eyes of true faith fixed on the throne of the Lord. I knew that negro people had souls!"

"Yes sir!"

"Brothers and sisters, the bosses employ preachers who tell you God is a tetchy old man in the sky who is ready to damn you

272

for the slightest transgression from the day you're born! They say if you have faith in the fact that Jesus walked on water, that same kind of faith can repair the profit machine. So, while the bosses sit and wait for a miracle, you people, poor black and poor white, sit and starve. The boss's church tells you if you're good and stay quiet you'll go to Heaven; if you don't stay quiet you'll go to Hell. How can that kind of blackmail mean anything to the poor blacks and poor whites of this country? *You're living in Hell already!"*

"Livin' in Hell, yes sir!"

"My Jesus is the Jesus you let into your hearts who fights pain, disease, economic oppression, war, and racial bigotry. He is the force that helps man fulfill the divine in himself. Brothers and sisters, how long shall I speak?"

"From now on!"

"Brothers and sisters, I hope that this strike can stay solid. Brethren, Jesus's blood was red, the International Workers' flag is red. It means, regardless of race, all our blood is red. It's the one color of mankind symbolic of solidarity and brotherhood.

"Yes, I'm red, I preach a religion of Jesus, not a religion about Jesus. My religion means the same thing the Marxist means by class consciousness. Now if there's truth in Marx and Lenin, which I believe there is, then there must be God in Marx and Lenin.

"All through the Bible the righteous are placed with the poor, and the wicked are placed with the rich. The class fight of Marx and Lenin is the same old Bible fight between God and Mammon. You people are impotent because the country is in a depression; that depression puzzles you. Nobody will enlighten you, because they know that once you understand the puzzle, you'll want to smash the cause. You people are hungry in mind and body. You need physical food and mental food so badly, it's impossible to put one concern in front of the other. Your minds are starving for the knowledge that will explain why your bellies are empty, and just how they can be filled.

"Now I believe men cannot live by bread alone, *but cannot live at all without it!* And if man doesn't live, how can he love, and God is love! You are the only people who can make the changes to help you lead a more secure life, because nobody else will. And to do that you have to be united. Jesus was powerless until twelve followers got together and formed a union! All men of different creeds and color have to follow Jesus and form a union, a spiritual and practical union. A long time ago in Nazareth a carpenter organized his twelve apostles."

"Yes sir!"

"You remember how the fishermen stayed with Jesus three years before he got lynched?"

"We do!"

"Those fishermen didn't understand at first. They were told to go to Jerusalem and wait until they got the power. And how did they get the power? They became of one accord. That means they were organized!"

"Amen!"

"But each race can't do it on their own. We've got to work together so the planter bosses can't divide us along our weakest line, the color line. We can't let them break this strike!"

"No!"

"That's what trade unionism is, solidarity of black and white. It's the most Christian thing in the world! All of us, black and white, working together!"

A white man suddenly jumped up.

"By golly preacher, you just 'bout got me convinced on some of them ideas o' yours. But d'you mean to tell me a damn nigger burrhead is as good as I am?"

"Not as good as you, brother," said Claude, "but certainly as good as me."

"Amen!"

"Read the Bible! The Bible tells us there is no creed or color in the religion of Jesus, there is only one race, the human race. We pray to Our Father, not a white man's father."

"No!"

"Not a black man's father."

"No!"

"But *Our* Father. Thy will be done on earth as it is in heaven. Thy will be done in the *union!*"

"In the union!"

"What we have to do together, both black and white, is build the kingdom of God on earth. That kingdom is not of this world, but *in* this world. What Jesus meant by 'world' was the social order, not some old pie-in-the-sky paradise. He said,

'Seek ye *order* founded upon my principles.' That means an order of justice and brotherhood for *everybody!*"

The speech had a great effect on Inshroin. He returned slowly to town, swimming in a sea of adrenalin.

Lucy was sitting on the bed in her hotel room, when the door opened, and a huge bunch of flowers was pushed in. "Who's there?" she called.

Inshroin followed the flowers, crawling in on all fours. "I've come to ask for my job back. If you listen hard enough you can actually hear the remorse I'm suffering from."

"Remorse is out of fashion."

"It was a trump card when I first went on the stage." He sat up on his haunches. "I've been walking around all night thinking about the fiasco I caused. I can show you the corns."

"No thank you, and why may I ask are you holding that cushion?"

"I carry it around with me all the time now; if I fall in the gutter again, I can sleep comfortably. Can we try again please—you'll only have to swing the old clock back once."

"I can't stop you coming back; I'm not the producer. In any case we rescued the performance after you'd gone; I expect most people have forgotten about it by now."

"Out of sight, out of mind, eh?"

"It may not be what you're used to, but in this case I should be grateful if I were you."

Inshroin looked at her in silence for a few seconds, then said, "I've just heard an incredible speech by the man who's leading the strike, and I've had a few ideas."

"I didn't know you were interested in politics."

"I got the sack from Drewstone's because I got caught up in politics. I try to be a realist; the only trouble is I sometimes get channeled off into idealism. Anyway, I thought we could do something about the strike."

Lucy shook her head. "I think we should stay clear of getting involved directly. Saying something about Hitler or Stalin is okay, but this is too partisan. The strike committee is organizing a picnic for Saturday and there will be a lot of people in town. I've been asking around, and what everybody wants most is what we're supposed to be best at, drama. I think we should stick to Shakespeare and do it properly."

The phone rang and Lucy picked it up. "Hello . . . Yes he's here. It's for you, the receptionist says she's got your call through to Hollywood."

Inshroin took the receiver.

"Hello . . . Yes you may . . . Tell him it's Sir Edmund Jones of the British Film Institute . . . Mr. Drewstone of Drewstone Films? How do you do, sir, my name is Edmund Jones of the British Film Institute. Up to a few moments ago my wife and I were on the verge of a divorce, but we discover we still love each other. As a consequence we thought we'd go out for a meal, and then take in one of your marvelous movies. Can you tell me what you have showing tonight at your theater on Forty-second and Third in New York? Thank you."

Inshroin put his hand over the mouthpiece. "He's checking . . . Hello, I see, *The Blonde Wore Pants*. Most edifying. By the way, is Phillip Inshroin starring in the film? No, I see. Well, please make a note that the public is asking." He put the phone down and smiled at Lucy. "If we do Shakespeare, we should break it up with a little more comedy. Will you stop laughing, what do you think?"

"It certainly can't hurt."

"I've thought of some things."

Lucy wiped her eyes then reached out and held his hand, "Tell me about them."

Notices were placed all over town for the picnic day performance, and rehearsals went on for three days, fourteen hours a day. The production opened on Saturday at half-past six, but a line had begun forming by five.

We see the main street of the town from inside a moving car. Traveling along with it for a minute, we catch a crowd of people scattered along the sidewalk—a blur of faces. We pass a brightly lit store window, then leave behind a Wrigley billboard and arrive at The Limit, the front of which is now covered in a mass of handwritten posters.

LUCY ARMITAGE. SHE JUST ACTS. NOT ALL PERFORMERS CAN BE EXPECTED TO DANCE AND WEAR EXPENSIVE DRESSES.

LAST WEEK'S PRODUCTION? A SUCCESS AS USUAL.

A GRAND GALAXY OF STARS WHO ARE GOOD AT EVERYTHING. FUNNY THINGS, OTHER THINGS, EVERYTHING BUT OLD AND BORING THINGS.

A DOZEN COMICS WHO ARE THE FUNNIEST PEOPLE ON EARTH OR IN THE AIR.

A DOZEN DANCERS WHOSE FEET ARE PERFECT POEMS.

PHILLIP INSHROIN, HE ONCE LAY DRUNK IN A DITCH, BUT SWORE HE'D RETURN A STAR. OF COURSE HE EARNS MORE THAN THE PRESIDENT. HE DOES LESS HARM.

ANY PERSON MAKING A FUSS WILL BE INJECTED AT ONCE!!!

NO DRINKING ALOUD INSIDE. BUT THE BEST OF LICKERS CAN BE OBTAINED IN THE BAR NEXT DOOR.

THE SHOW CLIMAXES WITH EVERYBODY BURSTING INTO A BRILLIANT PERSPIRATION.

COST OF ADMITTANCE? PRICELESS. BUT TO YOU FIVE CENTS.

At seven o'clock, Inshroin stepped from the wings onto the stage and looked out into the packed theater.

"Our production has arrived!" he said. "There's no pretending we're not excited about it, because we are. The cast is about to throw the product of their minds before you. Watch and listen. I'm not going to make any rash claims, but I do promise you the grandest story ever told—great drama, and some screamingly funny stuff.

"The depression this country is going through is dead!!!!! *Deader'n'ell!* Yes sir, *Deader'n'ell!!* Get out the crepe! Sound the doleful drum, let the trombone croon its agonizing dirge, ring the bells! Old man depression is dead, he is shot full of holes, punctured and perforated from his peanut head to his peanut toes. Depression is gone and will give us no more trouble. He has as much chance of a comeback as a snowball in Hades! All this is because our production has *arrived*! Ladies and gentlemen, members of the cast will play a number of different roles in the production. We all hope you enjoy the show."

Inshroin bowed and moved toward the wings. As he did so, the curtain lifted.

SCENE: *A courtroom packed with people. Everybody rises as the judge enters. Judge Jenkins's arm is in a sling, and his face is covered in claw marks as if he has been attacked by a wild cat.*

"No smoking in court!" said the judge.

"Nobody is," said a man on the jury.

"I don't care, the law must be obeyed," said the judge. "I'm sorry about my appearance, I got into a little scrape last night over a card game. In spite of my looks I think I got the better of the fight. My gouging was pretty good. I got my thumbs into his eyeballs, and this morning they look like old inkwells."

There was a smattering of applause as defense and prosecution counsels arrived.

"Where's the first guilty criminal?" asked the judge flicking through some papers. "Ah yes, Sadie Johnson."

"Yassir, that's me!"

"Thirty days in jail, that's me! Next case."

A man got into the box.

"How old are you?" asked the judge.

"Twenty-four, your honor—just."

"You'll be fifty—just—when you get out. Next case!"

Defense counsel stood up. "I would be obliged if your honor would take things a little slower; I'm afraid I cannot keep up."

The judge scowled, then said, "Bring in the next prisoner."

The accused, played by Inshroin, walked onto the stage, and before he stepped into the box, stooped down and removed a dirty pair of boots. He then hung a sign on the outside of the box that read, PLEASE WAKE IN TIME FOR LUNCH.

"Will the accused remain standing so the court can see him?" asked the judge.

Defense counsel rose to his feet. "Would you like him passed around, your honor?"

"That is an improper remark."

"It was provoked by an improper suggestion."

The judge ignored defense counsel and addressed the man in the dock. "Prisoner, you are accused of being drunk and disorderly in a hotel on Fitch Street. Can you remember what happened?"

"I'm not sure what happened before my arrest, but I think I was taken into custody by two officers."

"You think?"

"I can't remember the incident too well."

The judge sighed: "Drunk I suppose?"

"Yes sir, both of them."

The judge pounded his gavel in the ensuing laughter. "Silence in court!" he shouted.

The sheriff stood up and produced a bottle full of liquor.

"We searched the accused's room, your honor, and found

this bottle of illegally distilled whisky in one of his jacket pockets."

"I know nothing about it," said the prisoner. "It must have been there when I purchased the jacket."

The judge beckoned with his hand. "Give me a drop to keep up the circulation?"

The sheriff handed the bottle up to the bench and the judge took a gulp. "That is the strongest whisky I've had in years." He smacked his lips. "I wish I could have that feeling forever. There are folks who say whisky was invented by the devil; in my opinion it's the pure juice of paradise."

"We found five similar bottles under the accused's bed," said the sheriff. "All empty."

The judge sat back, stared up at the ceiling, and said, "Huw-wee!" loud and clear. "This is a very serious offense. Now let me see, what's the usual procedure in a case like this?" He shook his head slowly, strummed his fingers on the bench top and sucked in air through his clenched teeth.

Defense counsel sniggered.

"It seems to me, judge, some of us learn law at school, while others only manage to suck it in through their teeth."

The judge immediately began to swell up with wrathful words. He got bigger and bigger and seemed on the verge of bursting. With a great effort he controlled himself and leaned forward.

"You're being offensive, sir!"

"We both are, the only difference is I'm trying to be, you can't help it."

"I shan't warn you again," said the judge. "You are beginning to disturb my peace of mind, and I get very angry when my peace of mind is disturbed."

Defense smiled. "Will the court please note that the judge has admitted to having only a piece of mind?"

The judge was on his feet in an instant.

"You essence of skunk boiled down, just you get out of this court and stink yourself to death, you unburied cuss, you!!"

"Order! Order in the court!" shouted prosecuting counsel.

The judge sat down wiping his forehead. "Well," he said, "he got to me, and I'm just spoiling for a fight." He shuffled a few sheets of paper to collect his thoughts, and then said,

"Sheriff, how did the accused get hold of this liquor? Is his hotel near the distillery?"

"Quite near, sir."

"How near?"

Defense stood up. "Two miles, three hundred yards, two feet, eight and a quarter inches."

"How can you be so accurate?"

"I expected some damn fool would ask that stupid question, so I measured it."

Another titter ran around the court. There sat the judge, looking as if he weighed five hundred pounds, he was so swollen with anger. Then he blew out all his pent-up rage with such force, it nearly burst his vest. The smoke of his torment poured out of his pants pockets and buttonholes in great clouds. He jumped up, grasped the seat of his baggy pants with both hands, and jumped up and down while roaring in a way that made the windows jangle, and brought down bits of plaster from the ceiling.

"You damn pinko commie-loving Yankee!" he screamed. "You're the totality of all human abhorrence, you sniggering varmit you!!!" Then the judge collapsed into his seat.

"Easy judge," said a voice from somewhere in the court. "Never fly off the handle when you're conducting a trial."

The judge was on his feet again. "Who said that!!!? I fine that man fifty dollars for contempt!!" He rose on tiptoe trying to catch a glimpse of the offender. He didn't, and sat down again.

"I guess it was nothing but the wind," said the same voice.

The judge glared at the prosecuting counsel. "Have you anything to say?"

"Well, your honor, why don't we do what we usually do?"

"What's that?"

"Give five dollars to the jury if they find the defendant guilty."

The judge started waving his hand, trying to get prosecution counsel to shut up.

"That, sir," he said, "is a highly improper suggestion."

"I'm sorry, your honor, I meant no offense. I didn't intend giving five dollars to the whole jury, I meant five dollars each."

The judge sat strumming his fingers, and a man sitting over by the courtroom window got up and rubbed a dusty pane with his cuff. Then he put two hollowed hands on either side of his face and peered out into the street. Suddenly his body went rigid. "*Coons!* Six of 'em crossing the road. A pa, a ma, and four young uns!"

"Court adjourned!" shouted the judge. "Where's my gun, fresh meat for dinner!"

There was the sound of a gunshot from the corner of the theater balcony. A woman began screaming violently and piercingly, while everybody on stage scattered in all directions. Without warning, a man jumped from the balcony, looked up, shook his fist, and shouted something foreign. Then he was gone.

"Strikebreakers!" someone called from the audience.

The doors at the back swung open, and a line of armed men filed in. The one leading the column said, "Everybody will stay perfectly still! Nobody will get hurt if you don't move."

The audience froze into silence, but from the balcony the screaming went on and on, the sound now mixing with the buzz of male voices. The noise above seemed to move toward the door at the back, then it could be heard coming down the stairs toward the lower part of the theater. More men appeared at the door. Some of them were wearing Union army officer uniforms of the Civil War period, others were in black suits and stovepipe hats. They forced their way past the armed group, who had come in earlier, shouting and punching in all directions. "Stand back, the President has been shot!" They carried the body of Lincoln down the center aisle toward the stage. Mrs. Lincoln, played by Lucy, came behind screaming, and trying to break through to her husband. The bottom of her dress was red with blood that came from a wound in Lincoln's head. The group passed up onto the stage, and went out the same way as the man who had jumped down from the balcony. After they had gone, the noise of shouting and screaming stopped instantly, and the man who had ordered the audience to stay where they were signaled for his men to leave.

The theater lights were lowered, and as everybody sat down, a spotlight picked out Inshroin and another man standing in a corner of the stage in front of a furnace. Inshroin was sifting through a trunk of clothes. He paused now and again to look at an article he pulled out. He held up an eighteenth-century jacket with lace cuffs, turned it this way and that, sighed, and pushed it into the furnace. The other man prodded the burning material with a rod, until it caught all over. Occasionally sparks flew out and lit the two faces luridly as they worked.

A bundle of letters tied with a pink ribbon went in next, then a dagger, a sword, and some long wigs. After they had been pushed into the flames, the trunk was knocked to pieces, and the wood, along with the ropes that had bound it, were also thrown in.

"Is that everything?" asked the man with the rod.

"That's all. Everything has been burned. There's nothing left to remember my brother by."

Somewhere in the theater a loose shutter banged against the side of the building and boomed through the silence.

"What time it is, Garrie?"

"Nearly six-thirty, Mr. Booth."

"My brother performed many times in this theater before he shot Lincoln. I expect they will want to pull the building down now?"

"I expect so, Mr. Booth."

"It's late Garrie, go home. I'll stay a while, and see the furnace is put out."

When he was alone on stage, a brighter spot was turned up, and Inshroin was pooled to the front of the stage. When the actor arrived at the footlights, he stopped, sighed, and spoke the lines from Julius Caesar's burial. He then went on to *Othello*, and some *Hamlet*. After reciting for half an hour Inshroin called Lucy onto the stage, and together they did some passages from *Macbeth*, *King Lear*, *The Taming of the Shrew*, and *Romeo and Juliet*:

> But, soft! what light through yonder window breaks?
> It is the east, and Juliet is the sun!
> Arise, fair sun, and kill the envious moon . . .
> Her cheek upon her hand:
> O! that I were a glove upon that hand
> That I might touch that cheek.

The only other sound in the theater was that of rustling paper, as people turned the pages of their family Shakespeares. Everybody was packed in so tight, a dime wouldn't have fallen between them. At the end of the performance, an elderly man from the audience came down the aisle to the stage. He held up a dollar bill.

"Here! Here!" he said. "Hit's wuth more! Hit's wuth more! Take it. The ticket was too cheap."

After he'd changed, Inshroin stopped off at Lucy's hotel for a drink. He watched her pouring out a Scotch. "I finally pulled everything together," he said.

Lucy smiled. "You did very well. You reminded me of the soldiers who came back after the war."

"How's that?"

"At first everything seems hopeless. You've lost your drive, nothing seems to go right, you can't see a way out, everything is as low as it can get. But something will turn up you never counted on; it always does."

"I suppose so," said Inshroin. "I think things can only get better now. I thought we did very well in *The Taming of the Shrew*, but I bet you didn't know your stockings were nearly falling down, they were bunched an inch thick around the ankles."

Lucy pulled up her skirt to look, and Inshroin smiled.

"I've always liked trim legs in seamed stockings."

"Have you? There's only one way to succeed with suspenders and stockings; you have to bully them. Show you're afraid, and they'll slip, twist, and wrinkle all over the place. I'll show you."

Lucy put a foot up on the bed, undid a stocking and rolled it down.

"Now, you must take your time at first, fit it around the foot like this. Do it carefully, then pull it up so, getting it nice and smooth over the knee. Make sure the seam is straight, then yank and pull, and drag it. When you've drawn the thing up as far as you can, pull it another inch at least. The damn thing will creak and snap, and pretend it's going to split, but if you give it the treatment I've just demonstrated, it'll know its place, and stay as smooth as the skin on your arm and bottom."

Inshroin went over to the bed, took her chin in his hand, and kissed her on the mouth. She said nothing as they drew apart, but looked up at him through half-closed eyes. Then she sighed and fell back into the pillow. Lucy pulled her dress up to the waist and bumped herself to the edge of the bed. She wasn't wearing any underwear. Inshroin stood between her legs toying with a cluster of curls—she nodding slightly like a water lilly swaying in the wind when its cup is full of rain. Holding her legs up, she reached around under her thighs and pulled herself open—lips a tempting pout like the cleft of a burst apricot.

Inshroin undid his pants. Within a minute he was completely distracted, holding Lucy under the buttocks and wiggling her around like a man maneuvering a pinball machine. After a few more minutes he stood back and helped her to turn over so that she was kneeling on the bed. When she was comfortable, he entered her from behind. Inshroin pulled her hair back tight with both hands, then began to pant softly. The panting grew faster and louder, faster and louder, then stopped with a catch of breath.

Inshroin shriveled quickly as he drew away. Semen flowed like lemon juice over a wide surface of caviar. Lucy's lips folded behind him delicately, but remained slightly open at the bottom, leaving a thin mauve line visible. Carefully she got off the bed, sighed, then turned and looked up into the actor's face.

"You're a nice clean-looking young man with lovely eyes," she said. "I like you, any girl would, but you had no damn business to make love to me like that. I never let men make love to me without being asked. You did it properly even though you didn't ask; now you'll go away really pleased with yourself. Who do you think you are? Who do you think I am? Do you think I'm a girl in a whorehouse? You have a lot of cheek."

Lucy sat on the edge of the bed.

"None of you women have a sense of humor," said Inshroin.

"You know why that is, don't you?"

"Why?"

"If we had one, we'd spend all day laughing at men."

Inshroin sat down beside her. "You're just playacting with me now," he said.

"No I'm not. The stage and life are two different things. In life we don't have time for rehearsals."

"Would you consider marrying me?" asked Inshroin.

Lucy smiled. "One actor husband is enough!"

"I'd like to punch your head," said Inshroin.

"And instead I'm punching yours—that is, if it's punchable. Just thank God I didn't accept; we'd do murder living with each other. I can put you out of my heart, so you can put me out of yours." She smiled and put her hand on his shoulder. "Now kiss me like you did before."

As the actor left he glanced at the hall porter and noticed that apart from his extreme ugliness, he had the same large blue eyes as Lucy. The man looked back and scowled. "Who are you staring at?" he asked. "Do you want to remember me?"

"Sorry," said Inshroin, "it's just your lovely blue eyes."

A car drew alongside Claude Williams and a black union steward as they left the theater. The two men were thrown into the back seat between a couple of masked men with guns. The car rolled away down the streets, passing through top-crust, middle, and bottom, ending up on a patch of open ground surrounded by trees, somewhere on the outskirts of town. A circle of cars had been drawn up, and their spotlights beamed to a single pool in the middle. The two prisoners were dragged out, and their hands tied behind their backs.

"Strip 'em off," someone said.

When the two men were naked, the man who had ordered the stripping led them into the center of the circle, and said to the black steward, "Get down on your knees." He then turned to Williams. "You like niggers so much, you're gonna lick his arse while we tickle you with a pipe. If you stop lickin' we've got a dozen rifles stickin' on yer ear and we'll blow your brains out."

"Who runs this town," asked Williams quietly, "the law or scum like you?"

"We're a very law-abiding people around here," said the man. "We're just saving the law the trouble. Besides, the law is too slow in situations like this. We're dealing with a threat to our national security. On your knees and start lickin'."

The men began taking turns flogging him with a length of rubber hose that had been split into long ribbons. Each of the ribbons contained holes, so that every time the lash came down, it raised, and at the same time broke blisters.

The pain was excruciating, but Williams never made a sound. Six men stood around him, pushing their rifles up against his head. After ten minutes of the beating, the two men were forced to change positions.

"Now you're gonna lick the commie's arse, and we're gonna whup you so you won't forget. Next time you see a white man it'll turn your stomach. You'll just want to stay in your cabin and fuck them six nigger wives you live with."

"I've only got one wife," said the steward. "An aristocratic, white Christian gentleman like you should understand that."

The last remark was made with such withering contempt, it took everybody's breath away. There was a moment's silence, then somebody said: "When niggers get uppity like you, a beating ain't good enough, we usually burn 'em."

For a moment the only sound was that of Williams's heavy breathing. Someone in one of the cars flicked the headlights on and off a few times, and the voice that had ordered the two men stripped said, "I think it's best if we just have a little celebration tonight, gentlemen; I don't think the sheriff wanted anything grand this time."

The two men were found semiconscious an hour later, beside the main road leading out of town where they had been dumped.

As Williams was helped into the car, he said, "If the road runs forward, the cross can't be dodged, nor its eternal lesson. A crucifixion, even in a small way, is necessary before each of us is aware of the nature of evil, and our frailty against it."

The following morning Inshroin and the company left town for their next engagement one hundred miles further along the track. At the station there was a lot of noise and confusion, performers leaning out of the train windows, others pushing bags and trunks into the boxcar. People seeing them off waving and shouting. For the first time in fifty years the train didn't leave on time.

A mile out of town there was a bend in the track, then a steep incline, so the engine slowed down. As the car containing the theater group passed some rocks, a ragged man and woman rose up out of the ditch and slid underneath. Doubled up they crawled from sleeper to sleeper, then took hold of the rods that ran between the wheels.

"Make sure you hang on tight," said the man. "Remember what I told you."

"I will, Charlie," she said. "I will."

The whistle blew, and when it reached the top of the incline the train picked up speed. Underneath, the couple hung side by side, gripping the rods, suspended a couple of feet above the rails. The man shouted: "Dolly my gal, I'll keep hollerin' instructions. Make sure you holler back!"

"I will, Charlie, I will."

After a few more minutes, he could see she wasn't going to make it. Wind, gravel, and dirt blew into their faces; she was hit in the face by a stone and started screaming.

"Hold on Dolly, and keep your mind down to business!"

He caught a glimpse of her white terrified face looking over at him. He did all he could—shook his head up and down, then sideways.

"Don't let me go Charlie, please don't let me go!" At this point her hair slapped hard into his face, then whisked away—and he was alone . . . The wheels carried the man further away from where the mangled woman lay still in the middle of the track. The train rushes on and turns into a blur of whirling newspaper headlines:

"A GREAT RETURN FOR PHILLIP INSHROIN!"

Another whirl of newspaper headlines:

"PHILLIP INSHROIN AND LUCY ARMITAGE GREAT SUCCESS!"

Another whirl of headlines:

"PHILLIP INSHROIN A TRIUMPH!" Etc. Etc. Etc. . . .

IF, AT THIS TIME OF RESURRECTION IN HIS CAREER, Inshroin had been able to lift his eyes to the horizon and beam them down to Drewstone's, the actor would have witnessed a strange event in the life of the company. Some of the Chief's younger executives had arranged for him to meet and see the work of the newest Hollywood rage, the Spanish surrealist painter and filmmaker Salvador Dali.

In the cinema room at Drewstone Castle, a Dali film was being fed onto the projector, while assistants bulging with excitement and expectation rushed around. Amid all the activity, the Chief sat in an armchair smoking a cigar. Flicking ash into a coffee cup, he asked, "Where's he from, anyway?" The executive who had arranged the meeting turned from the projector: "He's from Europe, Spain actually. He's mainly a painter, but he's made some really exciting films."

"I didn't know they made movies in Europe anymore," said the Chief.

"Of course they do. You must have seen some French

movies, they're the ones where FIN comes up in the last frame."

Salvador Dali arrived and was introduced. The Chief tried hard to hide his amazement. Shoulder-length hair, one half of the upper lip clean shaven, on the other a long greased moustache that grew out beyond his ear. A yellow silk suit, orange boots.

"Mr. Drewstone," said Dali, "it is an honor to meet you. You are the greatest surrealist in the world."

The Chief looked puzzled, glanced round suspiciously, and asked, "Is that good?"

Dali smiled. "It means your films are more real than realism, they are super-realism."

"Oh a kind of super-colossal realism?"

"That is right."

"Well, I certainly understand that, I'd like to know more."

Dali spread his arms in wonder. "You? But you know more about it than anybody. Nobody knows more. You are king of surrealists."

The Chief's chest went out like a pigeon's. "How can I help you, Mr. Dali?"

"I want to make a film with you. I want to create a film of dream sequences. It will be a masterpiece of absolutely colossal realism beyond all bounds!!!"

He sat down. "You see my film of surrealism."

The lights were turned down, and the projector started to roll.

1-2-3-4-5-6-7-8 . . . . . A man picks up a razor, he turns to a wide-eyed girl, and cuts her left eyeball open. It slithers down her face. She runs away through endless rooms chased by the man. Close-up of a door covered with decaying ants. The girl reaches the last room and crouches in the corner. The man strains toward her, but he is held back by giant cables attached to his shoulders. He strains and strains; nothing happens. Shot of two grand pianos filled with dead donkeys, their heads are sticking out dripping blood on the white keys. Shot of two pianos: They are moving along the floor dragging some priests who are attached to the pianos by more cables. They hold up open Bibles and their mouths move silently in prayer . . .

There was the sound of someone being violently sick, and

288

when the lights went up, the Chief, blanched white, was hanging over the side of his chair.

"Super, super realism!"

"Staggering colossal realism beyond all bounds!"

"King of surrealism!"

Dali reported to the press, "A great success, Mr. Drewstone was absolutely speechless."

T HE POPULARITY OF THE FEDERAL THEATRE was now reaching a climax all over the country. Sixty thousand people bought tickets for *Power* before it opened in New York City.

The play *Lysistrata*, written two thousand years ago in Greece, opened in Seattle with a black company. It was considered too risqué for the audience, and the theater doors were locked after the first night.

Southern audiences flocked to see *Altars of Steel*. They praised it, they fought over it. One critic found it as dangerous as *Uncle Tom's Cabin*. Another called it a document as fundamental in its facts as it could be. In Chicago 250,000 people saw the all-black *Swing Mikado*.

Flash of newspaper headlines: A COLORED CONVULSION, A RAZZMATAZZ THAT BEATS A WHITE HOT TEMPO! A KILLER-DILLER BOUND TO SHAKE THE FOUNDATIONS OF JACKSON BOULEVARD! BIGGER AND BETTER CHORUS LINES THAN YOU EVER SAW IN A WHITE MAN'S SHOW! THE MOST DELIRIOUS OUTLAY OF UN-BRIDLED TRUCKING AND CAKEWALKING THE CHICAGO STAGE HAS EVER SEEN! THE HOTTEST SWINGEROO TO HIT TOWN SINCE THE KING OF JITTERBUG ROCKED THE WINDY CITY!

The Los Angeles Police Department said: "We want you to know that the Federal Theatre is playing a big part in our crime prevention program. It has cooperated with us in putting on shows in high schools. We want to go on record at this time asking for its continuation. Any decrease would directly hinder us in efforts to reduce delinquency."

In many places in Georgia the children were taught to make puppet theaters and puppets. A little girl tried to smuggle the puppet she had been making home under her dress. When it was discovered, she refused to give it up. "Hit's mine, hit's mine, hit's the onliest thing I ever had that was mine."

All the parks in New York City put on open-air performances in front of tens of thousands.

A writhing mass of children are crowded as close to the ropes as the law will permit; young legs protrude from under the spotlight platform, and dangle out of the trees. When the play begins in the twilight, they all move forward as though pushed . . .

PANORAMA

Stalin will get me in the end. If he lives long enough he will get every single one of us who has ever injured him in speech or action. That is his principal aim in life. He is completely dominated by a vindictive passion. He will lie back and wait, ten, twenty, thirty years, secretly plotting to achieve an exquisitely appropriate revenge upon an enemy.

L. P. Serebriakov

BY 1937 BOLSHEVISM WAS DOMINATING RUSSIA as completely as Hollywood was dominating America. Lenin was dead, and Stalin had won the battle of succession against Trotsky. As absolute as any Czar, he sits across the country, a monumental presence.

Where Trotsky had wanted Russia immediately to go to the aid of revolutionaries all over the world, Stalin first wanted to consolidate power, and build Soviet influence from a firm industrial home base. The battle of succession came to a head on this point.

In China, the Nationalist Chiang Kai-shek, who had made an alliance with the communists, did an about-face, and began a bloody purge against them. Stalin seemed compromised, for it was he who had strengthened ties with Chiang, suggesting the creation of a great Sino-Soviet bloc against the British empire.

Trotsky accused Stalin of betraying the world revolution by such an alliance, and eighty-three well-known government figures backed him. With great cunning and intuition Stalin succeeded in discrediting Trotsky before the majority of the Congress, which decided to exile him.

Stalin knew that Trotsky would find a way of being heard by the Russian people if he stayed at home, and ordered him deported. Trotsky spent the last years of his life living abroad and was finally ice-picked to death by a Stalin assassin in Mexico.

Now the sole heir to Lenin, Stalin began his program of industrialization, which would involve the uprooting, starvation, and death of millions. His program would continue until the German invasion of 1941.

Eisenstein was back in Moscow after he had finished filming in Mexico with Upton Sinclair. He did very little directing, but headed the national film academy in the capital. He began all his courses by telling students that they would not be able to make pictures unless they were familiar with Shakespeare, Dickens, and Dostoyevsky—unless they knew Beethoven, Tchaikovsky, and Rimsky-Korsakov. When a director emerged with his degree from Eisenstein's academy he was as much at home in a concert hall as he was in a cutting room, and he knew the philosophy of Marx as well as he knew how to use a makeup box.

In a small room in the darkened palace of the Kremlin, Stalin was being shaved by the Chief of the Kremlin guard, a Hungarian called Pauker. He was the only man Stalin trusted with an open razor near his throat. He played the same role to the Russian dictator as Bormann played to Hitler, but he was funnier and like a court fool kept Stalin entertained.

The dictator stood up, and wiped some shaving soap from behind his ear. He gazed out across the Kremlin wall to a factory chimney that had appeared on the Moscow skyline.

"That is where our future revolutionary power lies," he said, "not going to the aid of every little workers' strike around the world. If we had done that, as Trotsky suggested, the capitalists would have divided us up, and cut our throats. We need to measure everything with money and bayonets. Once there is enough money, and enough strong bayonets, then there will be a world revolution, and it will be the result of our armies and our gold.

"The little skirmishes stirred up by European revolutionaries are insignificant. The great revolution will come when our troops, the tartar hordes of Eurasia, enter every capital city from here to London. We can ignore the Western proletariat in the major part of that revolution; they are as weak and despicable as the bourgeoisie. If they had any character, they would have seized power as we did."

In Munich the great German Museum has been taken over, and now houses a gigantic exhibition for the education of the German citizen called "The Eternal Jew." A thirty-foot-high yellow and black picture of Shylock has been placed outside to advertise the show.

Inside there are a variety of displays: "Jewish ritual knives for circumcision," photos of Kosher butchers "massacring defenseless cattle." There is a "Chamber of Horrors," with a seven-pronged candlestick, and blood-stained ceremonial robes.

Another room is described as "a true replica of the inside of a Masonic Temple." Maps, diagrams, and charts are everywhere, claiming to illustrate the sinister influence of Jewry through the world and the centuries. Records of Richard Tauber singing, and Yehudi Menuhin's violin solos are played incessantly on slightly off-center turntables to illustrate "degenerate Jewish music." Charlie Chaplin is postered up on the wall (moustache carefully removed) in the "Rogues Gallery of Notorious Jews" which included Prime Minister Disraeli.

At his Bronxville home, Sinclair Lewis is giving a party in honor of his idol, H. G. Wells (he had named his first son after the author). Alice Longworth, daughter of President Theodore Roosevelt, is there also. Wells, who is very vain about his tiny feet and hands, sits talking to Edith Haggard, the literary agent. The two of them are the center of a heated discussion. Wells is saying there will soon be a new world war, and everybody laughs.

"I can tell you exactly when it's going to start."

"When?"

"In the autumn of 1939."

Everybody sniggers, the man is obviously old and senile.

"Just as soon as the harvest is in," he adds gently, as if he is speaking to a group of backward children.

FINIS OF PANORAMA

THE FEDERAL THEATRE'S FUNDING came up for review, and because of its popularity, everybody expected that the government would allocate more money.

Inshroin's group had now arrived in Cleveland, and was preparing some new things they hoped to have ready by the fall of 1937. Before rehearsals started, Inshroin (who needed extra money) decided to take a break for two weeks, go back to Hollywood, and put the tower up for sale. Lucy went with him, to visit an agent who had written her suggesting she should do some film work.

When the couple arrived at Hollywood Station, Inshroin phoned his real estate agent, and discovered the key to the tower had been left with the Chief. He phoned Drewstone and arranged to go over to collect it. Lucy went off to see the agent on her own, and Inshroin stepped out of the station and hailed a cab.

As they turned onto Sunset Boulevard, the driver hit a bump in the road, and the car shuddered.

"Jeez," he said, "if anything goes wrong now, I ain't got the dough to fix it."

"A bump's good for the liver," said Inshroin.

"Not for the temper it ain't. Gee, dames squawk if I drive over a dime on the way home from one of them illegal operations. That's the movie world to me, Mr. Inshroin."

"You remember me?"

"Saw all your movies, read you'd been abroad."

"For a while. Ever wanted to travel?"

"Naw, not now. If I was younger, I'd go to Bermuda for next to nothing."

"How?"

"Lotsa sex on ships with rich old dames who'll pay for the trip."

Inshroin stared out of the cab on his way from the station to Drewstone's. Downtown Hollywood looked exactly the same as when he left, except there seemed to be a lot more exotic pet shops. The driver's brick-red face turned in Inshroin's direction.

"Have you heard about Drewstone's latest? I drive a lot of his people, and they tell me he's gonna do *Robinson Crusoe*. I reckon the guy will put the lid on Hollywood with that one. I read the story when I was a kid, and I've always thought it would be a great movie."

When he arrived at the Chief's office, Inshroin paused at the door and looked in. The Chief was sitting at his desk looking the same as ever, while a man standing at his side was handing him some eight-by-ten glossy pictures of another man who was sitting over at a piano playing some boogie-woogie. The performer suddenly stopped when he caught sight of Inshroin, and Drewstone looked up.

"My God," he said, "you look ill. Are you still on the booze or doesn't the stage agree with you?"

Inshroin walked into the room. "It's hard work, but I enjoy it. I think I can keep going for a few more years yet."

"Can you?" said his old boss. "Can you? Well, I've heard the Federal Theatre Project is getting into hot water over some of its productions. Seems a lot of your performers are red, and the

American public is getting wise to it. I was saying last week it would be a miracle if you lasted another six months and I don't believe in miracles."

"Really?" said Inshroin. "That's amazing considering it's taken a succession of them to keep you out of prison."

The man with the eight-by-ten glossies smiled. "The Chief's right, the Federal Theatre is too radical. Take out *c-a-d*, and you still have *l-i-a-r*."

"True," said Inshroin, "and *star* is *rats* spelled backwards."

Drewstone was in a good mood, and remembered warmly all the money Inshroin had made for him.

"Sit down, Phillip, have a drink, I'll phone down for one of the staff to get the key to the tower." He poured out a Scotch, phoned downstairs, then introduced Inshroin to the two other men.

"This is Terp Crosby, agent for Cass Grant. We're thinking of using him in a movie we're doing of *Robinson Crusoe*."

The men nodded at each other, then the agent handed the Chief another photo. This one showed the actor full length, in profile, smoking a pipe, and wearing a trench coat.

"He looks a bit like a trussed chicken," said the Chief.

"Anybody who wears a Humphrey Bogart coat looks like a trussed chicken," said Terp.

In the next picture the young man was wearing a sailor suit and smiling coyly at the camera. A third showed him in a checked shirt, thick pants, and boots. He wore a frown indicating a serious state of mind useful in a Steinbeck "problem" story with a message.

Terp threw back slabs of creative hair. "I think that one is the best; it shows an intense pouncing animation waiting to be unleashed. It portrays a swift gritty personality gripped in an elusive turmoil of vitality. He'd be great for Crusoe."

The young man at the piano suddenly stopped playing and got up. He stomped around the room performing the black bottom.

"Okay," said the Chief. "I'll give him a try. What do you think of the bits I altered in the story?"

A silence fell, and everybody looked at everybody else.

"We've been having a talk," said Terp, "and although your alterations are fantastic, Chief, there's one thing you haven't pushed for enough."

Drewstone was immediately on the defensive.

"Oh, what's that?"

"Sex."

The Chief tapped his forehead, and a flashing lightbulb seemed to hover over him.

"Easy enough," he said. "We'll make man Friday, girl Friday, and Crusoe can fall for her."

"We thought of that," said Terp, "but what about the color bar? Man Friday is colored, and we can't show a white guy in a cuddle with a colored girl."

The Chief paced up and down for a while snapping his fingers.

"I've got it! We'll make her a white girl Friday, a blonde. She can get shipwrecked as easily as a colored dame."

"That's a great idea," said Terp, "but there's a problem with that too. Would a white girl be allowed to travel unchaperoned? How could a single, beautiful white girl get washed up on a desert island if she was chaperoned? It doesn't make sense."

The Chief scratched his head thoughtfully. "We'll have to bring the story up to date." He snapped his fingers. "Here's what we'll do. We'll get a whole yachtful of blondes and have them washed ashore, a whole yachtful!"

"What about some music?" said the pianist.

"Music. That's it!" exclaimed the Chief. "Crusoe is a man about town, a multimillionaire who has to go into hiding on a desert island because of gambling debts. Back in town a chorus line from a night club hankers after him. They charter a big yacht, or a deluxe liner, and set out in search of him. We'll have Crusoe a bit of a crooner—it could be his crooning to the moonlight sea that catches the ear of the lookouts on the liner."

"Great idea!"

"Hell!" said the Chief, "who cares about Crusoe anyway, we'll call it *The New York Wanderer*. Let me see . . . cost one hundred thousand, acting fees twenty thousand." The Chief drew an imaginary axis in the air, then slashed it through with a straight line. "Easy," he said, "I should make in the neighborhood of one hundred thousand, and that's my favorite neighborhood."

He picked up the phone and dialed his accountant.

"Hello Bill, we've got the outline for the Crusoe movie

worked out. Will Mrs. West get a big cut now that she's a company executive?"

He listened for a while, then heaved a sigh as big as a fist. "Okay, okay, draw me up one of your leathery contracts. You know the kind, one that'll stop a strong female shark getting her teeth into it."

He put the phone down and sat back in his chair. Everybody waited in silence.

"So Mrs. West has moved up in the organization," said Inshroin.

"Yeh, I cut Olive's contract, and I had to make up for it somehow, or get sued."

"Why did you cut the contract?"

"Have you seen Olive recently?"

"Not since I left Hollywood."

"Well, she's aged fifteen years, and drinks a lot. Mrs. West keeps spending a fortune on expensive doctors, and these days, every time she sees a dollar bill, she gets so excited, I have to get some of the boys to hold her down. Anyway, she's off my back for the next few weeks, she's gone to Italy for a vacation."

"Did Olive go with her?"

"Not this time; she went last year. Funny really, there was a time when Mrs. West wouldn't let Olive out of her sight; that doesn't happen much anymore."

The door was thrown open and a girl of about twenty-two tripped in. She was wearing a tennis outfit, and carried a racket in her hand. The newcomer sank into a chair and said, "Oh my God, I'm absolutely *dead*! What a day! I've been playing tennis since breakfast." At this point her head fell forward onto her chest, her sweet lips pouted and quivered, while long dark eyelashes closed over her beautiful eyes. There was a gentle sigh then silence. The Chief opened a drawer of his desk, took out a checkbook, and wrote out a check. He then got up, tiptoed over to the girl, and placed the money between two limp fingers of a hand that was draped over the arm of the chair. Immediately the fingers grasped the check, and the girl's eyes opened; she stretched and said, "I do feel so much better now."

"Good," said the Chief. "Go out and enjoy yourself. Stop working so hard or you'll be useless on the set."

The Chief watched her leave. "That's Jenny Dill, she's one of a bunch of new girls I'm building up. Great sense of humor. Last week we came out of a restaurant, and this guy comes up and asks for money, said he was starving. Jenny told him she wished she was suffering from his condition because she felt sick, and couldn't eat another mouthful."

"I can see she covers every aspect of Drewstone fun in toto," said Inshroin.

"That's because she's got her feet firmly on terra cotta. We all do in this organization."

Drinks were poured. Inshroin had another, and as the conversation became louder, a girl ran past the open door screaming.

"What's the matter with her?" asked Inshroin.

"Ignore her," said the Chief. "It's nothing. She just doesn't have any self-control."

"She should take some lessons from Lucy Armitage. I've been working with her, and she's got self-control down to a fine art."

Terp looked interested.

"Are you working with Lucy Armitage?"

"We've been doing some things together. She's come back to Hollywood with me to see an agent about film work."

"She is one of *the* best," said Terp. "Chief, you should try and get her to do something for us."

"I don't see why. She's too old, and besides, the stuff she does is all highbrow."

"You're talking about one of *the* queens of acting," said Terp crossly, "and from what I've been reading in the press about the popularity of the Federal Theatre, our public might be ready for a few heavier things."

The Chief stared at Terp, made a mental note of this display of insubordination, then asked Inshroin who Lucy was going to see.

The actor shrugged. "I don't know exactly. I know she's got one appointment with Warner."

"Has she? What's she like?"

"It's hard to put into words," said Inshroin. "Offstage she's very quiet and modest, but when she's acting I'm always getting smothered in her wet but firm kissing."

"Are you," said the Chief, looking interested. "I suppose we could meet and have a chat."

A butler brought in the key to the tower, and Inshroin got up to leave.

"Have you been invited to the party tomorrow?" asked Terp.

"What party?"

The Chief hesitated, and frowned at Terp. "Mussolini's youngest son and some German film people are in town. Mussolini's son has made some good pictures; we might be doing some co-productions. I've arranged a party and a dinner for them at the Porters'."

"The Hollywood banker?"

Drewstone nodded.

"Why there, if it's your party?"

"Mrs. Porter's been getting jealous of the parties we have, and as I do a lot of work with her husband, I thought I could smooth things over if I let her play host." There was a pause, then the Chief shrugged. "Come if you want to," he said. "If your friend Lucy sees me tomorrow, I'll ask her to come as well. I don't want it said that Drewstone movies ignores theater people."

The two men walked to the door. The Chief smiled and held out his hand. "By the way, nobody's been near the tower as far as I know, but I've been using the cages to store a few of our film birds. Be careful. You've got a vulture up there, and some parrots we used in *Lust of the Islands*."

"As long as I'm not expected to pay for their upkeep," said Inshroin.

Outside, Inshroin crossed the road between two new production buildings, and came across a large Victorian cemetery that hadn't been there when he was working for the company. Behind two large iron entrance gates, a man with a smoke machine was pumping fog into, and around, the gravestones. There was the sound of bridles jangling, and a glass-sided hearse pulled by four black-plumed horses turned the corner and made its way toward the gates.

A camera crew was being pulled along on a trolley beside the hearse but seemed to be filming something immediately behind it. Inshroin waited. As the vehicle drew past, the actor saw that the star was Bim Bim, the Chief's actor-dog, following the mortal remains of its master. The performance was impeccable. The hearse stopped at the gate, and the coffin lid opened half an inch, and a voice said in a stage whisper: "Here boy! Here boy!"

Bim Bim cocked his ears, then with a single leap jumped up on top of the coffin, and lying prone, rested his head on his paws and looked even more melancholic. Inshroin could swear he saw a trickle down the animal's muzzle. With cameras rolling the funeral procession continued into the cemetery.

Inshroin now crossed the road and followed the iron railing of the cemetery, which was bordered by streets lined with false wooden housefronts. People began to appear in greater and greater numbers, carts piled high with vegetables, men and women in costumes of the 1870s.

There was a sudden commotion back at the graveside, and as Inshroin looked round, he heard someone shout, "Quick, get on the phone to the Chief, we've just backed the hearse over Bim Bim's head. I think we've killed him!"

In his office, Lucy shook hands with the Chief. She smiled, and he sat looking at her through half-closed eyes—his version of looking. She was doing nothing he expected. She wasn't playing coquette or chastity flaunter, and was offering no pretend ogles.

"Do you mind if I smoke?" he asked.

"Not if you don't mind me being sick all over your furniture."

The Chief didn't light his cigar.

"I read somewhere that you drove an ambulance in the war."

"Yes, I did."

"I expect it was tough?"

"We had a philosophy."

"Oh."

"Yes, either you were at the front, or you weren't at the front. If you weren't at the front, you were okay. If you were at the front, either you were under shellfire, or you weren't. If you were under shellfire, either you were hit, or you weren't hit. If you were hit, either you were killed or you were in the hospital. If you were sent to the hospital, you were okay. If you were killed you were okay, too, because you had nothing else to worry about."

There was a pause. "Very interesting," said the Chief. "Can I see you do something?"

"Sure," said Lucy. She stood in the center of the office and began to perform. The voice was by turns melancholy, tragic, light with happiness, then blistering with bitterness. Laughter ran through it, gentle sobs and moans—not a note of the gamut of emotions was left out.

The Chief sat listening and was impressed. When she finished he said, "What was that from?"

"It wasn't from anything. I just recited the alphabet in Polish."

"Well, I've never heard it done like that before."

Lucy raised her eyebrows. "Really, and when was the last time you heard it?"

The Chief looked nervous: "I can't exactly put my finger on the date, but it was some time ago. There's only one problem, you breathe with your stomach. Come here and I'll show you how I train all my best girls."

Next door, Drewstone's secretary jumped up quickly as a howl of pain rang around the office. The door of the Chief's inner room flew open, and Lucy appeared looking slightly out of breath. She was holding a heavy ledger book in her hands. The secretary caught a glimpse of her employer, red in the face, doubled over, and holding his crotch.

Lucy turned in the doorway. "Pull yourself together, you silly little person, and grow up! If you were any smaller, your shoelaces would be flapping in your face."

Twenty minutes later, the Chief left for the party. He walked with a slight limp, the villain of the incident swinging painfully between his legs.

As the interview between Lucy and the Chief was taking place, Inshroin was leaving for the party. He took a chauffeur-driven company car from the tower, and when they got down to Drewstone's studios, the driver had to pull over to let a truck pass. Inshroin noticed it was carrying a huge slab of black marble. At first he thought it was the one he had sent the Chief when he left the company. It was a monument, but the epitaph was different:

> HERE LIES
> BIM BIM
> A DOG BORN IN HUMBLE CIRCUMSTANCES

WHO
BY STRENGTH OF CHARACTER
AN HONORABLE AMBITION
AND UNCEASING PERSERVERANCE
WON
THE LASTING LOVE
OF A POWERFUL PATRON
MR. DREWSTONE (THE CHIEF)
WHO
HAD HITHERTO
DISLIKED
THE CANINE RACE.

After some maneuvering, Inshroin's car was able to get out onto the road.

At his host's house five miles farther up the coast, Mrs. Porter lifted her dressing gown and sat down on the toilet. Because of the loudness of her gushing urine, she didn't hear the door open or see the young man in a butler's uniform walk in. Ignoring the noise she was making, he began dusting the mirror.

"Good evening, madam."

Mrs. Porter (chin cupped in her hand like Rodin's "Thinker") glanced up. "Good evening, Billings. Have you decided what you'll do?"

"Marry her, madam."

"Is that fair to her?"

"Fair to her, madam—how do you mean?"

"I suppose, Billings, like many young men, you think you can repair the damage of a seduction by marriage. I don't want to imagine the girl living with a cad like you. Why not get out of her life, and give her a chance?"

"I'm thinking of the child, madam."

"Well don't," said Mrs. Porter. "Illegitimacy is no longer the proud privilege of royalty and aristocracy; it'll soon be perfectly respectable for any girl to have a child out of wedlock. Besides, illegitimacy has never been a word in a mother's dictionary."

Mrs. Porter took her hand away from her chin and straightened her back. "However, I don't want a man like you to escape all the penalties. I believe in a heavy maintenance order even if the girl is to blame. There must be a check for her somewhere in the situation. Now pass me that fresh roll of toilet paper; I can hear people downstairs, and I have to finish dressing."

Among the first guests to arrive was Inshroin. He gave his coat to a butler, glanced into a beautifully candle-lit conservatory off the hall, then walked into the main room.

He was soon talking to a group of Germans from the Reich Film Society. "Certainly I've heard some of Hitler's speeches," the actor was saying, "and they worry me."

There was a lot of jovial laughter supported by demands to know why. "We think as members of the Nazi Party that Hitler is quite a decent man," said one of the translators. "So what is worrying about that?"

"It's hard to explain," said Inshroin. "I suppose we are all men and women of the world, and I bet most of us would repeat a funny story about a prime minister or a president. I do, because I reserve the right to treat my leader as an equal. You all appear to be realists, but is there one of you who is prepared to say Hitler is less than God?"

The laughter stopped after the question had been translated, and there was a sudden silence. No one spoke, and every face was deadly serious.

"That is a little joke?"

"No," said Inshroin. "Am I asking too much? All I want is that one of you should admit that great as you think Hitler is, as majestic, as sublime, he is still less than God."

This time the silence was unbroken.

Inshroin took a drink from a passing waiter and wandered over toward the piano as the room began to fill up with more guests.

A young man was picking out a tune on the sweet and mellows. A girl climbed up on the piano and lay down on her stomach facing him, chin cupped in her hands. She was smoking a cigarette, and its smoke curled up toward a yachting cap that was cocked over one eye, exposing a little spit curl stuck to her forehead. She bent one leg at the knee, tapped her bottom with a heel and started to sing: "A shady nook, a babbling brook."

Inshroin went upstairs to the bathroom, which was off the study. As he walked across the room, he passed oak cabinets displaying sports trophies, shields, and medals. In the middle of the room, in front of a desk, was another cabinet containing a dozen old birch canes. Inshroin glanced at them, then went into the toilet.

Each room on that side of the house had french windows with a balcony and looked down the drive to the gates. As he peed, the actor looked out at the night sky. The sound of laughter came up from somewhere below, and in the distance an owl hooted.

Four dots of flickering light appeared and moved slowly toward the house. As they got closer, Inshroin saw the lights came from four flames burning in conic shells attached to the corners of a Rolls-Royce.

When the car pulled up, the back door opened and the Chief got out with Tabby Royal, who was laughing and chewing gum. A small powdered nose peeped into the world between two fluffy bundles of yellow hair, while her chocolate box-top blue eyes were constantly on the lookout for a man to give her an expensively good time. Next to get out of the car was Mrs. Drewstone, followed by a man in a long saffron robe.

The group disappeared from view as they passed under the balcony and entered the house. Tabby's screams of delight echoed around as she recognized other guests.

Inshroin was about to go back into the study from the bathroom, when the study door opened and two men came in. One the actor recognized as the owner of the house, Mr. Porter; the other was a young man of about twenty-two, a well-tanned beach boy in a smartly cut evening suit. Mr. Porter closed the door behind him quietly, walked over to one of the cases and flicked a switch, bathing the interior in light.

"These are the cups I wanted to show you, most of them are for rowing, but three are for swimming."

"Fantastic," said the younger man.

They came to the case of canes, and Mr. Porter sighed loudly.

"These are particularly happy links with the past. They remind me of the times I was punished for lighthearted boyhood misdemeanors. When I became head of the bank, I went back to my school and bought up all the canes that had been used on me."

"I didn't think they allowed caning in American schools."

"Not usually, but mine was one of those private places,

modeled on an English public school. The fees my parents had to pay were unbelievable!"

Mr. Porter sighed nostalgically. "What I'd give to be caned again."

There was a long silence, then the young man coughed discreetly and said, "If you really feel like a caning, I'll do it for you."

Mr. Porter gasped, "Would you?"

"Sure, why not?"

"Do you know, I really think I must. The past beckons in a way I can't resist."

Mr. Porter lifted his jacket, rolled down his pants to his knees and bent over. His youthful companion took a cane from the case, swished it in the air, then delivered six vigorous drives at the proffered target with such force that Inshroin's eyes watered. When it was finished Mr. Porter got up unsteadily, eyes brimming with emotion.

"Wonderful," he said as he put the cane back and locked the case. "Let's go back downstairs, and I'll introduce you to Mr. Drewstone."

The rooms were already packed with people. The young man still sat at his piano struggling with his musical problems, but he was now surrounded by a cross and quarreling confusion of female admirers.

Over in the corner Tabby Royal was talking to admirers and reporters. Inshroin took another drink and stood on the edge of the group.

"Okay boys," she said, "ask me any question you like. Tell me what you want to know, and I'll speak honestly and freely."

"Is it true, Miss Royal, that you're still going out with six men at the same time."

"I'm a little quieter than I used to be; it's down to three now. But don't get the wrong idea, I ain't exactly taken the veil. Sure, I'm oversexed, but I don't call it that; I call it just right.

"Pardon? Speak up fella. No I had a poor childhood, where did you get the idea my family was rich? Pop didn't click as a moneymaker.

"When I came to Hollywood I discovered movies as the last great Klondike, and I'm gonna hang in until I've sifted enough of the dirt. At the moment I'm making a fortune and collecting everything money can buy. You name it, I've got it. Silks, food, cars, servants, mansions in the sky, everything. I started doing all this buying several months ago, and I ain't quit yet. My new pic will be a wow! It's called *The Saturday Night Gal*. Say that's me all over! Did somebody mention a book? I've got one."

She turned to the Chief and asked in a stage whisper, "Can I say something about the colored maid? Yeh? Okay boys, here's a new angle for you, 'cause I've never talked about my staff to the press before. My fast friends have started cutting me for being so familiar with the coloreds in the house, but my maid adores me, and I adore her."

A man standing next to the Chief who appeared a little drunker than the rest, now lunged forward and kissed Tabby on the lips. She pushed him away with a shriek.

"Keep yer hands off; you ain't got the science. When I want gum joy, I'll ring!"

"Men kiss you all the time on the screen, Tabby."

"If I sell my face for a thousand dollars a pucker, that don't mean it's poaching ground for every amateur who ain't got the dough." Tabby suddenly swayed and put a hand to her head; "I feel the pressures of existence overcoming me again; where's my spiritual adviser?"

Ram Rambone was at her side instantly, and Tabby put an arm around his shoulder. "This is Ram Rambone, fellahs; I never go anywhere without him these days; I'm absolutely cracked on mysticism and learning. I never used to go for mysticism and learning, but Ram ain't high-hat and swanky with it. My sister married a swank from a swell boys' college, and the way he treats me you'd think I had measles."

"So with the guru's help, you're learning a lot from the East?"

"I can't begin to tell you how much. Now I don't want you to think I've given up the faith I was given at birth by Mom and Dad, 'cause I ain't. I'm still a Catholic, and I've always wanted to be a nun. No kiddin'!!!! I know dozens of Mother Superiors, and I'd love to be a nun and live a life of sacrifice, but I can't spare the time. I'm practically a nun now. The only difference between me and a qualified nun is that I smoke, drink, talk dirty, chew gum, and screw around a little. Apart from things like that, I'm a nun. Guru, tell the boys about my destiny, them things you discovered in my tarot."

306

Ram Rambone folded his arms across his chest and closed his eyes.

"Miss Tabby has a great number of planets in the ascendant. Mercury gives her a fertile mind, Jupiter provides justice and honor, Venus provides beauty and grace. There is an aura of nativity about her, which shows she was born to sway the world. Theosophically I should say she is going through her eighth reincarnation as an actress. If everybody was as good and pure-minded as Miss Tabby, there would be no sin in the world."

Inshroin took his leave with a trick he had learned as a boy. He snapped a coin he had hidden in his hand against the glass at the moment it touched his lips. It made a noise like he had bitten a piece off the lip of the tumbler. Then he swore loudly, and spat out a mouthful of crunched ice, which looked like glass when it was flying through the air.

"Are you hurt?" screamed Tabby.

Inshroin doubled over, hand to his mouth. "Bleeding to death . . . I'll go to the bathroom."

As he maneuvered his way through the crowd, Inshroin suddenly came face to face with Olive. She was leaning on a man's arm. It was unmistakably Olive, but her face was fattened out, the skin was very lined, while the eyes were hidden behind thick makeup. When she finally focused on Inshroin, her dulled expression didn't change. She greeted him as though she'd seen him only yesterday.

"Hello Phillip, I didn't expect you to be here." There was a pause, then without looking at her companion, she said, "This is my friend Tom Mix, he's been marvelous, he helped me get over the death of Sage Lolland, the one great love I had in my life before we met."

"I don't remember you knowing anybody called Sage Lolland," said Inshroin.

"He was killed in France during the war. He won a lot of medals for bravery."

Inshroin raised his eyebrows.

"I can see you don't believe me," said Olive. "You think I'm lying, don't you?"

"I don't mind if you are. I'm a bit of a liar myself, and I've always enjoyed listening to people who can tell a good lie."

"Now you're laughing at me," said Olive. "I suppose you

think you're better than the rest of us because you work in the theater. Sage would never have let you laugh at me. Sage hated people who had cheap and nasty minds." She clenched her fists. "My God, you've got a cheap and nasty mind; you're like all the rest."

The conversation ended abruptly when the band broke into the Italian national anthem. Inshroin became separated from Olive by a wall of bodies that instantly materialized and pushed toward the door to witness the grand entrance of Il Duce, Jr.

As the guest of honor appeared, the anthem softened dramatically. Above the reverential hush, Tabby Royal was heard to shriek, *"Keep your paws to yourself, fuckface!"*

The Porters settled their illustrious guest on a sofa by the massive fireplace and the press of people fell silent to hear the conversation. Well to the front stood the Chief, with a firm grip on Inshroin's elbow.

"How do you do," said Mrs. Porter, extending her hand. As the arm came up, Inshroin swore he heard juiceless sinews creaking.

"Romano Mussolini at your service."

"It's lovely to meet you," said Mrs. Porter. "I do so admire what your father is doing for Italy. You know the phrase 'Give Rome a Napoleon, and in twenty-five years it will have an empire'?"

"I find I have not heard the saying, but I appreciate your kind words about my father. Are you a Fascist?"

"I'm not quite sure what the word means," said Mrs. Porter. "I think you have to be either a German or an Italian to be a Fascist. On the other hand, you don't have to be a Greek to admire Greek architecture."

"Exactly. I don't think it's particularly Italian or German to be Fascist. Fascism means an extreme love of one's country."

"Well, if that's all it is," said Mrs. Porter, "I can't see anything wrong with it. When we make our European tour, we shall see for ourselves."

A maid who was putting down some drinks sniffed and said, "Pooh, ve shust game from dere."

"If you are going to Europe, madam," said Mussolini, "there is no shipping line better than the Italian. When do you expect to travel?"

"Early in the spring."

"The weather is often very bad at that time of the year."

"The rougher the better," said Mrs. Porter. "My father was a sea captain, and I know I'd love it."

"Will you be perhaps taking your children?"

"I have no children, I'm afraid," said Mrs. Porter. "I have my figure to think of."

Mussolini smiled sweetly. "Doesn't your husband want any children to carry on the family name?"

"Alas no, he's a very pessimistic man. He thinks our President is in league with those who will destroy our way of life. He says our children would just get used to wearing silk when it would be torn off their backs and rags substituted. He thinks it's a trend of the times. He says the champagne age is passing, and people will drink beer, and he hates beer."

"Do you believe him?"

"It's hard to tell. I sometimes wish I was married to a man with illusions."

A floating red balloon nudged the young Mussolini's ear; as though to punctuate Mrs. Porter's profundity, he playfully pricked it with a swizzlestick. The onlookers murmured appreciation, but one angry face suddenly appeared holding a string: Attached to it was the ragged neck of the balloon. He wore a badly fitting morning coat and a pair of striped pants; his thick eyebrows and moustache looked false. They seemed to have been stuck on to his face as an afterthought. A passing uniform bumped into him accidentally. The man frowned, jerked his cigar from his mouth, twitched his eyebrows pneumatically, and said, "Whatever happened to the old-fashioned Nazi who said sorry when he bumped into you, eh?"

"Baron von Howitz!" said Mrs. Porter. "How are you enjoying the party?"

The man with the moustache peered closer. "Ah Mrs. Porter, I didn't recognize you. My, you've lost weight. You're so thin you must have to lean up against a wall to give vent to a good cuss. I could pick you up by the ankles and whip a judge with you." He kissed her hand passionately.

"You like the new look, Baron?" said Mrs. Porter.

"You're no raving beauty, so play up the good parts like Dietrich does her legs. You have an interesting pair of hands. They look lovely stripped as they are of any ornament except for those extraordinary nails bitten down to the quick. Some people might say they're a deformity; I'll always swear they're hands. But don't overdo things; never go out in public without your gloves on. Look, there's Sybil Raintree! Coo-ee Sybil! She said she'd do anything for a fur coat, now she can't do it up . . . Thank you, I'll have a brandy. My these glasses are as big as oxygen tents, and the ice cubes could be explored by Scott of the Antarctic!"

On the way into dinner, the Chief walked with two of the Germans, talking animatedly through the translator. At the door a retired executive from Coda stopped and asked the Chief how he was feeling.

"Not so bad for my age; I get a bit of muscle cramp now and again."

"You should exercise more," said the Coda man. "Look at me." He put his arms above his head, and keeping his legs straight touched his toes. He repeated it four times, then walked off to his dinner place.

The Germans stared openmouthed, then through the translator, one of them said to Drewstone, "We knew you were important in Hollywood, but the bow that man just gave you was for a God!"

The table arrangement had been copied from a picture book of banquets at Buckingham Palace. A table on a raised platform stretched diagonally across the floor, while two longer ones, joined to the head table at either end, ran the length of the room. In all there was enough space for one hundred diners. On two of the walls were huge paintings of Mussolini. One showed him in profile wearing a plumed velvet hat, the other was a frontal view of the dictator in a steel helmet that half covered his eyes. In both pictures the jaw line had been darkened and gave the impression that it was physically jutting out over the heads of the guests. The room was lit by dozens of candles set in glass holders on the tables, and waiters dressed in the uniforms of Vatican guards hovered around the seats.

As the hors d'oeuvres were presented a dozen men in cowboy outfits simultaneously took out six-shooters and put them beside their plates.

When the soup was served, one of the cowboys drank his very loudly, then demanded a second helping. The man

310

immediately opposite laughed loudly, causing the first man to ask what was amusing his honorable friend. A short and loud argument followed in which both protagonists swore to cut out the other's liver. Other cowboys broke up the quarrel, hands were shaken, drinks were drunk, and the next course was served, which happened to be fish.

The first cowboy now remarked that there was somebody else at the table who was a queer fish.

"Who?"

"You."

"You're a damn liar!"

Panic followed. A fight broke out that involved all the cowboys. Shrieks, curses, and calls for fair play bounced off the walls. Mrs. Porter suppressed an urge to get up and run out of the room.

Inshroin stood up. "Ladies and gentlemen, quiet please . . . *Quiet!* . . . Thank you. Now before we go any further, I would like to say a few words about Mr. Drewstone. The Chief, as he is affectionately known, has always aimed at giving the public and his employees the best he possibly can. We may have had our differences in the past, but I cannot deny that here in Hollywood, Mr. Drewstone sets the whole industry an example by copying the 'strength through joy' program advocated by Herr Hitler, and we are all better people for it."

A congressman smiled at his wife. "A very fine observation," he said. "I wish I'd said that. I'd say it myself if I thought there were the slightest chance I'd be re-elected to public office afterward."

Inshroin continued, "Yes, Mr. Drewstone's films always have the right ingredients that go to make up a successful movie. Sexual titillation without much sex, an element of fun, and above all a passionate adherence to the craze of the moment. His dialogue is a breathtaking breakthrough in simplicity, and requires very little brainpower to decipher its meaning and see how it applies. When he's making his cinematic essays he works extremely hard, as every one here can testify, and—" (much table thumping) "—and the intellectual effort required in making them he always finds an exciting and rewarding exercise, especially after he's had a good night's rest and really feels up to it." (The Nazis nod as officials translate to them.) "It is perhaps one of Mr. Drewstone's lasting achievements that every one of his movies is a true reflection of the fine man who makes them. *However*, as we can all testify, they are most emphatically not representative of real America any more than they resemble true films." Here Inshroin bowed to his former employer. "An achievement, ladies and gentlemen, of which anybody can be justly proud."

"*Hear, hear!*"

The Chief didn't follow all the speech, as he was caught up in the fight that had preceded it. The words sounded right, but coming from Inshroin, they didn't seem as right as they sounded. He was even more amazed when he caught sight of a blond-haired man throwing himself across a table, and pawing at the dress of one of the guests. Dozens of waiters appeared and started to serve food.

At the head table, a Nazi guest drank a toast to the Chief, and called on him to reply. Drewstone took a quick glance at some notes he had prepared, and wiped his forehead with a handkerchief, leaving a lot of black smudges on his face. He dug his knuckles into the table, hoisted himself into a position to reply, but at a remote table away in the distance, Baron von Howitz rose and addressed the diners through a megaphone, thus drowning out the Chief.

"Thank you, Herr Ritz. Ladies and gentlemen, honored guests, I am new American what I cannot talk English until I took a lesson often. I'm surpassing at it now, what you can speculate since I been reading at you."

"*Hear, hear!*"

The Chief ordered a waiter to go down and stop him, but the speaker waved the menial aside with a gesture of contempt. Notes began to arrive begging him to stop, but he slapped each one into a ball and tossed them behind his seat as he continued speaking.

"But can we get the good Reich movie? Write the script goodly and make them stay uppermost, you'll ask myself. The German industry in the far future will be given shortly facilities imposed in a multiplication vast, vast you her said!" He paused to sip his drink, smacked his lips and held up the glass. "What jolly, what delinquency!"

The diners' meals were being enhanced by a number of interesting diversions: Plate tilters and dribble glasses; a meat that turned the teeth green; hot toothpicks that burnt the

312

mouth; collapsing knives and forks; rubber bread rolls; and excellent reproductions of dog mess here and there under the chairs.

The speaker plunged on: "Dare I ask if acting people must be carefree cowboys."

"*No!*"

"I see, let us drink more wine, this thirsty is drinking work. That after we joyfully discussion when the Reich Hollywood is established."

Inshroin smiled at the Chief. "They're loving it, boss. This man is the latest fashion. He is the newer nonsense, the larger lunacy, the higher goofiness, the ultimate crazy, the complete dippy in the dream box."

A waiter pressed a note into Inshroin's hand, which he read quickly. "Good God, that's terrible news, terrible."

"What's it say?" asked the Chief.

Inshroin leaned forward. "Chief, it's very important you" (here the actor lowered his voice to a whisper) "aska umble apid irgan ayey loof stooger, *loose a lot of money* garvid of the fishing grew!"

"What was that? Will you speak up?"

Inshroin looked surprised. "Chief, if you don't make a decision quickly, les inam atic namble cur eft rigeroff probable *million dollar loss*, if ego juster flot!"

"Let me see that note."

Inshroin passed it across, and as the host read, his mouth fell open.

Dear Mr. Drewstone:
We the undersigned regret to inform you that we can no longer serve the enemies of democracy. We have thrown the rest of the food into the garbage, and all spat in what you are now eating.
Signed, THE STAFF.

The Chief stood up and told someone to call the police; as he did so the chair he had been sitting on was removed by a waiter and another put in its place. He stood there, legs planted firmly on the ground. Scowling around, he lit a cigar.

Baron von Howitz was now concluding his speech: "Finally ladies and gentlemen, a shaggy dog will pass amongst you. Once upon a time there were two Jews . . ." A dozen voices replied, "*Now there are millions of them!*"

All the lights in the room went out, and a general battle ensued among the cowboys. When the lights were restored, men lay in heaps across the table, while one individual swung by the neck from a rope attached to a glittering chandelier. "Good God," said the Chief, "is he dead?"

He put a hand to his head, dropped back into a chair, and fell through the bottom. Drewstone's arms shot up to control his balance, and it looked as if he were tossing his hands to the ceiling in a violent double Fascist salute. All the men who had been fighting jumped up and put their arms out, "Sieg Heil, Chief! Sieg Heil! . . ."

Inshroin slipped away to the front door, and as he stood waiting for his coat, he began to feel pleased with himself. He hadn't drunk much all evening. A few glasses of champagne, some Scotch, some wine . . . there was the sound of a woman's sob, and it seemed to come from the conservatory. As the actor listened, he heard Olive's raised tearful voice say: "Why can't you?" Then more emphatically, "Why can't you explain it to me? You've got no idea how miserable and unhappy I am, have you? Do something for me, will you? Why don't you kill me? I'm not scared, honest to God I'm not. You're the one that's afraid, not me, you cheap coward. What have you ever done in your life to be afraid of, you mummy's boy? You're a cheap dirty coward, I really could admire you if you weren't, I really could. I'd reverence and admire you. I would. I'd do anything for you. I'd lay down and let you crap all over me if you wanted to. I would. I thought you were strong and powerful. But I was wrong, you're all the same, you men, you're all cowards and liars. God, I loved you once, but I don't believe in you anymore, can you understand that, can you? Darling, for God's sake why can't you explain things to me?"

Inshroin tiptoed over to the conservatory and glanced in. Her escort sat on the sofa smoking a cigarette while Olive sat beside him twisting a handerkchief around in her lap. Her face was swollen up like a balloon, and makeup was running in streams.

When Inshroin got back to the tower, he found a note pinned on the door.

The trouble with Drewstone is that he weighs 180 pounds, and thinks 175 of it is tucked down the front of his pants. I've gone back to New York, I'll write when I'm settled.

Lucy

314

Goebbels was obsessed by films. He went out of his way to cultivate friends in theater and film circles. His attitude toward these persons bordered on worship. They, in theory, could do no wrong. Many an erring actor or actress found personal scandal hushed up by the intervention of Goebbels in the years of his power. As his aide Rudolph Semmler observed, "His motto is like that of Frederick the Great; artists must not be bothered." Even on the busiest days he found time to see the latest film and write about it. He understood film as well as any industry executive, and probably better.

David S. Hull
Film in the Third Reich

Du Liebling schenke mir
Einige Silberlinge
Daraufhin zeig 'ich dir
Sehr interessante Dinge
Zwar wenn die Sonne steigt
Muss du aus meinem Zimmer
Doch was ich dir gezeigt
Vergisst du nie und nimmer.

(Darling give me
A few shillings.
Then I'll show you very interesting things,
It's true that when the sun rises
You must get out of my room,
But what I've shown you
You'll never, never forget.)

A. H. Brodrick,
Casual Change

IN GERMANY ALL HITLER'S DREAMS HAVE COME TRUE. He is now absolute power, and seems as impregnable as a force of nature. The people are paying him a homage that is cosmic, and with them he is about to launch his revenge war. When he meets foreign leaders, he seems a citadel of silence and reserve force, a man who can be ominously silent in fifty languages. Put a swastika around the sphinx's neck, and you'll have Hitler in stone. He is cold, impressive, and always makes his visitors reveal their intentions first. His mental power, physical resources, and memory are the marvel of those who watch him, while his mind seems ever fixed upon a distant purpose he alone perceives. It was Napoleon's way. It was Bismarck's way.

While the Chief waits for the police to arrive at the Porters' house, it is early morning in Munich. The Führer is in the city for the day to watch the procession of "Two Thousand Years of German Culture."

The show doesn't start till two, so Hitler has a few hours to devote to other interests. He meets with Peter Kreuder, the German jazz king and piano virtuoso, the man who put swing and trick melodies into Hitler's favorite versions of Lehar's *Merry Widow*. Finally, before lunch, a quick discussion with Joseph Thorak, the artist who is designing some plaques for the new Palace of Art.

At two o'clock Hitler arrives at the Podium of State to watch the procession. He gets out of his car, greeting town officials with a series of seal-like flaps of his right hand. Around him are dozens of gray uniforms slashed with crimson. All the surrounding streets have been closed to traffic, and the lower parts of the shops and houses are hung with black crepe, making the route look like a long winding canal of darkness.

Hitler climbs the steps of the podium, stands rigidly at attention, firm, monumental, and as silent as the opposition benches in the Reichstag. Then he puts his arm out to greet the army, which is leading the parade and has just turned into the street.

They goosestep by in their tens of thousands, complete physical fitness, unity, and determination. *Down* come the feet in absolute unison, every muscle in their bodies taut and tingling. They are followed by thousands of men and women in costume, and hundreds of floats pulled by horses.

The first part of the procession holds Hitler's attention, but now his mind begins to wander. He starts to daydream about his own funeral—it will be the most magnificent in German history.

Late at night, the mourning nation stands around a vast artificial lake that has been built in front of the Berlin Gate. At the center of the expanse of water is a huge floating mausoleum that contains the Führer's body. In the distance, on a hill, an orchestra plays Wagner. The conductor has a little gas container attached to his wrist, which tips the baton with a blue flame. It flickers back and forth, representing the spirit of the departed Führer rising to join the Valkyries.

The center of attention is the contraption in the water, which is lit by searchlights dotted along the shoreline. It is neither boat nor raft, but a combination of the two, a rectangular chest resting on a huge flat-bottomed raft. None of its building planks are visible, because masses of black crepe hang down from the sides and sweep the surface of the water. The chest is covered by a black canopy, the four-corner supports of which are life-size figures in full silver armor with closed visors. Each suit is surrounded at its feet by trophies and ancient war implements.

A black velvet altar under the canopy contains Hitler's body. He lies in a copper coffin, with a swastika-inscribed shield at each corner, his head resting on a crimson cushion. Immediately at the foot of the body stands a broad rectangular pedestal, eight feet high, upon which is a huge silver lion, three times lifesize, with its head resting on its paws. Beneath this figure, and right at the front of the raft, is a winged female statue in long flowing robes. She is also silver. Both arms are stretched toward the horizon, and she is holding a gold plaque inscribed with the words:

ADOLF HITLER
FÜHRER
CUT FROM THE LAND OF THE LIVING
HE FELL ASLEEP SOFTLY.
SURELY HE HATH BORNE OUR GRIEFS.
HIS END IS VICTORY.

The searchlights beam down on the silver and the rich deep black, producing a feeling of profound melancholy among the mourners.

The parade organizer has to cough twice to regain the Führer's attention. It is time to leave for an evening gala behind the Nymphenburg Palace, home of the former Bavarian kings.

Hitler enters the park through lines of blond members of the League of German Girls, who throw flowers at him. Thousands of guests in their finest uniforms or summer clothing sit at tables around a clearing in the wooded park, SS guards in white uniforms serve food and drinks, while pretty girls in elfish uniforms flit about the tables and among the trees. In the clearing, the best German ballet stars and actors take turns performing.

Girls ride in bareback, to show that the woman of earlier times was a keen huntress and a joyful comrade of men in the noble chase. After a little galloping around to the sound of horns, men ride in, and a mock battle of the sexes takes place. It is described in the program. "Swords and shields ring out, figures on horseback charge each other; some flee or again take the offensive. Sometimes it looks as if one side then the other is winning, but the battle rages on in a hot struggle."

J. Valtin, the German-American author, was being held at prison camp Fuhlsbuettel for questioning concerning left-wing, antistate espionage.

All through the night of "Two Thousand Years of German Culture," high-spirited SS guards went into the cell opposite Valtin's to kick and beat a middle-aged Jew, who had been accused of attempting to seduce a Hitler Youth girl. Through-out the night the cell door was repeatedly unlocked: the sounds of curses and blows as truncheons were used on his genitals, then hoarse whimperings until the beating resumed. By day-break the man was dead.

At seven in the morning, prisoners were marched out into the yard and separated into two groups—Jews and non-Jews. A group of Jewish prisoners was already there, and they had dug a deep hole. As everybody stood at attention, the naked body of the dead man was brought out on a stretcher, and dumped at the feet of the diggers. Several put hands to their faces when they saw its condition, while three fainted. All were cuffed with sticks until they stood straight again.

The prison commandant then ordered the men to drop their

pants and masturbate. Those who were slow to respond were beaten with truncheons. After this, the corpse was kicked into the hole, and each man was ordered to climb in, stand on the remains and shout, "I am a race polluter."

When they had all taken a turn, the corpse was removed from the grave, and the Jewish prisoners were forced to roll it from one side of the yard to the other shouting, "We're all race polluters!"

While this was going on, political prisoners repeated over and over at the top of their voices, "We are red pigs in prison for high treason!"

When the guards had tired of the entertainment, everybody was marched back to the cells, and the corpse was taken to a furnace in the cellar.

Senators, I think this activity is a fine thing for us. After all, our little brief authority here will not go very far. We shall soon be forgotten; it is a great thing to know we have this great activity for which we may appropriate money, and which will make us all actors on the stage forever.

The play to which I refer will probably be reproduced longer than *Hamlet*, and people will be talking about the Senator from New York instead of the Prince of Denmark. When most of us die we are forgotten almost before the resolution to pay for our burial is passed. But down yonder at the WPA there are playwrights who are putting us down in books, so that we may become part of the permanent literature of the ages. Men will walk the stage a thousand years from now representing us in our proper persons and our dignity. It is the first time, I think, that the Senate ever won immortality.

Senator Bailey of North Carolina,
Congressional Record, February 22, 1938

FROM MID-1938 TO THE END OF THE YEAR, the House Committee to Investigate un-American activities (Chairman

Martin Dies), conducted hearings against the Federal Theatre. The hearings were instigated because institutions that were being attacked in productions wanted the theater project discredited, then terminated.

The Director Hallie Flanagan was called to answer certain questions.

Dies said, "We are combating un-American activities." Flanagan said, "I have been engaged over the last four years in combating un-American *in*activity."

"Do you consider the theater a weapon?"

"The theater is all things to all men."

Senator Starnes suddenly waved an old copy of *Theatre Arts Monthly* in the air.

"Do you see this?"

"Yes."

"In it you describe a meeting of workers' theaters in New York in 1931. Were you active in setting them up?"

"No. I wrote an article on them called 'A Theatre Is Born.' I was simply a reporter to the event."

"How many people has the Federal Theatre played for so far?"

"About twenty-five million."

"Where do your audiences come from?"

"The people of America."

"Isn't it true, you couldn't get audiences for anything but communist plays?"

"No. Our list of productions shows we had a wide variety of plays."

"I'd like to return to your article, 'A Theatre Is Born.' You described them as having a certain 'Marlowesque madness.' Are you quoting from this Marlowe?" asked Starnes. "Is he a communist?"

"No. Put on the record that he was a dramatist in the period of Shakespeare, immediately preceding Shakespeare."

"Can you give us one play dealing with a social question where organized labor doesn't have the best of the other fellows?"

"Certainly, *Spirochete*, the history of syphilis, a production endorsed by the Surgeon General of the US Public Health Service."

The chairman waved the example aside.

"Doesn't the play *Power* imply public ownership of utilities is a good thing?"

"We don't pick plays by choosing a side in a controversy."

"Have you produced any anti-Fascist plays?"

"Some people claimed Shaw's *On The Rocks* was anti-Fascist, some said it was anti-communist. We had the same discussion over Shakespeare's *Coriolanus*. We never did a play because it had a political bias; we did a play because we believed it a good play."

Titles were produced that showed the influence of red Russia and the Kremlin: *Love 'Em and Leave 'Em, Up in Mabel's Room, A New Kind of Love*, Molière's *School for Wives*, and Sheridan's *School for Scandal*.

In the middle of the hearings, on Sunday, October 3 at eight p.m. EST Orson Welles and his Mercury Theatre of the Air begin their radio performance of H. G. Wells's *War of the Worlds*. In the CBS studio, Welles puts on his earphones, cues in the Mercury theme, then begins to read. "We know that in the early years of the twentieth century, this world was being watched closely by intelligences greater than man's, and yet as mortal as his own . . ."

The introduction was followed by an anonymous announcer pretending to be caught in a routine bulletin, who told the listeners that strange objects were appearing in the sky over America. Millions of people now tuning in had missed Welles's introduction and heard what appeared to be a straightforward news broadcast about an invasion from outer space. When it was announced that the mysterious objects seen in the sky had fallen to earth at Grover's Mill in New Jersey, pandemonium erupted. Within minutes the nation was in a state of panic from coast to coast, and people were taking to the streets to flee landing Martians.

A frantic mayor of a midwestern town phoned the studio. He reported crowds in the streets, women and children huddling in churches, violence and looting: a state of affairs repeated all over the country.

As the Mercury Theatre of the Air concluded its broadcast, the building was suddenly full of police. The members of the cast were taken to a back office and held incommunicado while network employees frantically destroyed or locked up all the scripts and records of the broadcast. Then the press was allowed in.

"What do you know about the fatal stampede in a Jersey hall?"
   "How many traffic deaths have there been?"
   "How many suicides, murders, rapes, etc., etc?"

Hours later the players are released and creep back into the streets, which have now returned to normal. At the Mercury Theatre, there are more reporters, more cameramen, more questions. For the following few days, editorials condemning the radio production are delivered by the Mercury press-clipping bureau in sacks.

The Nazi propaganda department is quick to respond. Dr. Goebbels comments: "Berlin Nazis weep for US naïveté. If Americans fall so easily for a fantastic radio broadcast of an invasion from Mars by Orson Welles, it explains why they so readily believe Nazi atrocity stories. What is the lesson? Let us weep for our American contemporaries who accept such atrocities as true. Naïveté is a gift of God, but it should not be abused. How much less naïveté is required to accept as true, atrocity stories about Nazi Germany? This explains a lot for us in the Old World."

The Dies Committee Report was filed with the House of Representatives on January 3, 1939. Six months of sensational charges tapered down to one short paragraph:

> We are convinced that a rather large number of the employees of the Federal Theatre Project are either members of the Communist Party or are sympathetic with the Communist Party.

There was to be no more funding from Congress, but productions went on all across the country for another six months. On June 26, 1939, *Florida Wheel* by Hallie Flanagan was presented on an NBC national hookup in a special broadcast for the Federal Theatre from Hollywood. The program included Lionel Barrymore, Edward Arnold, James Cagney, Dick Powell, Joan Blondell, Walter Abel, Edward G. Robinson, Al Jolson, Bette Davis, Henry Fonda, Gale Sondergaard, Ralph Bellamy, and Gloria Dickson.

We played Ohumpka, and they came by oxcart,
They came in with lanterns to see Twelfth Night.
An old man barefoot helping children from the oxcart
said, "They may be pretty young to understand it
But I want they should be able to say
They've seen Shakespeare—
I did once when I was a kid . . ."

At midnight on June 30, 1939, *Sing for Your Supper* ended at
the Adelphi in New York. Performers sang for the last time,

"Aint it lucky, ain't it swell?
I ran all the way home to tell.
I'm so happy it's just like ringing a bell—
Papa's got a job!"

The production reached its climax in *Ballad of Uncle Sam*
which later became *Ballad for Americans*, used by the
Republican party as an anthem. That night it was sung by Paul
Robeson over a nationwide hookup, and CBS was buried under
an avalanche of mail saying, "This was the voice of America."

The curtain came down on a coast-to-coast theater, on
thousands of people, their lives and their efforts. A million
dollars worth of equipment that had been bought over a
four-year period, from gifts, and admission charges, was locked
up in government warehouses, and disappeared.

Inshroin went to a good-bye party for the Federal Theatre at
the Curzon music hall in Hollywood. At four o'clock in the
morning he staggered out into the street between two friends,
his head lolling forward as if his throat had been cut. He
stopped, reeled back, took a swig from a bottle, then fell to his
knees, and rolled over on his back.

His companions were drunk also and couldn't lift the actor
from the gutter. In the end, one of them dropped a sign he had
picked up at the party across Inshroin's chest, and then they
staggered off singing. The actor lay on his back under the night
sky, his eyes fishlike and glazed. His back was arched while his
hands dug into the road. Champagne bubbles pumped up out of
his mouth as if they were being forced up by the strokes of an
internal piston. The liquid spread over Inshroin's face, covered
his eyes, and ran down through his hair, collecting in a dark

pool at the back of his head. A gray form sniffed the liquid then hopped away squeaking. The sign on Inshroin's chest told anybody SHOOT ME WHILE I'M STILL HAPPY.

THE PRINCE OF WALES we met at the party on Long Island had become king, but was forced to abdicate before he could marry Mrs. Simpson, "the woman I love." From the day of his abdication to his death, he would spend his life wandering aimlessly with her from one expensive and exclusive resort to another. His brother George, who was nervous, stuttered badly, and would have preferred to remain in the background, was obliged to assume the crown.

The new king arrived with his wife for an official tour of North America on May 17, 1939, sailing into Quebec harbor on the *Empress of Australia*. Canadian and American photographers realized the significance of a picture taken as the royal couple came down the gangway, when for the first time in history, a British king and queen would set foot on North American soil. As soon as a picture was taken, it was rushed to the Chateau Frontenac, where darkroom facilities had been set up. In little more than one hour from the moment the king and queen stepped ashore, the first picture was in the newspapers of twenty cities in Canada, Britain, and the USA.

On May 21, 1939, George VI unveiled the Canadian National War Memorial in Ottawa. In front of a large crowd, he stood on the steps leading up to the memorial and made a speech.

"It is my privilege as your King to unveil today in your capital city, this noble memorial to Canada's spirit of sacrifice in the Great War. It has been well named 'The Response.' Surmounting the arch through which the armed forces of the nation are passing are the figures of Peace and Freedom. To win peace and secure freedom, Canada's sons and daughters enrolled for service during the Great War. For the cause of peace and freedom 60,000 gave their lives, and a still larger number suffered impairment of body and mind. This sacrifice the national memorial holds in remembrance for our own and succeeding generations. The memorial, however, does more than just commemorate a great event in the past. It has a message for all generations and for all countries—the message which called forth the Canadian response. Not by chance do the crowning figures of peace and freedom appear side by side. Peace and freedom cannot be separated. It is well that we have in one of the world's capitals a visible reminder of so great a truth. Without freedom there can be no enduring peace, and without peace no enduring freedom . . ."

The one feat alone—that of dying—by which a mean condition could be resolved into a grand one, Fanny had achieved.

Thomas Hardy
Far from the Madding Crowd

FOUR MONTHS HAD GONE BY since Lucy returned to New York, where she had taken a job in a small theater off-Broadway. Her performance, like the production, was uninspiring and listless; she wasn't involved; her mind was elsewhere; she began to feel herself drifting—aimless. A stomach-cramping fear for her future would descend without warning and stay with her for hours. It was a kind of fear she had never felt before, not even when she was driving the ambulance under fire.

One evening late, we find her writing a letter. She is bent over the page writing with a dip pen, a habit she has not lost since the war. She crumbles a sheet of paper and starts again:

DEADLY:
This being away from you. What I do every day is much the same while what I think is very different. I sometimes glance at the papers to keep up with current affairs, but no matter how hard I try, current feelings are all I seem able to cope with at the moment. I wish I had star eyes to carry me over the horizon that keeps you invisible. Is the sky looking at you like it's looking at me? I'm a little

to the right of the moon below a cloud, I think you're further west, but I'm not absolutely sure; wave to me.

My friend, now don't get upset, that way of talking to you isn't cold. I couldn't come down in your direction without being a friend first. Phillip, I think I could love you, and if I can't say more, it's because words say so little, do you know what I mean? I know now that the war altered me completely, it made me so careful about my feelings, taught me to hold back, never show a sign of being happy, in case the cause of that happiness was taken from me. I think I've been running away from you (and from myself) ever since we started working together. Do you know what I mean? . . .

Reloads the pen from the inkwell, then a fresh splutter of thoughts and feelings she chases along the page . . .

I'm not that old, can you imagine any children? You me and the potential third. It'll have a combination of your face and mine, what a funny face. Do you have any green-eyed ancestors? I do.

Before she could mail the letter, a telegram arrived from a Doctor Simpson telling her Inshroin was very ill, and could she come down to Hollywood. She left immediately, and while she was on the train the conductor told her that Germany had invaded Poland.

When Lucy put her head through the secret trapdoor of the tower, she couldn't see at first, things were so gloomy. The room was illuminated by one small light beside a camp cot over which a man was leaning. Lucy climbed up into the room and stumbled over bottles that seemed to be littered everywhere. "God," she said to herself, "he must have drunk enough to launch a battleship."

The man bending over the cot looked up. "Lucy Armitage, I recognize you from your pictures. I'm Doctor Simpson; I sent the telegram."

"How did you find my address?"

"Mr. Inshroin asked me to phone your agent."

"How is he?"

"He's very bad, I'm afraid, he's been in and out of a coma for two days. His liver is like a piece of coral, and there's a lung complication that's turned into pneumonia. I wanted to move him to a hospital, but he wouldn't let me." The doctor shook his head. "Were you very close?"

"We were getting to know each other better."

A spider let itself down to the floor on a long thread and hid in the dust, dust that had settled like seeds, germinated, and grown. A small monkey ran chattering across the room.

"The place is just like a zoo," said the doctor. "I don't know how he could live in such a mess. Did you see the pigeons and vulture in the cages downstairs?"

Lucy nodded and looked around; for a moment she thought she was back in the trenches. The place was full of uniforms, rifles, and packs from *The Heart of Turbulence*. Old tin hats were stacked everywhere. The only furniture in the room was the cot on which Inshroin was lying, and a small table with a radio on it.

Lucy looked down at Inshroin as he started breathing heavily. Except for the drink belly, the actor was skin and bone. Finger cords showing tight like violin strings, forked blue veins looking like a map of the land of death. He turned over on his side: Thin shoulder blades stuck up, tiny wings ready to sprout for the flight. Lucy felt his pulse.

"You seem to know what you're doing," said the doctor.

"I was a nurse during the war."

"Then I can leave him in capable hands; I've done everything I can for the time being. I'll be back in the morning." He picked up his bag. "Mr. Inshroin asked me to release the pigeons, so I'll open the cages on my way out. Tell him when he comes around."

Lucy nodded. As soon as he had gone, Inshroin began coughing and then started to scratch, flaking skin on his chest until he was drawing blood. The only thing Lucy could find to stop him was a pair of boxing gloves, which she put on his hands and laced up.

At the base of the tower, the doctor released the pigeons. There was a connecting entrance from the vulture's cage, and before the doctor had time to slam it shut, the huge bird had hopped through and then flapped to the door of the pigeon cage. The doctor backed away slowly.

The bird stood there for a while, the pink neck resting back on its body, then it decided to lift off. It spread its wings and rose slowly, paddling against the thickness of air. The wings flared and folded like hinged fans. Mounting an updraft, it swung away to the right and sailed like a kite past Inshroin's window.

Inside the tower the actor had taken to hitting and pawing himself, since he couldn't scratch the itching skin. As he punched his chest, which seemed the most painful part of his body, he looked as if he had knocked himself down and was continuing the fight without benefit of a referee. Lucy sat down by the bed and started the vigil that would last through the night.

At midnight Inshroin opened his eyes and glanced around. His gaze settled on Lucy.

"So you finally came."

"Yes, my dear boy. I was writing a letter to you when the telegram arrived. I left right away. Is there anything I can do for you?'

"I want to hear the broadcast from London on the German invasion of Poland. It should be on around twelve-thirty. If I fall asleep, will you wake me?" Then he drifted off again.

Lucy went to the window and looked up into the sky. The vulture had not left, but soared back and forth over the tower.

At twenty past twelve, Lucy went over to the radio and turned it on. The machine looked very shy, totally unfit for the historic announcement it was about to make. Lucy turned the dial, exposing a static noise that sounded like waves at sea. She interrupted a voice that came clean out of the air in full flight. The station ran off downhill as she turned the dial. From a point two inches to the right, a new, but no less genial voice was picked up telling another story she didn't want to hear; she pushed on to the strains of music, discovered it was opera, and dropped it. Right on the edge of waveband 217, something was stirring—a sudden burst of music that can be whistled—the British national anthem. A little more this way, a little more that way, again the radio choked as Lucy fiddled with the dial. She lifted the set up and shook it against her ear, as history spluttered and faded.

"Leave the damn thing alone. Are you trying to dance with it?" asked Inshroin. He was conscious and propping himself up on his elbows. Suddenly they could hear Prime Minister Chamberlain's voice. "This morning, the British Ambassador in Berlin handed the German government a final note stating that unless we heard from them by eleven o'clock that they were prepared at once to withdraw their troops from Poland, a state of war would exist between us. I have to tell you now, that no such undertaking has been received, and that consequently this country is at war with Germany."

Inshroin sank back on the pillow, and Lucy said, "So, it's started all over again."

In England a message was signaled from Whitehall to every transmitting station and studio of the BBC. Engineers opened sealed orders—only two wavelengths where people at home could pick up British broadcasts. A foreign-language service was started for listeners in Europe. The British television service that had been on air for two years faded. The last thing seen on the screen was a Walt Disney cartoon showing a caricature Garbo. She faded murmuring, "I tank I go 'ome."

At the same time propaganda from Germany was intensified.

"Britain, we have ringed your cities with loudspeakers, and each one is loaded with words from us. Each of our microphones is an invasion point. From today you are the center of our front lip offensive. From this moment starts the coming of the mysterious and terrible voice of truth, and you will never be able to silence it. Our transmitting stations are aerial lighthouses, and only the keepers know the secret of controlling the magic beams. In your radio headquarters, the managers are pulling their hair out and screaming at the operators, 'Louder, louder, drown them out!' You will never drown us out."

Inshroin propped himself up on his elbows, and beckoned Lucy over.

"I want to send three telegrams."

Lucy found a pencil and paper.

"The first is to Fritz Veid, film overseer of the Third Reich. 'Will do co-production on funeral of Hitler. Expense no problem.' Sign that L. J. Selznick." The actor winked. "That should help to make him a little more political. The second one goes to Hitler himself. 'If all happy and well fed in Germany, why is Goering so fat and the rest of your countrymen so thin?' Put the Chief's name to that. The last one is my own, and it goes to Churchill. 'Dear Winston, I expect you will be in the fight. Please book two seats, front row center. Will try to attend.' "

Inshroin started coughing blood, and a trickle ran down his

chin. "I'll soon be like a potato," he murmured. "The earth will be my true domain." Suddenly the air was filled with the wail of an air-raid siren. "Practice downtown," he said.

Lucy smiled. "They're quick off the mark." Again she went to the window and looked out.

"There must be dozens of producers out there thinking this will be their opportunity to make the billion-dollar epic. Can you imagine the slush and nonsense most of them will come up with?"

She shook her head and looked down on the glittering lights of town. Against the background of that wailing siren, it seemed possible to imagine the whole of Hollywood was turning itself into the vast set of a world at war.

Swarms of men and women in uniform as far as the eye can see. Soldiers are maneuvering and forming the word *MOM* by ranks. The studios appear to have been converted into hangars, and women are crawling over aircraft riveting and wiring. They are pilgrim daughters again, but this time they have their own frontier, the mechanization of modern war. Under the brand name semiskilled females, GI Janes hold pneumatic riveters to bomber skeletons. They work under the command of male mechanics who often fall asleep because of the long hours they work. When they do, their mouths are open—the women doze off too, but much more prettily. Bright blondes are growing dingy at the scalp, and because acetate is being used in ammunition, there is no nail polish remover.

Fighter pilot jargon is used to describe adventures on dates. "I took evasive action."

"Rub and scrub, ye women who sacrifice to speed our planes. Burn your buttocks on that red-hot baby of a stove especially designed for you. If the toilet falls apart, refrain from complaint, hide away in nearby trees to answer nature's call."

Beside all the workers, men and women, is a huge billboard lit with electric lamps. On it is written:

IT IS A REFLECTION OF THE FREE DEMOCRATIC WAY OF LIFE THAT YOU ARE DOING A MAN'S WORK. NO LIPSTICK, OURS OR ANYBODY ELSE'S, WILL WIN THE WAR. BUT IT SYMBOLIZES ONE OF THE REASONS WHY WE ARE FIGHTING. THE PRECIOUS AND SACRED RIGHT OF WOMEN TO BE FEMININE AND LOVELY—

UNDER ANY CIRCUMSTANCES. YOU WILL FIND WHEREVER THE
LIPS OF OUR ALLIED MEN AND WOMEN MEET, THORNE'S
MODIFIED COSMETICS ARE EXCHANGED.

In the foxhole the officer pointed at a map of his section of the
line. "Her legs are uncrossed there," he said. "She'll probably
be violated again."

Lucy looked immediately down below the tower, and instead of
the usual Drewstone lot, she was looking out onto the back of
St. Paul's Cathedral.

The city of London is completely dark. In the moonlight,
balloons are visible everywhere, those close at hand looking like
silver fish—those father away looking like silver eggs. It is A.D.
1939. Britain is darker than it was in Julius Caesar's time; they
had fires; now there is nothing alight. London has become a
frontier town, like Daniel Boone's stockade in Kentucky. The
Indians have arrived, and the settlers have rushed inside and
slammed the gates behind them. Notices are everywhere
addressing the population as citizens, something they have not
been called since the threat of Napoleon's invasion. The capital
has been given up as a physical city, and the citizens stand
and stare harder at their buildings, storing up in their
minds structures that might not be there the next day. Time
has turned into tension, as the second hands on clocks jump
jerkily.

Lucy looked up into the night sky. A cat purred, arched its
back, and S-shaped itself between her legs. In the moonlight
the vulture soared and soared.

The drone of bombers getting louder and louder. German
planes, fires flickering in the wake of their engines, are
sweeping in. They have flown out from Germany, turned in the
Atlantic toward London, and followed the beacon of Dublin,
the only city still alight between Moscow and New York.
    As the bombs fall, Madame Tussaud's is hit, and H. G.
Wells, the king and queen, Hitler, and Stalin are all melted
into a single corporate state. A young woman stands near
the building, hands over her ears. She makes the mistake of

clenching her teeth, and as the bomb explodes, her skirt is lifted above her head, and all her teeth shatter into dust.

Through the center of London, flames, smoke, and bursting bombs. Broken gas mains flaring. A cauldron from which rises a dull red glow shot through with vivid white flashes. Dust and sparks billowing up, causing the moon to change from pale green to rich orange. A battery of heavy guns is going off like giant firecrackers in an iron drainpipe. A bomb drops near the BBC; the floor jumps sideways, swings to and fro, then settles back to normal. The newsreader pauses to remove the ceiling from his script, then continues.

Through all the noise and confusion there is the constant sound of whistles from rescue parties. They are never close or loud, but can always be heard.

In the middle of Oxford Street a broken gas main flames up fifty feet, bringing into sharp relief the tiny figures of the auxiliary fire service. There is so much shattered glass in Regent Street, it looks like New York after a light snowfall. All the burglar alarms have started by concussion, screaming the message that coats in their windows are now unprotected.

At an airfield outside London 11:30 P.M. Trucks carry Australian crews to their ships in the grass. Engines start and the pilots run their hands over the instrument boards as if they were piano keys. Slowly and noisily the aircraft form in line on the runway, and lift off into the night. Those men who aren't flying line up waving billiard cues and pint beer glasses. As each bomber takes off, pilots and gunners in their little glass blisters flutter a finger good-bye in the air . . . As the planes pass into Germany, flak starts to prod the machines. Searchlights grow more frequent. The sky is searched independently for a while, then lights converge on the sound and keep the quarry in sight. Occasionally a plane is hit, and as it begins to sink toward the earth, parachutists glide from the fuselage and explode like puffs of popcorn.

Coming toward Berlin. The city was pitch black and still—contracting its mainspring. Suddenly it was as bright as day, as thousands of beams of light were catapulted upward, each one making quick intense jabs at the nerves and lives of the fliers. Night fighters swept down on the Australians. The atmosphere was electric with radio calls and gunfire.

"I can't see anything in front of my eyes."

"He's going to crash into us!"

"Where?"

"Get the hell out of his way! Jesus Christ, all the glass is gone!"

"Are you wearing your goggles?"

"Ten of them heading your way, nose on! Oh Christ, I'll never get back to London now."

"I suppose I'll be grounded. Jesus, that burst was terrible."

"Going higher kangaroo can you hear me? Going higher."

"Bill, the fucking communication's been shot away."

"Get your head away from that glass dome, it won't stop marbles."

"I'm trying to ring the bail-out bell."

"No, only a few holes."

"Did my legs get hit? It feels hot down there!"

"Six o'clock and coming in fast!"

"No, they can't hurt me. I've got to get back to my wife, I've got to shoot them down, got to get back to my wife, promised her . . ."

IT SEEMED LIKE HOURS HAD PASSED, but when Lucy glanced at her watch, only a quarter of an hour had gone by since the declaration of war. The view outside the tower rewound itself back to the usual Drewstone lot and Hollywood horizon. She glanced at Inshroin, who had started coughing again. When she bent over, he must have felt her breath on his face, because he opened his eyes startled.

"I'm still here, my dear, don't worry."

"You won't leave me?"

"Of course I won't."

As she sat down, Lucy noticed some papers sticking out from under the bed, and picked them up—script sheets they had used while working together, some of the pages scrawled and marked with red pencil.

"I'll read to you," she said. "We'll have to start rehearsing again soon."

For the next hour Lucy read to him continually, hoping that

he could hear, and that it might be soothing. He showed no sign that he knew what she was doing, but his breathing grew softer and less strained. Later Lucy would think it extraordinary that she concluded on the passage she did.

Page thirty was turned, and:

> "But soft! what light through yonder window breaks?
> It is the east, and Juliet is the sun!
> Arise, fair sun, and kill the envious moon . . ."

As she read, a sort of convulsion cut across her face, pushing her eyelids up sharp. Every now and again she put a hand to her temple as if she were shielding her brain from the full implication of the words she was reading.

> "Her cheek upon her hand:
> O! that I were a glove upon that hand,
> That I might touch that cheek . . ."

For a second she thought he was joking with her. His hand, covered in its boxing glove, rose up slowly and rested across his forehead. She felt his pulse, but it was so faint she realized he didn't know what he was doing. She took his arm back down to his side, turned the page to the next excerpt, and continued reading:

> "How oft when men are at the point of death
> Have they been merry! which their keepers call
> A lightning before death: O! how may I
> Call this a lightning? O my love! my husband! . . ."

Inshroin stirred slightly, and Lucy put out her hand in case the glove came up again.

> "Death, that hath sucked the honey of thy breath,
> Hath no power yet upon thy beauty:
> Thou art not conquered; beauty's ensign yet
> Is crimson in thy lips and in thy cheeks . . ."

There was a slight contraction over Inshroin's left eyebrow, and he opened his eyes, but they immediately went back in his

334

head like someone fainting, then closed altogether. She thought he was gone, but suddenly his face cleared, and his eyes opened full on her, bright, quick, and so young.

"You made a mistake," he said, "You read, 'O my love! my *husband*, Death, that hath sucked the honey of thy breath.' It's Romeo who's speaking. The line is 'O my love! my *wife*.' "

Lucy looked startled. "I didn't realize I'd said that, it must have been a typing error." Without warning her voice gave way, interrupted by sobs that shook her whole body. She put both hands to her face and dropped her head down into her lap, then her hand reached out and twisted the sheets on the bed, knuckles showing white. She stayed like that for a few moments, then quickly got to her feet spilling script pages in all directions.

"You think you can throw your own life down the drain! Millions killed, dammit; you had a choice! I'm a good nurse, they didn't kill me, I'm a good nurse! Aren't you fucking clever!"

She looked down at Inshroin, but it was obvious he hadn't heard, his eyes were glazing over and turning up toward his forehead . . . Lucy froze . . . Like a candle flame that bends and wavers in a draft, he flickered uncertain for a few seconds, then without a sound his breath collapsed and he was gone, taking her heart with him.

Lucy dropped to her knees. She couldn't stop herself, it felt as if all the bones in her legs had decayed, her whole body was shaking. Throwing her head back she screamed and screamed. Excited by the sound, the monkey sprang from a cupboard and ran screeching over Inshroin. The animal then snatched up the First World War helmet from the foot of the bed, placed it over its body and disappeared completely except for the tiny dancing feet.

Drewstone was sitting at his office desk reading a script when Lucy came into the room. She stood by the door, her face white and drawn, the eyes red. The Chief glanced up, and his mouth fell open. For the first time in her life, Lucy realized how stupid that expression of surprise can look.

"How are you?" she finally asked, getting tired of saying nothing.

"Sure, sure," said the Chief, "what are you doing here?"

"I've come to tell you Phillip has just died."

The Chief leaned back in his chair. "I thought you looked upset. You must have got to know him well."

"We were quite close."

There was a few seconds of silence, then the Chief got up. "Sit down, you must be tired." He stood in front of his desk. "He made some very popular movies when he was working with me."

"I'm sure *Variety* will point that out in its obituary," said Lucy. "Did you know Britain has declared war on Germany?"

The Chief looked startled. "No I didn't. This place is slipping, I should have been told. How long ago?"

"It was rebroadcast on the radio last night. We won't be out of it for long. Phillip wanted to hear the announcement from London."

"Did he?"

"Yes . . . I wonder what'll happen when this one's over?"

The Chief shrugged. "There'll probably be another jazz age. What are you going to do in the meantime?"

"I'm thinking of going to England. With my experience, I might be able to help."

"I thought women were supposed to condemn war?"

"Why? Do you think all women hate war?" Lucy shook her head. "There may be a lot of women who'll condemn it, but there are thousands who won't. In war, the boredom of everyday living is wiped out instantly. This war will spread quickly, and it will change the lives of women all over the world. It's going to be mechanized, and we'll have to work the factories and the machinery. We'll be part of the adventure. For the first time, men won't be able to fight without us; we'll be equal partners. You're very stupid if you think all women hate war. I can feel a kind of excitement, so there must be others who feel it, too. If you expect us all to stay home weeping, it must be because you believe all the nonsense you see in the movies."

The Chief's face brightened, and inspiration began slowly to churn up at a deep and profound level.

"That's a very interesting idea," he said thoughtfully, "a story about an American girl ambulance driver. If I can come up with the right material, I've got just the girl who can roll up her sleeves, and show the world the power of this country's womanhood. She's a young blonde, nice figure, good legs; she can be a Joan of Arc type who'll love the wounded like Florence Nightingale." His voice started to rise with excitement. "I'll make her a mother, and her three sons can be at the front. I'll have her winning a lot of medals for bravery, then returning home and becoming America's first woman President." For a second the Chief's eyes seemed to revolve in their sockets, then righted themselves. He went over to the phone and dialed through to the accounts department.

Down on the Drewstone lot, a production was in progress. Indians swarmed around a wagon train, and as volley after volley was fired into them, men and horses fell spectacularly. A number of the animals had been hooked to long wires that were staked out directly behind them. After a fifty-yard run they fell end over end, a beautiful shot but usually fatal. When the scene was finished, the men got up and walked away, but most of the horses stayed down or tried to get up on broken legs. After another take the Indians and settlers took a break for coffee while men went around shooting the wounded horses that lay all over the set.

The city of Hollywood wound up its day's activities. In the rich part of town, huge letters were silhouetted everywhere. A controlling rheostat was turned up to a high pitch of brilliance, and ECSTASY was spelled out twice every ten seconds in the heads of people.

In the poor part of town, flames were licking above the rooftops, accompanied by a sound of singing and whistling. It was as if cracking flames (like water running in a bath) inspired people with a desire to make music. Someone was whistling Beethoven's Ninth. The interpretation was loud, inaccurate, and soulful. Above them all that morning the vulture still soared and soared.

Gentlemen, in a hundred years' time they will be showing another fine color film describing the terrible days we are living through. Don't you want to play a part in this film, to be brought back to life in a hundred years' time? Everybody now has the chance to choose the part which he will play in that film a hundred years hence. I can assure you that it will be a fine elevating picture. And for the sake of this prospect it is worth standing fast. Hold out now, so that a hundred years hence the audience does not hoot and whistle when you appear on the screen.

Goebbels to his staff, April 17, 1945,
as Russian troops advance on Berlin